SAILING

out of

DARKNESS

A Carolina Coast Novel

Normandie Fischer

Sleepy Creek Press

SAILING OUT OF DARKNESS

Copyright © 2013, 2017 Normandie Fischer

2nd Edition

ISBN: 978-0-9971855-2-2 (ebook edition)

ISBN: 978-0-9971855-3-9 (print edition)

To my darling mama, Ella Meadows Giesey, who always listens and whose love is unconditional. And to the next Ella, Mama's first great-grandchild, my daughter's daughter, Ella Cosette Meadows Scoville, who made her appearance on August 21, 2013.

I have been blessed and surrounded by the love of family and friends. But I've met others who weren't so fortunate. I also dedicate this story to those who feel overwhelmed by loss and by guilt. Who imagine themselves friendless or condemned, some of whom have chosen a final solution that offers no true peace.
May we who know love be the ones to listen when someone cries in the wilderness of their pain. May we reach out to those who have followed their heart into an unhealthy place that has left them feeling lost and alone and desperate. May we who know Love, offer it unconditionally.

1

SAMANTHA

Black night's emptiness, the bed reeks of nothing.
Cuckoo sings the melody, but no one hears.

Samantha Ransom smoothed her palm across the silky sheet, stopping when she touched a feathered mass of pillow. Just that movement roused a whiff of Jack's aftershave, along with traces of sweat and man, and memories flashed—of his touch, of his fingers, oh, and of his kisses. They danced in her head, unbidden. Unwanted.

On a moan, she tossed the pillow to the floor and pressed a fist against the wrench in her gut. The sound oozed from her belly, growing louder as it hit the air.

Long minutes passed before her cries quieted to ragged breaths. She kicked free of the tangled top sheet and waited for a sleep that would not come. The minutes became hours as the cuckoo in her old clock intoned their loss.

Something crunched on the gravel outside her open window, sending her heartbeat's thurump to double time. She balled her fists. An intruder would give her something to fight against instead of this self she couldn't control.

But no one came.

The silence echoed off the walls, reminding her of childhood nights when she'd bit her lip and squeezed shut her eyes to keep the bad away. "Let it go," she whispered now.

At the first gray of dawn, she eased out of bed, snatched at the sheets, and let them lie in a heap on the floor as she took her used body into the bathroom. Climbing in the shower, she tried to scour away the night and her misery with a lavender body wash.

The unscrubbable followed her to the laundry room, where she stuffed the sheets in the washer and turned the water temperature to hot. It settled on her as she ground coffee beans and placed the kettle on to boil.

Samantha's, her coffee/kitchen shop, was closed today. Church would happen all up and down the Neuse, but she wouldn't be there. Not today. Not this week. Not when her chest blazed its scarlet *A,* and God seemed un-found. Silent.

She wandered the downstairs rooms, waiting for inspiration, for something that would occupy her hands and perhaps her thoughts. She'd vacuumed, dusted, and polished during yesterday's storm. She didn't want to cook. Or pull weeds.

Perhaps she'd tackle her little boat's brightwork. The rain had kept her from sanding the mahogany on the centerboard trunk or touching up those peeling spots of varnish on the bowsprit. Besides, working on the *Alice II* always calmed her.

Leaving the coffee untouched, she donned her grubbies and headed toward the river. The wind lay still. The sky shimmered a light blue as the sun rose higher in a day that ought to hold some joy.

With one hand on the rail that led down the bank, she

glanced at the dock. And squinted as she looked again, because it couldn't be.

Her boat's mast listed a good thirty-degrees to port. Dashing down the short flight of steps, Sam tried to grasp the hows, let alone the whys. She always left enough slack in the lines to compensate for the rise and fall of the tide—unless she'd been careless when she'd last secured the boat. Because of those other things on her mind.

Alice strained against the dock. Thank heaven Sam had tied off the boom so it wasn't dipping over the left side, adding its weight to the rest. The bailing bucket, lines, and a sponge slopped around in a cockpit half-filled with water.

Her pulse beat a jitterbug as she knelt and leaned out and over. Nothing there. Perhaps forward?

Lying on her belly on the hard wooden dock, she stretched to check under the raised gunwale near her.

And there they were, a series of small holes just below what would normally have been the waterline. At each indentation, starburst cracks in the boat's interior gelcoat radiated outward.

She pushed herself up, studying the outside of the hull to be certain *Alice* hadn't hit barnacles or rubbed against a piling. But that wouldn't explain the starburst cracks. Those meant someone had stabbed from inside the cockpit.

Thank God, she'd messed up the dock lines, tightening them instead of leaving them loose enough for tidal changes. If she'd cleated them properly, any holes below the waterline would have sunk *Alice*. Whoever had poked those holes hadn't expected the short lines and the very low tide to keep the boat lopsided instead of at the bottom of the river.

Sam wanted to weep, but no tears came. She felt like retching, but what good would that do? About as much as railing aloud to an empty river.

The name flashed: India Monroe.

It must have been India.

She saw again India's face, the binoculars dangling from her neck as Sam and Jack sailed back to the dock. She felt again the hurt when Jack leapt from the boat and went to India's side to escort his old girlfriend away from his new girlfriend's boat.

He'd phoned Sam after he'd settled India at home, after he'd soothed—or somethinged—India. What was it, only days ago? It felt like years.

"We're through," Sam had told him then, her voice full of the tears that streamed down her cheeks. "This isn't working. I can't see you anymore."

"You don't mean that." Jack hadn't even pretended to believe her. Instead, he'd smiled behind his words, hadn't he, resurrecting a half-forgotten image of Jack-the-boy not taking her seriously and of herself, two years younger, stamping her feet at him.

She'd curled her toes and banked her frustration. "I do. This time, I do."

"We've been through this, Sam honey. I'm not with India any more. You know that. I don't live there. It's you I love. It's you I need."

Why couldn't he see? "I can't be the person who makes another woman hurt like that. Imagine what she saw through those binoculars." Sam bit back a moan that wanted to climb right out of her belly. Memories of what they'd done, of what India might have witnessed...

"It's wrong," she finally said. "We're wrong."

India's pain was only half of it. The smaller half. Still, it was obviously the half that had holed Sam's boat. But neither India's pain nor her own disgust at herself had stopped Sam from opening the door to Jack. She always opened to him.

A gull squawked and waddled at the end of the dock. With the tide coming in, she had to do something about those holes before the rising water loosened the lines and let the river sink her precious boat.

Sam found another bucket and line in the shed and prepared to bail. But no, she needed to fill the holes first, because an emptied *Alice* would bob upright, putting those holes under water. Into the bucket went epoxy, hardener, filler, and fiberglass cloth, along with sandpaper, thick gloves, solvent, tape, and a roll of paper towels.

From her awkward position on the dock, stretching out and leaning over to sand and clean the area, the prep work took hours. By the time she'd mixed and slathered on thickened epoxy and added a layer of fiberglass cloth for strength, patches of her skin were rubbed raw, and a few seldom-used muscles screamed for relief.

The repair job wasn't pretty, but at least it would keep the water out. If only she could patch her own self as easily.

JACK'S WORDS when she phoned to tell him about *Alice* set her teeth on edge. "It's got to be kids, though I admit this is getting way out of hand."

Why wouldn't he admit it might be about him? About them?

"Jack, really? You know it's not kids. Besides the fact that none live nearby, why would anyone randomly pick me as a target—again?" She waited for him to get it and finally spoke into the silent phone. "What about calling the sheriff?"

"Sure. Maybe he can figure this out. In the meantime, you want me to send someone over to mend the boat?"

"Like you did when my tires were flat and my screens slashed?"

"I'd come myself," he said, "but I told you, I'm heading out of town in about an hour. All goes well, I should be back next Sunday."

"I've already patched *Alice's* holes." She kept her tone flat instead of the round and mad that stayed just out of reach.

"Well, good."

"Jack." Her voice had pancaked to the point that the stupidest person should have been able to see she was on the brink, and Jack wasn't stupid.

"What?"

What did he mean, *what?* "You need to speak to India," she said. "She's the only one with a motive."

"Honey, she wouldn't. Look, I've known India Monroe for ten years. She's got issues, but I can't imagine her hurting you or anyone else."

"Then you're naïve."

His loud sigh made her want to kick something. She'd have used his shins if he'd been nearby.

"Fine, I'll call her. Hold off on the sheriff."

"I will for now, but you need to tell her that won't last. And don't forget to assure her we won't be seeing each other anymore. Maybe that'll get her to leave me alone."

"I can't say that, because you know it's not true."

"It has to be. This time, it has to be."

Three strikes, and you're out. She'd had her three —and more.

"I'll talk to her, but I'll also see you when I get back." He didn't wait for her answer.

Sam stared at the silent phone and slowly set it down. How had this disconnect happened? She said the words. He talked right over her and then walked right in. But could she blame him? Even the mess with her screens hadn't stiffened her spine enough for her to bar the door.

She glanced over her shoulder at the back porch. It had

been another morning like this one, sun-drenched and clear. She'd padded into the kitchen to the scent of fresh brew and filled her mug before heading to the porch to welcome the day. She could still feel the burn from the sloshed coffee on her wrist and fingers.

Someone had ripped down her screens.

No, not ripped. Sliced. Knifed.

She'd set her mug on an inside table, dabbed her hand on her bathrobe to dry it, and stepped out.

Boards had creaked under her feet, but she'd focused on one particular section of screen where the red letters of half a word still hung straight, leaving a *B* and an *I*. Flopped toward the floor had been three more, their shapes distorted by the folds of dangling mesh, but still guessable. She hadn't wanted to touch them, or touch anything at all.

The corner of a chair had hit her thigh as she'd backed away. Stumbling, she'd grabbed the wall, turned, and fled, locking the door behind her.

Now, on this morning of regret, she pictured blond hair surrounding a face contorted with anger. The sting of tears replaced the slamming of heart against ribs. Because she'd known, then and now.

Only one person hated her enough to wreck such damage.

GRAY OBSCURED the room when she woke the next morning, as if cataracts fogged her lenses. She rubbed her eyes to clear them and climbed from bed. The cuckoo in the hall reminded her it was time to get a move on. Work waited. The world waited.

She showered, dressed, and applied armor before she faced town: a dab of concealer under her eyes, a heavy application of blush, and a flick of waterproof mascara. She pulled a turquoise silk shirt off a hanger, slipped into black slacks and black flats, and added a pair of small gold hoops.

She packed a salad for lunch. *Samantha's* offered baked goodies for those who came in looking for a tall cup, or who wanted new knives or blenders or a cookbook so they could stir-fry in their new wok. Maybe she needed fattening, but not with espresso brownies, because she couldn't help thinking that once she got started, she wouldn't be able to quit. And today was not the day to get started.

Not unless she wanted to turn into her daddy's cousin Lulu, who'd blimped to 368 pounds when her husband ran off with his boyfriend. One brownie at a time had segued into one cake at a time and then into two cakes plus a gallon of ice cream. Lulu had died of heart failure before she hit forty-nine.

Maybe Sam's heart hadn't yet been completely shattered like Lulu's, but it surely had fissures big enough to leak the life right out. And she'd carved a slew of them herself.

Still, she had both of her shops, the first of which she'd built from nothing before the coffeehouse craze hit Raleigh, the second, post-Greg, a little closer to home. And she had her beautiful little sailboat, along with her newly restored cottage. And, of course, the twins plus one and a half. Lulu'd had no one. Not even her cousin.

That one-and-a-half still took some getting used to. She liked her daughter-in-law and the prospect of that new life Cindy carried. But it wasn't so very long ago that Daniel and his twin sister, Stefi, had been children on top of each other and her, their voices echoing, the thump-thump of their music swelling until it almost burst the walls of the house they'd all shared in Raleigh. Sometimes, when fixing breakfast for herself, she imagined the twins sitting behind her, begging for waffles: "Please, Mom, just one more?"

Her once-upon-a-time babies had morphed overnight, one into a husband and soon a father, the other, her sweet girl, into a design student in Florence, Italy. They were barely twenty-two.

Sam could feel wrinkles sagging her arms, her neck, her world. She was almost a grandmother. Soon, she'd need bifocals. A walker. A wheelchair.

That image provoked a bark of laughter.

"Get over yourself," she said, scrubbing harder at a splatter of oil on the counter.

Clouds darkened the sky as she finished putting away her lunch fixings, and the first spatters of rain hit the gravel as she headed out of her driveway and into Beaufort. Good thing she'd fixed *Alice's* holes before the rains returned.

Sam beat a tattoo on the steering wheel in time to the slosh of her wipers. She ought to get the radio fixed. Or put in a CD player.

She'd scheduled another training session for her Beaufort assistant, Tootie, on some of the software both shops used, and Rhea was supposed to call with a report from the Raleigh *Samantha's* at ten. Her morning would be busy. Busy was good.

Busy might keep her from...what? Calling the sheriff? Banging her head against the wall?

By closing time, Sam barely had energy to get herself home, like a horse that had been ridden hard and put away wet. "Yeah, right," she told her Toyota. "I'm more like wrung out and hung up wet, and I'll be wetter if this rain doesn't slow."

She picked up a ready-made spinach salad and an already roasted chicken at the grocery store, along with a loaf of freshly baked multigrain, and headed home. Where she found a voicemail from Jack.

"Missing you. I'll be back Sunday, if all goes well. I love you."

He loved her, but he hadn't mentioned speaking to India. He loved her, but he wouldn't stay away when she begged him to.

Well, of course not. Why should he believe she meant it?

She stabbed at her salad and tried to chew a bite that included greens and a chunk of goat cheese. It needed more salt. Pepper. Something.

She sipped her wine, which should have mellowed her, shouldn't it? When the phone rang, she jumped but let it go to voicemail.

Another sip, another stab, and curiosity propelled her to check the message. It was Rhea's voice this time, saying, "We need to talk."

Sam hit the *Call* button. "You rang?"

"I did," Rhea said. "Honey, you didn't sound so good today. Oh, I know you didn't mean to let me hear it. But this is me, remember?"

Sam picked up her glass and carried it to the couch. Sliding down against a fluffy pillow, she sighed. "Oh, Rhea. It's bad."

"Tell me."

"I found holes in *Alice* yesterday. Looked like an ice pick had made them."

"You thinking what I'm thinking? That it's the old girlfriend up to her tricks?"

"Who else?"

"So, why'd she come after you this time? I thought you'd shuffled·that man all the way out of your life."

Sam twirled the wine in her glass, but she couldn't bring herself to drink. Or to speak.

"You didn't? Oh, honey. I told you what you gotta do."

Rhea had. Rhea'd been steadfast when Sam's Raleigh church friends had sent worried looks and cold shoulders, as if her divorce were catching. So, of course, Sam had clung to Rhea's friendship. And big-mouth Sam had told Rhea all about meeting up with her childhood best friend, Jack. About him working on her house. About how fun it was to play on *Alice* with Jack.

It hadn't taken Rhea long to jab her finger on the tabletop when Sam had visited Raleigh. "Honey, you gotta flee." Then those fingers had fluttered in a little wave as if to shoo Sam out the door. "The Lord's really clear on this. You hear? Temptation like that? You gotta run fast as those legs of yours will carry you." She'd said it more than once since she'd learned the truth.

But in the beginning of the mess, the voice in Sam's head had whispered contrary messages. *You can do it. You're strong. Just say no.*

Who'd ever come up with that platitude? *Just say no.*

Sure. Right. Great idea, and workable for a saint, which Sam obviously wasn't.

No, Rhea's had been the better advice: "Hightail it out of Dodge."

"I know," Sam said. "I wish I'd listened."

"So, now what?"

"What do you mean, now what? I've made a mess of things." Her voice quavered. She didn't want to cry again. That's all she seemed to do these days when Rhea called to check on her. Rhea was the One Who Knew All.

"Girl, are you closing off again?"

Sam didn't answer.

"You stop that. Right now."

"It's so hard. I want to be good. I do."

11

"Well, honey, you tell me how you're gonna do that, right there in that town with him? A man you trusted 'cause he was your buddy way back when? And after all that mess with Greg?"

"I know. I know."

"So, now what?"

"You already asked that."

"I did. But you didn't answer."

How could she? She hadn't a clue. "You said flee. But that's not an option. I mean, I've got two shops and a house and a boat. And now I'm a grandmother-to-be."

Rhea hooted.

Sam pulled the phone away and stared at it. "What's so funny about that?"

"That baby's not coming for a long time. And you think you're indispensable at the shops? You think you haven't trained me and that girl, Tootie, to do just fine without you hanging over our shoulders? What's got into you? You've got Stefi studying in Italy, right there in that beautiful country. And don't you try to tell me you can't afford to go visit her."

Sam pulled up her knees and hugged them to her chest. She hadn't even considered traveling. And to Italy? *Oh, my.* "I always wanted to see Rome, Florence," and on a whisper, "Venice."

"You think I don't know that? How many times did you tell me that fool husband of yours promised to take you? You think I wasn't counting? That I didn't see your face time and again when he disappointed you?"

Dropping her feet to the floor and letting out a breath from deep in her gut, Sam nodded to the room and to her glass of wine, which she tilted to her lips. The dark liquid slid down her throat. Maybe it would help her decide what to do.

"You think it's really possible?" she asked, her voice smaller than she'd heard it in a while. "That I could leave everything?"

"Honey, it's not just possible. It's a got-to-do."

"And you think Tootie could manage without me?"

"Why not? I'll only be a couple of hours away. I can help her with the bookkeeping and payroll. Didn't you say you'd hired a part-timer?"

"Her fiancé's older sister. I told you about Holland, the banker."

"And how's that working out?"

Sam laughed. "We'll see, won't we? At least Holland's a good foot taller than his sister. He can stand at Tootie's back if she needs him."

This time, Rhea's laugh loosed humor. "So, you go on and buy yourself a ticket. Get healed and free."

The idea settled, took hold, and started to bud. "I'll try."

"Good. Now you call me with the details soon as you make them, hear?"

"Thank you."

"No need to thank me. You just come back whole enough not to need some man to fill in the gaps."

"Yes, ma'am."

Sam disconnected and wandered outside to the top of the cliff. The rain had stopped, and the sun eased below the horizon, throwing everything in shadow. *Alice* bobbed below, salvaged, but not yet beautiful. If she left, someone else would have to take care of finishing that job. Or maybe she'd just haul her boat in for the season.

Was leaving really possible?

She turned on her heel and headed inside to her computer. She'd just check on fares and schedules. Find out how much she had in her savings account. How much she could spare.

For healing.

Did ex-wives and ex-lovers attend some sort of twelve-step program? Or did they just evolve and explore until they found new ways to cope? New words to define themselves after all the old ones failed.

Maybe this could be her Betty Ford Clinic Abroad.

2

TEO

Lonely isn't lonely if one looks from outside in;
It's just the inside out that makes a person feel so thin.

Theodore Anderson clawed his way up the bank, grabbing handholds and pressing against rock with his bare feet. Why wouldn't his legs work? *Come on, move, move.*

Kicking only tightened the bindings around his ankles, at his thighs. What was wrong with him?

The hulk skidded along the asphalt. Tires shrieked and air brakes hissed as the engine howled in protest. Teo turned. The massive silver grille reflected oncoming headlights, blinding him, and all he could do was raise his arms to protect his face, because he was too late. He'd never escape.

And, dying, he woke.

He inhaled slowly, letting the breath whoosh out between pursed lips. He was in his room, wrapped in a sheet. No demons roamed, and, while that truck may have jackknifed years ago and thousands of miles away, it was not here in Reggio sul Mare, on the Italian Riviera.

So, why the dream now and in this place?

He tossed off the covers, slipped on a pair of jeans and a shirt, and slid his feet into loafers. He couldn't run off the tension, but he *could* walk. The tap of his cane on the sidewalk echoed in the pre-dawn.

Like eyelids closed against the night, metal shutters hid the shop windows. He could picture the butcher's just there, slabs of meat hanging from hooks, fowl complete with head and feet, prices by the kilo. He passed the greengrocer's, two stores down. Next, the *tabaccaio*, which reminded him that he needed to buy stamps when they opened. He knew the shopkeepers by sight after five years of walking these streets, even if he didn't know all by name.

In the distance, an engine revved. Most in town would stretch and yawn as they slowly woke. The bakers, though, were even now sliding dough into ovens, yeasty morsels he could buy in a few hours to nibble with a strong espresso. But not yet.

His tap-tap continued down the hill to the shore where he stepped onto the rocky sand and rebalanced. Waves crested and broke, hidden by the fog, though lights from the nearby hotel illuminated enough beach to keep him from falling. He kicked off his shoes and moved to the water's edge, then whispered, "*Sono qui.*"

That elicited a smile. "I am here," he repeated.

Not there. No longer *there*.

"Okay, I'm up and out." He aimed this message skyward. "I assume that's what you—or someone—wanted."

The sea wrapped his ankles and splashed the tip of his cane. The walk had cleared his soggy brain, and the eerie quiet of a mist-clad sea sat well with him. He stood still and listened to the soft slosh as the waves hit sand. But no one spoke, neither God nor man.

He'd begun to turn away when she stepped out of the fog, white on white with a touch of gray, followed by a flash of light skin and dark hair. Puzzled, he stared.

Slowly, her form emerged, and a bright smile bridged the dimensions. She beckoned. Did she wave at him? Teo peered over his shoulder and down the beach, but he was alone with only the sand and the sea and this vision before him. He expected to hear witchy moans next—or see a bubbling cauldron. Surely, this wasn't an angel.

"Che succede?" he called, wanting to know what was up, along with a why or two, but she didn't speak. Perhaps she couldn't.

The sea sucked the wave, as if the sand inhaled then exhaled, breathing in water and filtering it out like a fish's gills. He backed away, sliding damp feet into his shoes.

Lights from the new hotel, the Albergo dei Romantici, illuminated the froth, showing off upturned rowboats that lined the sand like an army slumbering till day. Teo rarely ventured close to the developed boardwalk, but at this hour it seemed appropriate. No one else stirred. He was free to explore.

This stranger's appearance wouldn't seem so odd if she had flesh and form that he could touch. Instead, she shape-shifted in the half light, one moment showing no more than a wispy outline, in the next, substance.

There, now: a three-dimensional image. She didn't possess Sophrina's soft curves or that long, wavy hair. Her lips eased without seduction, an art she didn't seem to know. Her lashes lowered, but not to shadow Sophrina's penetrating stare. They dropped to hide her pain.

How could he know that? He shook his head, puzzled when the understanding dropped into his mind with no prompting from either of them. His eyes snapped closed, then opened to scan the area. Perhaps he was merely dreaming.

A pleasant dream to make him forget the nightmare? His mind playing tricks?

He kicked the sand, then scored a trench with his cane. The effect seemed too real for a dream. Besides, a dreamscape normally stopped and rewound before either repeating the sequence or adding some new element.

Why did his sleep-deprived brain conjure this woman, whose image he didn't recognize? He'd left his bed, full of the need to walk. He should return and hope for rest.

Right. As long as this haunting didn't follow him into sleep.

Someone laughed from around a corner. A second hushed the first. These two may have been the only others yet abroad this night, their voices echoing in streets silent except for Teo's tap-tap-shuffle as he headed home. He leaned heavily on his cane. The damp had crept in, knife-like to his bones.

Unlocking and pushing open the heavy outside door took energy, but the elevator to the penthouse floor chugged on its own, gears squeaking, to drop him in the small foyer. He used a second key, and he was home, wishing his eyelids felt as heavy as his body did.

His computer beckoned from across the room. Perhaps writing a line or two would make him drowsy enough for bed. He eased onto his desk chair, flipped the switch, and waited as the system booted up. His fingers dashed across the keyboard, trying to capture and keep the image. He ignored the grit in his eyes and the fatigue that hunched his shoulders as letters grew into words.

He saw her long before he met her.

Gag. He hit the backspace key, tried again.

He dreamt her into being years before he saw her smile.

Jab, jab, jab. His index finger shot the words off the screen.

She had seemed so real. Why couldn't he find the words to begin?

Surely, she'd shown herself so he could create her. Fit her into a story.

He rolled his chair away from the keyboard, flicked up on the three-way switch, and squinted at the screen. With a sigh, he backed the brilliance down again. It wasn't the light.

Just because he made a career of recording Sophrina's antics, did that mean he couldn't branch out? Add a new heroine? Or a hero this time? What was wrong with having a hero?

Fine, he couldn't sell his first hero-laden story, but that was years ago.

He closed his eyes and waited. And there she was, again showing herself, this new *her* with dark hair windblown and stabbing out behind her head from one of those silly things women wore to make a stubby ponytail. Why was she even out in the wind? Was she running? From whom?

Her eyes hid behind dark glasses until she doffed the tortoise-shell frames and smiled. They were deep brown eyes, reflecting hints of yellow. She was more striking than pretty, but that may have been her age. She was older than he, of course.

Why of course?

He longed for a drink. A tumbler of lovely amber liquid that would slide down the throat and spread its warmth, its relaxing warmth, through his limbs.

Right. And straight to his brain, making it soggy and useless.

No. He wouldn't touch anything more potent than a few sips of wine. A humorless laugh was all he could manage as he imagined life in Reggio without at least that half-full glass of red near his plate, obviating the need to explain his past when someone tried to offer him more. The Italians either didn't have an alcohol problem, or it didn't worry them. His sigh as he remembered how the liquor had dulled more than his physical pain sounded loud in the room, because quitting didn't automatically erase the memories or the occasional—all right, sometimes more than occasional—longing for oblivion.

Hunger and the need to escape again assailed him, making him restless, fidgety. Shutting down his computer, he wandered to the window. The sky had brightened perceptibly. He slid his bare feet into shoes, grabbed his windbreaker and cane, and lumbered down the stairs and out the front door. The neighboring *tabaccaio* remained shuttered, but he heard noises from the bakery, smelled yeasty bread from the *forno* as he limped past. His cane clacked along the sidewalk. He picked up his pace, wanting to get to the sea before the sun slid up over the horizon.

A Vespa scooted to a halt as he reached the corner.

"*Buongiorno, Teo! Cosa fai stamattina?*" A grin revealed Nicco's gleaming new teeth.

Teo smiled back. What exactly *was* he doing? "Heading to the beach," he said, because at least that was a destination. "You off to work?"

"*Sì.* Adele wishes to see you. You come soon? We make a feast, *mangiamo insieme.*"

"I will. You thank her. Tell her to pick a day."

"*Va bene. Ciao!*" And the scooter zoomed off toward the hills.

Teo watched until Nicco vanished around a corner. Their chance encounter boded well for the day.

So what if he had a bit of writer's block? He'd get over it.

Without wind, the glassy surface of the Mediterranean caught the sun's flames and bounced them skyward. Teo watched the colors ease from purples to reds and yellows and oranges, blending shades of each in both the sky and sea. A few masts bobbed on a swell. Gulls squawked and cawed overhead.

The sand kicked up under his loafers and cane as he wandered toward the town landing. An espresso called. An espresso and a bit of fresh bread.

Perhaps the words hadn't formed yet, but hazy snapshots flicked into his mind, pieces of her image blinking behind the veil. Perhaps she would remain a mirage, but he certainly hoped not.

He'd like to have something new to show his editor when he visited the States. Val prodded him to write another Sophrina mystery, but perhaps he could convince her to take on someone different, his illusive vision. Especially if he didn't completely toss Sophrina to the wolves, but merely added a new twist, a new persona to his repertoire.

He'd like to savor something new, a fresh taste on his lips, a different world.

After all, he was a writer. He should be able to create worlds to inhabit, shouldn't he? Even if only for himself.

3

SAMANTHA

Pilings chafe and barnacles rip
At a body tossed on a word of truth.

An owl hooted. Sam stopped packing and listened, knowing what would follow. At the mournful response and quick riposte, she sent up a prayer for wandering barn cats. She didn't want to imagine talons swooping to capture the unwary. The two birds of prey spoke in the night stillness, while she stood, a fistful of underwear clutched to her chest.

Would she hear owls in Italy? Or be able to watch shore birds plunge after fish? How could she just up and leave it all?

Again.

What had it been? Eighteen months since she'd packed, changed homes, and started another shop, another life, two hours east and a lifetime away from Raleigh? No, more than that. It was the end of summer now. It hadn't even been winter then.

Divorce was such a harsh word. She'd purposefully left it out of her vocabulary, hoping it might never happen. Twenty-three years made creases in a life that didn't just iron out when someone said, "So long, good-bye, I never loved you." Amazing that after years of words, those would be the last ones in a marriage. At the very end, Greg's eyes had said, *I hate you.*

And here she was, no better off. What had she told herself when he left? That most men were creeps, interested in only one thing. She'd asked God or her own self or something to show her if her thinking were skewed, to show her a man who wasn't a clone of Greg. She'd declared to whatever wall happened to be listening that if a single man of good character existed, one who had enough gray cells to make decent conversation and who wasn't buying Jags and lacing fingers with teeny boppers, she wanted to meet him. She could still hear her own voice say, "Maybe not anytime soon, but surely before all longings drain out and I become a stick tossed about by the wind."

Well, she'd met a man all right. And look how *that* had turned out. She'd imagined him a gift, but considering the mess she'd been in when she'd first returned to Beaufort, she should have hunted up girlfriends. Sure, some of the younger women had tried to befriend her, but it had felt like too much work to fit into the happy-ever-after world of Tadie and Hannah and all those others.

She really hadn't given them a chance, had she? Not after Jack had shown up, grinning past those shades of his. She'd told herself the women were at a different place in their lives, half a generation behind her. Maybe if she lived in town, instead of isolated here at South River, making friends with them would have been easier.

She closed the lid to her case and headed to the shower. Turning on the exhaust fan, she undressed with her back to the mirror. She didn't want to see the cheekbones exaggerated from weight loss or the dark circles under newly sunken eyes.

She'd had the same look before, hadn't she, bony protrusions once softened by flesh? Then, her body had been unloved, untouched by her husband for more than a year. She remembered a time in the spring before he said good-bye when he'd turned away, limp and useless. She'd chalked up that failure to overwork and stress—she'd even felt compassion for him. What a fool she'd been. It had been overwork all right. He'd been overworked by Gail's young and very voluptuous body.

Now, guilt and regret were the culprits that stole Sam's peace, the things that devoured both belly and breasts. Her legs and arms would be next. Anorexia of the soul.

She slumped over the sink. It was a long time before her shaking fingers found the shower spigot and longer still before the sound of splashing water became the only noise that echoed off the tile walls.

~

Morning dawned and, with it, a profound melancholy. The ties to Beaufort, once so exhilarating, had become shackles. No more tears. No more weeping. It was time.

She said her house good-byes while she sipped a strong latte. With her palm pressed against the back-door screen, she stared out over the river. A gull dipped and cawed. A fish jumped. She bit her lip and turned, closing the door, locking it. For a moment, she stood there, her forehead touching the glass panel, one hand clutching her mug, the other still on the lock.

Greg's demands had forced her departure from Raleigh and from the marriage he'd discarded. This time? This time it was her own gotta-haves.

That thought brought on the shakes, her too frequent companion these days. She leaned her forehead against the door frame and repeated the litany she'd memorized: *You can, you must, you can, you must.*

Jack kept calling with messages that said the same thing: "Sam, where are you? I miss you." Next, "Sam, it's looking good for my return on Sunday. Why don't we sail?" And this morning, "Remember, I love you."

Love? Hah!

Well, she wouldn't be here to open the door when Jack knocked. Never again would she open her door to him.

You can, you must.

A knock at the front startled her. "Back here," she called as Tootie waltzed in, flashing her bright hair and her wild-child clothes, her dangly earrings and lavishly painted mouth, today a burnt orange.

What a fortunate day it had been when Tootie's Aunt Ruth had recommended her to Sam as an assistant for the Beaufort *Samantha's*. "Child's real name is Mathilde," Ruth had said while showing Sam the space that would become her new shop. "Maybe it was my son—or one of his friends—who first called her by that ridiculous nickname, but there you go. It stuck." Ruth, the realtor, had also found Sam's cottage. And reintroduced Sam to the contractor who would make it livable. Sam's old childhood buddy, Jack Waters.

Sam batted away that last thought. *Enough.*

Tootie was an elf on steroids: hair that changed color on a whim, earrings that dangled past her chin, clothes in hues that popped, all in a package that exuded a love of literature, an ability to set up shop windows and shop shelves that invited customers to browse and buy, and a personality that won converts to friendship in this otherwise staid town.

"All ready?" Tootie's grins lighted her whole body, reminding Sam of a mongrel the twins had owned, who'd wiggled, loose-jointed from head to tail, at Daniel's call or Stefi's laugh. Not that Tootie wiggled, of course.

Sam sighed. Jack said that people who were always happy must have a few screws loose.

That showed what *he* knew. Tootie had her screws set perfectly.

Sam pasted on a smile as she rolled her big suitcase toward the door. "Here I come."

"Let me get that," Tootie said, reaching to help.

Sam waved her away. "You can practice setting the alarm and locking up."

Her gaze swept over her small acre with one final, lingering look at the cliff steps. Then she climbed in the passenger side and concentrated on arranging her purse at her feet, on fastening her seat belt. She wasn't sure she'd have the courage to leave if she had to see her little sailboat again.

"Don't worry. I'll take care of it." Tootie started the car, nodding toward the house. "All of it. You just concentrate on having fun."

Fun? If only.

"I know you'll do fine," Sam said. And she'd be free. Or, at least, on her way toward freedom.

Gravel crunched under the car's tires. Sam angled toward the window, ignoring tears that slipped down her cheeks and dripped off her jaw.

Neither spoke until Highway 101 met 70-West in Havelock. Then Tootie said, "It'll be fine. Everything, *Alice*, the shop, your house. You've taught me so much. And, yes, I remember all you showed me yesterday, the electrical panel, the hot water heater, the furnace."

Sam pulled a tissue from her blazer pocket and swiped at her damp cheeks before blowing her nose. "That's a lot of responsibility I'm heaping on you."

"Sam, listen to yourself. You're letting me live in your wonderful cottage, letting Holland take me sailing in your beautiful *Alice,* which, by the way, he's dying to work on, so you don't need to worry about a thing there. And you're trusting me with the shop. You're doing me a huge favor."

"It doesn't feel like that from here."

"Pooh." As a few drops of rain hit the windshield, Tootie hunched over the wheel to peer up at the sky. "Was it supposed to do this today?"

"I didn't think so. Maybe it will quit soon."

"I hope." Tootie flicked on the headlights and the wipers. "I told you Jenny's opening this morning, didn't I?"

Ah, business. Good, a distraction. "You still think she'll work out?"

"I do."

"I hope she understands you're the one in charge."

"You made that plain. We won't have any trouble." Tootie shot her a big-toothed smile. "Besides, if she gives me any grief, I'll just sic Holland on her."

"That's what I told Rhea. What an image."

Tootie steered the Volvo toward Raleigh and asked, as if she'd just thought of it, "Are you sure you don't want me to take you all the way? I could, you know. It's not that far."

"No. It's time you met Rhea face to face, and I have some papers to give her. She lives this side of town, anyway."

Rain streamed down the side windows. Sam willed it to stop before she had to change cars, but the splat-patter continued. The wipers swooshed to the right, to the left, and back again in a grating rhythm that sometimes missed a beat when a blade stuck on the glass. A passing car sprayed a fan of water, momentarily blinding them.

"What's with these guys?" Tootie asked. "Haven't they heard of oil slicks?"

Sam didn't comment. She could barely see the highway, and Tootie's posture made it clear that the girl was nervous, especially when cars zoomed past in this fast zone. But the Volvo held steady.

As they approached the by-pass around Smithfield, she directed Tootie toward the exit leading to the outlet mall and then to a parking lot on the west side. "Rhea will meet us here."

Her stomach felt fluttery from too much caffeine. Or too much fear.

She hated the way she was doing this, leaving the world she'd created and heading off like an escapee instead of a woman on the brink of adventure. She shut her eyes again, just for a moment, and tried to conjure the image of a Tuscany landscape that had hung for so long in the Raleigh house as a focal point for dreams. Then, she'd imagined traveling as one of four. Not this way, the mama running off to visit her daughter because she had to go *somewhere*.

Mama, the mess. Mama, the....no, she wouldn't even *think* that word.

"Here?" Tootie asked, rousing her.

"That's fine. Rhea should be along soon."

Tootie shifted into park and left the engine running. Reaching into the backseat, she produced a book. "I got you this to read on the plane."

Sam studied the blurb. "Another Theo Anderson mystery. And how very apropos, with his heroine Sophrina sleuthing in the Apennines." She pulled the girl into a quick hug. "Thank you so much. You know I enjoy your uncle's stories." She tucked it away in her shoulder bag with her getaway stash: her ticket, credit cards, Euros, passport, and antiquated cell phone, which wouldn't work once she left the States.

"I wrote Uncle Teddy's phone number in the back, in case you get a chance to call him. I already told him Stefi's in Italy, because, you know, I thought he might help her. Make her more comfortable, having sort of a relation there. I mean, my relation, not hers, and she doesn't know him, but she knows me, sort of, anyway. Through you. And Uncle Teddy's great. I know he'd like to meet you both."

"Thank you," Sam repeated, scanning the parking lot for Rhea's car. All she could think about was escape, not making nice with anyone, even Tootie's uncle. "I don't know where I'll be or what I'll be doing, but thank you. If nothing else, I'm sure Stefi will be glad of another contact."

"I'm going to miss you, Sam. You will be back in time for the wedding, won't you?"

"You said Christmas."

"Doesn't that sound wonderful? All the lights, the trees. It's such a perfect time of year."

"It is. Absolutely perfect." She touched the young woman's hand as it lay between them. Tootie's turned and squeezed.

"Rhea promised to be here for you," Sam said, drawing back. "Anything you need to know. I'd never have made it without Rhea. She's a darling. You both are."

And on that, Rhea's blue van circled, looking for them. "There she is," Sam said. "Blink your lights."

"She saw us. Now you stay here while I get my umbrella."

"I'm not going to have you get wet!"

"Don't worry. I can change clothes. You can't."

Between them, Tootie and Rhea managed to transfer Sam and the suitcase with only a few splashes on each. "Yes, I know." Tootie held the umbrella over Sam. "Stop worrying. I'll e-mail you with details, and you'll call me." She leaned in around Sam. "Glad to have met you, Rhea. And thank you so much for offering to help me. I'll need it."

"Not a problem. I imagine Sam's taught you like she taught me, so don't you be worrying your pretty head about the shop.

I'll only be a phone call away, and you and me can get to know each other, hear?"

"Thank you, thank you!"

Sam put a steadying hand on Tootie's. "Get out of the rain. And drive safely back to Beaufort."

"Yes, ma'am." Tootie started to shut the door. "Will you please get a phone over there?"

"Fine, fine. Now, go."

The door closed. Sam blew her a kiss through the window, and Tootie blew one back, mouthing, "I love you."

As her one link to Beaufort splashed out of the parking lot, Sam took a clean tissue and dried the rain from her face, but the wet continued to form in her eyes. "I'm sorry to have dragged you out in this mess. I should have flown from Simmons-Nott Airport."

"Where's that?"

"Oh, right." Sam smiled as she remembered her grandaddy's obsession with New Bern history. "You probably know it as Coastal Carolina Regional, but my grandaddy knew the Simmons family and how the senator had honored Lt. Nott, a Marine pilot who'd been killed at the time Senator Simmons was dedicating the airport. Grandaddy insisted we call it by its original name."

"Well, honey, I needed to clap eyes on you again before you take off." Rhea pointed the car west.

"Sorry it had to be like this."

Rhea tapped the steering wheel with her long fingers. "You got no cause to be sorry. You're doing the right thing."

Sam eyed the milk-chocolate profile, with its fine nose, round puffy lips, and crinkly black hair pulled back so it stuck out like a fuzz ball from the bright red clip that corralled it. The clip matched the shirt peeking from under a tan raincoat and was just a shade darker than Rhea's lips and fingernails.

The tug on Sam's heart tightened. Rhea'd been her best friend as well as her employee for so many years that the thought of not being near enough to hear Rhea's laugh whenever she wanted just plain hurt.

"You seen him again?" Rhea asked, with a quick glance Sam's way.

"Jack?" Sam eased a deep breath between her teeth, slowly so it wouldn't whistle. "No," she said. "It's why I'm leaving today, so I won't be there when he shows up."

"Good. Only thing to do, girlfriend. You know that."

The memories, images she'd never be able to erase, brought a shudder. Sam slammed shut her eyes and bit the inside of her cheek.

After passing a lumbering truck, Rhea eased her van into the right lane again. The traffic was heavier the closer they got to the sprawl of the Triangle, but at least the rain seemed to be easing.

If Sam rode too long with her eyes closed, the bile would rise in her throat. Focusing ahead, she concentrated on the slower pace of the wiper blades and the hum of the tires on the wet road.

Rhea hit the turn signal and exited toward RDU Airport. "You won't believe who came into the shop yesterday." Straightening off the turn, she didn't wait for Sam's response. "Your ex. With *her.*"

Sam felt the wince in more than her eyes but tried not to let it show, because wasn't she supposed to be over that one? One mess down, one to go?

"Have you seen them since Daniel's wedding?" Rhea glanced over at Sam with a martial gleam in her eye that would have boded ill for Gail if she'd been there.

Sam almost smiled, until the image of Gail sashaying down the aisle in that miniskirt flashed front and center.

Gail, entering the front pew with Greg, sliding past Stefi, pretending she cared about Sam's grown-up boy and girl. "No, but I sure remember the diamond she flashed at Stefi."

"You mean, at you."

"Did I tell you she said she'd bought the suit because Greg was taking her to Italy?"

Rhea snorted. "Not now, I hope?"

"No. Daniel says they've gone and come back."

"But I bet you hated hearing that, him taking her on your trip."

"When she said it, I wanted to claw both their eyes out. Now?" Sam pictured the curvy Gail, whose melons pushed out the front of her too-tight tops while Sam was blessed with barely-theres. Gail swished when she walked and fluttered her lashes to make a point—whatever that point was. "You know what?" Sam said. "I'm almost glad she has him. So I don't have to."

Rhea loosed a laugh that sounded like a bark. "I kept my eye on her as she circled the aisles of the shop, oohing and ahhing, but she did buy a couple of mugs, picked those two with that blue-brown glaze we both like."

"Really?"

"Yep. Anyway, while I was packing them up, Greg leaned over, whispered to ask how you're doing."

"And?"

"I told him you were great, happy and fine. Best not let him know differently."

Sam grunted. "Absolutely not. And I will be."

"That's true. You will be. You're a whole lot better off without that sleazebag—or the one who followed." Rhea squinted in her rearview mirror. "Oh, glory, now what?" And she hit the signal to pull off to the side, but the state trooper's car dashed on past. "Thought he mighta been bored enough to stop me, speeding or not."

"Men." Sam didn't hide her disgust.

Rhea laughed. "Bound to be a good one or two out there someplace, but they sure haven't come our way, have they?"

"Afraid not." Her thoughts wandered again to her ex-husband's leave-taking. "Did I ever tell you what Greg's parting words were? That he'd never loved me?"

"Girl, he didn't say that!" Rhea shot her a look of disbelief. "*Never* loved you? That's not what it seemed like before. Greg may be a creep now, but he wasn't always. Was he?"

"I didn't think so," Sam admitted. "We had fun in the beginning, when the twins were young. But you knew that Gail wasn't his first affair. Or even his second."

"Did I?"

"Spilt milk." She leaned toward the cold window, longing to pound her head against the glass, as if self-inflicted pain might ease her now.

Ridiculous. Hair-shirts never worked, except perhaps to make the wearer itch. They certainly didn't expiate sin.

"Cheating and lying, like my ex," Rhea said. "Found out last week, Bry's got two babies other than my girl."

"No!"

Rhea nodded. "The mama of number two came calling last Wednesday night, looking for Bry, who hasn't lived with us goin' on three years now. So how come she's searching for him there? The man hasn't changed his colors, not a whit," she said. "I know we gotta forgive them, but it's hard."

"Especially when your sweet baby's bound to want her daddy," Sam said. "When did she see him last?"

"Considering he's been dodging support payments these last years? Not since she was two."

"Poor thing."

"Least yours were grown before Greg lit out." Rhea paused. "I know it broke your heart."

"He said selling the house would give me my freedom. Who wanted freedom?" No, she'd wanted her home, a place for the twins to visit and for grandchildren to find family. "The cottage is better, though," Sam told the window.

"Listen to us." Rhea's pursed lips poofed out a harsh sound along with a breath. "Moving nearer the coast got you another *Samantha's*, it got you Tootie, and it got you that pretty piece of land. And me? I got my baby and you and God. I don't need nothin' else." The ponytail bounced as Rhea made her point. "I know I'm preaching to the choir, but, honey, you and me gotta stop this complaining."

"And who started it?" Sam raised her brows then sighed. "I know. It doesn't matter. We're both better off. So, you're right, no more complaining."

"Amen. And you're about to go on a great trip."

"Which," Sam said, "wouldn't have been so rushed or so necessary if I'd been a stronger, better person." Her tone turned to disgust as the words again showed up in her head. "I'm pretty sure I taught the just-say-no philosophy. Too bad I failed at follow-through."

"We both know why," Rhea said. "I'm hanging the blame on Jack. He's the one had two women. He's the one with those smiling ways that suckered you *and* her. I don't care if he did move out of her house. He's the one ought to have known better."

Wouldn't it be comfortable if Sam could blame Jack for all her woes? But her moral compass should have pointed her away from him. Jack hadn't pretended to believe. She had.

Rhea's turn signal blinked and blipped as she maneuvered toward the terminal. "You just remember to take care of yourself over there, hear? You're doing the right thing. Besides,

Stefi's going to be over-the-moon thrilled, her mama coming to visit. It was a good thing, her being able to go, what with Daniel getting married suddenly like that."

"She felt kind of lost, didn't she?" Sam pictured it. Her beautiful Stefi, eyes wide with forced gaiety at the wedding, calling Cindy her sister as if the word had trouble rolling off her tongue. Thank God that the last-minute opening in her school's Italian program had offered an escape route. Something of Stefi's own.

"The twin thing," Rhea said, as if that explained it all.

It did. "They were each other's best friend. It's hard."

Rhea merged into traffic and the airport round-about, eventually zigging the van into a place at the curb. She climbed out and came around to open the side door, saying, "Stefi'll find her way. Don't you worry."

"I know." Sam hefted her bag to the sidewalk before pulling Rhea close. "Thank you. For everything."

"I love you. You take care, hear? And call me." Rhea sniffled, trying for a smile.

"Yes, ma'am. I'll check in regularly." Sam turned quickly so she wouldn't have to watch the van drive away.

SHE LEANED against a wall at the boarding gate. She'd tried sitting to wile away the hours before her flight. Had even paced from one end of the concourse to the other to work out some of the kinks. Now she just wanted to get on that plane and get this part over with.

She studied the folk preparing to fly the friendly skies with her. It sure didn't look like the world's economic recession had caused a slowdown here. Kids huddled around their parents, dropping crumbs and spilling juice. Businessmen and women two-fingered keyboards faster than Sam could have typed with ten functioning digits. Thumbs flicked over Androids or iPhones. A couple of grungy-looking youths lounged on their backpacks.

They called her boarding zone. Her cell phone jangled Daniel's ringtone as she headed down the ramp, but she ignored it until she'd settled in her seat and tucked away her carry-on.

This would be the last time she'd be able to use this old phone until she returned to the States. "Mom, get a new one," had been her children's litany. "One that actually does stuff." They called her a technological dinosaur, but she used a computer for all sorts of business tasks every day. She merely refused to send or receive text messages on a phone. That did not make her a dinosaur.

Blowing stray hairs off her face, she hunched away from the passengers who'd fit themselves in next to her and slowly punched in the familiar numbers.

Daniel's voice hiked an octave whenever he was worried. His, "You sure you're okay?" hit the top end of the tenor range. "You've got a place to stay when you get there?"

She watched out the plane window as a train of baggage carts wheeled past. "I booked a room near the Spanish Steps. I'll be fine."

"And Stefi's waiting for you?"

They'd been over this, she and Daniel, at least twice. "She will be," Sam said. "I'll head to Florence in a couple of days. I've made all the arrangements."

"By train? I heard you have to book seats as well as find a ticket."

Not by train, but she didn't say so. Better he think her safely on public transport than loose on the highways. She laughed quietly. "You've been searching on the Internet."

"Of course. What do you expect after calling me with three days' notice to say you're leaving the country?" At least he'd moderated his tone, sounding more like her in-control son. A business major, Daniel liked things to make sense, especially as he'd lost temporary control of his own life this last year. Still, he'd whipped it back into a semblance of order by marrying Cindy.

That had helped and had given Daniel other things to worry about than his mama. "I'll be fine," said that mama. "I have traveled before. And in Europe."

"But not for years and not by yourself."

A disembodied voice announced that they were closing the airplane's doors. "I have to go. We're taking off."

"Call me when you get there?" The tenor was back.

"Soon after. You don't want to hear from me in the middle of the night."

Sam hit *End* and held the button down to turn off the phone. Then she settled in to read *Apennine Angles* and the antics of Theo Anderson's heroine.

Hadn't Tootie been cute, hoping Sam would meet her uncle? The likelihood of running into a mystery writer in a country almost twice the size of Florida was so remote that she had played along with the girl's dreams. As far as Sam knew, the man might live down in Italy's toe or heel, which were not on her list of destinations this go round.

She tried to concentrate on the heroine's romp from the Italian Riviera south as the sleuth followed a thief who'd made off with one of her baubles, but the words swam on the page. The in-flight movie wasn't worth watching. She closed her eyes and tried to sleep. But memories intruded—no matter how much she wanted to squelch them.

Her life had flipped from flat to jagged to flat and back to jagged faster than she could snap her fingers. She was back in the flat zone now, but jagged had been her *modus vivendi* for much too long.

Out of one mess and snap into another. Like a magnet attracting nails, that had been Samantha Ransom.

She eased her seat back and adjusted the neck pillow she'd brought, then tried to focus on the abruptness of change to distract herself from fantasies of Greg flat on his back in a body cast, of Jack tumbling into the sea, even— *please*— of Jack's girlfriend, India, bound and gagged. If she let those in, she'd soon hear an imagined siren's wail and a jail door clanging shut.

She needed an expletive. A good, solid curse to shout at anyone listening. But, oh, it was hard flailing against all those years of zipped lips.

And a plane over the Atlantic, while providing too much time for reflection, also wasn't the ideal place for an explosion of language. Besides, she was supposed to pray, not blather ugly words.

Did she even remember how to pray? So far, her attempts to reach anyone in power had accomplished zip, zero, nada.

Exercise was the only thing that calmed the stress pushing her toward an early grave—and that wasn't hyperbole. Her own mother had worried herself into so many physical ills that she'd orphaned Sam as a babe of twenty-five. No, if Sam didn't relieve these raw emotions in some healthy manner, she'd end up heading that way too soon. She'd like to imagine her own end would be heaven, but she wasn't sure she rated an entry pass any longer.

She popped an antihistamine. Maybe its soporific powers would let her sleep without the after effects of a sleeping pill— and without embarrassing her by being too effective. She'd taken a sleeping pill once on a red-eye across country and awakened to find her mouth open and drool running down her chin.

Isometrics helped stave off leg cramps, but nothing else. She plugged in her iPod to tune out the caterwauling of the miserable baby in the row behind hers and as a distraction from the seat-kicking of the baby's brother and the imploring voice of their mother.

But neither music nor an audiobook corralled her thoughts.

"Can I get you something to drink?" the attendant asked.

"Hot water?" She turned down the food tray, but asked for crackers. "Have you got any?"

"Sorry. Only cookies or nuts."

"Nuts, please."

The attendant handed her two packages of peanuts and the steaming cup into which Sam dunked the chamomile tea she'd brought along. The task of eating one peanut at a time and sipping the tea very slowly occupied a few moments of brain space, but not enough.

"Hey, you gonna eat those extra peanuts?" the man next to her asked, pointing to the unopened bag on her tray table.

Sam looked from the nuts to the man's belly protrusion. "Help yourself," she said, surprised into offering them.

Had she wanted to eat them? Probably. Later. So why couldn't she have said no?

Typical. Weak and lily-livered.

She straightened in her seat. No, that was the old Sam. She wasn't going be that way any longer.

She wasn't? Then what about the peanuts?

She glanced over at the man. He had the bag upturned over his shiny lips. Now he was chewing. Too late for the peanuts.

Sam shut her eyes again. *You can, you must...* She would be strong. She would flee from the old and become a new person.

She would.

Her nose started to clog as her eyes fogged. She sniffled and squeezed her lids against any spills.

"Excuse me, ma'am, would you like something else to drink?" the flight attendant said in a bored voice.

Sam shook her head, willing him to leave her alone. She didn't want a soda. She hated sodas.

Because on that day, that very first and fateful day, Jack had handed her a can of soda, a Pepsi, as they'd sailed *Alice.* Before he'd kissed her. Before he'd done more.

Before she'd let him.

First the soda and then the *more.*

With a deep sigh, Sam pressed the seat back, trying to change its angle so the kid's feet couldn't land a direct hit. The man next to her readjusted his bulk until his beefy arms pushed hers into her lap.

His thigh intruded. She edged as close to the side of the plane as she could get, but the thigh followed, oozing under the arm rest.

She glared at the thigh and switched audiobooks, trying to concentrate on the British reader. When he announced Chapter Three, she realized she'd missed all of Chapter Two. She punched over to music.

Why wouldn't that pill work? She wasn't even drowsy.

The sky darkened as they sped east, away from her friends and the day-to-day running of her shops.

Choices. One always had choices. If only she'd run sooner.

Culpa mea.

4

JACK

Bat's in the belfry,
Supper's on the hook,
Pigeons taking pot shots,
Where is one to look?

Jack Waters didn't do churches. They made his back sweat and his heart rate surge until blood pounded like a jackhammer in his neck. Which meant he must be a fool, standing in front of this one, thinking about entering its frigid darkness on a day when the sun shone and the breeze blew from the right direction. Sun and breeze didn't come every day.

He scuffed the toe of his shoe against a flagstone. Yep, a fool or a coward.

In or out?

Sam should have answered her stupid phone. She knew he'd call the moment he arrived. That he *had* called. More than once. She was playing at hard-to-get again.

"Excuse us," a young and very pregnant woman said as she

waddled past, followed by a man hefting a diaper bag. *And* a toddler.

Jack winced. Obviously, there were worse things than being childless. Poor guy. But a drooling gurgle from the toddler stopped his blood-hammer long enough to let him concentrate again.

He ought to be on the river, sailing, not standing in front of this ivy-draped stone façade. He was bone tired and deserved a few hours of fun before he had to head out again.

Muttering a word that didn't belong on the steps of a church—and would have gotten his face slapped or his ear tweaked if his pop were still alive to hear it (the hypocrite)—he pushed open the heavy oak door and sucked in a deep breath, releasing it slowly as he crossed the threshold. She'd better be inside.

His eyes adjusted to the darkened entry, then again when he stepped into the sanctuary, where sunlight filtered through the stained glass.

"Welcome," a smiling man said as he tried to hand Jack some folded bit of paper.

Jack narrowed his eyes at the fellow. Either that dark brown rug thing was a toupee or a bad dye job. Still, Jack supposed he ought to say something back to a face that continued to beam at him like he was some long-lost brother. He waved away the extended paper with a, "No thanks," trying to sound polite, but failing. He cleared his throat. "Sorry." No sense getting tossed out before he'd looked around.

A keyboard, guitars, and a set of drums showed off up front. What had happened to the organ and choir? Not that he even liked organ music, but that's what he remembered from his last visit inside a steepled building. Had to have been thirty-some years ago.

He waited until the congregation had seated itself and he

could see over heads. He picked out Tootie's orange hair easily enough, but there was no sign of Sam's brown fluff. His gaze scanned the rows. Wait, was that…? An unknown woman sat up straighter. No, she was too short to be Sam. And there was a kid next to her.

As the service began, Jack turned and left, his frustration drumming in time to the beat from inside.

Where was the fool woman?

He'd been phoning the house for the last week, but she hadn't answered. This morning, he'd returned to town just long enough to pick up some papers he needed for tomorrow's sale. The equipment in Pittsburgh had been a dead end, but he was on the trail of a good generator that would hit the auction block in the morning.

Sam had been a mess the last time they'd talked, blubbering, saying he needed to leave her be. How could he? They belonged together.

He'd be able to smooth things over…once he found her.

Well, that would have to wait. She wasn't working, or at home, or sailing *Alice*. And she wasn't at church. She never stayed gone long, not when her house and boat were here. So, he'd be back.

And then he'd find her.

It was only a matter of time.

5

SAMANTHA

If ever I were wanting, if ever I were free,
I'd find myself a Chinese junk and sail up the yellow Yangtze.

Sam tapped a palm against her thigh, keeping time to the
music in her head as she stepped off a curb and crossed
toward the Fontana di Trevi. She wedged herself through the
crowd to the rail, and there it was, the famous fountain, just as
she'd imagined it from the movies.

This was good. She was in Rome. The sun shone, the water
splashed and bubbled, and she finally felt rested.

She ogled the carved figures and all the coins that visitors
had tossed in the water to bribe one god or another. Ah, but
she, Samantha Ransom, would keep her purse closed.

It wasn't a day to tempt fate, and—as far as she knew—God
couldn't be bribed.

Which really was too bad.

Turning from that thought, she checked directions to the
Spanish Steps. Her stride lengthened and her limbs loosened,
and she tucked the guidebook away in her bag.

The scent of baking breads, of garlic and herbs, and of coffee wafted from doors as she passed. Students and tourists perched on the tall steps, some reading, some chatting, some merely basking in the day. Well-dressed women strolled arm in arm. Cell phones seemed permanently attached to more ears than she'd expected.

Who cared about Jack or home? Not Sam. At least, not at that moment. She had cut loose bonds that had nearly strangled her in Beaufort. She imagined flinging them to the wind.

When her stomach reminded her that the chocolate gelato had long since worn off, she stopped for lunch in a little *trattoria.*where the waiter spoke English. Lovely waiter. She studied the menu and asked for a recommendation. He brought her a plate with four light, sweet, incredibly succulent mushroom ravioli, dribbled lightly with brown sauce and freshly grated cheese.

She moaned at the first bite.

The waiter returned. *"La signora* is certain she does not wish a small glass of wine to accompany *i funghi?* Merely the water?"

Tempted, because, after all, this was Italy, she said, "Do you have a suggestion?"

"Un momento, signora!" A smile lit his face, and he hurried off.

The small glass he gave her to sample was a light red, almost translucent. She'd expected white.

Sipping, letting it roll over her tongue, she wanted to purr. "Please, yes."

He filled her glass and stepped back, obviously delighted with himself. Well, she was pleased with him, too.

When he cleared away her empty plate, he asked what she'd like for the *secondo.* Four large ravioli, and he supposed she'd want more? "Fine," she said. "A small salad."

A couple of very handsome and very young men sipped something at a nearby table. One spoke, an invitation perhaps. She ignored him. The other's lifted glass and toast of "Bella" slipped through the language barrier. She appreciated the compliment—who wouldn't—but she'd read that Italian men flirted with anything female, no matter her age. Ducking her head between bites, she tried to emit no-talking vibes. No men allowed. No chatting or smiling or speaking. Period.

Thank you very much.

Wine with lunch meant a nap. After her tramp through the streets and her visit to the Colosseum early that morning, bed sounded like luxury. She left a hefty tip for the waiter and wandered back out into the sun.

Her stomach did a little lurching thing, as if it knew home, when she turned the corner and saw the sign for her quaint hotel. Retrieving her key from the desk, she thanked the bent and smiling clerk and climbed the marble steps to the second floor and her room, which overlooked a small courtyard. There, she eased out of her sundress and slid between the cool sheets.

Sleep should have been inevitable. She lay with closed eyes until images she'd tried to bury danced across her lids: Jack laughing as *Alice* bucked on a wave, reaching for her. And India, standing in the background, furiously pointing a finger. "He's mine."

Sam tossed off the sheet and grabbed her book. Sophrina had tracked the jewel thief to Bologna and was hot on his trail, but the words began to jumble and mix with India's voice crying Jack's name, with India's voice screaming Sam's.

Oh, God, please.

Noises filtered through her window. Siesta had closed the

shops. In the interlude, pots clanged and people talked and laughed. Sam wished she could be a fly on the wall, one who grasped this foreign language and could share the humor. Here, in Italy. Not there, in North Carolina, in the life she'd left behind.

∾

By MORNING, she felt ready to try the touristy bits again. She breakfasted in the hotel's parlor on espresso and a *pane al cioccolato*. Sweet chocolate in a semi-sweet pastry. She could get used to this. And get fat from it.

Well, maybe not right away. She still had pounds to put back on before she looked normal.

The crisp morning air made the trek to the other side of the city invigorating, and she lined up with the hordes to visit the Vatican. She'd never seen anything quite so awe-inspiring as the Sistine Chapel ceiling, although craning her neck while cheek to jowl with those hordes did nothing for her comfort level, in spite of the guards who stood everywhere, shushing all to silence.

She imagined Michelangelo, flat on his back, high above the floor with a paintbrush in his hand. How could he have had enough prospective to create such paintings when he couldn't move back far enough—without climbing down and then up again—to make sure that hand fit where it ought and that robe hung as it should? How had he imagined the scenes? God's finger reaching out, God breathing life. The history of mankind that had led to the coming of a Savior. The scenes from Christ's life. And there, at the front of the chapel, a crucifix.

The death. The resurrection.

What hours of preparation had gone into the planning, the

drawing, the crafting of a vision that still sent people to their knees? She'd have fallen to hers if she'd been alone.

And then a shout startled her and everyone else in the room. "My money!" In American-accented English, no less.

The crowd did its best to part as a guard rushed forward, and Sam could hear the man's words along with the frightened mewling of a woman who must have been his wife. "Look here. Someone unzipped my waist bag. How? I didn't feel a thing!"

Sam touched the small purse that dangled between her breasts and under her shirt. As she watched the crowd, another worry added itself to her load: pickpockets clever enough to lift valuables with no one noticing.

She exited the Vatican and headed back across the Tiber using *un ponte*— a bridge—slightly upriver from the first. Repeating the Italian word, she committed it to memory as she stared down at the narrow canal that was the Tiber River. The water looked deep and brown and very unappealing.

She tried to focus her attention on the streets, the bridges, the buildings, but a dark head or a certain look—or even the sight of water flowing past—brought a rush of memory. Jack, finger combing his dark hair. Jack, calling her to sail, to play, to forget her world of hurt.

The trouble with trouble was that it didn't go away just because you wanted it to. Why had she imagined a foreign place would automatically do the trick, as if the miles would wipe clean her brain's hard drive?

So, she walked. And then walked more. Finally exhausted, she carried a slab of onion pizza back to the hotel instead of braving another elegant dining experience at a table for one.

Perched on her bed, she opened the pizza box and bit into the thick crust. It was laced with rosemary and sprinkled with Romano cheese. She did her best to enjoy all the flavors that zapped her taste buds, putting off those phone calls.

They had to be made. And her daughter's needed to be first.

Stefi asked again when Sam would get there. "Soon," Sam promised, unwilling to limit herself to a specific day. She'd reserved a rental car for Thursday, but she might want to stop somewhere between Rome and Florence. An entire country lay before her.

Son Daniel must have been distracted by his pregnant wife when Sam called him. Or perhaps he took his tone from his twin sister, knowing his mama had actually made it to Europe and so out of range of his control. At any rate, he began to cheer her on.

The conversations with her children had almost worn her out, but her managers needed to hear her voice. Or she needed to hear theirs.

Rhea answered at the Raleigh shop, her warm tone like honey flowing over Sam. "I've checked in on the girl to see how she's making out. Seems to be fine. We have a date to meet next week."

"Thank you."

"You've got no call to worry about either of us. You just take care of *you*. Hear? You know what you gotta do, so stick with it."

Sam wrinkled her nose at the phone. "Yes, ma'am." She was trying, wasn't she?

"You don't make it back in time for the quarterly reporting," Rhea said, "I'll do it for both stores."

Tears filmed Sam's eyes. "How did I ever get so lucky as to find you?"

"Honey, wasn't you finding me. It was the Lord rescuing me by sending me into *Samantha's* that day."

Neither of them would win that argument, because Rhea had always given more than Sam could ever repay. It was probably time to make Rhea a partner, at least for the Raleigh store.

The talk with Rhea buoyed her enough to punch in the Beaufort number. Tootie zipped right on past the small talk. "I know you probably haven't had time to call my uncle yet, but did I tell you how to pronounce his name in Italy? They call him Teo instead of Theo. Isn't that cute? They spell it T-e-o, so I guess the *e* makes a long *a* in Italian? I should study the language. For when I visit him. You won't lose his number, will you?"

"I'm sure I won't." Obviously, Tootie wouldn't let her.

The girl giggled, reminding Sam how very young she was, barely older than the twins. Had Tootie undone her bright orange hair yet? The one constant delight was Tootie's ever-changing palette.

"How's the house? Are you comfortable?"

"I love it. I'm taking really good care of everything. Holland's coming over this afternoon to work on *Alice*. And he said he'd take me sailing this weekend. We'll be extra careful. You don't have to worry about a thing."

"I'm glad he's there to teach you. He's a keeper." Sam wished he could stay at the house as protection for Tootie. "Just be sure you set the alarm every night, okay? I don't want anything happening to you."

"We don't get who might have wanted to hurt you."

One sharp-eyed flight attendant? Sam didn't answer, but she had another excuse for staying far from home—the thought that India might escalate damage beyond Sam's stuff.

6

TEO

Strangers touch, and strangers see.
Lowering the bar, holding out a hand, that's the part that's up to me.

Teo returned to the pebbly beach, glancing over his shoulder, hoping his mystery woman would reappear. He laid his cane beside his shoes, waded out, and climbed up on a rock, his bare feet dangling on the shore side of the breakwater. Behind him, waves dumped their spume, splashing up, backing out, up and then out.

And suddenly he heard a whisper. "I need," she said. "I need."

The sound licked his ears, her trembling words barely audible over the persistent splashes. He turned but saw only rainbows in the water drops.

What did she need? If only she'd raise her voice, let him hear the timbre, the heft of it.

"*Sono qui,*" he called, his voice pitched to carry over the water.

Oh, right. She spoke in English. He translated. "I'm here." And then, "Speak to me."

A sob tumbled out of the nothingness.

No, not nothingness. Something crafted the words, those sounds. But who wept? How could he comfort her if he didn't know? "Please, let me help."

Prismed colors collided, and there she was. For a moment, her eyes stared into his. The lids lowered, and another sob caught on a breaking wave.

He sat there while the rock beneath him cooled and his trouser legs siphoned water up his calf. But she did not return, and eventually the chill in his feet and buttocks forced him up. Damp toes slid grudgingly into loafers. He ignored sand that scraped at his heel, kept his head bent forward as he trudged up the hill.

The soles of his shoes flapped against concrete. The tap of his cane joined a cacophony of cars and motorcycles and voices that all centered him in this place. Her voice, though, remained silent, even as he pushed open his apartment door and settled his cane against a chair.

He'd be heading to the States soon to meet with his editor and grab a little family time. He should let them know. He sat down, dusted the beach remnants from his feet, and picked up his cell phone.

It took only the sound of Tootie's lilt to draw a smile from him. "Uncle Teddy! Where are you, what are you doing?"

He laughed. "Still in Reggio, my pretty. I'll be knocking on your door in a matter of days."

"You'll have to come see me at the store. I'm just visiting Mom, because Sam left me in charge of *Samantha's* and her house."

"She did, huh? And why is that?"

"Oh, she's gone to visit her daughter. I don't think things

were going well for her, you know, since her divorce. And other stuff."

"Ah."

"I gave her your phone number and your new book. I told you Stefi was in Florence. You remember I sent you her number so you could call her."

"I haven't had a chance to yet. And after my visit stateside, I'll be heading to Greece for research."

"Greece! Oh, I wish I could come!"

Wouldn't it be fun to see the islands through young eyes? "I wish you could, too, but as newly appointed head honcho, you won't have much free time."

A sigh came through the phone, and then the chirpy voice returned. "Sam's in Rome right now. I know she'd like to meet you."

He shook his head. His niece, the matchmaker. "And I'm sure I'd enjoy meeting her."

"Well, you want to talk to Mom?"

"I do. See you soon."

As he waited for his sister to pick up the phone, he began plotting the stops for his trip, rebooting his computer to figure logistics. He'd bought his plane tickets, but he needed to confirm the rental cars, decide his route.

He had places to go and people to see. That was the best way to live. To keep moving. Think about the task at hand and not the would have been, could have beens.

7

SAMANTHA

An indented circle of naked flesh,
Where banded gold once staked a claim,
An unadorned finger wiggling at air...
Does this proclaim freedom or merely contempt?

Sam handed her reservation number to the man behind the counter at the EuroCar Rental Agency.

"Lei parla inglese? English?"

"Un po'. A little," the agent answered as he waited for his computer to upload Sam's information.

A woman in a smart lemon-colored suit spoke in Italian with another agent. She seemed to be having some sort of difficulty.

"Signora," Sam's agent said, "it seems we find a mistake. This reservation was for yesterday, *sì?* And so we have it no more."

"Yesterday? No, that's impossible. I asked for a car for today. I'm sure of it."

The man slid the paper across the counter and pointed at the date, then at the flip calendar at the end of the counter.

Sam looked at both and then at her watch. She had to squint carefully to see that it said the same thing. Today was not Thursday, as she'd thought, but Friday.

A day had vanished. How had she lost an entire day?

"But I must get to Florence. My daughter expects me." She had checked out of the hotel. Her bags were here, at her feet.

"*Mi dispiace.*" He shrugged with his face as much as his shoulders. "An auto for today is not possible. Perhaps the train?"

She wanted to be angry at him, but how, when the fault was hers? She pressed the palm of her hands flat on the counter and glanced around helplessly. The other customer, the well-dressed woman, watched. And then she spoke.

"My dear," she said with an accent Sam couldn't quite place. "May I perhaps be of some assistance?"

Sam merely stared back. How? By waving a wand to procure an extra car? "I seem to have misplaced a day."

The woman's laugh was a soothing gurgle. "So I heard. Do you know how to drive a gear stick, by any chance?"

"You mean a manual? I do indeed."

"Then perhaps we can help one another. My reservation was for an automatic. It seems to have vanished into the same black hole that took your car. But, I do have one with a gear stick—I mean, a manual transmission—and no way to drive it. And today I go to Firenze."

"Really?"

"This is today's destination. I will ultimately need to be in the north, but I am sure I can exchange for a better car first. This kind lady," —an arm swept toward the agent in front of her— "assures me that there will be a very fine automatic car awaiting me at the agency there."

Sam held out her hand. "My name is Samantha Ransom, and I would be pleased to act as your chauffeur."

The woman's eyes twinkled. "Delighted, my dear." She shook Sam's hand once. "Martine Paoletti."

~

SAM'S COMPANION pointed the way with a casual wave and asked, "You travel to Firenze to see the sights?"

"Yes, and because my daughter, Stefi, is studying interior design through her college's semester-abroad program."

"It is a wonderful city for art." Signora Paoletti smoothed her fine white hands down the yellow skirt. "I married while *una studentessa* in Roma thirty years ago."

"Married?" Sam swallowed. Stefi and dashing Italians?

"Do not worry for your daughter. She will return home, I am certain. But I, I am European. This was not such a change for me."

"Europe is bound to seem glamorous even to modern American girls."

"Would it be so terrible?"

Sam bit her lip. Losing Stefi to Italy might not be the end of the world, but it would come close.

Signora Paoletti spoke into her silence. "My darling Tonio awaits me at our home. It is near the sea."

"Ah." And wasn't that lame? But she hated that a daughter could grow up as quickly as her twin brother and make choices that distanced them all.

She had to let it go. Let them go.

But only yesterday they'd been dimpled and in diapers.

The signora's abrupt gesture focused Sam's attention on her driving. "There, to the right! You must follow that road."

Sam made the turn, grateful for fast reflexes and traffic that eased enough to let her in.

"I am so very sorry," Signora Paoletti said. "I was not paying the proper attention. So, do you stay long with your daughter or will you continue to travel?"

"Stefi has classes, and you know the hours students keep. I want to see the city and then perhaps rent another car and just wander."

"We are in Portofino. You must come. It is very lovely, and the tourist season will soon be at an end, so it will not be as crowded."

"Thank you, Signora." How fun. A destination.

"Martine. You must call me Martine. May I call you Samantha?"

"I prefer Sam."

"Sam." Martine rolled out the word with a cadence that had much of the Italian in it.

"You know, you sound more Italian than English. I love the accent."

"English is merely my second language. I am one of those odd creatures who was born in France and schooled partly in England. My father was an Englishman who married into a French family. He wanted me to have both, you see."

"And so you speak French, English, and Italian?"

"Yes, and also German and some Spanish."

"My goodness. I can barely manage a school-girl French."

As they zoomed north, Martine described places that remained names on signposts. Too soon, they were off the *autostrada* and into Firenze.

Sam pulled up in front of the rental agency. "Thank you for making this trip so delightful."

"The feeling is mutual, my dear. Do you know where you must go now?"

Sam dug out Stefi's address. "I'm sure a taxi driver will be able to help me."

"Perhaps your destination is on the same route I must travel to my hotel."

"My daughter said it's near the Duomo."

"Then we will share the ride, if you would like."

Of course Sam would like. Martine flashed a smile at the man behind the rental agency counter. She must have asked about a cab, because he immediately picked up the phone and punched in numbers that resulted in a ride awaiting them in very few minutes. Sam paid attention. Martine was obviously a woman who knew how to accomplish things.

"You will visit me?" Martine asked as the cab driver headed out into traffic. She extracted a calling card from a small case in her purse, jotted down her phone number and address on the back, and handed it to Sam. "And you said you miss your little boat. We, too, own a sailboat, but Tonio has been too ill to take me recently. Perhaps you would agree to?"

Sailing? On the Mediterranean? "I can't imagine anything I'd like more," she said, tucking the card in her wallet. The Italian Riviera and a sailboat.

"I will look forward to your phone call then, when you travel to the north. *Va bene?*"

"Thank you so much."

"Signora?" The driver pulled up next to a battered stone building and popped open his trunk.

Sam tucked a few folded Euros into Martine's hand. "You must take this. You paid for the rental and the gas to get us here. Let me at least pay for the taxi."

"I will look forward to seeing you soon, *cara.*"

As the taxi drove off with her first new friend in this foreign land, Sam hit the buzzer for Stefi's apartment. Soon, feet tromped down the stairs, Stefi flung open the door on a squeal, and, enveloped in her daughter's arms, Sam entered stage two of Mama's Healing Moments.

~

THE DAYS ROLLED one into one another as she and her daughter trekked around the city when Stefi wasn't in class. By her fourth day, Sam was determined to see the statue of the David tucked inside the cool stone walls of the Galleria dell'Accademia. None of the books or postcards did justice to Michelangelo's genius. She'd seen the two-dimensional artist in Rome, but oh, my, this larger than life, three-dimensional masterpiece amazed her.

She grinned. Interesting, wasn't it, that this study of the male form, this *huge* and very nude male, didn't send her running, considering her recent misadventures. Of course, she'd seen naked before, but neither Greg nor Jack could compare with this fellow. What man could?

A wistful yearning coiled inside her. The artist had caught the boy-man David, the one who had known rescue from the lion and the bear and now expected God to perform the same against Goliath. So why had Michelangelo carved worry lines on David's face?

Had he pictured David wondering as he held those smooth stones if maybe he'd misheard the call? Could the artist see the grown man, the king, who would become an adulterer, a murderer? Had Michelangelo thought of those times and of the days David had spent on the run from Saul while he chiseled winkles in this David's brow? She'd really like to know how David lived with himself in the days and years after Bathsheba.

She forced herself up from the bench and circled the statue once more. Stefi and the gorgeous Italian boy, Guido—who draped himself on, over, and around Stefi with too much freedom for this mother's comfort—would be waiting for her to squire them out to dinner again, so she'd better get moving.

She cast another glance over her shoulder and, doing so, could understand Stefi's infatuation. Guido might have been a direct descendent of the man who'd modeled for the pretty-boy David.

Stepping out into the sunlight, Sam pulled on her dark glasses and turned in the direction of Stefi's flat. They'd go to dinner—Sam treating, so she hoped the *they* wouldn't include too many of the roommates—after which the kids would want to go to a dance club. The very thought made Sam feel arthritic. Not that she was, but *really*. Had she ever had that much energy? Better to bow out tonight.

And try not to worry about her daughter in this too free, too foreign place. Yesterday, she'd tried to warn Stefi, quietly, gently, about the danger of quick intimacy. But Stefi had just hugged her hard and promised to be good.

Right. Stefi's mother had promised exactly the same thing, and look where she'd landed. Here, and wishing she could put a chastity belt on her daughter and throw away the key. It was way too late for Daniel, but she prayed Stefi would be more careful. And perhaps remember a few of the things her mama had taught her.

Divorce stank. So did its aftermath.

SAM LET herself into the flat Stefi shared with three other girls. "Hey, love," she called, setting her purse on Stefi's bed before joining her daughter in the living room.

Stefi sat cross-legged on a ratty old couch, the string from a tea bag hanging over the rim of her mug. "You have fun today, Mama? You want some tea?"

"No, thanks. And I had a lovely time. Saw the *David*." Sam eased down on the couch.

"Oooh, isn't he the yummiest thing?"

Sam raised her brows. She'd missed this amusing girl of hers. "Well, I'm not sure 'yummy' is the word I'd pick."

"Those hands. I'd love to touch hands like those. And the lips. It's probably a good thing the statue's so big. Can you imagine the lip-locks it would get when the guard turned his back if that mouth were in kissing distance?"

"Cold, though, don't you think? Who'd want to kiss marble lips?"

Stefi grinned. "There is that."

"Where are the others?" Sam asked, glancing behind her toward the back bedroom.

"They headed out early to get seats at this concert. I thought maybe you and I could hang out by ourselves. Go get pizza or something."

No Guido? But instead of asking, she checked her watch. "Are you hungry already?"

"I'm always hungry. Besides, it's been a while since I ate."

"Give me time to take advantage of the empty bathroom for that shower I missed this morning, and we'll head out."

Hot water was always at a premium where beautiful young women shared a space, and the faucets had run a tepid stream by the time Sam's turn came that morning. She grabbed her towel out of Stefi's room along with a bottle of Stefi's shampoo and climbed in and under. She'd learned not to leave the water running during her full shower, so she turned it off while she lathered and turned it back on to rinse. Clean clothes, a quick blow dry of her hair, a dab of blush, and she only needed shoes.

Stefi had changed from jeans with holes—fashionably placed holes—to a comfy yellow top and white pants. Sam raised her brows with a pleased, "Nice," and then checked out the obviously new sandals on Stefi's feet. "Like the toes," she said when her daughter wiggled the painted nails. "They match your lovely hair."

Stefi squinted down. "You think so? I didn't mean to make them auburn. I was trying for more red."

"They work well with those yellow sandals. You match all over."

"What are you going to wear? Your clodhoppers?"

Sam tried to look affronted, but she couldn't help the grin that surfaced. This was an old discussion. Sam had given in to some extent, but she'd never understand why anyone chose style over comfort. "For you, I'll wear my flats tonight." She dug the black shoes out of her suitcase and slipped into them.

"Thanks, Mama. They're much prettier."

Sam hoped they wouldn't pinch. "Where to?"

"Pizza?"

"I shouldn't have asked. I'm in the mood for a little elegance." She lifted one foot. "In honor of my flats and those pretty sandals of yours."

Stefi slipped her arm through Sam's and hugged. "Then the place across from the Duomo."

Which meant only around a couple of corners, no foot-pinching required.

A waiter seated them and offered menus. Sam honed in on the choice of mussels. "Me, too," Stefi said and pointed to the squid antipasto. "Let's live dangerously."

White wine arrived. "To my beautiful daughter," Sam said, lifting her glass. "I'm so glad to be here with you."

"Oh, Mama, I'm so happy you came. It's been so much fun."

"It has, but you know it must come to an end."

Stefi's glass clinked on her salad plate as she set it down. "Why? When? You just got here!"

"Four days ago." Four nights were long enough to camp

among the younger set and play at dorm living. "It's time to move on, honey. Do a little more traveling on my own."

Stefi ran a finger around the rim of her glass, studying it as if the liquid held the answers she needed. "You'll come back? When you've traveled more?" Worry clouded her lovely eyes.

"I'm sure I will, sweetie. But there's so much to see, and I need the time."

That inched the worry up Stefi's forehead. Sam longed to smooth off the lines, but she didn't have the power to do that, not unless she could pretend again that everything was fine. The smile she dug out must have been weak.

"You're still not over Dad?"

"Divorce is hard." If only Sam could lay the full blame there. "I just...the thing is, I'm still trying to figure out who I am as a single woman. Can you understand that?"

"I think so," her loyal daughter said.

"I got so busy starting over again that I didn't take the time I needed."

Stefi waited barely two breaths before inserting a timid, "Jack?"

Picking up her glass, Sam focused on it and took a slow sip, hoping Stefi wouldn't see the alarm in her eyes. Where had *that* come from?

"Mama, it was obvious that you and Jack spent a lot of time together. And that India Monroe wasn't exactly a part of it."

How on *earth* did mothers have conversations like this with their too astute daughters? "Well," Sam began and then lost the thought. She tried to hook another one. "Let's just say that the situation made me uncomfortable."

"That's gotta be hard. You always told me to run from temptation. I'm proud of you for being courageous enough to come here."

"You are?" But Stefi didn't know the truth of it—how Sam had run too late for it to count.

"I love you, Mama. I'm so sorry you've had to go through any of this."

Their waiter cleared his throat. Ah, the *antipasto*. And more bread. Wonderful. Another distraction. Sam nodded her thanks to the waiter, while Stefi said, *"Grazie,"* like a native.

Sam broke the bread and swirled it in the olive oil. She forked a piece of the perfectly cooked and marinated squid, smiling around a mouthful at her sweet, sweet girl, and that same sweet girl smiled back. They spoke of Italy and travel and school and Daniel and Cindy—but no more of Jack or of Italian boyfriends.

Later, as they prepared for bed, Sam reached for Stefi. "You're my beautiful girl, and I'm so very, very proud of the woman you've become."

"Thanks." Stefi swiped at tears that had begun during the embrace. "You'll call me? And you'll come back?"

"I will. I've lots of minutes on this calling card."

"You need an international cell phone, Mama. Really."

"Fine. As soon as I use up these minutes."

"And a computer or an iPad. Then we could talk and see each other on Skype."

"I know. But it's just another thing to carry around. Another thing to lose."

Stefi loosed a deep and very loud exhalation, ending with a shrug that said she'd quit nagging, but she wasn't happy. As Sam lay in the dark that night, she thought about daughters and mothers and all the mistakes she'd made. And she prayed that the compounded interest from each and every one of hers wouldn't have to come out of Stefi's account.

8

TEO

Every fork in the road is a moment of truth,
And a choice that leads to the next one.

An interesting place, New York, but not a city in which
Teo would want to live. He'd checked into his Soho
hotel and changed his shirt before heading to Midtown for a
late afternoon meeting with his editor, Valerie Thornton.

Val was one of those strong women whose office attire
consisted of jeans and a blazer with the sleeves folded back
twice. She gave him an air kiss and led him to her office, long
silver spirals dancing from her earlobes, her dark hair even
more closely cropped than he remembered from their last
encounter.

Pointing him to one of a pair of visitors' chairs, she took
the other.

"Things look about the same around here," Teo said, waving
at the piles of manuscripts that littered her desk. "Why don't
you just use a computer?"

"I do." She propped her booted feet on a coffee table,

crossing them at the ankles. "The thing is, I work better from printed copy."

"Lots of paper there."

"Yours is often among them. You have the outline ready?"

He nodded, handed over his ideas for Sophrina's next adventure, and asked, "With all that to wade through, how do you get your changes online to send me and all your other authors?"

"Gaby. My new slave."

Poor Gaby, deciphering Val's squiggles. He'd seen Val's handwriting, and it wasn't pretty or particularly legible. But then, neither was his. Waiting as Val studied the typed sheets, he tapped fingertips on the brass handle of his cane and let his attention wander to her bookshelves.

His occupied a corner, upper left, top shelf. He shot her a silent thanks for her early faith in him. The spines of others caught his attention. Colorful. Some actually blazed with reds and yellows.

"You haven't detailed who's to be the victim," Val said, clipping the pages together. "Someone on the yacht? And you'll puff it with Aegean mayhem?"

"I will. It's gelling." He cleared his throat. "What I really wanted to talk about is a new heroine, not quite fleshed out yet, but getting there."

Val's brows arched.

"To be honest," Teo said, trying for smooth and confident, "I was thinking of trying something a little different, something other than a mystery."

A scowl replaced her hiked brows. "Your brand is mystery."

His bland expression resulted in a deep sigh and more questions. Clearly, she was not convinced.

"Don't worry," he promised. "I'll send you the finished

proposal for Sophrina's Grecian adventure after my trip to Athens. It's coming together."

"Good." She slid her feet to the floor and stood.

That hadn't gone so badly. Perhaps he just had to sneak the new proposal in at the same time he sent her the full manuscript of Sophrina's book.

He didn't hear laughter from any of the workstations as Val led him past staff who scooted back into position when they saw her. At the elevator, Val hit the button, combed fingers through her spiked hair, and blew out a long breath.

"Okay. Fine. Send me an outline of your new story idea," she said. "We'll see. But you may lose readers if you switch genres. A pseudonym?"

"Not a problem." He returned the barely-there good-bye hug, one cheek forward, brushing lightly.

So what if he hadn't a clue how to manage book signings as two different people. He wasn't sure they advanced his career appreciably anyway.

When the taxi stalled in traffic, Teo tried to make conversation with the driver and received only stares in return. Perhaps the fellow had just arrived off the boat from somewhere quite a bit east of here.

He picked up a latte from the coffee shop next to his hotel to tide him over until dinner and headed upstairs. His hotel room insulated him from the screeches and howls of rush-hour New York. He opened his laptop, set it up on the desk, and while it booted up, sipped the coffee, swiping at the mustache it left on his upper lip.

The caffeine provided enough oomph to get his fingers moving. But no matter how many keys he hit, how many sentences he wrote, he couldn't seem to make sense of his vision's last call for help. What he remembered was her silence, a silence still in force in spite of his offer to help. Noises surrounded him, but they weren't the ones he yearned to hear.

Spiritual things had once seemed important, but even back then, visions had never been part of the equation. Apparitions obviously involved spirits of some sort—unless he actually *was* crazy—and he'd be much more comfortable if he knew they had something to do with God and not the other guy. Like Jacob's wrestler or the extra man in the furnace. *Not* like something conjured in a séance or through a Ouija board.

He positioned his fingers above the keyboard, his wrists resting as he punched in words, sentences, paragraphs. Then he shook his head and pounded the delete key to erase the nonsense. The shivers he felt from *her* weren't remotely spiritual. No, sir. They were all woman.

Only, not real.

What was wrong with him?

He shut down the computer and slipped it back into its case. He obviously wouldn't be writing that evening.

Interesting that he hadn't told Val about the detailed notes he'd made of his encounters. Probably because what he had was plotless, consisting only of a few word pictures. Telling Val would have exposed the lack of substance.

Why couldn't he enlarge the story—*what story?*—and make sense of it all?

He tipped back in his chair and remembered returning to the beach in Reggio right before he'd left for the airport. A couple of wind surfers had struggled to stay upright. One, a bikini-clad young woman, had squealed as she steered and balanced.

Next thing? It had hit him. *Bam.*

His woman sailed. Of course. That's why he'd seen windblown hair and sunglasses. No, she hadn't appeared that day. No face nor body had come attached to the knowledge, no words on the wind. Just poof! He'd known.

Enough. He needed a shower and some food. Shower first.

The nozzle pointed spray at his tired flesh. He braced his hands against the plastic surround and leaned into it, letting the water pound the kinks from his muscles. If only it would empty his mind.

Sailing was an alien experience, right up there with bungee jumping or skydiving. Why would he conjure a heroine who messed with something so foreign? Sailing stories were bound to be full of odd and difficult technical details. Granted, he was a researcher, but settings were easy. Take a trip, write a new book. The murder/police procedural details came from interviews in each country and from a lot of reading. But sailing?

Maybe he could catch a ride on someone's boat when he went to Greece. Two birds and all that.

Did he know anyone who owned a sailboat?

Yes, he did. But Tonio hadn't been well in recent months, so he'd best get a charter, either in Greece or back in Reggio.

Still, maybe he was wrong about the sailing. After all, he was on shaky ground with the whole *knowing* thing. Maybe her hair was messy because she was a biker. He could do biker. Or maybe she just didn't use a comb.

Not likely. Who wanted to read about a hygiene-challenged female? Or to know one? Only Napoleon, and *that* story was enough to make a modern man gag.

In Italian, the word was *pazzo*. Crazy. Too much time alone.

At the thought, some old song flicked on in his head, something about being alone in a crowded place.

Yep. That was his life. People all around, friends, sort of, to dine and chat with. But no soul-searching conversations. No touch of intimacy. No skin on skin or mind to mind.

Not a healthy train of thought when it brought a stirring in his flesh, the sort that made him yearn for lips and breasts and...

Enough.

He could turn off the hot water, cool himself down, but the idea didn't have enough appeal. He wasn't masochistic—at least in the physical sense. Maybe he was a mental masochist.

But, as he couldn't wash away this or any of his other issues, he flipped the lever to *off*, wrapped himself in a big, fluffy hotel towel, and climbed out of the glassed-in shower. Steam clouded the mirror, hiding his scarred form from the judgment of his eyes.

They didn't snap shut soon enough as he lowered the towel to dry his legs, and he remembered why he was still celibate. He pulled on a robe and spread his hands on the basin, leaning forward. Heaven help him, he would *not* make himself vulnerable again. Ever. No other woman would have the chance to cringe from him, from even the *thought* of him, as Janet had.

Deep breath. Let it out.

He picked up a comb and ran it through his hair, trying to look at himself dispassionately. He was wealthy. He had a moderate following among readers. And like all wealthy, reasonably successful, reasonably personable men, he attracted interest from the opposite sex. Many of those women were beautiful, but none knew him. None looked beyond the romantic distinction of a brass-handled cane to the reality of those broken legs.

Who would, could, want a cripple with skin mottled in colorful lumps and ridges? No, he would not undress in front of a woman anytime soon.

∾

HIS LAPTOP KEPT him company on the flight to Richmond, Virginia, the closest airport to his parents' place on the Rappahannock. His laptop and thoughts of mysteries, Sophrina's very predictable ones and this new blip in his viewfinder.

He rented a shiny black Mustang at the airport, put his bag in the trunk, and headed out of the parking lot. Because it wasn't rush hour or a summer Friday when sand huggers clogged the freeway, he picked up the pace. Speed felt good.

Maybe spending time with his family would put things into perspective. Shake up his brain and let the pieces settle back into place. He'd been doing so well before *she* showed up and started roaming around in there.

Traveling began to take its toll, and his vision blurred the highway lines. He looked for somewhere to eat, turning off when he spotted a big pig and a neon sign advertising barbecue. The plastic tablecloths and country music sent him back to the Mustang to eat his take-out under a tree. The sweet tea tasted so good, it might have been worth braving the local ambiance just to have a free refill, but he could spring for another one after a nap. With the seat pushed all the way back and reclined as far as it would go, he closed his eyes.

And there she was, waving as she cut across the street and hurried around a corner. He woke slowly, the image stuck in memory. A perfume, barely there and unfamiliar, lingered in his nostrils.

"Who are you?" he asked.

But no one answered.

THE ONLY THING that marred the visit with his parents was a nagging guilt because he so rarely went this far out of his way to spend time with them. They seemed happy interacting in their busy community and bird watching from their aluminum jon boat. But when they spoke of visiting Deb and her family in North Carolina last spring, his dad's expression grew wistful. "Would have been great if you and David could have been there, too."

So, he promised Christmas—at least for himself. Who knew what David would do.

And then he waved good-bye and headed south on Route 17. He had hours to cogitate, which was usually a diverting experience. Because he usually thought about writing.

Not this time.

He loved his life in Reggio, but had he been selfish in making the choice to move that far away?

Say he lived in North Carolina, as his sister did. He'd still have to travel for his writing, and he'd still be busy at his computer when home. Would he get up to Saluda any more often?

Did Deb? He loosed a pent-up breath. No, she didn't.

The truth was, his parents liked to see him, and he liked to see them. He'd work on the logistics and be back for Christmas. Maybe bribe his son to join him.

Trying to focus on a feisty radio talk program, he finally crossed into Beaufort and found a parking space down the street from the store where Tootie worked. He straightened his sport coat, pulled out his cane, and added a spring to his lopsided gait.

Tootie handed a cup of something to a customer as he pushed open the door at *Samantha's*. He eased up to the counter. "An espresso, please."

She whipped around, cried, "Uncle Teddy!" and came flying toward him. He braced himself, holding out an arm to catch her.

She smelled of lavender, subtle enough to be from soap or shampoo, but unlike her usual. Did she use her boss's? That thought made him wonder about the boss and how she fared in Italy. It was amusing that Tootie wanted them to meet, but he was here, where the boss normally worked, while the boss was over on his turf.

"I didn't think you'd get here so soon." Her grin, that wonderful, wide grin she'd inherited from her dad, lit her face.

He ran a finger down her short nose. "Stopped to see my favorite girl."

"You mean *first?*" She reached up to give him a quick peck on the cheek and headed back around the counter.

"It sounded like a good idea." He rested an elbow on the polished surface as Tootie tamped down the grounds for his espresso. "Maybe you can help me figure out where to take you all to dinner."

"Woohoo! I'd love to go out, and Mom's been canning all morning. Putting up the last of the tomatoes and spaghetti sauce."

The image of his sister in an apron, manning a ladle and stuffing canning jars, surprised him. So, Deb canned her own food, the perfect farm wife. Amazing how different their lives were, his and his sister's.

He remembered the older sister who'd spent her gangly teen years holed up in her room with books, then her college vacations hobbling across the country in her beat-up VW camper that sort of ran, sometimes. Deb had wanted to see the world. When she'd fallen for a boy from North Carolina whose family farmed, she'd dumped the leggings and baggy sweaters for jeans and work shirts.

But it was easy to see where Tootie got her pizzazz.

The dark liquid spit into the small cup. Tootie passed it across to him. "Did Sam call you yet? Is she with Stefi still?"

His niece with the one-track mind. "I haven't heard a thing, but did you expect I would, really?"

"I guess not. It wouldn't do any good, would it, not with you traveling so much."

The other customer approached and slid his empty cup toward Tootie, but he directed his words to both of them. "You're discussing Stefi? And Sam?"

"Jack," Tootie said, without a particle of enthusiasm. "Uncle Teddy, this is Jack Waters, an old friend of Sam's. He fixed up her house."

"Theo Anderson." Teo extended his hand.

The other man's lips stretched in what would have passed for a smile if the eyes had reflected something more than a stare. Teo felt the calluses as they shook hands, but not much strength. Rough hands and a weak grasp seemed contradictory. He checked out the face again, the skin pasty, as if the man had been ill. Dark circles shadowed even darker eyes. Illness would account for the seeming weakness in hands that obviously knew manual labor.

"Sam?" the man repeated. "You know her?"

"No," Teo said, bringing his attention back to the man's obvious anxiety. "I'm afraid I haven't had that pleasure."

"Oh. I thought..."

"I'm hoping he'll get to see Sam. And Stefi." Tootie rinsed the dirty cup and set it aside. Her tone again bright and friendly, she continued, "Uncle Teddy lives in Italy. He can be someone for Stefi to call on when Sam comes home."

"Ah, yes, well." Jack Waters set a couple of bills on the counter, nodded at Teo and turned toward the door, pausing to ask casually, as if it were an afterthought, "Do you happen to know when that will be?" At the shake of Tootie's head, he flicked them a wave, turning on these words. "Tell her I asked, will you?"

"Sure, but how's India doing?" Tootie picked up the bills and added them to the cash drawer, not looking at Jack.

Teo caught the raised eyebrow as the other man said, "Fine. She seems to be fine," and left.

"Odd fellow," Teo said, one eye on Jack's retreating back as he carried his untouched coffee to a nearby table. "Come sit with me."

Another customer got ready to leave, and Tootie called out, "See you later, Clay. Say hey to Annie Mac for me, will you?"

"Will do."

When the shop had emptied, Tootie joined him. "That was our local detective. Good man."

"Ah, the police frequent here, do they?"

"Everyone has started coming in." She splayed her fingers on the surface in front of her.

Teo grinned and nodded at her diamond. "Nice ring. Good taste."

"Holland's mother's." Her smile blazed. "I can't wait for you to meet him."

"How about dinner tonight?"

"I'll ask. I'm sure he'd love to."

"Good. So what was that all about, that thing with Jack?"

"Oh, him." She waved her hand dismissively. "It's an odd situation. Jack used to live with India Monroe, a flight attendant. She grew up in Morehead City, so she's considered local."

"The one you asked about."

"Yes."

"But you used the past tense. He 'used to' live with her."

She began to draw invisible circles. "Jack and Sam were friends back when they were kids—they're both from Beaufort —so it wasn't all that surprising that they spent time together when they met up again here, mostly sailing on Sam's boat.

Jack moved back to Beaufort about a dozen years ago,, but Sam just returned a year or so ago. After her divorce. Anyway, they had the sailing thing in common. Plus their past."

Okay. So old friends got to know each other. Obviously, there was more.

"I don't think it made Ms. Monroe, India, very happy, especially when Jack moved out of her house. She has a place over on Emerald Isle."

"Ah." Ah, yes. That would explain Tootie's discomfort. She was, in many ways, an innocent. A very conservative innocent.

Her gaze wandered to the street and then back again. "After Jack left Ms. Monroe's, some strange things started to happen to Sam's house and boat."

He perked up at that. "What sort of things?"

"Vandalism. Jack says kids did it, and that's what Sam pretends to think. At least with me. But I'm pretty sure she believes Ms. Monroe did it, only it's one of those things we don't talk about." Tootie slid his empty cup across the table and stood to carry it behind the counter.

He expected another comment. When none came, he asked, "Why not?"

"I don't know," she said, her back to him as she turned on the water. He had to strain to hear. "Probably because there's no proof, and Sam's too nice to go gossiping."

"But not too nice to break up their relationship?"

She swiveled around and shot him an angry glance. "Uncle Teddy. You don't know anything about it. That was mean."

It was. "You're right, I'm sorry."

"The whole thing makes for an interesting mystery. And I can't blame Jack for preferring Sam to India, but it must have gotten out of hand, or else Sam wouldn't have left so quickly." Setting the clean cup to dry on a rack, Tootie wiped down the counter. "I've tried to warm up to Ms. Monroe, but she's just plain strange. Sometimes really friendly, like when she sent flowers to the shop soon after we opened, but other times, she's weird. I remember once I got here just as she flew out of the store, flapping her arms and cursing. Really ugly curses, too."

"I take it that wasn't her normal behavior?"

"Not from what I'd seen before. She ordered two pounds of coffee, then just up and ran out. Sam retreated to the office. Didn't say a thing."

"Jack doesn't look like a healthy man," Teo said.

Tootie's gaze returned to the street. "I saw that. He used to be really tan and fit. Maybe he's worried."

"Because Sam is gone?"

"I don't know. It came as a shock to him when he found me at her house."

That's right. Tootie said she was taking care of the place. What if this mess spilled over onto her?

"Nothing has happened at the house since you've been there, has it?"

She shook her head. "No. And I don't think it will now that Sam's in Europe."

"You can't be sure."

"No. But you remember Pete? Aunt Ruth's son?"

"Tall, lanky kid?"

"Yeah. He's a deputy now. He said he'd drive by every so often."

"That's good." But Teo would let her take him out to see the place. After all, who better to look at the scene of a crime than a mystery writer?

9

SAMANTHA

She stares in the mirror, empty eyed,
At worlds she made and lies she told.

T he mountains around Bologna fit Sam's mood—green here, gray-brown rock there, tunnels and curves and cars speeding past. She drove into the old city, found a place to stay and a small *ristorante* at which to sup, and curled up on a lumpy mattress as she awaited daylight.

When had the world stopped being fun? And when had she lost the ability to see beauty all around her—to enjoy the moment?

She tried to recapture these the next day by pausing at a sidewalk café to watch the passersby. If only the faces didn't blur, the voices, lilting or harsh, didn't slide past her eardrums without connecting neurons. At the Basilica San Petronio, her chair had a view of a magnificent altar, all gilded and glorious art. She squinted at it, hoping the squint would help her concentrate and allow the beauty to touch her core.

Disgusted with herself, she hit the north-bound highway.

She should have eaten something before she left, but Modena wasn't far. Perhaps it would have something to offer, something that would awaken more than her exhausted self.

She pulled off the toll road as images began to blur. The last thing she wanted was to fall asleep at the wheel. No matter how depressed she felt, suicide wasn't an option—it couldn't be.

And didn't that drive her thoughts to new convolutions? She was still believer enough to think murder wrong, even if she were the intended victim. And with a wreck, there could be more than one hurt. Not a pretty thought.

Besides, showing up at the pearly gates with so much on her conscience would be foolish in the extreme.

She'd done the I'm-sorry bit so many times she ought to feel forgiven. She knew self-flagellation wouldn't get her to the other side of here. But it sure would be great to move forward, from *here* to some sort of peace, without raking up all those scars from the cat-o-nine tails that were her thoughts.

Sighing, she searched for a parking lot that would take her car. And then for a small restaurant that would feed her. She found both, ordered, and then merely stared at the *spaghetti alla bolognese* when it arrived. She forced herself to eat a few bites, to drink a small glass of the local red, and then wandered the town in search of an affordable hotel.

As she lay on the very comfortable bed, on what felt like a down mattress pad, she stared at the ceiling and the intermittent light that shone from a flashing sign outside. Her stomach hurt. And her eyes. Yes, definitely her eyes, dribbling tears down her temples, past her hair. She turned on her side, and the tears fell toward the pillow.

Why was she crying? It didn't make any sense.

She'd broken free. She'd never let herself be in that position again. And she was, after all, in Italy.

She brought a tissue to her nose and blew hard. Who cared that she was a walking disaster?

Finally, sleep came. And when the morning sun filtered through the slats in the blinds, she got out of bed, dressed, and went downstairs to the next-door coffee bar. Armed with a croissant, an espresso, and a little box of orange juice, she returned to the room to get ready for a new day.

She was going to conquer this thing, this business of being alone and full of self-pity. While she ate, she studied the map. A day or two here—where was here, exactly?

Oh, right, Modena. Lots to see in Modena.

So, she saw the lots: the Romanesque cathedral, the Ducal Palace. And in between these and the hotel were shops and restaurants and people.

She stayed two days. And then picked out her next stop, Piacenza, slightly to the north. She ducked off the toll road, found a hotel, and settled in for overdue phone calls before she went after food. If she ate first, she'd become too lethargic to bother. Oh, the responsibilities of being a grown-up.

Yeah, right, Sam. That's you.

She punched in the numbers she'd need to reach Daniel and listened to it ring. Maybe she'd only have to leave a message.

He answered. Yes, he was fine, his wife was fine, the pregnancy was going well. "You fine, Mom?" he asked, and when she said she was, he chatted about his classes and how well he was juggling it all. She hoped it was true, that he wasn't merely trying to stave off her worry.

Her next call was to Stefi.

"Yes, I'm driving carefully. Conservatively," Sam promised when Stefi asked.

Even though cars passed with kamikaze pretensions, the Italians did seem to honor the passing-only-on-the-left rule and kept that lane clear for vehicular samurai. Sam didn't mind hugging the right shoulder, not even when it meant moving at a snail's pace.

"What are you seeing? Is it helping?" Stefi, who'd begged her mama to phone nightly, continued to need reassurance.

"I'm eating and touring and having a lovely time, sweetheart. But don't you think you should concentrate on your life there and let your mama off the leash?"

Stefi's answer followed a very loud and very elongated sigh. "But you'll call me often? Maybe not every night, but often?"

"I promise. Don't worry, please."

"I'm trying."

Which was all Sam could ask of her, especially as Sam held a graduate degree in worry herself.

The new girl in Beaufort answered the shop phone. Yes, she loved working there, all was great, lots of customers, and she'd go fetch Tootie from the stock room. Tootie could barely control herself as she told Sam about her uncle's visit.

That was good. Tootie's uncle in the States meant no nagging for Sam to look him up.

"I'm glad your assistant's working out well," Sam said to change the subject.

"Oh, she is. And she has a whole slew of other friends who've started coming in every day. Business is great."

"Rhea says the same thing about the Raleigh store. Perhaps I should have left town sooner."

Tootie giggled, as she was supposed to. "You're a hoot, Sam. By the way, Clay stopped in. He said the same thing he always does. No way is he going to swill that junk they brew down at the station house. He's so funny. When I told him you were off in Italy, he said to tell you 'hey.' And Hannah was here this morning with her two. You met them, didn't you? Louis and his sister, Linney? She asked where you were visiting. Said you had to come see her when you get home so you can compare trips."

"I forgot Matt had taken her to Italy."

Hannah happily flitting from place to place with her husband versus Sam's miserable and very alone self barely registering her surroundings? Not exactly the bubbly conversation Hannah would expect.

Tootie's words didn't register until she said something about Hannah's newly adopted daughter. "Seems Linney's been feeling poorly. You think the child's condition makes it harder when she gets sick? I don't know much about Down Syndrome."

"She's sure a sweet thing, isn't she?" Sam said, remembering the talk in town when the two children had been discovered hiding out behind Hannah's church. "I suppose they were visiting Down East Creations?"

"Business seems to be thriving there, too."

"Good news all around." At least there was good news in Beaufort. Good news somewhere.

Get. Over. Yourself. The words showed up as if shot from an old ticker tape machine. Click. Click. Click.

With a sigh, she hung up and dialed Rhea's phone. The thought of more conversation made her throat constrict. "I'm having a *grand* time," she assured her friend and, hoping to cut short the call, added, "No, no, I'm not depressed or moping. How could I be, here in this incredible place?"

Fine, she lied. So what?

~

THIS BECAME HER DRIVING TOUR. Each morning, the map and the route. Each evening, a place to rest. If she liked the look of the resting place—and how could she not, considering that this was the land of gorgeous, old, and welcoming places?—she stayed a day or two.

The towns blended into a tapestry of quaint and interesting. But days of travel, with only a phone card to link her to others, began to take their toll. She needed to stop. To put up her feet and stay a while. To speak English.

Portofino and Martine's invitation to visit got Sam thinking west and then south. She opened her guidebook to research the area.

Ah, yes, well, she should have known. She'd never be able to afford more than one night in a place like Portofino, a high-end—meaning expensive—seaside resort, very much on the beaten path. She flipped to the next page. Tucked in among the natural hyperbole were two paragraphs suggesting that the smaller, supposedly cheaper Reggio sul Mare might be the place for Sam, near enough to Portofino for her to call Martine and invite her for lunch. Or something.

The little rental descended a treed hillside into the smallish resort town. She topped off the rental car's tank, looked around with curiosity, and asked for directions to the nearest inexpensive hotel.

The station attendant raised his brows at the word *economico* from an American's lips, but he jotted down several names, accompanying his notes with florid gestures and something about turning right and then left—or maybe that was left and then right—and how this one was up the hill, and that one was down. The Pensione Garibaldi was her next to last stop.

"*Posso vedere una camera, per piacere?*" she asked at the desk, quoting her phrasebook.

The landlady grinned over winsomely crooked teeth. With great flourish, she patted her flyaway hair and led Sam to a room on the third floor that boasted a distant view of the sea.

NORMANDIE FISCHER

It had a throw rug in bright blues to soften the terrazzo floor, a small desk, a bureau with a miniature television set, and a double bed, which Sam tested by sitting on it. A sink occupied one corner, but the toilet and bath were down the hall. Sam pointed to the shared toilet and shook her head, saying, *"No, no, troppo,* too much," to the quoted room price.

The woman suggested a sum by the week. Sam did the mental calculations and named a smaller number. The landlady grinned and nodded. The light in the woman's eyes probably meant she'd have taken less.

Handing over the keys at the local car rental agency gave Sam momentary pause, but she could leave whenever she chose, either by bus, train, taxi, or hired car. And she wasn't far from Genoa or Milan, which meant flights home when she'd tired of this journey.

And, no, choosing a place this close to someone she'd met had nothing to do with emotional dependence and everything to do with shoring up her walls. She'd come for adventure, but she didn't want to become a basket case again and find herself in trouble. Better to admit she needed friends and be close enough to visit one.

She sucked in a deep breath, released it, and nodded to the walls of her new room. This was good. She didn't need an AA meeting, but she might just need an English-speaking female friend.

Now that she'd decided to stay for a while, she looked at the town with a different eye. The other stops had been places to see. This was a place to savor while she saved money.

She grabbed her shoulder bag and set out to explore. And to eat.

A sign caught her eye. Any restaurant that advertised with a brightly painted fish in pinks and oranges and yellows swimming on a sea of blue at least needed sampling. A smiling waiter ushered her to a window table and brought her a bottle of water.

She ordered her favorite mussels. If they could prepare mussels well, she'd return. And the cost was a fraction of what she'd spent on simpler fare in the cities. She must have delighted restaurateurs in Firenze when she took Stefi and that young Guido to dine.

Speaking of Guido. That boy certainly knew how to flash his pearly whites. Naturally, Stefi imagined herself in love. But Guido had very little education, poor boy, and only spoke Italian. Oh, and hadn't he said his life's goal was to take over his uncle's garage? He'd bore Stefi to death in a month.

Sam forked a succulent bit of meat, chewed, and sighed. The waiter hovered. *"Delizioso,"* she said. He smiled.

Why on earth did her daughter date these totally inappropriate men?

Oh. Right.

Sam winced. Perhaps she should initiate the Samantha Ransom Dependence Recovery Program and invite Stefi to join.

Her mind kept capitalizing letters. That probably said something, though she didn't know what. Very like Stefi in her teen years.

She finished eating, paid and thanked the waiter, and started once again toward the seaside when a phone kiosk caught her attention. She really ought to report her new location to the troops.

The children's cell phones took messages. She tried Beaufort.

Tootie answered. "Oh, Sam, you won't *believe* how many people we've had stop in to buy things just today. I even sold one of those huge kitchen mixers to someone from out of town. And I'm doing fine with the spreadsheet program.

Rhea's been making sure everything is the way you want it. She's great. I just feel so privileged to work with you both." Tootie probably bounced to her toes as she spoke, with her eyes all glittery.

When Sam asked about the house, Tootie mentioned the autumn flowers and fun on *Alice*. It was a good thing Holland knew his way around boats.

"I'm glad you're sailing her," Sam said, trying to hide a wistful yearning.

"So, where are you now?"

"Well, I've decided to take a rest and save a bit on gas—so expensive. You remember I mentioned the woman I met in Rome, the one who comes from Portofino? Martine? Well, according to the travel guides, Portofino caters to the tourists, so I found a *pensione* in a little place to the north called Reggio sul Mare. It's—"

Tootie's sputter stopped her. "Reg— *Reggio*? You're there? Oh, Sam, that's where my uncle lives!"

"Theo Anderson?"

"He does!"

"Really?" Sam's heart slammed into overdrive. Had Tootie told her this? The pounding hit her temples with a dull thud, like a rubber mallet on a nerve or two.

An American ex-patriot and semi-famous writer roamed these streets. A man whose books Sam had read. Whose phone number Tootie had scribbled in a book. His book.

He'd think she stalked him. How mortifying.

Her first scrambled words made her cough and try again. "I suppose you must have mentioned the name of this town, but I certainly didn't remember."

"Maybe I did. Who cares? It's wonderful."

Seemed contrived to Sam, whose headache now burned at the back of her eyes.

"I forgot to tell you that I took Uncle Teddy to your house. I hope you don't mind?"

Her house? Sam wanted to ask why, but ever polite, said instead, "Of course not."

"He's gone off to see my cousin David at his school in California. And then there's a trip to Greece. Anyway, he'll be back in Reggio sometime or other. I'll tell him to look for you. Okay?"

"I only stopped here because of Martine Paoletti, the woman I traveled with. Who sails. She said I'd like Portofino. That I'd like to visit her. I mean, that's why I'm near there. Here." Sam clamped her jaw shut.

Tootie merely gushed, her voice full of laughter. "Now you will have two people nearby. Uncle Teddy will be *so* excited."

"I don't know how long I'll stay. I mean, I may move on. Soon." She'd paid for all those nights. How could she just up and run without using them? The pit deepened. Widened.

"Oh, don't. Please."

Sam tried to add a lightness that she was far from feeling. "We'll see. Anyway, I'll call you in a few days. And if you need anything, just send me an e-mail or leave a message at the front desk." She recited the *pensione's* number.

"I will. Oh, Sam, this is going to be so good for you. I just know it."

"Yeah, well."

Maybe Tootie's uncle would remain abroad long enough for her to see Martine and justify the expense of moving to another town. Or maybe he'd stay holed up in his rooms when he got back. He had to write, didn't he? That ought to keep him occupied and off the streets.

Her call to Rhea was harder still. The Raleigh store was doing fine, but Sam felt exposed, vulnerable, aching more with every sympathetic word Rhea uttered.

"It seems," Sam said, "that Tootie's uncle lives in this town. How did that happen?" She tried to turn her half-snort into a cough. "I didn't know that when I stopped. At least, not consciously."

"Just watch yourself, hear? Maybe he's single and free, but you don't want to go messing with anything that isn't right for you, you know?"

"I'm not." She wouldn't. She had no intention of even *seeing* the man, much less getting involved with him. She supposed Rhea just wanted to warn her. Mama Rhea.

"I know you thought maybe Jack would fit in the picture, bring healing, because of that whole kid-friend thing and you trusting him. But, honey, God never does things that way, does he? Hurting someone in the process?"

Sam shut her eyes against the memories of India. And of all those lies she'd fed her broken heart.

Rhea seemed to read her mind. "And just 'cause that woman he lived with has issues, you don't know what goes on in their home, in spite of him leaving. It wasn't right. To my mind, that man has his own share of problems."

"I know," she whispered. She did know. "But, then, so do I."

"We all do, baby. Look at us, not a one all fixed. Not a one with a bigger sin than the other. You know that, don't you?"

"Sin is such an ugly word."

"And so unpopular." Rhea expelled a loud breath as if she were trying to stifle one of her laughs. "A rose by any other name—or, in this case, a wrong called a right or black called white. Words can't wipe out the truth."

Sam didn't answer. Rhea dipping her toe in the literary didn't erase those plaguey images.

"Just remember," Rhea said softly, "it's how we deal with our stuff that God cares about. He knows we're gonna make messes. Look at David if you want to think of someone making a real mess. At least you didn't get India killed off."

That forced a grunt from Sam. "At least."

"That's right."

"I saw the statue of David in Florence. An incredible work."

"I've seen a picture."

"Doesn't do it justice. It's powerful. Really powerful."

"And look at that. All David did? Him being a murderer as well as an adulterer? God still said David was a man after his own heart."

"But that was David. Not me."

"Well, sure, honey. Me neither. But so what? It's the heart thing. You hear that? The heart. So you just get your heart focused where it's supposed to be and let it mend, then see what comes."

"Yes, ma'am."

"And watch out over there."

SAM LEANED against the headboard of her bed with the notebook on her lap and a pen in her hand. Journaling was new to her, but it seemed fitting, like a grown-up's diary to record the moments, the scenes, to complement the photographs she usually forgot to take. For later. When this trip was merely a memory and real life again foisted itself on her thoughts.

Because the time here wasn't real. But it was all she had at the moment.

The sea continued to amaze her. If she looked to the side out her window, she could see the turquoise that turned to cobalt and, further out, to a darker black-blue. And the mountains. So much green, so many rocks and stones, levels and heights. And the buildings, so old. No, ancient, with newer apartment buildings away from the center of town, so much uglier than the old.

She described it as best she could, the people watching, her frustration with the language. Language study would have been a whole lot easier at twenty. She'd learned to ask *quanto costa*, how much, and to understand numbers, to figure out how many euros to dole out and how many to expect in change. Calculating from euros to dollars and cents made her dizzy, so she just pretended they were equivalent, one to one.

And then there were the vehicles. She still couldn't figure out how four people fit into a Fiat barely big enough for one. And the three-wheeled trucks were a hoot. Scooters zoomed all over the place, but she could see their value in a country where gas prices would put most folk in the poor house.

Her pen dashed across the journal's pages as she made notes about the family Garibaldi, her landlords—mama, papa, aunt, grandmother, teenaged daughter, and schoolboy son. The daughter often worked behind the front desk and spoke beautiful English.

Lovely people. Everyone here is friendly, much more so than in the cities. I wish I knew how to answer their questions or understand their explanations.

If it weren't for that fellow—who's bound to think I'm one of those author-groupies if he finds me here—I'd park myself in Reggio for the next several months.

You know, until I'm no longer afraid to go home.

That drew her attention to the window and the sun streaming in. She slid the notebook back in a drawer, ran a brush through her hair, and headed down the stone steps to the lobby. Signora Bruneschi, manning the front desk, called a greeting. Sam waved, adding a *"Buon giorno"* to her and then to Papa, who was sweeping the front walk.

She didn't remember being quite so driven by the scent of food back in the States, but here she existed to eat. Her mouth watered at the thought of a thick slice of pizza, dripping with mozzarella. She stepped up and into the marble-floored pizzeria and breathed in the aromas of the wood oven, onions, garlic, and herbs. When it was her turn to order, she pointed to the slice she wanted, topped with olives, artichokes, and onions, and carried her trophy and a bottle of water down to the beach.

She slipped out of her walking shoes and waded into the shallows. Without a breeze, the sea was calm, a deep aqua melding into a dark, rich blue beneath the light that danced on the small ripples. She climbed on her rock, the one she'd discovered yesterday where she could dangle her feet on either side—toward the Mediterranean or the beach. Today, she faced Africa.

One bite of her pizza and she moaned. Chewing, she decided that the world felt rather perfect at that moment in time. Her children were well and happy. Her shops were thriving. And she was here, taking the time she needed. Tucking into a place like Reggio seemed to be just what Dr. Rhea had ordered.

For now.

She sniffed the sea, the salt and seaweed. People wandered the boardwalk, and sounds happened behind her, but she felt isolated, alone yet not lonely. A sip of water washed down another bite. She might want to finish lunch with a cappuccino or even an espresso.

Perhaps she'd stop again at the local coffee bar for a *pane al cioccolato* and coffee. She grinned, remembering the two men from this morning. They'd started chattering about something. A third had joined in, and then there'd been four, voices raised, hands jabbing the air. The show had been fun.

A wave splashed up and onto her rolled pants. Looking out, she saw the boat that had raised the wake and hiked her feet just in time to miss the second, less virile crash.

Oh, well. Back to the hotel for dry clothes. At least she'd had time to finish her pizza.

~

BY HER SECOND Tuesday in Reggio, Sam woke bloated and premenstrual. It was another glorious, sun-drenched day, but it might as well have been clouded and dripping. Signora Garibaldi's happy *"Buon giorno!"* irked her. A woman's laughter as she passed the fruit vendor's sounded harsh, rasping. The barkeeper's smile became a grimace. Sam sipped a cappuccino and ate, without relish, a brioche at the local bar, then returned to her room.

Perhaps she should go back to bed and start over. Her stomach felt lined with acid, her hips arthritic. She washed her face and brushed her teeth at the small basin in her room, then padded down the hall to use the communal toilet. Zia Francesca and her niece cleaned the bathroom daily, which made sharing it tolerable. Besides, after the German couple left two days ago, she was, at least temporarily, the only guest on the third floor.

She looked longingly at the tub. A good soak might ease this tension. But no, it would take too much effort to cope with that minuscule water heater—turning on the water to wet down, turning it off to wash, and turning it back on again to rinse, because the turn-on bit always meant temperature adjustments. Instead, she used the bidet and the basin and then climbed back in bed.

But sleep eluded her, replaced by images of Jack that

hovered almost close enough to touch. She imagined his lips, his caresses. Oh, how she longed to hear his laughter.

Stop it.

She scowled at the ceiling. Anger had propelled her here. Anger and shame, which meant she'd better stop romanticizing their encounters. She flipped onto her side, closed her eyes against all of it, good and bad, and finally slept.

And she was there again, with him. *Alice* danced on the waves as they laughed and told stories, remembering all the days of their childhood, the years in high school. And when Sam woke, she was still in that moment. The sounds of encroaching afternoon filtered through the window, but in her bed, under the covers, she was back on *Alice*. Back with Jack.

How many times had they sailed together, starting when she was what? Nine? Ten? And when they hadn't been sailing in the old boat he'd resurrected, they'd been fishing. How many fish had they caught and cleaned and eaten together?

She remembered the flounder and croakers and spot, the Saturday they'd thrown their lines in the shallows near an old wreck. They'd used their smallest hooks because the fish weren't very big, but they'd hauled their catch home, thinking dinner and wouldn't everyone be thrilled? Sam's mom had had a pot roast already in the oven and told them to take them to Jack's. Jack's dad had looked in their buckets and said he wasn't going to have anything to do with cleaning such sorry fish.

Jack had put his arm around Sam and whispered, "Come on, we'll do it."

They had gone to the outside sink by the back door and cleaned those fish, then taken them in to Jack's mama, who'd cooked and served them. Jack's daddy had eaten three all by himself, but never once did he tell Jack or Sam thanks or say he'd been wrong. Jack's brother, Jerome, wolfed his down, ignored them, and then didn't even excuse himself before he hightailed it out of there. Jack's mama only said there sure was a mess of them.

What good was that? The sting wasn't so bad, though, because Sam and Jack had each other. They could sail and fish and not give a hoot about fathers and mothers. On the water they didn't have to talk, though they did that, and they didn't have to go anywhere or catch anything, though they did that, too. They just had to *be*.

Feeling the salt spray, hearing the slap of the sail, she slept again, but barely.

This time, India waited at the dock with her shouts and her stormy tantrum, and Sam woke to a cry of, "No!"

Damp covers stuck to her bare shoulder. Thank God, she was here in Reggio, not in Beaufort. She deserved every curse India sent her way.

Splashes of cold water freshened her skin. She pulled on a pair of jeans and a T-shirt and set off toward the beach. The vastness of the sea, the pungent smells, the caw of birds, the teeming life: these had become her haven. A hideout from the self she didn't much like.

Waves swelled against the pebbly sand, rolled over rocks and touched the rim of her sneakers. She left prints, voids that filled once she had passed.

Her own empty spaces didn't fill. They echoed and wailed like specters near a grave.

10

JACK

A rock-strewn landscape, an unkempt sea,
A sky in tatters, dripping on me.

J ack stared at the drink in his hand. The liquor slipped
smoothly down his throat, but that's all it did. Fix his
pain? His thirst? Not a whit. India'd brought it, what, a
month ago? Sometime after she'd shown up at the dock.

No. It was after she'd found him at Sam's house close on
midnight. Her rage and her tears had needed cajoling, but he'd
managed to quiet her down.

He held the glass toward the light. Its contents didn't do
squat for the sledgehammer banging in his skull or the fire
behind his red-rimmed lids. And, no, he wasn't drunk. Or
hung over.

He shut his eyes and held the icy glass to his temple. Smart
move, bringing along his recliner when he moved out. India
hadn't liked that much, but it was his.

Why on earth had she come on to him again? "Jacky," she'd
said, her lips doing that little curvy thing. Made her look

wistful, needy, with her blonde hair cascading down her back instead of caught up the way she wore it when she worked. She'd stood right there in the doorway, her feet in those high heels she liked so she'd be taller, holding out that bottle like a peace offering. "I hope I'm not disturbing you. I just wanted you to know I don't harbor ill feelings because you chose Sam over me. Really."

A peace offering? Better than a repeat of the yelling she'd poured in his ears last time he'd seen her. "I appreciate it, India."

"Marty, he's the co-pilot who flies with me a lot, he got it from his brother. I thought of you." She'd looked shyly down at the carpet. "I love you, you know."

He'd reached out. A touch to her hand and the words, "I know. I'm sorry."

She'd nodded her good-bye, almost like the old India. Almost pretty again. No more sputtering and arm waving. No more ugly words.

He blinked, willing silence. He'd been a jerk, seducing Sam that way. He'd known how she felt about sex without marriage. That she was vulnerable. What had he been thinking?

Ah, but...

Hadn't it been worth it? Those minutes with her, the water lapping, the sails stilled? Her soft skin...

And then India'd been waiting with her field glasses.

Maybe his worst sin had been leaving Sam with the afternoon's shambles as he went off to placate India. He should have stuck with Sam. His soothing noises hadn't made it right with India, had they?

Not that he owed her anything. Not really.

Except for the years they'd shared. That imposed a certain emotional debt.

And Sam? Sam had finally packed up and run.

She'd threatened to. Each time. He should have paid more attention. He could have gotten her to stay if he'd only paid more heed.

But she had let him in. She had always let him in.

Until she hadn't.

Yeah. He should have married her.

Not that he'd wanted to get married. He'd said no to India enough times, hadn't he? But he had wanted, still did want, Sam. Seemed she had some fool notions of morality that got her all riled when she broke them.

See. He knew there was a good reason he hated religion. Look at how it had messed things up for him and Sam.

Now all he had was a bottle, a headache, and a sack-load of nothing.

He topped off his drink. He hadn't seen much of India after she'd shown up that evening, though she'd called a few times to see how he was feeling. Evenings were so lame, he almost missed her. When she'd appeared at his door that day, she'd seemed much more the woman he'd lived with for those years, instead of the crazy one from whom he'd fled.

Maybe if he picked up some Vitamin C and Echinacea, that would do the trick. Because if these symptoms didn't ease up soon, he'd be forced to see a doctor. His business wasn't going to sustain itself for long if he wasn't there to run it.

~

INDIA WAVED as Jack climbed out of his truck in front of the pharmacy. Almost as if he'd conjured her. She sidled up, touched his arm. "Jacky, you don't look so good. What's happening?"

He shrugged with the barest movement of his shoulders. "I don't know. I haven't been feeling well."

She squinted into his face, and her hand slid down his arm. "Why don't you come over, let me fix you something to eat."

"Not much of an appetite, India."

She sighed. "I'll make you some soup, something you can digest easily. Come on. You'll feel better with some of my homemade soup."

Maybe soup would be good. India was a great cook. Maybe he'd let her take care of him tonight.

He nodded. "I've got to stop at a job site. Six o'clock be okay?"

Her smile dimpled her cheeks. "That would be great. I'll see you then."

11

TEO

Yesterday, he sat on the pencil point,
His days pressing against lead.
Today, he's scribbled between blue lines,
And the yellow background matches his skin.

Teo eyed a plate of *fusilli* with fennel and sausage. Adjusting the linen napkin on his lap, he pondered the wine, still untouched in his glass, before forking the fresh pasta and a bite of sweet sausage. The flavors broke on his tongue. "Ahh..."

Was there anything better?

His eyelids dropped. That wasn't a question he particularly wanted to ponder while he dined alone. Again.

He swirled his wine, sipped. An earlier call to David had merely exacerbated his feeling of tethers unclipped and dangling. David's, "Glad you got back safely, Dad. So sorry, but I've got to run," had left Teo staring at his cell phone.

Wasn't California supposed to be a laid-back state? Teo

thought of the minutes he'd spent in his son's presence on that quick California trip, David claiming business—or was it merely busyness—when he'd apologized for not having time.

Teo hadn't felt this level of disquiet since those months after the accident when his future had drifted into the unknown. Unease at this stage seemed absurd, but like a chess game, his work required linear thinking. A mystery writer hunted for answers and didn't rest until he saw the line open, the next move that would bring ultimate victory. So why didn't this business of his mystery woman work the same way?

The waiter cleared *il primo piatto*. Teo touched the napkin to his lips, sipped again. *Il secondo* appeared, a plate of veal, *vitello*, with a hint of lemon. Ah, and garlic. *"Grazie, "* he said, sniffing as he leaned closer. The tiniest potatoes edged out slivers of carrot.

A man should rejoice with food like this. Not sit around stewing because he had lingering writer's block.

Yes, he had finally made arrangements for his stay in Greece. A little travel among the islands by boat. A zip over to Crete. And he'd found a broker offering a charter by sail. He'd made a reservation.

He raked fingers through his hair, sipped lemon water, and forked another bite. "Savor it," he whispered before he popped a potato into his mouth.

He tried, but between the veal and the salad that followed, his stomach began to churn its contents.

The waiter refilled his water glass.

"Il conto, per favore?" Teo asked, ready to bolt as soon as he paid.

It was too hot to wander far, so he ambled back to his apartment, limp-tap, limp-tap. Instead of working, he brewed a cup of coffee. The mug Tootie had slipped in his suitcase sat on his small counter. It was black with a gold *Samantha's* emblazoned across the front. It remained sterile, still unused.

As he rinsed it, his phone rang.

"My dear Tootie," he answered, amazed that the thought of her had conjured her voice. "What are you up to?"

"Just wondering how you're doing, Unc. And to tell you that Sam, my boss, is in Reggio."

"Here?" His gaze traveled to the drying mug with its lettering now upside down.

He heard a delighted laugh. "Isn't that wonderful? She drove north and stopped in Reggio because of a woman she met in Rome. Someone who lives in Portofino. You have friends there, don't you?"

"I do."

"I told her you'd be on the lookout for her. Shall I send you a photo? I've got one from Daniel's wedding. One of her and Stefi together."

"I'll be leaving for Greece tomorrow, but send it on if you think she'll still be here next week." Why did he say that? He drew a deep breath and scowled. The last thing he wanted was to have to entertain anyone. If Tootie's boss were here, you can bet it was because Tootie had mentioned him and, in the same breath, had said he was single and available.

"I think so. I'm not sure, but I hope so."

He sighed and turned on his computer. "I'm logged on. Send the picture when you will."

"Oh, I don't have it with me. But I'll get it to you in a bit." She was quiet for a moment, then said, "Unc, are you okay? You seem a little down. I thought so when you were here."

"What makes you say that?"

"It seemed like something was bothering you. Is your writing going well?"

"It's fine."

"It's just, it was so unlike you."

"I was probably thinking of all the new changes in your life. Holland, your job, the place you're staying. Have there been any new developments there?"

"Are you trying to throw me off? You do that in your books, you know."

"What? Ask questions?"

"See. You haven't told me a single thing."

"Ah."

"That must mean there is something, but you just don't want to say."

"And you, my girl, are just too smart for your own good."

"So?"

"So, what?"

"Uncle! You know what. Has something upset you?"

"No, honey. Nothing's upset me." If he weren't careful, she'd wear him down so he'd slip. He did not want to mention the apparition and have her think him crazy, too. "How are things at home? At the shop?"

"Fine at home. Dad's busy with tilling, and Mom's still canning. Making jam this time."

"Industrious pair, those parents of yours."

"I know."

"And at the shop?"

Again, he heard a pause and a deeper sigh. "Yes?"

"Things are going great as far as sales," she said. "I mean, more people are coming in all the time. I love the challenge. I'm learning so much. But when I talk to Sam, I worry. Which is why I want you to meet her. Help her over this hump."

"Me? What can I do?"

"Well, you've been there. Divorced and all."

He wondered if Tootie had been reading too many

romance novels. "Honey, how? Everyone's divorce is different. If she needs help, she should find a counselor. And if you're trying to play matchmaker, don't."

"Oh, I'm not. Really."

Right. He'd heard that before.

"It's just," she said, "you're such a good listener."

"Here's what I'll do. If I run into her, I promise I'll let her pour her troubles in my ear. Once. Over a cup of espresso. But that's all."

She giggled. "I'm being pushy again, aren't I?"

"Interfering might be a better word."

"Okay. I'll leave you alone."

"I don't want you to leave me alone. Just realize that I'm not interested in having a relationship with anyone. Not even if she's gorgeous and brilliant and all the rest of it. And, look, if what you say about your boss is true, I don't imagine she's looking for another one either."

"So leave it alone?"

"Yes. Please."

But Tootie's mention of Portofino reminded him that he hadn't checked on Antonio and Martine in a while. He'd chatted with Tonio just before he'd flown to New York. Something about Martine visiting friends in Capri and going with them to Rome. She was to rent a car for the drive home because she had a few stops to make on the way.

Was it possible?

Nah.

He flipped through his address book, then punched in their number. The housekeeper answered. Yes, Signora Paoletti was in.

"Teo, is that really you?" Martine's melodious voice asked. "Tonio said you'd called while I was away."

"How are things with you both?"

"Oh, Teo, it's been so hard. Tonio had another episode. He has been in the hospital for the past week. I just got him home."

"I'm so sorry. What can I do?"

"Visit? I know he would like to see you and perhaps play a game of chess."

"Sounds great. I'm off to Greece, but when I get back next week?"

"He'll be so pleased. Any afternoon, after the nurse has had time to get him ready, and he has had a light meal. He always takes a short nap afterward, but by three he is usually alert."

"I'll call you once I get back," he said. "Oh, and by the way, did you have company when you drove north?"

"How did you know?" He heard her surprise.

And his own resignation. "It's a very small world." And getting smaller by the moment.

"You know her? Samantha is so lovely."

He meant to laugh. It came out as a bark. "No, I don't know her. But my niece works for her."

Martine's laugh was real and tinkling. "I think this is perfectly delightful. I'm hoping she will visit me soon."

Teo ended the call, reiterating his promise to phone on his return. This really was too much. He didn't believe in coincidence, which meant there was something going on that was just a little bit scary.

Who was lining up the chess pieces? "God, is this you or not?"

If it were all happening for some divine purpose, he wanted to align himself on the winning side. But if the orderer of these seeming coincidences came from elsewhere, then he wanted to steer very clear of all of it.

How was he supposed to know?

~

IT WAS NEARLY midnight when he checked his e-mail a final time. There was a note from Tootie in his inbox. He clicked on the link to open the first photograph. And nearly fell out of his chair.

12

TEO

A dreamscape draws him out of self,
And he is there, not here.

With hoisted sails and a humming engine, the beautiful little yacht *Prosforo* headed out of Naxos harbor. The sky and sea were both a lovely azure, the breeze easy. Teo imagined a fun day on the water.

He took the offered helm in the interest of research, just to see how the boat handled. The skipper rubbed a forearm along his brow when Teo pushed the tiller the wrong way. He beetled his brows and made a rude arm gesture when Teo's efforts didn't bring the bow across the wind. As the sails slapped, the captain spit off the transom, barely missing Teo's arm. Teo relinquished the tiller.

And then the peaceful breeze became a nasty wind out of the mountains, and the waves grew. The captain shouted foul-sounding Greek words at a grumbling crew. Anger flashed almost as often as the boom crossed the deck.

All Teo wanted was off. Now. He imagined they all felt that

SAILING OUT OF DARKNESS

way, except perhaps the captain, who pushed and shoved and threatened the crew with death and dismemberment. Or so it seemed to Teo.

His muscles began to ache from hours of trying to hold on and not fly out and over and into the deep, dark sea. He was sure he'd drown or at least lose his lunch, especially when one of the younger crew needed Teo to hold his shoulders so he wouldn't fly overboard along with his stomach's contents.

Eventually, they made it back to the dock. As the crew made fast the lines, Teo shuffled from the deck to the dock boards and didn't look back.

Gripping his cane, he warily avoided cracks in the cobbles. Just a step up on a curb sent the muscles in his right thigh into overdrive.

He had certainly discovered one thing. He was no sailor. Give him terra firma any day.

But he did have pages of technical terms gleaned when the long-haired skipper deigned to speak English.

Why didn't that crew mutiny? *Prosforo?* Teo should have turned tail as soon as the taciturn mate said the name meant *an offering to God.* Like the Orthodox holy bread. Right. Teo could see it. Instead of bread, unwary clients were dashed over the side to appease some imagined sea lord.

He shook his head. So much for sailing.

It would be books or interviews about nautical lore for him from now on. His lips curved as he imagined writing a scene where Sophrina investigated the skipper's overboard demise. And it wouldn't be the crew members who did away with the man.

The café was crowded, but he found a chair. The waiter welcomed him and took his order for ouzo and various *mezethes*, those delightful small plates of food.

Wouldn't Tootie enjoy being here with him, watching the

sun dip into that brightly hued sea? That brought to mind the other *she*, the she who now had a name. Samantha.

His anise-flavored drink, potent and clear before ice and water clouded it, flowed in small sips, wakening his senses. Its murkiness seduced both his brain and his memory. He ran a finger around the glass's rim as he stared at the milky white substance. Ice cubes floated in the liquid until they melted.

Like images that appeared until they didn't.

A grimace contorted his expression. Hadn't *her* image, her face, been designed for *his* use?

He lifted the glass, toasting the air. His facial muscles relaxed, and he sipped. He'd probably already consumed too much, but who cared. Medicinal, that's what this was.

But, no. He was *pazzo*. Not that he wanted to be mad. He just figured that's where he'd landed. His own rabbit hole.

He shifted in his chair, sipped again, and decided he should have been a poet, a breed synonymous with mad capers. The image had appeared—when it appeared—ostensibly as some story's heroine. And yet no story came. Or, rather, no story in which she fit. Then, suddenly, she wasn't a character who needed naming, not one who needed taming and plotting. Suddenly, she was a real person, and one he saw in a photograph. A woman from North Carolina who was now staying in Reggio, *his* town. A woman he was supposed to meet.

And, yet, one he already had.

Pazzo.

Or puppet. Perhaps that was it: a puppeteer with an odd sense of humor managed the strings, and Teo Anderson danced.

In that photograph, imagination and reality merged. And he didn't know what to do with either. Because how could he meet a woman, one who had shown up in his visions, and pretend he was seeing her for the first time?

He pictured the scene. "Hi, how are you?" he'd say with his hand extended. "We've met in those waves out there. On that very beach. And also over there, on those rocks. Oh, and you were crying."

She'd consign him to hell if he spouted such a line. And he'd think he needed a psychiatrist's couch once again.

He licked his lips. He'd figured out how to drink ouzo on that trip to Lebanon. Its slight licorice flavor went well with these *mezethes*. He broke off a piece of cheese pie, *tyropitakia*, scooped up an olive from a small plate, then took a forkful of skewered lamb. The lamb held hints of rosemary. Mint flavored the yogurt. He bit into another olive and sighed. Yes, Tootie would enjoy the food, the town. And what if she brought her boss?

What would that be like?

He hadn't a clue, because now that his dream had found flesh, that was all it was. She hadn't beckoned him into her world. And there was no way he'd be able to write her. It was crazy. Why had any of it happened?

He didn't read many fantasy novels or science fiction. He was an educated man, a literary man. Was he having a breakdown, some leftover bitterness or unresolved anger that pushed him past sanity? He'd seen plenty of angry people when he'd practiced law.

Perhaps he should order another ouzo. There was half a plate of lamb left. And if he were going crazy, what did intoxication matter? He hadn't taken a sip of Scotch in two years. Not that he had ever been a drunk, but he had frightened himself, knowing he could have graduated. He allowed himself that glass of wine with dinner. No more, and yet here he was, tempted over the limit by an absurd Greek drink.

Would he be more insane with the alcohol, or would he merely become a wandering lunatic who appeared perfectly sane?

This mess smacked of too many coincidences. Val would roll her eyes and say he was striving too hard to make things work if he submitted a storyline with half the puzzle pieces lined up like this. It was almost as if a *deus ex machina*, god of the machine, had dropped into his life—and not into his literary one. He was a puppet. She was a puppet. They were all puppets of the one who pulled the strings.

Now, if the god at work was *God*, that was fine. God was supposed to work in a benign fashion for everyone's good. Right?

But what if it weren't God-Jehovah? What if it were some force that was out to get him?

That thought provoked one of his grosser laughs. What, did he feel persecuted?

"Well, wouldn't you?" he asked the air. "You saw it back there."

He was talking to himself.

Of course he was. Everyone else spoke more Greek than he had on hand.

Perhaps in *Aegean Travesty*, Sophrina could meet a man slightly off-kilter. Or perhaps Sophrina could fall down the rabbit hole herself and wander dizzily for a while.

He raised his glass and toasted Sophrina, the only safe thing in this world of his. She would travel with him by ferry back to Piraeus tomorrow, away from these rocky paths where they searched for murderers.

A last sip, and he pushed the glass aside, paid his bill, and stepped out into the cobbled street for the short hobble around the corner to his room.

Amazing, wasn't it, how a chance photograph could be the death knell of an idea? How odd that *she* had seemed so in need of him. He knew that a world full of otherness surrounded the flesh-woman. As he had his own packed world of people and obligations, everywhere or anywhere he wished to go.

~

He woke to darkness and a ticking clock that sounded loud in the otherwise silent room. A bathroom visit, a return to bed, but no sleep came. He rose again, followed his feet in their course to the room's small table, where he sat and pondered...nothing.

He didn't want to lose his hold on sanity. He no longer found the idea of an apparition that looked like a real woman the least bit appealing. An apparition was a spook. A something he wanted no part of.

If it were spiritual, which he had already decided apparitions were, then he wanted it gone. Or explained.

And the only one who could explain it was the fellow they called God.

Fine. Teo ran fingers through his hair, yanked on a longish lock. He had used that amorphous naming thing again.

All right. *He* called him God.

"God."

The word, the *name*, sat heavily on a tongue that rarely used it. Sure, he had thrown it out pejoratively, but whenever he had asked for a clue or two, there had been silence. Only, right at this moment in time, God seemed to be the only one who could help him come close to understanding.

The only one who could keep him, Teo, sane. Who could

explain enough for Teo to find peace amid the contradictions and odd happenings.

"Please?"

He stared into the darkness, waiting. But all was still. Only his breath uttered sound in the noiseless room.

13

SAMANTHA

If you've not flown with wind or words,
If music hasn't captured you,
If beauty doesn't set you free,
Then maybe it's not meant to be,
And maybe you should stay there.

Hormones were such absurd things. One minute, she was drowning; the next, she felt sane and in control of herself. Maybe she should see a doctor, get a prescription or an herb or *something* to combat the edginess, the physical cravings.

But when it was over, she forgot the horror. Until the next month.

She climbed the coast road, high above the shore. Villas perched on the slopes toward the sea sat hidden by high stone fences or iron gates camouflaged by evergreens. She occasionally glimpsed an elegant garden or a patio overlooking a private cove and imagined living in one of the villas. And then she imagined the cost.

Her calves felt the pull of uphill walking, but exercise was supposed to be good for stress. Perhaps it would keep her young.

The rhythm of the sea and life in Reggio began to seep into her psyche. Today, she could smile at the noise of scooters changing gears around curves in the road, at the shouts of school children and vendors for whom whispers or subdued voices seemed unknown.

Turning back to the beach, she picked up her pace. Soon, her shoes left the concrete and dug into rough sand. She stripped them off and rolled her jeans, dipping her toes in water as she strolled its edge. The small waves swelled at her feet and then receded, in and out, constant in their ebb and flow. She stared at the impressions she made as the water carried sand into them, sand it had sucked out moments before.

And she flashed to a memory of Jack extending his hand, offering to sail with her. His friendship had flowed into her emptiness, swelling around her until she lay heaped on the sand. But as the waves of need had receded, she'd coughed it out— *him* out—and had finally begun to breathe again.

What had been, what might have been, and what could never be sometimes whispered on the wind, yet in the midst of her sadness, she spied patterns, old and new, the new yet to be created from pieces of the old. She longed for absolution. Barring that, she longed for forgetfulness.

Suddenly self-conscious, she stopped and glanced around to make certain no one else stood near enough to hear her thoughts or see her tears. If she didn't hold herself in check, if she let any of this loose, the tears she swiped from her cheeks would flip right over into hysteria. And wouldn't that bring on a crowd?

She turned from the water, hurrying toward the rocks,

where she sat and dusted off the sand before slipping her feet into her shoes.

She was absurd. *Waves of need receding?*

Melodrama City, here she came. Her *need* hadn't receded. She still longed and she still wanted and she still felt needy enough to open that door again if Jack knocked from the other side of it.

What had finally gotten through and pushed her out of Beaufort hadn't been anything receding. It had been a bleeding gut.

She climbed the rocks that barred her path, stopping to perch just above the lapping waves. There she raised her fist out over the water. Opening her fingers, she imagined releasing Jack to the water and the wind, releasing her hopes and her need, as if they were ashes that could float and dissolve and become one with the sea.

Forgive me.

When a chill crept through her jeans from the damp rock, she headed slowly back to *Le Stelle*, the bar that fronted the public beach, and ordered *un espresso*, trying to slur the words together as an Italian would.

The barman handed over the dark brew. She tore open a packet of powdered creamer and added a spoonful of sugar. The first time she'd committed this sacrilege, she'd seen him grimace. His hand had swooped to grab the used creamer packets as if they were offal, before he'd wiped up the mess.

"*Grazie,*" she said.

He returned a facial shrug that involved his lower lip and his eyebrows, accompanied by the odd sounding *"Beh,"* which could mean anything—or nothing. Of course, if he stocked a pitcher of cream, she wouldn't need the packets. *Cappuccino, sì. Caffè con crema, no.*

Other than a few men sipping their morning *caffè* as they

stood at the bar and one hiding behind a newspaper at a nearby table, the place was empty. Sam set her cup down and pulled out a chair. The newspaper lowered.

She recognized the face from the grainy image on the back cover of his books. He nodded. She nodded back. They smiled.

"I haven't yet had the pleasure," he said, "but Tootie did send me your photograph."

"You're Uncle Teddy."

"Yes, though perhaps Theo or, as here, Teo?" He waved at a chair across from his. "Won't you join me?"

She picked up her cup. "Thank you."

The smile stretched his lean face, tucked in the lines, and brightened his eyes. "Tootie said you'd stopped in Reggio."

She winced. "I didn't know you lived here. I made a friend—"

"Yes, I know. Martine. I put two and two together."

Sam didn't know what to say. "Tootie?"

"She happened to mention that you were here because of a new friend from Portofino. I had a reason to phone Martine, and she said she'd come north with you."

Sam frowned. She did the math on the too many coincidences and didn't like the answer. "A friend of yours," she said on a sigh.

"Of long standing. Her husband, Tonio, has just come out of the hospital."

"Oh, I'm glad he's better. I haven't spoken to Martine yet, but someone who seemed to be a housekeeper mentioned the word *ospedale* in conjunction with *il signore*. I made the leap."

"Ah."

"It's a small world." She sipped, staring at the dregs of her espresso. What could she say? "I hope you don't think..." This was so difficult. He must be imagining all sorts of things. "I mean, really, I didn't know."

"If you had, I'd be flattered." His lips quirked.

He was laughing at her. Her hands flew to her reddening cheeks. "But I didn't. Really. At least, not consciously."

His fingers appeared to rest negligently on the table, relaxed, at ease. She slid hers to her lap so he wouldn't see them tense.

"Whatever brought you here, I'm delighted," he said, still with that hint of amusement. "And Martine will be very pleased if I take you to visit her. She asked me to stop by sometime to play a game of chess with Tonio."

At the mention of chess, some of Sam's tension dissolved, taking with it the heat from her blush. He couldn't think too badly of her if he'd suggested a visit to Martine.

"Thank you." She unclasped her hands and smoothed them over her thighs. To change the subject, she said, "Tootie told me you went to Greece. How fun that must have been."

"Gorgeous place. Have you traveled there?"

"No, but I'd love to sail the Aegean."

"*Hoh*, I did, and it was appalling."

"No! Why?"

Sam grinned at the way he told the tale. When he mentioned his plan to immortalize the captain in his next story, a gurgle of laughter escaped. "It sounds as if your Captain Bligh deserves a foul end," she said, "but I'm sorry you had such an experience. Sailing can be wonderful."

"You're a sailor." He didn't make it a question.

"I am. I have a small boat in North Carolina."

"I'm sure you miss it."

He was back to polite again. Why? Had her tone or something she said put him on guard? If his only sailing experience hadn't been so wretched, he'd know how a sailor longs to be on a boat.

"Tootie said she showed you my place. You didn't see *Alice*?"

"No. She mentioned troubles you'd had at the house. I went to see for myself."

"Ah, the protective uncle."

He angled his head in a quick assent. "She seems to be fine. And her cousin patrols the area."

"Your nephew?"

"No. From her father's side."

"I never met him. I did meet her Aunt Ruth."

"The deputy's mother."

Okay. She should go. She'd exhausted all the small talk she had in her.

He stopped her with an innocuous, "How have you been getting on with the language?"

She'd have thought him as bored by the conversation as she was. "I stumble around, trying to make myself understood. I suppose you're fluent."

"My accent's appalling." His smile twisted slightly before he curved it up. "I can't carry a tune either." A smile really did transform his face, the hardness lost in laugh lines.

She eased back in her chair. "It must be my age, but I feel so frustrated and stupid. Just when I think I've made some progress, I hit another wall of words that don't relate to anything I know. Everyone has been helpful, especially the Garibaldis, who run the *pensione* where I'm staying. And the shopkeepers seem to like that I try, but learning a foreign language was so much easier when I was in high school."

"Don't I know it. But the eagerness of the Italians to help is one thing that makes them so charming." He finished the last of his caffè. "Could I get you another? Or something else?"

Oh, were they staying? Was she?

She paused, weighing her options. He was, after all, fulfilling her desire for conversational English. The thought brought her own smile forward. "An *acqua naturale*?"

"Something amuses you?"

"Only thinking how much I've missed speaking English with a fellow American when what I ought to want are Italian lessons."

"I know. When I was in Greece, I wanted more than anything to find someone—anyone—whose language I understood."

"Not that you're just anyone," she said.

That drew him up short. "Nor are you." He slid from his seat and then reached for a cane.

She hadn't noticed the cane. "I'm sorry," she began. "Why don't..."

"It's no problem. I'll just tell Giorgio what we want. He'll bring it over."

"Thank you."

He leaned rather heavily on the brass-handled stick, ordering at the bar in what sounded like flawless Italian. By the time he returned and slid back into the seat across from her, the barman was following with his cup. "Excuse the awkward leg. Can't quite manage the way I used to."

"I'm sorry."

"No need to be." He accepted his cup and waited as Sam opened her bottled water. "I've gotten used to it."

Did she dare ask? He *had* mentioned the leg issue first, and some people liked to talk about old injuries. Of course, some people hated to. She took a sip. All he could do was shoot her down. "Do you mind, I mean, would it be impertinent to ask how it happened?"

"Truck driver on drugs." He picked up a spoon to stir his coffee. "The tanker company neglected to do a background check. The guy had a history of trouble, including traffic violations involving substance abuse in various forms."

"But don't they *test*?"

"All he had to do to pass was to keep clean for a few days. When he hit me, he was high as a kite. The jury found the company negligent, and here I am."

"That's terrible. Is it still painful?"

"Much less than it used to be." Though his tone made the pain sound negligible, she knew that broken anything hurt. And he did limp. He lifted his cup and stared at it. "My sister says the jury's settlement is the silver lining in a rather unpleasantly dark cloud, and I suppose that's a good way of looking at it."

"I imagine you'd rather be pain free."

He shrugged again as if Italian-reared, head and face and rarely hands. "Everything has a price," he said. "Before, I slaved sixty to eighty hours a week, trying to bring in enough billable hours to keep my partners happy. I felt tied to my law practice. Now, I have time for a siesta in the afternoon and hours to spend writing at my computer. And my sister and her husband have restored their old farmhouse, my son's enjoying the college of his choice, and my parents are secure in their retirement. All things worked together for good, so I'm not going to complain."

"What a nice way of looking at it." Sam caught herself before reaching to touch his hand. Heat again spilled onto her cheeks.

Why was her first reaction to touch? Hadn't she learned that touchy-feely with men was *not* healthy for her? She shut her eyes to block the images and snapped them open as she hunted up another topic for discussion. They'd mentioned the language, his injury, sailing. She didn't want to resort to the weather. Had she exhausted family?

"You all must be quite close," she finally said. "I know Tootie adores you."

"She's a great girl—woman. I can't quite get used to the fact that she's an adult now. And engaged. Makes me feel very old."

"I know. My son recently married. And," she said, giving in to the easier memory, "when traipsing around Firenze with Stefi—I felt ancient. I was very glad to find a quiet place to pause after that."

He shifted positions. She imagined discomfort, but his face remained clear and calm. "Reggio is a good choice if you're looking for quiet. Italian, as opposed to tourist-laden. You'll have a much better chance of finding Italians who let you into their world. I travel a lot, and I'm always surrounded by strangers, always returning to a hotel room. Here, I'm comfortable. And I have friends."

He gazed out toward the sea. Watching him, she began to wonder what had brought him so far from home.

"My husband and I spoke of traveling."

The blush returned. Why had she said that? Too much, way too much information.

"But you didn't?" He asked as if her answer mattered.

Her thoughts ping-ponged back and forth from did/didn't to should/shouldn't. She could almost see them lobbing across the net. "I suppose I was the one who talked about it, and he grunted in what I thought was agreement. We never went anywhere. So at least I'm finally out and about, even if it's on my own."

"Now that you're here, perhaps you'll allow me to show you some of the sights."

His offer surprised her. He probably felt an obligation. Because of Tootie. Because she'd shown up here, foisting herself upon his notice.

Not that she'd meant to.

She'd come abroad to recover, to become independent. She had not come to clutch the first hand extended her way.

He was kind. That was all. He must be a very busy man. And a famous one.

Famous men were always busy.

"So, then," she said brightly to avoid answering. "Tell me about your son? What's his name, and where is he?"

Teo's twinkle returned. He certainly did that well. And looked years younger with the change of expression. "David is studying finance at Berkeley. He already wants to manage me and my money."

"Oh, yes. How well I know that. My daughter's always trying to fix my wardrobe and my life. Her brother is a little better, but maybe that's because he has his hands full with a pregnant wife."

"You're almost a grandmother?"

She didn't know whether to feel flattered or not when his brows hiked. "His having a baby was a little premature. But I'm certainly old enough."

"You don't look it."

Okay, flattered, but that meant it was time to move on. She slid back her chair. "It was so lovely to meet you," she said, standing and holding out her hand. "Perhaps we'll run into each other again."

"I hope so." He also rose and took the extended hand. "May I take you to dinner tonight?"

No, no, no. He couldn't. She wouldn't.

But *dinner*? Really?

What did that mean? Was she supposed to say no and let him off the hook? Is that how this was done?

Or should she consider whether or not she *wanted* to go to dinner with him?

She did, didn't she? She'd be a fool not to. A date. For dinner. In Italy. Um, *yeah.*

He waited. He didn't push, but she felt the expectancy. It gave her the courage to nod.

⁓

HE ARRIVED AT SEVEN. An early meal, they'd decided. Early worked for her, although seven would have seemed late at home.

She ordered a shellfish stew. He chose veal. They eased into conversation, and she tried not to let the butterflies in her stomach gain control. They dunked fresh bread in olive oil and discussed the weather and some of the places she'd visited after Florence. Their main course arrived, along with another round of fresh bread. He passed the basket to her.

"I don't want to embarrass you," Teo said, breaking off a crusty piece and studying her closely enough to embarrass her no matter what he said, "but Tootie seemed to feel we have something in common."

"Oh?"

"Yes. She mentioned that you, too, have had to deal with an unpleasant divorce. I think she imagined I might help you through it."

Sam felt her mouth gape. She shut it quickly, hoping he hadn't been disgusted by the rows of silver fillings. "That's absurd. Why would she think I need help and why from you?"

"Ah." He had the grace to look rueful—as well he should. "I shouldn't have said anything. I'm sorry."

She excavated a bit of meat from a clam shell before setting her fork down with a sigh. "Well, you're certainly more direct than I'd expected. I don't know you at all."

"True, but there's Tootie."

"Who talks."

"She thought we might commiserate."

"What, divorced solidarity?" Sam squinted at this man who seemed to bend—or ignore—the rules of early, polite conversation. Of course, she had done the same thing when asking about his accident.

He raised a brow. "I think I asked Tootie that same question. I may have even used those words—or something to that effect. I remember telling her your life wasn't any of my business."

Sam almost choked on the bite she'd taken. She coughed, sipped water, and said, "Is that how I sounded?"

"I deserved it."

"Perhaps we should..." They did still have the meal to get through. "Shall we begin again?"

The rueful, apologetic look returned. "You know," he said, studying the veal he'd cut in slivers before staring back into her eyes, "I'm usually a bit more adroit when meeting someone. I do apologize, and if my curiosity makes me too pushy, please just say so."

"Well, we are here, far from home and linked by something, if only Tootie." As she paused, he took a bite and watched her. "I suppose your way breaks down barriers more quickly. Gets one past polite conversational beginnings. And it's not that I wouldn't have liked to do the same thing this afternoon. I mean, ask more than I did."

That provoked a deep laugh. "What, ask questions? Now that I've done the feet-first dip, feel free."

She sipped, waiting.

"Or feel free to tell me to shut up," he said.

"Do people ever do that?"

"Too many. Especially when I was trying to win a case."

"Yes, of course. I've known a few lawyers whose tongues needed singeing." She picked up her fork, looked at his raised brows, and laughed. "Greg's attorney was a slime ball who went after my boat so I'd sell the house."

"Deserves to be hanged."

"It was easier to give in than fight a battle that I may or may not have won, even though I'm sure my lawyer would have made mincemeat of Greg—and his attorney—in a court battle." She paused, then said, "You never think about those things, do you? Not when you assume your marriage is forever. But can you imagine anything more unpleasant or harder on the children than seeing their parents haggle over *stuff*?"

"What about your business?"

"Oh, my lawyer locked that away from Greg's greed when she drew up the incorporation papers. He couldn't touch the things closest to my heart, not once I had *Alice*. And, besides, what's a house anyway?"

Teo waited, but she'd already said too much. She picked up another shell and released its meat onto her fork, then dunked bread in the broth.

"So good," she said. "These are cooked perfectly."

"As is this veal."

Their silence finally felt comfortable. When a piece of meat dropped off her fork and splashed broth, she rolled her eyes and laughed with him. Someplace between swallowing bread and sipping wine, she realized that she hadn't let him speak of his own troubles. "What about you? You said ask."

"The divorce?" He shrugged. "Not pleasant when it happened, but a good thing in the end."

"It's hard, though, isn't it? I mean, at first?"

"Janet couldn't quite handle the sight of my broken frame." He swirled the water in his glass. "It didn't take her long to find someone who could still take her dancing. I was at the rehab center for a while, you see. Of course, I'm convinced now that she did me a huge favor."

Sam allowed her sigh to relax into a small smile as she broke off another piece of crusty bread and toyed with it. She was eating way too much starch, but it occupied her fingers. "When Greg left for greener pastures, I thought I'd never recover. It's taken a while to get to the place of being glad and a little time on a rather slippery slope, but I'm beginning to think life can be good again." She *was* happier—and not only without Greg, but without good old Jack, too. "Italy's a wonderful place to discover freedom."

He held up his glass, inviting her to join him. "Here's to freedom and second chances."

She lifted hers. "To second chances." Or to third (one day, if she were very good), but she kept that to herself.

How quickly life could do an about-face, what the Italians called a *voltafaccia*. When, as they spooned bites of crème brûlée, Teo invited her on a tour of Cinque Terre two days hence, she lingered over her last bites of sweet and the question of whether or not one could actually have an uncomplicated friendship with the opposite sex, where neither had expectations the other couldn't—or wouldn't—fulfill.

The answer did not exist in her spoon.

"Yes," she finally said. After all, a guide who knew the territory and could describe it in English wasn't something to be rejected, was it?

14

TEO

We leave off our hats and pretend we're not fools,
While laughing at moonbeams and dancing on stools.

Sentence by sentence, Sophrina's adventures emerged and slid onto his hard drive. Teo could even appreciate that wretched sailing trip as he slipped in its lingo and used his anger to work the murder-investigation angle. He reread his notes, adding another scene and ignoring the stack of mail on the hall table that cast a lure in his direction.

"Just another few pages," he said over his shoulder to the seductive pile. "Almost there." He meant to reach his quota of words for the day.

Their appointment was for tomorrow. Today, he was supposed to work.

He certainly did not want his in-the-flesh specter to interfere. His tilted universe.

His fingers hit the keyboard. Sophrina bought a ticket from Naxos to Athens and then took a taxi to the airport. But something stopped her from boarding the small plane.

What was it? Was she supposed to return by ferry as he had?

Fingers hovered. He stared at the screen, reread the paragraphs above, went to the chapter beginning, reread more. Typos leapt out. He fixed them. Then he rewrote a line. Another. But still she wouldn't get on board. Why not?

When no answer came, he sat, puzzled, before deciding to leave it for a while and let it gel. Saving the file, he collected the mail and flipped through it until he came to a letter from his lawyer and ex-partner. If the envelope were thinner, he'd snatch it open eagerly. He enjoyed Robert's epistles. But fat meant trouble.

And there it was. Robert had forwarded a long, ungainly letter from Janet.

The rest of the envelopes contained notices, a couple of bills. Nothing from family. He hadn't heard a peep from his sister or son or Tootie. But that just meant they were busy. He hadn't called them either.

He shrugged. It was what it was. Right?

Popping the cap on a bottle of *limonata*, he wandered between rooms, distracted now. His brain churned in spite of his attempt to ignore Janet's letter, which was bound to revive a stench he couldn't seem to exorcise.

His back to the pile of mail, he stared down at a street teeming with the post-siesta crowd. He didn't want to think of his ex-wife. Her letter would not be good news.

Janet Elizabeth, born Watkins, became Anderson. Still was, though he couldn't figure out why, except that the hulk she lived with had a name like Hapsnopter-something. Teo didn't know why the guy didn't just drop the last few syllables. Foreign, as in non-Anglo, was not Janet's style.

Not Janet of the beautiful body and crippled soul.

He flopped on the couch, pulled the letter out of the

envelope, and spread it open. Her flowery script sprawled across a page of expensive, perfumed stock. She wrote like a schoolgirl, penciling circles over each *i* in place of dots. He had once thought it cute.

Several paragraphs of "Oh, Teddy, remember when?" were her attempt to soften him before she cut to the chase with a plea for money. Eighty thousand dollars' worth of money.

Asked for a loan, wanted a handout. For a down payment on a new house, she said, so she could be comfortable. She was sure Teo wouldn't miss that measly (*Measly? On what planet?*) amount, not with his books having done so well and all that investment income.

How did she know about his investments? He certainly hadn't mentioned them. She even threw in the line about being the mother of his son. As if he needed reminding.

Sorry, Janet, no more bailouts. Robert had been right. He'd scribbled a note on the bottom of his typed one. "Don't let her con you, boy. You don't watch out, there'll never be an end to that gal's whining."

Teo could hear Robert talking past the cigar perpetually unlit but drooping from his lips. Robert's wife, Lizzie, laid down the law, said she'd leave him if he didn't quit smoking. She'd rather be divorced than watch him die of cancer or have to listen to him talk through one of those tinny boxes his brother had. She pretended she didn't notice the hastily chewed mints or the smell of mouthwash.

Robert had once asked how Teo could write so sympathetically about Sophrina when he acted so blamed mad at women otherwise. "Because," Teo had said when he'd moved past admiring Robert's turn of phrase, "I like Sophrina. She makes no bones about being self-centered, then goes out of her way to help people."

"Means you know there are types other than Janet," Robert had said.

"Sure, but I'm not about to put myself in a place where a woman has power over me again."

A fresh cigar had crackled as Robert rolled it. "Never say never." One of Robert's favorite lines, that one was right up there with, "Never say you won't ever until you haven't ever." You'd think Robert were seventy instead of fifty-eight.

He loved to pontificate, spent a lot of phone time telling Teo to forget about Janet, go find someone better. Get on with life. "Your leg and hip were busted, boy, not your balls." If Robert had a gut and gray hair to go with the stogie, maybe a white suit and shoes, he'd epitomize Hollywood's Southern lawyer. Instead, he was a grown-up preppie with the build of a linebacker.

In spite of Robert's words, Teo knew the truth about himself: he was a man of broken parts who had once lain in a hospital bed with a non-functioning libido. No matter how hard he had tried to stay positive in those days, a leg muscle contracting in spasm or a moment of loneliness priming him for a pity party had brought Janet's whining to full throttle. How had he ever imagined loving such a voice?

Like loose metal in a tin can the scene jangled in his brain. No matter how often he tried to stuff it under other thoughts, the memory surfaced. He slammed shut his eyes to ward off a rewind. It didn't work.

He saw it: his cracked body lying tilted in the hospital bed as he attempted to anesthetize himself with a made-for-TV movie about a murder in Wilmington, DE. Hard to believe. Wilmington didn't seem like the place for real-life soap operas, although Teo supposed bad could happen anywhere. As an anesthetic, the movie had failed miserably, mostly because he identified with the criminal's frustration. A modern Lady

Macbeth, the guy hadn't been worried so much about getting out the spot as trying to sink in the deep blue sea a cooler containing the body parts of Mistress Number Two. No matter how many holes he shot in that cooler, the thing had refused to sink.

That part of the memory amused Teo. Sophrina would have laughed that fool of a murderer out of town, especially when he came up with the theory that his Mistress Number One had pulled the trigger.

Teo hauled himself up again and limped to the window, trying to think about dinner and not the scene that had played out that day. He propped one hand against the frame, but he didn't see what was out there. His gaze focused inward.

His own repeat-play melodrama began with Janet's swishing entrance into his room at the rehab center. He remembered her long nails, red and sharp against the tan leather of the briefcase—his new, barely used and very expensive briefcase—that she had flipped open. She'd reached inside and shoved some papers across the tray table.

"Need you to sign, Teddy, bottom of the fourth page." The red tips had slipped under the top right corners, and she'd counted under her breath until she reached number four. He'd glanced down at the words, uncomprehending.

"I just can't take this whole scene anymore." Her mane of unnaturally bronzed hair had walled part of her face as she refused to make eye contact. "It's just too much, you see? I mean, you can't expect me to put my life on hold any longer, and who knows what kind of shape you'll be in if you ever do get out of here. I mean, trauma does things to a man. You even told me you couldn't... I mean, that it doesn't, you know, so..." Janet had shrugged, as if she weren't talking about the most vital part of his anatomy. Then she'd rammed the knife home. "And I'm real sorry, Teddy, but those scars, well, they really—

and, look, I don't mean to hurt you, you know I don't," and here she'd let her gaze catch his for a brief moment, "but they...well, they turn me off. Big time."

He'd just stared at her, not quite comprehending. When she'd handed over a pen, his gut had twisted.

Years of marriage blown off with a paper and a wave. And him, left lying in that bed, wondering, imagining.

Not get it up? Ever? Hadn't that just been a temporary setback? The accident, the surgery, the rigors of rehab?

Okay, so he'd worried when nothing had happened, no matter what, but he'd thought it was bound to come back. Wasn't it?

And then—so what if he had gotten it back? He'd still have to deal with this mutilated shell.

In those days, when he wasn't being yelled at and prodded and forced to put one leg in front of the other for his own good, he'd fretted. Then he'd prayed. Then he'd begged.

Then he'd shrugged. "No matter." At least, he had come out flush from the trucking company's settlement (thanks to Robert), and if he were gimpy—or whatever—at least now he was a rich gimp.

Right.

As if that made it okay.

Dream on, buddy.

His head fell forward, and the regrets washed over him. Tomorrow he'd work again. Tomorrow he'd get out of this slump. There was always tomorrow.

But there wasn't, was there? Tomorrow he'd be playing host and tour guide. Why had he made that offer? Yes, Samantha seemed nice enough. And certainly attractive. But she was recovering from a divorce, and, if Tootie were right, something since then with that fellow Jack, who was bad news, if Tootie were to be believed. With a girlfriend who ought to be locked up, supposing she'd been the vandal at Samantha's place.

No, he needed to avoid this in-the-flesh vision and whatever baggage she carried. And he would. After tomorrow.

Taking her to visit Cinque Terre would fulfill whatever host obligations he had. And tonight, Nicco and his wife had invited him to dine at their flat. That would be fun. It always was.

~

SATED after a hefty plate of fresh greens that Nicco's wife promised would improve digestion, Teo leaned back in his chair and smiled at his hostess. *"Delizioso, Adele,"* he said as he patted his stomach.

She beamed. *"Vuoi di piu? Forse un espresso?"*

"Niente, grazie. Nothing more."

Nicco passed the carafe of *vino rosso* around the table. Teo, whose first glass still held a few sips, offered to pour some for Adele's latest matrimonial candidate.

The woman extended her glass. *"Grazie,* " she said as her lashes drooped and lifted to regard him once again with acute interest. She was a beautiful woman. No, a stunning one. Her dark hair fell in luxuriant waves below her shoulders. She was also a widow who obviously thought him an excellent prospect for husband number two.

The conversation swelled around them as Nicco and his brother discussed the latest soccer tournament. The team from Padua was ahead by two wins, but Nicco waved this away. "They have not the fortitude to go all the way to victory."

His brother disagreed.

Teo watched the interchange, acutely aware that the beautiful widow wanted more from him. They had spent a pleasant evening with lively conversation, mostly about travel. She and her husband had visited many places, including New York. And she would very much enjoy a return trip.

When the party began to break up, Nicco suggested Teo drop the woman at her flat on his way home. He'd agreed and then wished their silence on the drive were a comfortable one, but her expectations weighed on him. He walked her to her building's entrance and helped with the key to the heavy door. She looked up at him. He bent and kissed her cheek. She sighed.

"Would you enjoy to come up for a while?"

"I think not," he said, making his tone gentle with a hint of regret.

"Perhaps another time."

"Thank you. Perhaps."

"Buona notte, Teo."

"Anche a te."

She turned, and he waited until the door closed softly behind her.

He was a fool. A beautiful woman obviously offered herself, and he turned her down. He could at least have cultivated a friendship. She was intelligent and kind.

But she wanted more than friendship, and he didn't have it to offer. He tried to picture intimacy with her. He could imagine himself sitting over dinner with her, enjoying conversation with her. But he could not imagine more.

It was too bad.

$\sim$

IT WAS PAST MIDNIGHT. He reread the words on the screen before him as Sophrina busily wove herself through the story. She stood on the deck of a mega yacht, dressed in a flowing caftan and holding the wrong end of a loaded gun. A muscled and oh-too-handsome (which made Sophrina's heart flutter) deckhand extended his palm. She dropped the gun into it and pointed to the wife of the shipping magnate. "That is your murderer," she proclaimed untruthfully, before all hell broke loose.

Teo rubbed one hand down his trouser leg and grinned. Somebody was going down.

Of course, the somebody wouldn't be the wife.

His fingers rushed across the keys. The phone rang. He ignored it, then blew out a loud breath and answered.

"Unc, it's me, Tootie."

Sighing, he tried to disconnect from the story. "What's up?" He looked at his watch. "And why are you calling at this hour? Is anything wrong?"

She laughed. "I figured if you didn't want to answer you wouldn't, but you're always up late, aren't you?"

He sighed. "I guess I am."

"Anyway, I just wanted to say hello and find out about your trip. I'm here with Mom and Dad. He's grilling steaks. And Mom said she hasn't heard from you either, so here we are. Calling."

His silence had been intentional, hadn't it? But he couldn't tell her or Deb that.

"Well, let's see," he said. "I learned that I'm not a seaman. I chartered a boat for my research, and a storm came up. The captain made Bligh look like Santa."

"Poor Unc." Her pause lasted for one quick breath. "So, have you seen Sam yet?"

A tremor massaged his throat. He swallowed it away, saying, "Yes, yes I have."

"Did you like her?"

Tootie sounded so eager—and so young—that Teo couldn't

be upset, although remembering the embarrassing moments from the night before, he wished his friends and relatives would leave well enough alone. Fine, he enjoyed good company, but women invariably wanted more. "She's very nice. I invited her to visit Cinque Terre tomorrow—no, make that later today. After I sleep for a few hours."

"Really? That's great!" she said, ignoring his hint. "Where's Cinque Terre?" He heard a voice in the background, and Tootie said, "Oh, here's Mom. But how do you spell that place so I can look it up?"

He told her and waited for his sister to pick up the phone, answering her queries mechanically, assuring her that he was well. And, yes, enjoying himself.

He was, of course. Always.

15

SAMANTHA

Choices threaten, choices come,
Choices beckon, choices run.
Choose to listen or choose to flee,
Choose to cower or choose to be.

Sam spared very little thought for her outing with Teo—until she woke that morning. She finished her ablutions and headed downstairs for a *prima colazione* of tea and fresh bread. None of that brew pretending to be coffee for her. No, tea would do when she breakfasted at the hotel. There was nothing better than a good Italian espresso, but she was too spoiled from years of sampling luscious roasts at *Samantha's* to be interested in the Garibaldi's attempts at *caffè Americano*.

She'd play it cool with Teo. He had offered his tour-guide services. She'd accepted. They would visit the five hillside villages that hugged the sea, and then he'd go back to his writing, and she'd...well, maybe Martine would be available for lunch one day soon.

He arrived in an elegant Fiat that was worlds away in design and cost from the lowly rental that had brought Sam north from Firenze.

"Nice," she said as she slipped onto the leather seat and smoothed her palm across its edge. The buttery feel of it made her hand tingle.

With Teo driving, Sam could watch the passing scenery, and his easy handling of the powerful vehicle allowed her to relax—instead of trying to press imaginary brake pedals as she'd done whenever Greg got behind the wheel.

They parked at Monterossa al Mare, the village most easily accessible by car. "Come," Teo said, helping her out and leading her to the waterfront. The charm of the place, the splash of color in sea and buildings and people, the lazy sunlit day, caught her imagination.

Teo didn't seem bothered by the pace she set or by her silence. When the walkway filled with jostling tourists and one loud fellow bumped into Sam, he motioned them forward. "Which would you prefer? Train or by foot?"

She thought of his leg as she shaded her eyes and studied the rough path that headed up the hills and into vineyards. "It's quite a distance, isn't it?"

"We can take the train to Riomaggiore, the last village, and walk back as far as Manarola. The hike between the two is easy, and there's a wonderful restaurant by the sea."

The train ride took minutes, the tour of Riomaggiore not above an hour. "Been there, done that," Sam said as they began the walk back. But she said it under her breath and doubted that Teo even noticed. Hiding under her broad-brimmed hat and with a faint breeze off the water, Sam could enjoy the rustling silvery leaves of the olive groves with always the view of the water on one side and hills on the other.

Teo led her into the cool darkness of the restaurant. She ordered *spaghetti al pesto,* he a salad and slice of steak. She slurped the ends of her pasta, dashing bits of basil-garlic sauce on her chin. Teo's eyes smiled as she dabbed it off.

She felt the tension of the past weeks ease as they chatted. Thinking of him and his writing world, she nodded toward the town. "Will you use this place in one of your books?"

He leaned back in his chair and lifted a cup of cappuccino to his lips. "Maybe some time or other, even if only in reference."

"So how do you pick your settings?"

His eyes twinkled. "Sometimes I want an excuse to visit a place. Other times, a random twist in a plot idea just seems to point to a specific place. I'm fortunate that Sophrina likes Europe."

"I see." Wasn't that twinkle cute? "You're completely at the mercy of your character."

"You've discovered my secret."

She'd like to pick at the subject, but she'd need more caffeine if she had to work at it. The pasta and the exercise had made her sleepy.

They watched colorful fishing boats coming and going and, after lunch, headed out onto the stone jetty. Waves spewed surf into the air. Sam dodged the damp spray, laughing, and Teo snapped photo after photo, too often of her.

"Stop," she cried, holding her hand to shield her face. "Photograph something else, please. That bent woman over there, or look, the little boy with his fishing rod. I think he's caught something. Just turn the thing away from me."

"The widows," he said, staring through his viewfinder.

She followed the direction of his lens as it pointed to a group of ladies in black dresses, black scarves, leggings, and shoes. "This is like a story book. Doesn't it make you want to know about the people who've always lived here? What it was like for their grandparents, before tourists showed up? Were the towns rivals? Did they work together to tend the vineyards and olive groves or did each hold tightly to his little parcel?"

Teo dropped the camera to his chest. "Exactly. I visit places like this and wish I could get into the soul of the people, not the shopkeepers and waiters with their always smiling faces, but their families, the ones back up in the streets behind here, the ones we don't see. How much of the world do they know— well, not this generation, but the previous ones? Did they venture forth, as isolated as these villages must have been for years? What is their conversation? What are their interests?"

"They've been discovered now. I mean, by the world."

"I'm afraid so," he said. "I wouldn't want to visit in August when most Europeans take their vacations. Come on, let's catch the train to the next town."

Two hours later and back where they'd begun their tour, they sampled *gelati*. Sam ordered a raspberry ice. Teo held his cone of *cioccolato* to her lips. She grinned, licked, and shared hers. His eyes seemed to darken as he offered seconds. She demurred and turned to watch the sun-speckled sea. Had she imagined that look, that connection?

Biting the side of her cheek and turning her head so he wouldn't see, she grimaced. She really, really must get over herself.

On the return drive, she tried to do that. But she barely noticed the view as the car sped down the highway, barely heard the purr of the well-tuned engine, but she did listen too acutely to the sound of her own thoughts, which flitted from the scent of this leather and the feel of this seat to memories of Jack's refurbished MG on the way to the concert in Greenville.

Her eyes slammed shut and then opened almost immediately. She would not go there. She would not think of black hair.

She glanced at Teo's profile and as swiftly turned to the window. Light hair versus dark hair. Light eyes versus dark eyes.

Why was she doing this to herself? She would not substitute one man for another. Any man, even a delightful companion such a Teo. She didn't want a relationship. Not now. She wanted freedom from her needy self. Period.

Get a grip, Sam. *Breathe.*

She heard words, but didn't catch them. "I'm sorry. I was daydreaming."

His voice held a hint of laughter. "I only wondered if you'd like to visit Martine soon?"

Martine? Oh, yes, Martine. "I would, very much."

"I'll arrange it and let you know."

SUNLIGHT MADE the salmon walls of the Paoletti's cliff-side villa glow with a welcoming warmth. Bushes Sam didn't recognize lined the iron fence that separated the small yard from the road.

"Just wait," Teo said. "The hidden part is the best."

A housekeeper ushered them through the wide hall toward the back of the house, and all Sam could do was gape at the hills and the sea spread before them, the town beneath, dropping to the harbor. As Martine rose to greet them, Sam closed her mouth. "I would never leave home if that were my view."

Martine laughed and introduced her husband, Antonio.

"*Scusatemi*, please, excuse me," he said in a languid voice, waving at the chair in which he sat. "I apologize for this weakness."

Antonio Paoletti was a tall, thin man with a shock of white hair, but most notable were his deep blue eyes and a smile that put Sam instantly at ease. He motioned Teo to a chair across the chessboard, speaking to him in Italian. The housekeeper hovered.

"Something to drink?" Martine asked. "Tea? Coffee? Anything else?"

"Water, if you please," Sam said.

Teo agreed to a cup of tea.

"Come." Martine led Sam to chairs in front of the long windows. The view spanned the harbor where sailboats bobbed, along with dinghies and yachts of all sizes and shapes.

"Oh, my, look at all those," Sam said, unable to keep a wistful note from her voice.

Martine accepted her cup. "We must make arrangements for that sail, you and I. I would be grateful for someone who knows how to manage the boat and could share the pleasure with me. Tonio has not been able to take me in recent years." She sipped, set her cup on the table, and picked up a plate of small cakes.

Sam accepted one. "I can't believe you're inviting me to sail here." Waving outward, she said, "There. On that sea." She missed *Alice* more even than she missed her home.

Martine's silvery laugh brought a question from her husband. "*Cara?* "

"Sam has agreed to sail with me."

"Ah. *Ma, è perfetto*! You have wanted to go on the boat

again." He gestured toward his frail limbs. "And I, I cannot take you."

"Yes, I'd thought of using you for research," Teo said. "Wish I could have."

"Instead of the crazy Greek," Sam said with a grin.

"Exactly."

"I regret that we were not available. You would have been welcome."

"Sì," Martine said, "but he would have needed a better teacher than I could have been." She looked over at Sam. "But once you learn our boat, perhaps you could take Teo with you."

"Oh," Sam said, "I don't think... I mean, I couldn't."

"No, no." Teo waved away that suggestion. "I've had my fill of sailing, *grazie*, Martine. You two have fun. I'll keep Tonio company."

"When would you like to go?" Martine asked.

Sam glanced over at Teo. He shrugged. "Thursday? Will that work?"

"I will telephone to the boat yard," Tonio said. "They will do what is required." And to his wife, "As long as the weather agrees."

THREE DAYS LATER, Sam stared up at a pale hydrangea blue. Specks of white showed off in the western sky, as if extensions of the billowy sails, but overhead was an unrelenting sun-bleached blue.

They escaped the harbor using the diesel-powered engine with Sam at the helm. It was so simple really, but on first seeing the key switch and the labels *Off, Run, Preheat, Start*—in English, at least—Sam had raised her brows and pointed. The gas outboards of her experience required only a pump of the fuel line, the start button, and then forward or reverse.

"Ah. This I can do," Martine said. "The key goes to this point." She indicated the *Preheat* position. "You hold there for some seconds, *cosi*, so, and then over to *Start.* " She did this. "See, the engine goes. And now I loose it, and it falls by itself back to *Run.*"

The next bit was complicated by a crowded marina, not at all like pointing *Alice* into an empty river—a little like working one's way around the Neuse on race day, except here they dodged moored boats and water taxis, big yachts and small dinghies.

Once they escaped the harbor and the small boats moored cheek by jowl in their floating parking lot, they hoisted sail. And then there was nothing but the wind in their face, the scent of salt air, the slap of boat on waves. Sam crowed, and Martine clapped, laughing at Sam's joy. Soon they were out past the cerulean, bobbing over the cornflower blue, and onto the darker iris and then a blackened hue. *Belle Journée* slid along on a calm sea, the wind puffing just enough to move her forward.

A pod of dolphins cavorted off their starboard bow but soon leapt away, disturbed by the loud engine of a cigarette boat. Farther out, the wind eased, and Sam steered them closer to shore.

Martine finished reapplying sunscreen to her face and hands and asked, *"Hai fame?"*

"I know that one," Sam said, raising an index finger. *"Sì, ho fame."* Her grin widened. "Of course, I'm usually hungry."

"I know. I, too. I thought that would lessen with age, because the ability to keep off the extra pounds certainly diminished."

"Did it ever."

"I must exercise daily. But here on the water, one is always hungry, yes? I will bring the food that was prepared for us."

The click of the opening refrigerator sounded from the small galley. *Belle Journée* had a head with a real toilet and a V-berth forward, so much more room than on *Alice*.

When Martine returned, she carried a tray of cheese, *prosciutto*, and bread. "Do you continue with water?"

"*Sì, grazie.* This is so good for me, practicing the language. Just make the words simple, *per piacere.*"

Martine leaned against the cushioned seat. "*Senti*, listen. Is there anything better than to be on a boat when this is what you hear, the water so gentle, the birds calling to us?" She nodded toward a couple of terns with their black heads and orange bills, swooping across the bow and down the port side.

Sam shook out her ponytail. "Nothing better. And your boat is a dream to sail." And eating like this, instead of jostling for comfort on *Alice*'s floorboards, seemed extravagant.

"Tell me about yours." Martine lowered the bill of her boating cap to keep the sun out of her eyes as *Belle* fell off slightly to catch a breeze that had circled around the promontory.

"She's eighteen feet, made of wood, and her name is *Alice*."

"You love her."

"I do." Sam reached for the bottled water, opened it, and took a sip. "Of course, she doesn't have a holder for drinks. Or a comfortable place to sit."

"*Perché no?* Why not?"

"She's a daysailer. I sit on the aft deck to steer, using a tiller. And guests sit on the floorboards, on cushions."

"And you do not get tired? Your back does not hurt from this?"

"Well, no." Sam hadn't really thought about comfort on *Alice*, just about the experience of being on the water. "I suppose she's primitive, but she's really beautiful and lots of fun to sail."

"I see. But *Alice* is an odd name for a boat, yes?"

Sam grinned, remembering the day she'd picked up the new-to-her boat. "The builder was a widower who'd named her the *Alice II* after his wife. He asked me to keep the name."

"That's very sweet."

Sam checked ahead, saw that they were coming a shade too close to shore, and suggested they tack. "Ready about?"

"Oh, *sì, un momento.*" Martine set down her sandwich and readied the jib sheets, one to loosen and one to tighten. "*Pronto!*"

"Hard to lee," Sam said, turning the boat's nose into and through the wind. She managed the mainsheet, trimming it once they'd finished the maneuver and she'd pointed *Belle* further out to sea. Because of the Med's changeable nature and the winds that could come up suddenly, Sam tried to judge her course to make for an easy trip back.

"This is so fun, is it not?" Martine said. "Your friendship with Teo and his with us, as if perhaps it is something meant."

Sam cocked her head, curious but a bit wary. Was this to be Martine's take on the too many coincidences? "Meant?"

"Well, you have told me that you were hurt and so has Teo been. Perhaps you can find solace. All of the signs point you to each other."

Sam felt like a mimic, and yet she needed to understand exactly what Martine had in mind before agreeing or arguing the point. "What do you mean by signs?"

Martine ticked off the list on her fingers. "*Per prima cosa,* you work with, no, excuse me, you have hired the niece to work for you." Her correction accompanied a laugh. "*Secondo,* I meet you in Roma, and you become my driver. This is a big one, no? Because the timing, the arrangement that put you there at the same time that I need you. *Terzo,* I invite you to visit, not knowing at all about this niece of my friend, who has also told you to contact him."

"Yes, she told me to, but I didn't intend to follow through with that. And I certainly did not know he lived here."

"Aha!" Martine said, holding up a fourth finger. "*Numero quattro,* to come and stop in Reggio without this knowledge. *Il buon Dio* has been at work."

"Do you really think God does that? That he bothers?"

"Oh, yes, it is evident. From all around us. We must just listen to the wind and watch the sea. We must be still and quiet and wait." Her shrug was very Gallic—lips, eyebrows, shoulders, hands. "Too often, we hurry. This must happen *now.* We cannot wait, and so we find ourselves working and hurrying to make our world do what we wish. Is this not true?"

Thinking of Jack, Sam nodded. "Much too true."

"So, now, we see what will happen. We wait and we see."

"I'll definitely buy into the idea of waiting. I've seen what happens when I don't."

The wind changed slightly, luffing the mainsail. Sam reeled in the sheet and signaled Martine to adjust the jib.

"I don't know how often I've tried to control my world, but I've certainly gotten myself in trouble because of things that were lacking in me."

"Ah, yes?"

"I mean, I'm willing to do whatever God wants, of course, but I'm not sure how to do that. I feel as if I've a long way to go to get healthy."

Martine nodded. "Trust is very hard. And I find that we often have an enemy that comes to live in our head. You agree? A whisperer who makes us remember only that which is not good about ourselves."

"Oh, I've got that one down pat."

"Perhaps, my friend, you will learn to whom you must listen and to whom you must not."

Sam forced a smile and said, "I hope I will." She checked the way ahead and the dying wind. "I think we ought to douse these sails and start the engine."

The sweet little diesel roared to life. Sam had to admire an engine that worked on the first try and let them return to port at will. As they neared the harbor entrance, Martine went forward with the boat hook and used hand signals to help Sam steer the course she wanted. "There, point there," Martine called. "I will grab that ball."

Sam edged the boat's nose toward the mooring ball. All those boats in the way, so close together—she wasn't sure she could do it. She took a deep breath, eased back on the throttle to just above an idle, and managed to get the boat close enough for Martine to hook the tether line's float. Martine then secured the line to a cleat on the foredeck. That done, Sam backed the boat while Martine dropped a stern anchor.

"I wouldn't want to try that in any wind," Sam said.

Martine laughed. "Nor I. We will remember that. If there is wind, perhaps we will go back to the dock and get help first."

"Or pay one of them to do the job for us."

"Excellent idea." Martine pointed her index finger at the side of her head. "We will use brains, yes? Now, I will hail a water taxi, if you would like to gather our things."

A few minutes later, they stepped off the small boat onto the quay. As the boatman handed up their bags, Sam took one and said to Martine, "That was such fun. *Mille grazie.*"

"*Prego.*" Martine slipped a couple of Euro to the boatman with a "*Grazie, signore,*" waving away Sam's offered contribution. "No, no. I, too, had a lovely time, and you have done me a great favor. It has been much too long since I have been able to enjoy our boat."

"Any time. If you want to sail again, just let me know." A boat. The water. A new friend. *Please.*

And, perhaps, if she spent time sailing with Martine, the gnawing in the pit of her stomach would ease. The past would recede, and she'd be here, doing what she'd come to do.

Which would *not* include a new man. In spite of Martine's theories.

16

TEO

An egret dips, a pelican plunges,
A seagull swoops, but I...well, I forgot how to dance.

The computer screen darkened. Teo's fingers tapped the air, but they couldn't seem to find purchase on his keyboard.

Fine. Whatever.

He wandered into the kitchen, poured mineral water into a glass, and eased his aching hip down onto the big recliner. Outside, pale yellows splashed against the blue of the western horizon as the sun crept toward dusk. He stared out the window, unfocused on anything but an awareness of color.

He sipped and realized he'd forgotten to add a slice of lemon. He wasn't about to walk back into the kitchen to get one.

Perhaps it had been the pink glaze on Samantha's cheeks after her sail or the bright tint to her eyes that had stalled him when he tried to shift gears back into Sophrina's world. He'd promised himself, hadn't he, that a quick trip to Cinque Terre would fulfill his obligations? But then there'd been Martine and Tonio. How could he not escort her to see Martine? And to go sailing, when it obviously meant so much to her? It was, after all, only common courtesy.

It wasn't his fault that he enjoyed the occasional shared meal. The chance to speak English with a fellow American. And who wouldn't delight in showing off a favorite town to a visitor?

He dragged fingers through his hair. Fine. He also couldn't ignore the fact that her mere existence carried elements of the supernatural that he simply couldn't explain.

"I'd like to understand, please."

Nary a whisper in response.

"A clue here?"

He should get a cat. A cat might at least look his way when he spoke. Traveling, he could leave a cat at home and have his cleaning lady change the litter box, make sure the animal had food and water. And when he was home, he'd have something to talk to other than walls. Not someone. But an animal would be better than nothing.

Yeah, except cats didn't give a hoot about anyone but themselves. And they didn't talk back any better than the air did.

His rational self wanted an explanation. His literary self wanted to dig in and explore. His petrified-of-caring self wanted to catch the next plane out of town. Maybe he could justify a trip to China. Or Japan. He could send Sophrina off in search of stolen artifacts. Have her look for smugglers. Bad guys who dealt in jade or bronze figurines.

He closed his eyes. And concentrated on the street noises that filtered through his open patio door. A scooter sputtered to life. Children played something that involved a ball bouncing on concrete. A woman yelled for someone named Leonardo. She repeated her words, and a door slammed.

"Relax," Teo whispered. It was time to relax. Time to quit thinking about puzzles. Or women.

A woman.

Why did she have such a compelling slant to her eyes, so much liveliness when her lips moved? He'd watched her ease into comfort with him a few times and then back away like a skittish doe. How could he not be curious?

After all, he was a writer. Writers needed to know. That's all this was.

Simple curiosity. Research.

17

SAMANTHA

Life pours out the messy bits,
The rats and snakes and honey pits.
It's up to us to shut them out,
To close the door and bar the way.

S am climbed back toward her room as dusk settled over
the town. Lights shone out of still-open shops. Chatter
competed with the clomp of shoes and the noise of motors on
the street.

The sail had invigorated her, and she'd felt the first pangs of
hunger shortly after Teo had dropped her off at her *pensione*.
She'd dined on a bowl of *tortellini in brodo* accompanied by a
light salad, an excellent ending to the day.

The daughter of the house greeted her from the front desk,
waving a folded note. Sam took it, said, *"Grazie,"* and read the
scribbles as she waited for the elevator.

How odd. Her ex-sister-in-law, Lena, had phoned and
would call again at nine. She and Lena had never been close, so
why was Greg's sister phoning her here and now?

At nine, she was downstairs waiting. At nine-ten, the phone rang. The receptionist handed her the receiver.

"Darling," Lena said. "So glad I've found you. *Finally.* I tracked down your hotel through Daniel, and that was *so* laborious. But it doesn't matter now that I have you, because I've such news. Phil has clients who own a villa up on one of the lakes, north of you someplace. I don't know where, but I'll get out a map before we come. Yes, that's why I'm calling. We'll be there next Thursday. Well, no, I suppose it will be Friday morning. Anyway, Phil's clients are so pleased with his work that they offered us the villa. It should be divine, and the kids are thrilled. Can you meet us? Come for a week?"

"Well, it sounds..." What could she say? She didn't want to see Lena, certainly not for a week. The thought of Lena intruding on her idyllic little world appalled her.

"Oh, and tell Stefi she must come, too, even if only for the weekend. We want to hear all about her school. And we can celebrate your birthday. Wicked of you to take off without coming to stay here, without letting us at least wish you a happy. Now, you must agree to join us. The children will be devastated if you don't, and you know Phil adores you."

Sam inhaled and released the breath slowly. This was not a moment when the truth would work. "Well, thank you," she said, because hurting Lena seemed worse than lying to her.

"Why don't we visit you in your quaint little town first? Daniel says you've run into that writer-uncle of your shop girl —what *is* her name? Anyway, we'd like to meet him and see your environs. You're not far from Genoa are you?"

"Not at all. Or from Milan, though that would be backtracking for you guys."

"I'll see what Phil says. His secretary's booking the flight for us, and I don't know why she can't do it into Genoa and out from Milan."

"Do you want me to pick you up at the airport?"

"Heavens, no. We'll rent a car. But you could book us a night's lodging nearby. A suite, preferably. That way we can get off fresh the next morning to find the villa by daylight. You know what Phil's like when it comes to maps and asking directions. Much better if he's had a good rest."

Yes, she knew Phil, and she knew Lena, and the thought of spending days confined in a house with either of them set her fingers drumming on the countertop. As Lena chattered, Sam shifted position, tucked a lock of hair behind her ear, and scanned the room's furnishings without seeing them.

When she and Greg had been married, they'd shared the occasional Christmas dinner with his sister's family, the rare weekend in the city. But Lena's designer clothes made Sam feel frumpy, and her conversation made Sam want to put a sack over her head until she could flee.

Now she felt trapped by this unexpected invitation. Why hadn't she just said no?

Back in her room after promising to call Stefi tomorrow, Sam stood at her window, staring out at the dark sky. "No. No," she whispered to the view as she practiced the unfamiliar roll of the words off her tongue.

WHEN SHE REACHED her daughter the next morning, Stefi's screech blasted through the phone. "Mama, yes! I'd love to see the lake country. This is so great! I can miss a class or two. I mean, *really*."

Stefi would be the perfect buffer for awkward moments with Lena. Besides, Guido wouldn't be there, hanging on. Maybe Stefi would return to Firenze with a different perspective on her Italian pretty boy after spending four days with younger cousins who were bright, fun, and curious about life.

She collected a note from Teo on her way to the Internet café to check e-mail. Would she like to dine with him again? It took mere seconds for her to decide. Eat by herself, alone and unable to communicate, or eat with a witty author who seemed to enjoy her company and who made her laugh? Hard decision.

Besides, it was just dinner. Nothing more. It would never be anything more. She liked being with him. He seemed to like being with her.

A third dinner together meant nothing. They were Americans abroad, and he, the local, wanted to help her, the temporary visitor, over the hump of her linguistic limitations.

She answered e-mails, entered words in her journal, walked, paused for coffee and lunch, walked again. By evening, she couldn't wait to spend time with someone who spoke her language.

She met him in the lobby. "*Buona sera,*" she said gaily and felt a momentary guilt because she was having fun. Absurd, that guilt, but, as Stefi would say, so like her.

She hiked the smile back into place in time for Teo to offer his arm and say, "Good evening to you, too. Tonight, I thought I'd take you to Il Mare Turchese."

Her first impression was of an unpretentious place splashed with turquoise on the tables and walls. The maître d' greeted Teo warmly before seating them in a corner, away from the traffic pattern to and from the kitchen.

"So that's what it sounds like when an Italian pronounces your entire name," Sam said as they opened the menus.

"I like the way you say it." Teo squeezed lemon into his water. "He merely gives the syllables a different flair. It turns out, he is also a Teodoro."

The waiter arrived, took their order, and left, followed almost immediately by a young boy who placed a loaf of bread and a bottle of olive oil in front of them.

"Great service here," Sam said, returning the young Italian's smile.

"It's a family-run place. He's the owner's nephew. I don't remember his name, but I understand he's very proud to be promoted to dining room work. His father," Teo nodded toward the front, "is the mustachioed fellow behind the cash register, and his sister, the lovely Isabella, should be making the rounds soon."

"Friends?"

"On my first visit, the brother-in-law limped over to compare canes, mine to his ornately carved ebony one. We shared an espresso and war stories."

Sam tore off a piece of crunchy bread and poured herbed oil on her plate. "There's something about the Italians. Something we're missing. We're so busy, so isolated back home."

"I agree. I suppose that's one of the reasons I like it here."

And he seemed to fit in well. Had she ever actually belonged to a place? She'd imagined melding into the Raleigh world from all her years there, in that house, raising her children, seeing to her shop. And then, suddenly, she hadn't.

The same could be said for Beaufort, couldn't it? She'd been away so long and had no family left here. The never-belonging had always been the case. Would, she imagined, always be that way.

Blown by the wind, that was Samantha Ransom. Up and out and off and away.

"What?" Teo asked.

She shook off the melancholy and pasted a smile back on. "I'm sorry. Woolgathering."

"Thinking of home?"

"You really want to know?"

He nodded. "I do."

"I was thinking how well you fit here. Reggio seems to suit you perfectly."

"Ah." He swirled his bread in the oil and bit off a chunk, pausing to chew.

Which gave Sam the opening she needed. "Speaking of liking it here—" His brows rose in question. "You were. Speaking of it, I mean. Anyway, the point is, we need to change one thing."

"What's that?"

"The fact that you always pay for the meals. I must contribute."

"No, stop, please. I can afford this and more. Besides, I enjoy having company. Think of it as doing me a favor." A pause let his eyes reflect the smile she found so appealing. "Please."

"Is this to be my convenient savings plan? Eat with you and extend my budget?"

"Why not?"

"Sounds like a kept woman." Sam hiked her eyebrows.

Teo wiggled his own back at her. "Without the fringe benefits."

"I admit that viewing this world with a witty companion has distracted me so well that I only called my assistants once this week."

"That's down from every day?"

Oh, my, she didn't want to be affected by that twinkle in his eyes, but how could anyone stay aloof from a man who knew how to laugh at his world?

She sighed. "It was hard letting go of the shops, but Rhea

and Tootie both seem to be getting on fine without me—which says something about how important my role is."

"No, it just means you trained them well."

"I still miss going in every day. Do you? I mean, do you miss being a lawyer?"

"I would hate to go back to that pressure. Life is too short."

"But I feel so idle here."

And he wouldn't, not with his writing. She bit into oil-dipped bread. He seemed about to speak when their main course arrived, and they grew silent, tasting the food. She savored the hint of garlic, the rich blending of herbs that made up the sauce on her plate.

She revived the conversation by asking about his latest manuscript.

He forked a bite of pasta. "Ah, poor Sophrina. She's gotten herself in trouble. She fancies herself in love with a Greek playboy."

"But I thought she was always imagining herself in love."

"Now, Samantha," Teo chided. "Didn't you notice she takes care *never* to fall in love? No, she enjoys having men wine her and dine her, and she enjoys a little cat and mouse with them, but she never finds one quite clever enough for her."

"Hard being a gorgeous and brilliant sleuth, I imagine." She'd never had that problem. No, sir. She was neither gorgeous nor brilliant, as she'd proven again and again.

"Extremely. But in Greece, she meets her match. At least, she thinks so."

Sam raised her hand to stop him. "Don't tell me any more. I want to be surprised when I read it. But do you have anything I could borrow now? I've finished the ones I have and need something to do when I can't sleep." She wiped her lips. "You know how one gets in the middle of the night."

"The middle of the night and I spend many hours together. I know it well."

Compassion made her long to reach out. It came so naturally to her, that lifting of her hand to lay it on another's forearm, the tactile of "I hear. I care." But she'd robbed herself of that freedom, hadn't she, the freedom to touch and be touched. New rules meant hands off. Hands to herself. On the bread or her fork. In her lap.

She was probably certifiable.

"Does pain keep you awake?" she asked, working on casually concerned.

"Not really. I often write entire chapters in my head before I'm forced to turn on the light and put the words on paper. I can't go to sleep until it's all written out."

"Such discipline."

"I wouldn't call it that. More like self-preservation. Tendrils of ideas that don't unravel into complete thoughts drive me crazy."

"That, I understand." She took another bite of the goat cheese and escarole cannelloni and sighed deeply. "This, sir, is good enough to make me weep."

"As is this," he said, nodding toward his plate of penne with lamb ragu. "Here." He reached for her fork, stabbed a bite of his dish, and held it out to her.

She slid the morsel into her mouth...a hint of mint and savory. "Oh, my. That's incredible."

"I told you. One of my favorite places to eat."

"It has just become mine."

After consuming and moaning through a few more bites, she remembered to tell him about Lena's visit. "Do you happen to know of a good hotel for them?"

"I do." He scribbled on a folded paper he retrieved from his pocket. "With two young people in tow, they may prefer this one." He added a star next to one located in the larger town just north of Reggio. "More for them to do."

"Thank you. Lena hinted more than once that they'd like to meet you."

"That would be fun."

"You think? Just prepare yourself to be cross-examined. They're both lawyers."

"Reminders of times past. I think I can handle it."

"I hope so," she said, sopping up the last of her sauce and wiping her mouth with the generous napkin.

"Would you like anything else? A cup of coffee?"

"No, thanks." She set the napkin by her plate and, yawning, slipped her purse into her lap.

"In a hurry?"

She followed his gaze to the purse, surprised to find it there. "I'm sorry. It must be the food and all my walking today."

"Then I'll drive you home."

He signaled the waiter and paid the bill, offering his arm as he led her to his car. She waited when he went up to his apartment to retrieve one of his books for her and tucked it in her purse with a "Thank you" when he returned.

"Hope you enjoy it." He turned the key in the ignition, pulled away from the curb, and entered traffic.

And a woman screamed.

Teo slammed on the brakes. Before Sam could move, he'd climbed from the car and darted to the sidewalk. She opened her door as Teo called something to a woman leaning out an upper window. A few passersby paused to watch, but only Teo spoke to her.

"There, can you pull the car up into that space, out of the way?" He didn't wait for Sam's answer as he hurried toward the building's entrance. "Her grandson's hurt."

"Can I..." she began, but he'd already climbed the short stoop, caneless and limping, but at a clip that surprised her.

She parked, grabbed his cane, and hurried after him. Sobs led her up two flights of stairs and through an open door. A very young boy—three, maybe four years old—lay with his leg bent awkwardly. The poor little thing writhed and wailed, while other children bent toward him, some weeping, some staring. Sam counted five in all.

Teo knelt beside the little one and spoke soothing somethings in Italian. Waving his arm at the other children, he scattered them and tried to question the sobbing grandmother. Sam waited for direction.

"I've called for an ambulance," Teo said over his shoulder. "Now I need to phone the father. Will you sit here by the boy, see if you can keep him still?"

She lowered herself to the child's side. What had she done for Daniel when he'd broken a collarbone? She mumbled a prayer as she smoothed the boy's forehead. She couldn't imagine why the grandmother didn't have the boy in her arms. The poor thing had to be petrified as well as miserable, and all Sam had in her arsenal were English platitudes.

Teo was on the phone with the boy's father when the medics arrived. Their presence seemed to inspire awe in the other children and the old woman, but the child kept a death grip on Teo's hand, especially when the medics readied him for transport.

"The grandmother will have to stay here," Teo said as he picked up his cane. "Could you follow the ambulance so I can go with the child? I told his father I would."

"Of course. I have no idea where the hospital is, so don't lose me, okay?"

He touched her shoulder, spoke to the others, and accompanied the stretcher out the door and down the stairs.

Sam's heart ached for the whimpering child. "I'll be right behind you."

The hospital wasn't far. By the time Sam had parked and followed them into the emergency room, a doctor was already tending to the boy.

She would have recognized the man who finally burst through the doors as the boy's papa even without his frantic cries. Teo spoke and found himself pulled into a crushing embrace before the man turned to find his son.

Teo straightened his jacket. "Well."

"Well indeed. You did a good thing tonight."

That brought his head around. "I'm sorry. You were tired, and I was about to take you home, wasn't I?"

"You can certainly do so now. Looks to me like you need your bed, too."

His hand touched the small of her back as they turned toward the exit. "The boy thought he'd fly like Superman when he jumped off the bed."

"Poor little tyke. He must have been in terrible pain."

"I'm sure of it," he said, removing the warmth of his fingers to open her car door.

She snuggled back against the seat. It wasn't an even exchange.

"That's a lot of children for a grandmother to care for."

He snorted. "Too many, obviously. I wanted to gag her."

"But you didn't. Good man."

"Force of will." A streetlight illuminated his grin. "And the faces of those children."

"I'm proud of you." She surprised herself by just how much she meant the words.

How many men would have responded to the cry of an old woman and taken charge as he had? No passerby did more than pause. And there'd been other tenants in the building. She'd seen their faces peeking out of doors.

But Teo, a stranger, had offered help.

He pulled up in front of her *pensione*. She reached for her door handle, but he stopped her.

"Please, allow me."

At her door, he offered his hand. She stepped onto the curb.

"Thank you for tonight," he said.

"I did nothing."

"You were there. You calmed the child."

He turned her, his hands sliding to her upper arms, and his lips grazed hers before his fingers traced a path down her cheek and he whispered, "Good night, Samantha."

She stood, the expression in his eyes surprising her more than the kiss. Just before he climbed back into the car, she murmured, "Good night."

"Sleep well."

The sweetness of that kiss—and that look—lingered as she prepared for bed. There'd been nothing potent or frenzied in either, nothing to remind her of former kisses, former loves. But the difference told her she'd better do some serious thinking.

18

TEO

Fallen markers mask the path,
And curves ahead will blind us.

Teo drummed his fingers on the steering wheel, his jaw set, his eyes focused on the narrow streets for the short drive home. He parked, locked his car, and tap-tapped through the entrance door to his building.

The lift carried him to the third and top floor. Laughter, bleating horns, feet on concrete barely registered.

Still working by rote, he entered his elegant hall, made his way to the kitchen, and leaned his cane against the counter to pour a tall glass of water. Hydration, that's what he needed. He'd hydrate, and things would even out in his head.

He carried the glass with him onto his large terrace. He could distance himself here in this lovely alcove that overlooked the sea, and tonight he needed distance. Besides, there'd be no writing. Not tonight. And didn't that just send a chill to his bones?

Maybe he was merely exhausted. There'd been the

adrenaline rush when he helped the child. But that wouldn't have interfered with his work.

No, it had to have been Samantha. Her existence. Her essence.

But no woman should have the power to stop his words.

Why on earth had he kissed her? He hadn't meant to. Absolutely not. Neither of them wanted or needed a relationship. And hadn't he promised he'd remain aloof? From any woman?

Except.

Except what? He couldn't quantify the time he'd spent with her. She made him feel carefree, lightheaded. Things came alive when seen through her eyes.

And, yet, there remained that puzzle: the who, what, and why of the other *she*.

He had no answers. *He* hadn't changed. He still didn't like the idea of visions or mystical stuff. Every encounter with the fleshly Samantha made him wonder what sort of unreality he'd roamed in when he heard those whispery wails. And he hadn't a clue if they were merely the workings of an overactive imagination or messages sent for a reason. He did know they had put him on his knees again—figuratively, of course.

And now she, the real she, was here. And he'd kissed her.

Hey, God, a little wisdom would be much appreciated. I sure hope you're the one pushing the buttons. I mean, remember me? Theodore Anderson? Not your best representative. Lots of questions down here.

Right.

Teo set his lamp on low, eased into a recliner, and tried to clear his head.

Like a top tightly wound, Samantha seemed ready to unspin and twirl out of the scene at the slightest misstep. He had to be careful. Very careful.

Which meant, he shouldn't have kissed her, however lightly.

Fine. No more of that. She was a woman in obvious pain who needed a friend. He knew how to be that. Hadn't he been prepared to be merely a man who practiced prayer for her?

Her expression as they'd left the hospital had been filled with admiration. For him. Not because he had money or could write. But because of a simple act of human kindness. The sort of thing anyone would have done.

Perhaps meeting her sister-in-law—okay, ex-sister-in-law —would shed some light on the conundrum that was Samantha.

Samantha. Who came in from sailing with Martine looking as if she'd shed years and all the cares of her life, and yet who sometimes sat across from him with haunted eyes.

Maybe that's why he'd seen her before he met her. He tried to imagine how those eyes would have terrified him if they'd looked at him from the face of a randomly met woman. He'd have run so far and so fast...and he'd never have looked back.

Instead, the puzzle intrigued him. And, because he was intrigued, he pursued a relationship that he otherwise wouldn't have.

The fact that it also provoked him into seeing Samantha as an actual woman couldn't be discounted.

Teo Anderson, man on the run, had paused. And was taking stock.

Eventually, he shed his clothes and prepared for bed. He didn't want to write tonight. Instead, he allowed thoughts to fill him and take him where they would. A real person instead of an apparition was a gift he mustn't lose, but he might if he weren't careful. She was a butterfly with a broken wing. If he tried to capture her, all the fairy dust she carried might wipe off, and she could die.

He didn't want that on his conscience. Ever.

He'd like to understand the source of her pain. He was a writer, after all. Curious creatures, writers. They felt the need to know even when it wasn't any of their business.

He tossed, because, yes, his hip hurt, and no position felt really comfortable. Finally, he must have slept.

A parade of faces appeared, each calling something he couldn't hear. He didn't recognize any of them. Why did they cry out?

He turned into the pillow. And woke. Or thought he did. His eyes opened, and he saw her face, weeping pitifully. She was on a small boat, alone, while the sail batted madly back and forth, the sound a loud slap accompanied by a groan from the wooden spar and the grating of metal against metal. Why didn't she tighten the rope that hung by her side?

"Samantha?" he whispered.

She turned as if she heard his voice. So he said, more confidently, "The rope? Don't you want to grab that what-do-you-call-it? That line?"

Tears continued to stream down her face, but she reached out and took the line, then wrapped it around the metal thing...the winch. And the sail came under control.

"Thank you," she mouthed. "Thank you."

And then she was gone.

He puzzled over the dream as he prepared his morning coffee. Had he actually been awake when he spoke to her? If not, had there been some bit to understand, something he should take away from what he'd seen? Something about control?

But whose and how?

19

SAMANTHA

With you, I ventured out of sync, an aberration only,
A summer's whiff, a pretense...

Sam paced at the *pensione*'s gate, waiting for Lena and Phil. "Breathe," she told her body. *"Calmati."* She liked the Italian way of telling someone to calm down. She whispered it again. *"Calmati." Calm-a-tee.* Calm yourself.

All she had to do was stay strong against a personality that had always slammed her less-vocal one out of the way. Why, she'd like to know, did Lena hang on to the relationship now that Sam was down for the count? Did the other woman relish the game that much?

Lena was still the children's aunt. Sam got that. But right now she wished her sister-in-law had dumped her after Greg decamped.

She grabbed two of the wrought-iron spikes on the fence. Throwing a glance skyward, she said, "Fine, that wasn't nice. I'm open for improvement, you know." At least, she'd like to be. "Especially if we could speed it up."

A long and very fancy something stopped at the curb. Lena opened the car door, slid one slender leg out, and followed it to a standing position. She glanced around, then reached for Sam, kissing cheeks and saying, "Oh, my dear, so quaint. I never heard of this town of yours before, of course, but I can see why you decided to stay. Much nicer than one of the cities. Your hotel, though," —and here her gaze flicked over it— "does leave a little to be desired, but I suppose it's good for the budget. Frugal Sam." She patted Sam's hand and smiled. Used to this, Sam returned the smile with the same lack of humor.

"Where shall we go?" Lena asked.

Sam directed them to a café at the beach where they ordered cappuccinos all around.

"We just love the hotel you found for us," Lena said. "The kids wanted to take turns with the bidet once they discovered it, but they ended up giggling so much, Phil sent them out for pizza. We left them in the concierge's charge. So nice to have that service available so we could get away to see you."

"I bet they've grown."

"Oh, my, yes. But you'll see for yourself at the lake. This trip's going to be good for them. I don't know why we didn't bring them over earlier." She looked at her husband. "Why didn't we?"

"I think we decided they'd get more out of it when they were older. Which they now are."

"That makes sense."

"And" —he patted her knee— "you always felt you needed time away."

"Just the two of us. That makes even more sense. But," Lena said in a bracing manner, as if trying to convince herself, "the experience will be educational. I love to think of them trying to buy things with their smattering of French and Spanish. I wish I could watch from a distance."

Sam leaned forward. "Well, if the locals there are anything like the ones I've been dealing with here in Reggio, the kids will make fast friends and get all the linguistic help they need. Florence, on the other hand..."

"Not nice?"

"When did you last spend any time in the city?"

"I don't know," Lena said, checking with Phil. "It must have been ten years ago, wouldn't you say?"

"At least," Phil agreed.

"Well, there are thousands of gypsies now, so nothing on your body is sacred. One of the girls living with Stefi was robbed when a woman and a bunch of children surrounded her, and the kids literally climbed all over the poor girl. She lost her passport, camera, and money, all because she wouldn't slug the little dears or kick them away. I don't think she knew what was happening at first." Sam remembered how appalled she'd felt when the girl told the story, and how creepy the gypsies had seemed after that.

"How awful."

"I loved touring the museums, but I was ready to leave."

"I hope Stefi survives."

"She carries her money in a pouch under her clothes and tries to look Italian."

"Good for her," Lena said and then chatted gaily about inconsequentials, including the famous Theo Anderson.

"We should invite him to dinner," Phil said. "Perhaps he can recommend some place we'd like. Do you have his number?"

"I do." Sam fished in her wallet for the card Teo had given her. "But no cell phone."

Phil handed over his, and Sam made the call.

"Why don't we meet at the small trattoria near the beach café?" Teo said after accepting the invitation. "You remember it? Trattoria da Mario?"

"Where I had the mussels?"

"Exactly."

Lena and Phil drove back to their hotel, returning a few hours later, still without children. "They had so much fun with the person we hired this afternoon that we kept her on," Lena said. "Phil and I don't want them competing for attention this evening."

Of course they didn't.

Teo waited just inside the door. "So pleased." Lena's enhanced eyelashes waved at him. Phil extended a hand, and they moved to their table.

While the others studied their menu, Sam asked Teo about the boy he'd helped.

"I stopped by the grandmother's this afternoon. He seems quite proud of his cast. He even let me sign it."

"Turning the others green with envy."

"Of course," Teo said. "His nonna couldn't stop thanking me and apologizing for the trouble."

"No sign of the boy's mama?"

"I don't think she's around. From what the children said, they and their papa live with the grandmother—or she lives with them. Perhaps I'll discover more on my next visit."

"There'll be a next visit?"

Lena fluttered her fingers between them. "You can't leave us out of the conversation, Sam. Who are these children? What are you discussing? Tell me."

"I'm sorry." Teo gave the rough outline of the incident, which prompted Sam's, "He's not mentioning his heroics."

"Nothing heroic. Just simple humanity."

"Right. Who else stopped to help?"

Once Lena had oohed and ahhed and so-sorried, they ordered their food and drink, and Phil and Lena began chatting lawyer stuff and Washington stuff with Teo. They continued as Sam forked her way through a huge plate of mussels in garlic and lemon sauce. Over coffee, the three others discussed skiing and travel, then broached the subject of Teo's accident and his new expatriate life as a writer. Sam dipped biscotti and studied wallpaper.

She shouldn't have been surprised when Lena invited Teo to join them at the villa. Lena's ever-expanding circle always included people like Teo—the famous or the would-be famous. "Perhaps you could drive Sam up?"

"I'd be happy to, if you think you have room."

"It's a huge place. And besides, Stefi will be there. You must meet her. And we've decided to celebrate Sam's birthday —late."

"Well, in that case, I must come." Teo winked at Sam.

She longed for the evening to end. She was tired of the wallpaper and tired of trying to care about the conversation. Petty of her, perhaps, but she wasn't a lawyer and she didn't know the people they discussed. Nor did she care about any of it.

Fine. She was petty.

She glanced around the restaurant, hoping for some interesting faces to study. And found two, which gave her several pleasant moments while she imagined the life of that white-haired man and woman who seemed genuinely pleased with each other and with their meal. The man had more and fluffier hair than his wife—Sam checked the hands and found wedding rings on each—and he sat straighter than she did, but didn't he seem to delight in her? What must that be like, married and in love after all those years?

She had to look away. She concentrated on managing the smile on her face so it wouldn't droop.

The meal ended. Phil paid the bill. And the three of them squeezed into the Maserati.

Lena barely waited for Phil to shift into gear before waving toward the departing Teo and saying, "Very nice. I think you've done well this time."

"We're only friends."

And that's the way it was going to stay. Sam couldn't say that to Lena, who thought only of the emotional distance from Greg. If Sam could help it, Lena would never learn the rest.

"Well, he seems interested. Don't let him get away."

As long as Teo didn't repeat the kiss or try for anything more, she was perfectly happy to keep him.

It was the *more* she dreaded. More always got her in trouble.

∾

THE LAGO COMO villa exactly suited Lena's elegant style. And it didn't take long for Stefi to declare this her favorite part of Italy.

It *was* gorgeous. But Sam felt as if she'd been bustled here and pushed there, and if she had to agree that the vista was breathtaking one more time, she'd scream.

Lena and Stefi collected a fancy *torta* from the local bakery and decorated the villa with balloons and uncorked bottles of champagne for the birthday party. The fuss made Sam feel guilty for her bad humor. When had someone last held a party for her?

And this had all been Lena's idea.

Amazing.

When it was time to distribute gifts, Stefi handed her mother a pair of black leather gloves from the street market in Firenze. Stefi's hug and her, "You're the best," brought on sniffles.

"You darling," Sam said, returning the hug and dashing at

her tears. How had she ever produced such a gorgeous and wonderful daughter?

Lena and Phil always gave money, but this time they added a few lacy things. And a cell phone.

"It's time, my dear sister-in-law, that you joined the modern age," Lena said. "Here's the SIM card. I'm sure Teo can help you figure it out."

Sam blushed—of course, she blushed—at the lingerie, but wasn't that sweet of Lena to give her a phone?

"Or I can show you." Stefi turned to her aunt. "Thank you *so* much. Daniel and I have been trying *forever* to convince Mama to get a new one."

Lena waved Stefi away. "Yes, well, now she has no excuse not to keep in touch with every one of us."

Which made Sam wonder at this new interest Lena showed in Sam-the-ex-sister-in-law as opposed to the old Sam-married-to-Greg.

Teo's gift showed up next in Sam's hands. He must have passed it to her, but she could only stare down at the elaborately wrapped package. "Oh, you shouldn't have," she began.

"Stop. Just open it." Lena inched closer on the couch. "We're all dying to see what it is."

Sam tried to salvage the paper, which made the process agonizingly slow. Teo offered his knife to cut through the packaging.

Wrapped inside was the gilded antique music box she'd admired in the village. How had Teo known? She hadn't praised it more than other quaint or lovely things she'd touched, and yet it was perfect.

"Your eyes lingered on it," Teo said, answering the question she hadn't posed aloud. He'd been a dear since they'd arrived, even winking at her during one of Lena's name-dropping monologues. But this?

Sam lifted the inlaid top and let the notes of Vivaldi's "The Four Seasons" wash over her. "Oh, my," she whispered and bit her lip. Had any man—any *person*—ever given her so perfect a gift?

"There are other songs," he said. "I believe this has a choice of four."

"Thank you," she said, meaning it. Wishing she could give him a hug that wouldn't embarrass them both. At least there'd been no further pursuit, no more lip touching or cheek grazing.

After the cake and the gifts, Stefi went off with her cousins to play at something, and Phil offered to pour more champagne. His wife was the only taker. But as Lena and Phil corralled Teo into another discussion of something that held no interest for her, Sam had time to think about her music box, which led to thoughts of how kind Teo was, which brought her focus to him.

And to a study of his face. He didn't notice when she traced his profile—in her mind, of course—down the tapering nose, to his lips, and then to his strong chin. Had she been aware of that chin before? Or the expressive quality of his lips when seen from the side?

As if he sensed her gaze, he turned toward her and smiled. It was a conspirator's smile, slightly apologetic, as if he were saying, "I wish I could talk to you instead, but what am I to do?"

So she smiled back and nodded.

∼

"YOU LIKE THIS color better or this other one?" Stefi asked her mother, holding up two bottles of red nail polish.

"There's a difference?"

"Of course there is." She held the colors closer to Sam.

"I must be colorblind."

The terrace door opened, and Teo stepped out. "Ladies," he said. "Am I interrupting?"

"Only a discussion of red versus red," Sam said, and Stefi wiggled the two bottles.

"Sorry. Not my area of expertise. I came instead to tell you that I made reservations for dinner in the village, hoping I could convince you both to join me." And to Stefi, "Do you think your cousins can spare you for an evening?"

"Oh, yes." Stefi's eyes widened, and she gave him a dazzled smile.

"I'll let you get back to your colors then."

He left them, and Stefi gathered the polish. "Show me what you're going to wear."

"Now?" Sam asked.

"Now."

Upstairs, Sam pulled black silk slacks and a loose fitting shirt from a hanger and laid them on the bed.

Stefi studied the outfit. "Hold on a minute." When she returned, she carried a silk scarf in hues of blue and purple. "With this for color."

Grinning, Sam accepted the scarf. "Gorgeous. And you?"

"I'm thinking that reddish dress to match my nails, which I'm going to paint now." At the door, she turned to ask, "You sure you don't want some?"

"I'm fine." Sam waved her out, thinking what a show-stopper her daughter would be in red, red, and auburn.

≈

THEY LEFT the villa at seven. As Teo drove them down into the village in his elegant car, Sam imagined her daughter's fingers on the leather, mimicking her own. She remembered the little-girl Stefi, bouncing in the backseat on their way to a treat—a movie or pizza or shopping for new clothes. This nearly grown Stefi wouldn't bounce on the outside, but she was probably doing a fair imitation of it on the inside.

Walking into the dining room in front of her mother, Stefi turned and wiggled her brows. Oh, yes, Stefi liked the linen and the splendor and the dinner out with Teo. Sam wiggled hers back. Yes, ma'am. Nothing shoddy about this place.

The waiter held Sam's chair, while Teo held Stefi's. After they ordered, Teo asked Stefi about her classes. "Did you bring any drawings up with you?"

"I did."

"I hope you'll show me."

And Stefi toppled at his feet. Her mother sympathized.

WHEN TEO HELPED her escape from a dinner with Lena and Phil and some friends from DC, Sam felt like a teenager escaping parental supervision. When he ushered her into the small, intimate restaurant, she remembered another reason she liked being with him.

Over a glass of wine, he told a story she hadn't heard about getting lost in an alpine village on a research trip. He asked about her student years, her children, her decision to open the first *Samantha's*. They lingered over coffee.

And suddenly he lowered his cup.

There was nothing about the cup lowering that should have caused Sam to drop her gaze from his flashing eyes to his widened smile. But her hand stilled. She caught her lower lip between her teeth, mesmerized.

His smile vanished as the heat climbed from her neck to her cheeks. Reaching across the table, he clasped her hand. "What?"

She shook her head. She hadn't a clue.

A blush, a stillness. *What?*

Because she couldn't stop staring at *lips?*

"I must be tired," she finally answered.

"Yes, of course you are. I'm sorry. Are you ready to walk back?"

"The air will do me good."

He signaled for the check, slipped some bills into the case, and helped her stand.

A moon rose slowly over the lake, which showed barely a ripple in the light's refection. He offered his arm again, and again she took it.

How on earth was she supposed to learn independence when her mind and flesh seemed determined to succumb to a man's charm? *This* man's charm. Serial monogamy meant serial dependence. Why couldn't she just see him as an interesting friend?

There must be something deeply wrong, something innately lacking that made her afraid to be alone.

No, that wasn't right. She didn't mind being alone, but obviously some part of her longed to be part of a couple.

Which is exactly what had happened with Jack.

20

SAMANTHA

I hope: imagination soars;
I fear: night splits in shards of glass.

Food seemed to define her days and evenings. Breakfast, lunch, dinner. And dinner too often with Teo. Sam hated that she'd come to depend on his company to keep her *alone* from screaming in her ears, but no matter how disappointed with herself she felt, she continued to say yes to him.

Yes instead of no. Always yes.

When would she learn?

They'd returned to Reggio in a lighthearted mood. At least, he'd seemed full of good humor during the drive and while they supped on a small pizza. She'd tried to keep up the cheer and escape the nagging question of whether or not the time had come to leave Reggio.

Exhausted that night, she slept, but soon she was aboard *Alice*, reclining on the floorboards and staring up at a sail full of wind. All she could hear was the lapping of water against the bow as the little boat sliced through the waves. She said something; the words changed every time the dream replayed: "Isn't this great?" Or, "Don't you wish it could last forever?"

And then silence, always silence. She spoke again, but no one answered. She sat up to see why and found herself alone on the boat, the untended tiller swaying to and fro. She called out to Jack, to anyone. Nothing. She was alone in the middle of the river, while her boat sailed itself. She sat mesmerized, watching the tiller move. In the way of dreams, parts repeated, caught, stopped, backed up, and happened again. But the scene never resolved itself. She had no idea if she ever got back to land.

She still wondered what it meant when she woke the next morning.

The water took forever to warm. While it did, she brushed out her tangles and tried not to think too much. After her shower, dressed and patinated, she wandered down to the neighborhood bar where she ordered an espresso and a chocolate croissant to arm herself with caffeine and too many calories.

Then it was off to the Internet café to e-mail the troops.

She found one letter in her inbox, from Rhea. *All's fine here, except you-know-who showed up again. Almost made my stomach turn, seeing Gail.* Sam loved the visuals. *That is,* Rhea continued, *until Miss Sugar-Won't-Melt-on-Her-Tongue pulled out her wallet and handed over four hundred plus of those gorgeous green things for another set of stoneware. I grabbed those bills, Sam honey, and flashed her the biggest smile you ever saw. She can come in here and hand over her money anytime, far as I'm concerned. You think she's coming in here to see what's what? My guess? All's not right in that gal's world.*

Sam grinned and typed*: I'm thrilled she's spending Greg's money with us.*

When her new phone jangled in her purse, she dug for it

and found Teo's number flashing on the screen. She logged off and headed outside.

"Seems my editor wants to meet me in Milano," he said.

"But you just got back from there."

"The drive isn't that long. I'll be in Reggio again in time to take you to dinner."

"You don't want to postpone?"

"I'll still have to eat, and I'd rather do it with you than alone."

"Well, if you're sure."

Ten minutes later, her phone rang again with another call from Teo. "Martine just invited the two of us to their house for dinner and you for an afternoon of sailing."

"Really?"

"If you can catch the bus down to their place, I'll meet you there and get you home."

Sam jotted down Martine's number, called to make the arrangements, and asked how and where to catch the bus. Her smile almost split her cheeks.

Oh, yes, oh, yes, keeping busy on the water. This worked.

THE WIND DIED.

Martine's rueful expression accompanied her words. "I am so sorry. I forgot to check the forecast."

"It doesn't matter. I'm just glad to be out and on a boat."

They dropped sails, and Sam gazed out to the horizon. "Do you mind just drifting for a while?"

"It is so peaceful." Martine stretched out her legs and lowered her big-brimmed hat to shade her face.

The gentle movement of the boat lulled them as *Belle* bobbed with the current and the receding tide. The occasional light slap on the hull brought the only noise, except when a gull squawked in hope of a handout.

Checking off the stern, Sam noticed the shoreline growing less distinct. "I think we should start the engine. We can't very well paddle a boat like this." And it would never do to be too far from land if the engine quit on a windless day.

"Do you wish to head in?" Martine asked.

"I think it best. But slowly."

"Another day, we will sail more. I will be certain to listen to the weather reports."

Sam steered. Relaxed, she tried to pick out words when the VHF squawked occasionally in Italian or French. There were more boats on the water today, but no other sailing vessels. *Belle*'s small engine puttered them toward the harbor.

"*La Belle Journée,* she is a fine little boat, *n'est-ce pas?*" Martine's eyes twinkled.

"Ho-ho. You are going to work on my French now, as well as my Italian?"

"*È necessario.*"

"Ah, it is necessary. That's an easy one, but we're back to Italian."

Martine laughed, a pleased gurgle. "You will stay here, in Italy?"

"I'm not certain. Sailing with you makes me want to linger, but someday soon, I'll have to return to my home and my shops."

"It is permitted to suggest that my dear friend Teo may not be happy if you leave?"

Sam focused on the wheel, adjusting it slightly to starboard. "He's very nice."

"Of course, he is. He has also many times revealed to Tonio that he has no interest in another wife. He tells Tonio, you know? How his friends, they try to introduce him to women, but Tonio says he has too much hurt inside and does not wish to let himself grow close again."

"Ah. Yes, I see. Well, I've told you that I'm not angling for a man. It's much too soon for me."

"Of course. I should not have mentioned it."

Sam suppressed her sigh, but she heard it rooting around in there. "It doesn't matter."

She wouldn't discuss this. Certainly not with Teo's advocate, and the one who figured some sort of relationship was *meant*.

Martine stood and peered out past the shading bimini as a cloud obscured the sun. "More clouds seem to be coming from the south. It is good that we go in."

Picking up the mooring was easier this time. Sam beamed at Martine, who gave her a victory wave and called, "You are becoming the expert."

They secured lines, gathered their belongings, and closed up the boat before calling for a water taxi. The air had begun to cool. Martine had been right about the approaching storm. Sam hoped Teo would make it to Portofino before those clouds let loose.

THE HOUSEKEEPER HAD JUST BROUGHT in a light antipasto of lettuce rolls and condiments when Teo arrived. Martine rose to greet him and accepted the offered bottle of wine and the cheek kisses.

"*Benvenuto*," she said, the lilt in her voice as welcoming as the word.

Sam didn't rise. "You see us relaxing after a strenuous day."

"Hard work on the water?" Teo said and pointed toward the window. "I do believe we're in for a deluge."

The wall of misty rain advanced across the harbor. By the time the housekeeper announced that dinner awaited them, rain pelted the windows and the tile roof.

"Teo knows us," Martine said as they sat before beautifully arranged platters of veal, vegetables, salad, and bread. "We do not eat huge meals here."

"It's perfect."

"Lisette goes to her own dinner now. We can enjoy the meal without so much commotion, you know?" And with a shrug toward the back of the house, "Except for that which is outside."

Tonio patted his wife's hand. "It is well."

"You had the meeting with your editor?" Martine asked Teo, passing the bread basket.

"I did. She gave me the same line as always: The books are doing well, when will I send the next? By the way," he said, dunking his bread in olive oil and turning to Sam, "Val had an interior designer with her, a woman who has written a series of articles she wants to compile and publish. I crashed their party and mentioned Stefi's aspirations, which means that I now have a name, a contact, and a promise to look at Stefi's drawings whenever we can get the two of them together. Stefi is Sam's daughter," he explained to the others. "We met at the lake."

Martine's gaze flickered toward Sam.

"I can't believe you did that for her," Sam said. "She'll be ecstatic."

"I like Stefi. It's no big deal."

"It will be to her."

"Well, connections are important. Stefi seems to be working hard to learn as much as she can. And I liked the drawings she showed me. It'll be up to her now."

Martine extended the plate of stir-fried vegetables to Teo. "You've met Gian Baggati, haven't you?"

"I have." He turned to Sam. "The Baggati Castle's that big place overlooking Reggio."

"Quite a fortress," Sam said.

"He was in town this morning." Martine sliced into her veal. "Such a production."

"From what I've seen," Teo said, "he does everything that way. How many cars did they bring this time?"

Tonio speared a zucchini chunk. "*Almeno cinque.*"

His wife translated. "At the least, five, and very big ones they were. So many guards around him."

"Probably afraid someone will take a pot shot in his direction," Teo said.

"Pot shot?" Tonio asked.

Teo pointed his index finger and pretended to fire. Tonio laughed. "*Sì, esattamente.*"

Exactly? That roused Sam's curiosity to a new level. She'd seen the castle up high on the mountainside with its long, winding drive and the best view in the area. "He's afraid for his life? How do you know him?"

"I got into a conversation with the man himself late one night at a local coffee bar," Teo said, "and he invited me to a party he was having the next evening. Castello Baggati is quite a place, exactly as you would imagine a medieval replica constructed by Disneyland."

"You're kidding. You mean, it's not real?"

"It's certainly no older than the fifties. His father had it built with money he'd made in the United States. Steel, I think. Buying himself a setting for all that gold."

"You have spoiled our friend's illusions, Teo." Martine wagged a finger playfully. "She has been imagining an antique castle, perhaps from Charlemagne."

"I have indeed. So what does this son do up there?"

"As far as I can tell, nothing at all, except spend money and enjoy life. The place is worth a visit, even if it's not authentic." Teo reached for another piece of bread. "Great food, Martine," he said and, at her smile, bounced back on topic. "That castle might as well be a fortress. It would be very hard for anyone to sneak up on them, with those steep ridges behind and the ground falling off in front. The night I was there, limos lined the length of the pavement. I didn't know any of the jet setters, but there seemed to be diamonds flashing everywhere. I had a grand time watching them in between examining Baggati's collection of paintings and antiques. The castle may not be period, but the furnishings are, and someone up there has an eye for fine art."

"I'd love to see it." Sam imagined telling Stefi and Daniel about such an adventure. The idea of a fortress brought to mind those old black-and-white films of women in furs and cigarettes in holders. Jewel-encrusted, of course.

"Wouldn't we, also." Martine nodded toward her husband. "So mysterious. And to think our writer was invited."

"If I ever run into him again," Teo said with a wave of his fork, "I'll see what I can do."

"Will you write of him?" Martine asked. "The mysterious Baggati?"

"Who knows? Perhaps someday."

That reminded Sam of something she'd meant to ask. "Speaking of writing, do you ever imagine doing something exciting like the characters from your books? Chasing bad guys?" She'd caught him mid-bite. "Or do you get asked that all the time?"

He held up a finger until he'd swallowed. "Rarely asked. With a female heroine, I imagine meeting her, not being her. I like mysteries because I like to solve problems. It's like playing chess, figuring out moves three or four plays ahead. Of course, if I were better at chess, I'd be able to see straight to the end, and Tonio wouldn't stand a chance."

He stopped to translate that for Antonio's benefit and scored a laugh from the other man. "I try to fix my plot points toward the taking of the bad guy's king instead of the other way around." A sip of water, and then, "I suppose I may have created a few characters who are particularly strong or attractive or brilliant as compensations for my own needs, but I usually just write about people I'd like to know. And sometimes about people I'd hate."

"What about...?" And they were off, discussing favorite characters and plot lines. Martine joined in with her own questions, and Tonio managed to get off a few in English. Martine and Teo translated Tonio's Italian comments.

Sam hadn't felt this energized in months. She didn't want the evening to end.

When Martine asked her what sort of stories she most enjoyed, Sam thought for a moment. "I'm fairly eclectic in my tastes. For a while after Greg left, I'd pull ten books off the library shelves, take them home, and maybe actually get through three of them." She took another small sip of wine while she tried to come up with a good answer. "I like romance, mysteries, suspense. As long as they're not formulaic and are well written. I enjoy stories that are intelligent and a fun read. Like Teo's books."

"My humble thanks." Teo bowed his head, but his grin didn't look the least bit humble.

No, he looked like he was soaking up the praise. Happy to slather more on, Sam continued. "You keep me guessing right to the end. In *Alpine Trumps*, I was sure Evangeline had done it, and then when it turned out to be that meek little Rufus Becker, I was stunned." Her raised palm stopped any comment.

"Oh, only at first. You did a great job of making me say, 'Of course, it couldn't have been anyone else.'" She gave him a satisfied smile. "So, you see, you did exactly what you were supposed to do, and very cleverly. And that Sophrina. Great fun."

"Thank you," Teo said. "I rather like her myself."

"I, too," Martine said. "I'm afraid my dear Tonio is waiting for the Italian translation of your books."

"I speak some English very imperfectly," Tonio agreed, "but these days, the reading of it tires me." To Teo, "I used to, but now?" He shook his head.

Teo waved a hand. "Please, don't even think about it. I write purely for the fun of it, and there are many wonderful Italian writers who will serve as well. Or better."

Tonio inclined his head.

Sam shifted the focus. "I, for one, don't know how you manage to write so well from a woman's point of view."

"It is true," Martine said. "You do, Teo, and that is not usual."

Sam finished the thought. "Your stories make me grin, which doesn't usually happen in a mystery. Besides, as promised, no gore."

Teo's eyes lit.

"I hate it when writers think I want to visualize every wound or bit of blood in horrific detail."

"It is the same for me," Martine said. "Graphic descriptions do not please."

"*No, cara*," Tonio said, smiling and pointing to the wine.

Sam caught the affectionate glance between Tonio and Martine, along with a sparkle that seemed quite a bit more than mere affection. The yearning for her own bit of sparkle— healthy, happy sparkle—slammed into Sam, and she hid behind closed lids until the moment passed.

~

THE RAIN HAD FIZZLED to nothing by the end of dinner. Sated and mesmerized by the play of headlights on puddles, Sam leaned against the headrest as Teo drove the winding roads to Reggio. The next thing she knew, he had parked at the curb in front of the *pensione*. She rubbed her eyes.

"Did you have a nice nap?"

"I did."

He reached for his door handle.

She stopped him. "No, please. Don't bother to get out."

"I like to bother." His hand touched hers lightly before he withdrew it. "I just wish the evening didn't have to end."

"I know. But I think it should."

"Samantha?"

"Yes?"

He shifted in the seat. "Is there another man in your life?"

"Why do you ask?"

"Because I think you like me, and I know I like you, but I hesitate. Perhaps neither of us is ready for more?"

She clasped her fingers tightly together and stared at the dark shadows in the street beyond the lamplight. "No."

"Then there's no one else?"

"Not now."

"But there was. I mean, since your husband." He paused. "Jack?"

Sam's exhale echoed in the silent car. Tootie again.

"I met him in the shop," Teo said. "He seemed inordinately interested in your whereabouts."

"I came here to get over him."

"Ah..."

His monosyllable elicited a slight smile. "Ah, as in, you're not certain if you should ask anything more? Or you're wondering, now what?"

"Both," he said. "I'd like to ask, but should I? Will I want to know the answer? I doubt it."

"It's a little cold to sit here and talk, don't you think?"

"I am sorry. Would you like to go somewhere else?"

Exhaustion, brought on by the mere mention of her past, claimed her. "What I'd like, if you don't mind, is to go in and take a hot bath—or at least as much of a bath as I can muster—and go to bed. Perhaps, if you truly want to know the unhappy history of my love life, we can meet sometime tomorrow."

"Coffee at eleven?"

"At Le Stelle."

21

SAMANTHA

Time has a way of galloping when what we do is fun.
It passes slower than a snail's pace,
Leaving a gooey snail's trail,
When what we do is wrong.

Patterns of shadow flickered against the far wall. Sam climbed out of bed and padded to the basin, wincing at the mirrored reflection of straggly hair and baggy eyes.

Teo ought to see her now. He'd hop in that fancy car of his and never be heard from again.

She hadn't bothered with a bath the night before, so she raised the bathroom temperature with a portable heater, wet and lathered herself, and decided to go ahead and wash her lank hair, eking out the last drop of warm water as she finished. Never again would she take hot water for granted. A deep, steaming bath had begun to look like a remnant from paradise.

The bar was almost empty when she arrived a few minutes before eleven. A couple of old men sipped espressos. Another already held a glass of red wine. The bartender's wife stooped to add pastries to the case.

"*Buon giorno,*" Sam said to the room in general.

"*Buon giorno,*" the room chorused.

Teo pushed open the door behind her and doffed his sunglasses with a wave to the bartender. More *good-days* followed.

"An espresso?" he asked. At her nod, he ordered two and escorted her to a table.

The bartender delivered the coffees. While Sam stirred in sugar and powdered creamer, Teo stared out at the sea. "Is it okay?" he asked when she finally took a sip.

"Fine, thanks."

"You know, you don't owe me anything. Certainly not an explanation. It's none of my business."

Her smile faltered. "I know."

"I shouldn't have brought up the subject last night. I'm sorry."

She shook her head. "No. It's okay. Maybe talking about it will do me good."

He waited.

"Don't you think so?" As soon as she asked the question, heat hit her cheeks. Why did she care what he thought, what he wanted? She longed for a hole in the bar's floor big enough to crawl into and disappear.

"Only if you feel comfortable enough to tell me." He extended those long fingers across the table.

She stared at them, his fingers resting on the table, relaxed, so different from her curled ones. She had to speak, say something.

Or walk out and pretend they'd never met.

"I'll never feel comfortable about what happened. Comfort's not the issue." She closed her eyes, pressed middle fingers to her temples, and sucked in a deep breath. Okay. Better he know and run now than find out later.

"Let's talk about something else," he said gently. "Have you heard from either of your children?"

"No. Yes—no. I mean... You met Jack," she blurted, rushing her fences. "The thing is, he was my best friend from the time I was seven. We lived next door to each other." She could see it, see their small houses, side by side, the sound close, the river closer. "He taught me so much. I always loved him."

"But you didn't marry him."

"No, it was never like that. We were buddies. I mean, sure, I'd hoped for more when we were teens, but he saw me only as a tag-along kid, the neighborhood tomboy. You know, the one he took fishing and boating, the one he taught to sail, that kind of thing. He married the girl with the boobs." She stopped suddenly, and her hands flew to her face. "Did I actually say that?"

Teo's grin widened. "I believe you did."

Sam ducked her head, took several quick breaths, and looked up, struggling for a shred, a remnant even, of dignity. He shouldn't laugh. It really wasn't funny.

She sat a little straighter and, with as much pride as she could muster and with a wave of her hand, said, "Whatever."

Teo doused the grin and leaned back in his chair.

"So, anyway, Jack and I lost track of each other over the years until after Greg left. When I moved back to Beaufort and Ruth Bonner recommended a contractor to redo the cottage I'd bought, it turned out to be Jack. I'd had no idea he even lived in the Beaufort area, because the last I'd heard, he'd gone off to college somewhere on the other side of the state and had stayed away. An amazing coincidence seemed to have brought the best of my past to comfort me."

She could see it, that first meeting, Jack sauntering up in

jeans and boots, his fingers looped in his pockets, sunglasses hiding his eyes. He hadn't known her immediately, but she'd recognized the gait and the voice.

And then there'd been those early days of finding Jack waiting for her at the cottage, of taking solace from his presence, his laughter. Sailing with him. How good it had been.

Until it wasn't.

"So, what was the problem? Was he still married?"

"No. That hadn't lasted much past college. He lived with a woman named India."

"Ah," Teo said, but he didn't look very surprised.

Tootie again? Sam hiked her brows momentarily, but decided not to ask. Best just get this over with. "It was the sailing. I hadn't found anyone who loved to sail with me since Jack and I were kids. One thing led to another, and eventually Jack left India."

"And took up with you?"

Just mentioning those days brought flashbacks, first of Greg's words, then Jack's. Greg's actions, then Jack's. And then, of course, hers. "I was so happy to have my friend back that I ignored how India must have felt. Eventually, Jack said he couldn't stay with India now that he realized what he'd been missing. It was heady stuff. Of course, India didn't see things quite the way Jack wanted her to."

"No, I imagine she wouldn't. How long had they been together?"

"Too long. In some states they would have been considered common-law married."

"Not in North Carolina?"

Sam shook her head. "I don't know. Whatever their status, I closed my eyes to her pain. I also told myself that I could keep Jack at arm's length, that I was a strong, morally secure woman who knew how to steer clear of trouble."

Teo's expression sobered even more, very reminiscent of her father's when she committed a misdemeanor. She began stacking creamer packets and added sugar and artificial sweetener to the tower, straightening it when it threatened to topple.

"But I'm guessing you couldn't. Because one can't, you know." Teo kept his tone level. "You became lovers?"

The lump in Sam's stomach bounced and threatened to exit up her throat. One hand still on the stack of packets, she managed, "You do cut to the chase, don't you?" He didn't speak as she stared out the window at the sea. "It sounds horrible, stated so baldly. Makes me seem so weak and ugly, going against everything I believed in. But, yes, that's what happened. We became lovers. My emotions overruled my scruples, and there was no excuse, no matter how many I offered myself."

His hands splayed on the table. The veins bulged slightly, and light hair flecked to his knuckles. Their position exuded a restrained power, as if they waited to become fists. He slid them to his lap. One foot kicked a table leg as he readjusted his position. "I can't believe that he, this supposed best friend, took up with you like that. He may have left her, but he wasn't free. I'm sorry, I have no respect for two-timers. Or for those who prey on the wounded." He ran his fingers through his hair. That exquisite control seemed to have deserted him. "Seducing you and hurting her? Those were acts of a man who loves no one but himself."

"It was my fault, too." Sam straightened. She couldn't let Teo heap all the coals on Jack. "I could have said no. I could have told him to quit coming around, to quit calling me, to quit sailing with me, to quit making my life fun again." She clenched her teeth to bank the tears and control the shivers. "I could have told him not to be my friend anymore."

They brimmed then, those tears, and Sam didn't try to wipe

them. Teo reached over and touched her fingers, closing now-tender hands over hers, gathering them together. "I'm sorry. I shouldn't have said that. I've no right to judge you or him or anyone. It's just that I hate to see the pain you're in. You deserve so much more."

Sam licked away a tear that dripped onto her lips and sniffed, then eased a hand out of his clasp to brush at her cheeks. "I kept telling myself the same thing. That's why I'm here. To get out of that mess and start over again."

"Hampered slightly by a broken heart."

"Slightly. That's two breaks in quick succession, so you can see why I'm not exactly panting for another relationship."

"I can."

He handed her a handkerchief and waited as she dabbed at her cheeks and blew her nose. She didn't want to look up. She didn't want to see his eyes.

He cleared his throat, leaning closer. "How about an unencumbered friend? No strings on me or from me."

Now she did look up and at him, studying his expression, waiting. His smile gentled her nerves. His hand resurfaced and reached toward her, palm open. A moment later, she slid hers into it, feeling his fingers close slowly, gently, his grip light enough for a quick escape.

"Thank you."

Freeing her hand, she tucked his handkerchief in her lap and tipped her cup to swallow the last of the coffee. "I wish I'd never run across Jack again." She paced her words, wanting them said, wanting them silent.

Well, that could be managed. Just shut up.

Ha.

She'd exposed herself. And *why* had she done that? Some sort of masochism at work?

The spewed words made her want to come up with a finish

to the story. That's what flitted through her thoughts—*finish*—as if her words required a patina.

Absurd.

But it was that bit about being exposed. Naked in front of this man. It was one thing to tell a semi-stranger the crudities of her life. It was another to tell someone she'd come to admire.

She looked again into his eyes. His compassion opened the valve, just as it had before. "The thing is, this pain feels worse than Greg's infidelity because, this time, I'm guilty. *I* was the sort of person I hate—a taker. Self-centered and self-absorbed. I'm working hard to forgive myself."

"You must."

She shook her head. Boy, once she got started... "Easy to say. Two problems. There's India. And there's me. I never really felt as if Jack were free, you know. And India kept showing up. He always made excuses and placated her. He obviously still cares for her. Oh, and a third thing. The whole issue of broken commandments."

"Does India know?"

"She's bound to." Sam told him about the holes in her boat and tires, the slashed screen. About India and a pair of binoculars through which she'd probably seen way too much.

"Tootie mentioned the damage and your worries. But she said you and Jack claimed it was kids."

"I never thought so. I just didn't want to accuse India without proof." Her fingers splayed on the tabletop.

He reached over with a comforting caress across her knuckles. "You've got to let it go, Samantha. Consider instead how much courage it took to leave. How strong you've shown you are by quitting something that wasn't healthy. Not everyone can do that. Look at you," he said, his voice as soft as his touch. "You're shivering. Drink your coffee—no, you've finished, haven't you? Hold on. I know just the thing."

He limped to the bar, returning with a steaming glass of something orange. "It's hot *mandarino*. Drink it slowly. It's potent."

The liqueur lit a fire from her lips to her stomach. She coughed once pressing his handkerchief to her mouth.

"Slowly now."

She nodded and took a tiny sip. "It's lovely. But it feels like something that could make me quite drunk."

"Just sip it. You don't need to drink it all, just enough to warm you before I take you to lunch."

They sat in silence as she cupped the hot glass, using its warmth on her hands as well as her insides. As her shivers eased, Teo said, "I think I can see how this relationship with Jack came about."

"It's all so complicated."

"You probably wouldn't have exposed yourself to anyone except this childhood friend. He wasn't some random man showing up in your life."

"I know, but I'm an intelligent woman. I should have been able to recognize trouble and run from it. Especially after Greg's infidelity."

His expression turned rueful. "There are millions of 'should-haves' for each of us."

"Yes, but some are worse than others. You can't equate them."

"Stop it, Samantha. As vulnerable as you were, you don't have anything to kick yourself about." His tone grew harsh, disgusted, as he said, "This Jack fellow? He's a different story. He used your weakness and played with both of you. It sounds like he would have gone on juggling you indefinitely if you hadn't broken free."

She licked the sweet orange taste from her lips. "I hope he's miserable."

"Thatta girl." The twinkling eyes were back. They emboldened her. Or maybe it was the liqueur.

She giggled. "I try to be good. I try very hard to think positively about both of them and hope for the best for their relationship. You know, the whole praying for your enemies bit? But sometimes..." She stared into the remnants of bright orange liquid and pushed the small glass away. "This is so delicious, it could definitely become addictive."

"Not the little you drank, my dear. Now that you've stopped shivering, how about a walk on the beach before lunch?"

He left a tip on the table while Sam pulled on her sweater. The wind blew off the water to cool the already moist air as they picked their way across the sand-and-pebbled beach.

Her problems seemed to have distanced themselves, either because of the heated drink or confessing all to Teo. The sensation felt pleasant and gave a certain lightness to her step, but the pleasant could become addictive, and she'd flown all the way here to get away from addictive anything.

They walked slowly, barely speaking. She'd talked enough for a lifetime.

He guided her down the beach, his hand sometimes at the small of her back, a gentle pressure that gave her courage. The touch of a friend.

Turning her wordlessly toward town, he offered his arm. Her chin came up a little more.

"Pizza or pasta?" he asked as they approached a small restaurant where the smells from an open door made her mouth water. "These folks serve a mean zucchini-flower-and-arugula pizza."

Zucchini flowers? Ah, wonderful Italy.

They ate. When she caught his eye over a bite, he smiled gently, as a friend would who was glad to be here and satisfied with the company. It encouraged her to eat more than she might have.

Replete, she sat back and announced, "Siesta time." Sleep sounded like luxury.

Teo again offered his arm. She felt an easy smile form, the first easy anything for days, as they climbed the hill to her hotel. She leaned into his strength. Had she ever felt so at peace, accepted, in any man's presence? There'd always been an edge with Jack. And she wasn't even going to count the years with Greg. Today, Teo had heard the worst about her and still offered his arm with a gentle squeeze on her fingers when they closed on his bicep.

At the *pensione* door, she disengaged and reached up to kiss his cheek. "You're rather wonderful, did you know that?"

He hugged her with his free arm. "Sleep well, princess," he whispered, touching the top of her forehead with his lips.

If only she could. If only she were.

22

JACK

Truth cowers under stones, blameless in itself,
While I still hide from whispering words
Designed to set me free.

A drip hit Jack's cheek. "What?"

"I've a flight today. Will you be okay?" India dropped the washcloth in a bowl and extended a towel.

He wiped his face with the sheet. "Don't need that."

She huffed. "You're getting it wet."

He ignored her as he eased a pillow behind his back. She patted a second into place and stood studying him.

"I'll be fine. Thanks for taking such good care of me." His tongue stuck like cotton to the roof of his mouth. He couldn't even get enough spit together to wet it.

She handed him a glass of water, waited while he sipped, then set it back on the side table. "Did you get any sleep?"

"Not much."

"Well, I made you a muffin." She nodded toward the table and smoothed her palms down her thighs. "And a cup of tea.

We're only flying up to LaGuardia and back. I should be home tonight." She checked the room, seemed satisfied. "I've left a pot of stew in the refrigerator. Can you manage?"

"I'll be fine. I only have to run to the office for a little."

"Then it's back to bed with you."

Jack reached out, took her hand. "Then it's back to bed."

She leaned toward him. Her lips touched his forehead. "I think it's best if you don't drink anything alcoholic tonight. Just juice and water."

He nodded. "If this fever doesn't abate, I'll need acetaminophen anyway."

"I'll call you from New York."

He listened to the front door click shut behind her before swinging his legs over the side of the bed so he could get to the phone book. A few weeks ago, he'd have written his tiredness off to discontent, but he couldn't do that any longer. Not with these coughing fits and bouts of diarrhea. He reached for the bedside phone, dialed the doctor's office, and asked them to see him that morning.

India's odd behavior made him wonder what was going on behind that pretty face of hers. She'd been good to him, almost like he'd never moved out. But what about the occasional squint that puckered her forehead when she watched him? The flip side would be a peculiar brightness. Neither made sense.

Maybe they were both dealing with some new virus.

It took a full hour to get dressed and ready. Lucky for him, the doctors' offices weren't far.

The doctor who saw him—a Dr. Lennon—was a burly, balding man and the only one in the practice who could squeeze in an extra patient that day. His nurse drew blood, accepted a urine specimen, and left Jack to freeze in the air-conditioned exam room.

When the doctor finished asking questions and fiddling

with his stethoscope, he pulled up a chair. "Looks like you've got some kind of virus, Jack. Don't know quite how to treat it until I get the lab report, except to tell you to go back to bed. You said you had some chest pain this morning and you're always popping mints because you have a bad taste in your mouth on top of the other symptoms. It's a metallic taste?" He glanced up from reading the chart to catch Jack's nod. "Well, you don't have a fever, but that may be because you said you took acetaminophen for it. How long ago?"

"Two hours."

"Well, I doubt you've been chewing lead particles on the job." At the slight shake of Jack's head, he said, "Thought not. So, we'll just have to wait this one out."

"How long before you get test results?"

"A couple of days." At the door, Dr. Lennon turned. "Call me if those symptoms get worse, will you? I might want to get you in for a scan or two."

All Jack wanted to do was collapse, but decisions had to be made, orders given so his business would stay together. He longed to go home, pop a pain killer, and try, again, to sleep.

He drove to the office, made a few of those decisions and delegated the rest of it to his office manager and foreman. And then he went back to India's.

Food seemed like the devil, so he sipped water, and when the pain got to be too much, he gave in and poured himself another drink of the good stuff India had given him. A sip at a time. That was all, a sip at a time.

And, sipping, he dreamed of Sam. Sweet, sweet Sam, whose smile took his breath away. How come he hadn't seen that when they were kids?

Ha. Not him. He'd been too in lust to think with the head on his shoulders—then or now. He'd treated Sam badly. Hell, he'd treated them both badly. He could admit it. Sam had begged him to leave her be, and he should have done just that. Started slowly. Moved away from India without involving Sam. Fixed it so India wouldn't have been so hurt.

It would have worked. If he'd been smart about things. If he'd done it right, India wouldn't have been able to blame Sam or felt she had to go after Sam's house and boat.

Yeah, he knew she'd done those things. Even if he pretended it had been kids.

Maybe if he'd done right by both of them, Sam would still be here. With him.

23

SAMANTHA

An eye peeks through the shuttered door,
While all the rest is tucked up tight and safely locked
Against the light.

Teo eyed her over the rim of his cup. "Want to go to Venice?"

Sam's hand paused abruptly, splashing cappuccino foam. They'd met for coffee most days, occasionally dining together. They'd kept it casual. And now this?

"Venice?" She cleared her throat so her next words would sound less like a ten-year-old being offered a trip to the circus. "Oh, Teo." Okay, more adult this time, but still wistful. Well, of course she sounded dreamy. He offered her the chance to visit an exciting city with a friend. Instead of alone.

She wiped the spill off her hands and mopped dribbles from the wooden table. "I've wanted to see the canals, all those palaces. Much better than the Baggati Castle—although I still want to get in there, even if it is a fake. Don't you think you could wrangle an invitation?"

He laughed. "You obviously aren't up on the local news. We, my dear," he said, rubbing his hands together, "have our own local murder. The place is temporarily off limits."

"Murder at the castle? And I missed this?"

"Guess so. It was in yesterday's paper. It seems one of the semi-permanent guests, a Swiss playboy, was found done to death with a letter opener."

"Aha, a made-to-order story for you."

"I've begun clipping all the articles. But, of course, this is Italy. I may have to make up an ending as they're not likely to solve it in this generation."

"What a very prejudiced thing to say, dear Teo."

"Hey, if someone is wealthy and has friends in high places, a cover-up is easy. And there have been rumors that Baggati has Mafia ties."

"Good thing I've avoided a life of crime," she said, laughing. "No money and no important friends."

Teo raised his brows. "None?"

"Except for you."

"Ah." Down came the brows, and out came the smile. "How soon could you be ready to leave?"

"Tuesday?"

THREE DAYS LATER, she joined Teo in their very own Venetian parlor. An ornately framed mirror hung above a bird's-eye maple desk. Pale green satin covered the chairs, and a darker green velvet hung at the windows. Sam trailed her fingers over the satin. "Gorgeous. And the rooms don't even match, which means these are probably real antiques or at least very fine copies." She traced the bird's-eye, pulled on one of the brass knobs, and noted the joinery work inside the drawer. "Even the bathroom, all that marble. And gold fixtures. Are yours the same?"

"As nice, anyway."

"It seems palatial."

"Until now, my dear Samantha, you've traveled on economy tickets. It's time to experience a little luxury, don't you think?"

Well, of course she did, although the "of course" made jitters threaten. She wasn't supposed to covet more, was she?

Oh, pooh, why not?

Well…

But her thoughts were cut short when he threw open the long windows to lead her onto the balcony overlooking the Grand Canal. "Look at this view."

She leaned against the stone balustrade to peer into the dark water. A *vaporetto* picked up passengers and headed off down the canal. "Do you always stay in places like this?"

"Only for research."

She rewarded him with a smile. "I've never had a rich friend before. This is probably very poor-spirited of me, living off you like this."

"Let's pretend we're communists, sharing the wealth."

Her smile turned into a hoot. "Shall I buy a *bandiera rossa?*"

"And march with the people? Thank you, but I think I'll limit my wealth-spreading to family, friends, and my favorite charities."

"You'll never make a good party member, Mr. Anderson."

A gentle breeze blew from the direction of the lagoon and brushed across her face. On an arched walkway over the canal, a dog sniffed at corners, and a lone pedestrian paused to tie his shoe. It was still the time of siesta, a quiet and languorous hour when most of Italy recovered from stuffing themselves at the mid-day *pranza.*

Sam sighed. "It's just as I pictured it. Can you imagine living in a city where you either walk everywhere or travel by water?" She glanced over her shoulder and caught him staring, his expression sober. "What?"

"Nothing. I'm just enjoying your enthusiasm."

She turned quickly. She hated the weakness that made her susceptible, always susceptible to a kind or flattering word. "Why don't we go for a walk? We'll have the city practically to ourselves."

Behind locked grates on the winding, narrow streets, shops displayed the wares of Venice. Carnival masks were fancifully plumed and sequined, lacquered or gilded. Some had hooked noses, some upturned.

"Look at that—the gold one with those slits for eyes and all the feathers surrounding its crown. And that black and silver one." She touched his arm as she pointed. "Aren't they incredible?"

They wandered until shopkeepers began unlocking doors and raising grates as Venice woke from its nap. "You want to go in any of them?" he asked.

"Not today. Let's just keep going until something absolutely catches our attention. There's so much to see. Have you been here before?"

"Once, for my honeymoon."

"Ah. Fond memories or not?"

He laughed, but without humor. "Then, I thought it wonderfully romantic. Now?" He shrugged. "Now, I'm hoping to make new memories and see it with new eyes."

Hers were certainly new, at least for Venice. "Lead on."

They strolled up one alley and down another, pausing often to rest Teo's leg and have something refreshing—*un limonata, un caffè*. Some streets appeared hooded; their buildings, dark with age, obscured the light. In the Piazza

San Marco, pigeons swarmed and strutted across the pavement.

"Look over there." Teo nodded toward a man tossing bread crumbs on the ground. With each toss, dozens of pigeons scurried to eat. Some landed on him, most pecked at his feet. "Tomorrow we'll play tourists at the Basilica and the Palazzo Ducale." He slipped her hand under his arm. "But now, let's eat."

They secured a table at an elegant restaurant and supped on scampi and an arugula salad, laughed, talked of streets and squares and possible plots for Teo's next book. Over bites of the peppery salad, Sam said, "I can't imagine you any other way than now, the gallant squire for my fun days and evenings."

"One who's having a delightful time squiring you. But you're not talking about that, are you?"

"I suppose I'm curious. When we get to be this age—by the way, how old are you?"

Teo placed his hand on his chest in mock horror. "How old? You dare to ask?"

"Women get to. It's men who can't."

He relaxed his expression and forked some greens. "I'm old enough."

"For what?"

"For whatever comes up."

Sam squinted and pursed her lips. "Are you as old as I am?"

"As I don't know how old you are, how can I say?"

"I've two children in their last year at college. Considering that neither is a prodigy, I'd have assumed you'd done your calculations."

"Child bride."

She rolled her eyes. "Right. Don't I look it."

"Amazingly, you do. You must know you're beautiful."

Her hand paused in mid-air. "Don't be absurd. I'm not ugly, I know, but I've never been beautiful."

His eyebrows tented. "You are kidding me." When she shook her head, he sighed. It was a very satisfying sigh, because it made her believe he meant his words. "Well, let's just say that I see you as beautiful and young."

"I'll accept that and thank you for saying it." How could her ego not feel soothed by his words? "Just so you know exactly how heady that makes me feel, I'll confess that I turned forty-five on my last birthday. In August."

"Ancient."

"So?" She gestured with a forward wave. "Come on, your turn."

"Forty-one."

"Oh, my. A child-husband." A giggle wanted to surface, but she only loosed a swift grin.

He shrugged. "And father. We were very young."

"High-school sweethearts?"

"College. I graduated early, and we married that summer before I began law school."

"And then the accident?"

"Exactly. I told you she took up with someone while I was in the hospital. She said my condition repulsed her."

"Ow. That hurts. I am sorry."

"To be honest, I'm not. It's best knowing what they're like, isn't it? Even if we learn a little late in the game? The good thing about being discarded, in my humble opinion, is that once one gets over the pain of rejection, one is usually just a tad more discerning about choosing one's friends."

"Unless one isn't."

He reached over and squeezed the hand she'd rested on the table. "Yes, you fell into an unhealthy relationship, but you got out of it. And you're healing. That's all positive."

"I hope so. I certainly don't want to make that sort of mistake ever again."

"Stick with me, babe, and I'll fend off the wolves." He grinned, wiggling his brows up and down owlishly.

Sam couldn't help laughing. "You are good for me, my friend. Thank you." And then, because this had been worrying her, "What about that whole God-hates-divorce thing? How do we deal with that?"

"You mean because we can say we're glad they left and we're better off without them?"

She nodded.

"Well, I'm no Bible scholar," he said, pouring a few more inches of wine into both glasses, "but it seems to me that if we look at the heart of Scripture, we'll see it's full of God's compassionate understanding for man's humanity. It's not like either of us set out to divorce a spouse. We were willing to hang in there."

"I know. I would have, certainly. I thought I was supposed to. Besides, I kept believing it would get better." Remembering that particular delusion wasn't helping. She sipped and tried to forget the never-again promises she'd heard and believed too many times.

"I didn't even know Janet and I had a problem." Teo shook his head as if the idea still surprised him. "So I wasn't expecting to have to fix anything. I suppose my injury just brought the issues to a head. Janet would undoubtedly have tired of me at some point."

"We bored them."

His expression of confusion morphed into a laugh. "I suppose we did."

"But that may speak more to them than to us. I mean, look at you. How could anyone find you boring?"

"Or you." His brow did the wiggle thing that made her grin. "We just needed to find someone with a good sense of humor." She lifted her glass, clinking with his.

~

"How about a gondola ride?" Teo said. "We're tourists, after all."

"And no self-respecting visitor to Venice would miss it." She linked arms with him. "Lead on."

The air held just a hint of a breeze, not enough to make her feel cold, but enough to cool heated cheeks that showed up as soon as Teo tucked her in next to him on what had to be the most romantic vehicle in the world.

She tried to scoot over without him noticing, because having her hip touch his focused her attention on skin and not on the lap of water below them. She did not want romantic or romance—or anything even remotely related to those two.

When a little chirpy voice showed up in her head, she closed her eyes—as if that would stop its *blathering. But you do. You do.*

No. She. Did. Not.

With her eyes still closed, she leaned back and found his arm beneath her head. She quickly shifted, but his hand drew her closer, and she tried to relax.

That wasn't happening.

She shivered. The chirp grew louder.

As the boat slipped gracefully through the water, Teo's fingers began to caress her upper arm. He probably meant to comfort her. Instead, blood rushed back to her face. Thank heavens, the dark hid the color, and the stroke of the gondolier's long oar drowned out her quickening breaths.

The gondola approached the hotel entrance. As Teo helped

her out, she tried to hide both her confusion and the tension that had bound up her muscles. If she were alone, she'd pause for some stretches. Or jog.

"Will you sit with me on the terrace?" Teo asked. "To watch the lights?"

She'd love to. But no. "I'm tired, really. I'll see you in the morning."

She stretched the kinks from her muscles, shed her clothes, and took time to ready herself for bed, to slather cream on her skin and brush out her hair. In her gown, she paused before hitting the wall switch to admire the room again. What a lovely bed. A lovely room. A lovely hotel.

Count your blessings. Lots of blessings here.

She turned out the bedside lamp and slid under the covers, the silken sheets cool to her skin. Shadows played from lights outside the window and seemed to dance even on her closed lids. She turned to her other side and let her eyelids settle, but the pillow-topped mattress felt pebbled under her hip. She flipped to her back. Her pillow lumped. She fluffed it.

How long she lay there, trying not to feel the lumps and ridges and bumps under her, she didn't know. Suddenly she was flailing toward the water's surface, toward the light that must be sky. Her fingers scraped the ocean floor. She had no breath left to carry her up. All she could do was suck in sea and die.

Her cry woke her.

Shuddering, she felt Teo's gentle caress on her forehead. "It's okay, sweet Samantha, you're just dreaming."

She opened her eyes. "I thought I was drowning."

"It's okay. You're safe."

Releasing a deep sigh, she whispered, "I needed saving, and you came."

Which woke her abruptly. She shouldn't say something like that. Ever.

She covered her face with the sheet and willed him away. What a wretch she was.

His laugh was soft. She peeked. In the dim light coming through the open doorway, she could just make out his smile. "Darling Samantha, if you'd let me, I'd rescue you always." He clutched her hand as tears fell slowly down her cheeks. He reached over and wiped them. "I don't want you ever to be afraid again. Or to hurt anymore."

"I'm sorry, I shouldn't."

"Shush. You've done nothing."

"I don't deserve a friend like you." A hiccup caught on a sob, which made both worse. "How can you stand my whiny self?"

He drew her to him. "Shh...it's all right. Think of me as one who understands. I'm here for you. Whenever you need me. In whatever role."

Which, of course, increased the flow. She clung to him until the sobs lessened and she could dab at her face and honk into the tissue he handed her. On a last sniffle, she lay back and whispered, "Thank you."

He tucked the covers over her shoulders, then bent and kissed her forehead. "Sleep, dear girl. I'll be right out there."

"How did you hear me? Weren't you in bed?"

"My thoughts kept churning, so I was still on the balcony, watching the lights across the canal."

"Thinking about settings?"

"Among other things." At the door, he turned. "Close your eyes and dream something happy this time. Think of all the good things in your life."

She tried to do as he asked. She'd tried before that dream. And now her thoughts were peopled by Job's comforters. How did one know if they lied...or if they actually spoke the truth?

24

SAMANTHA

If sickness overwhelms you, and boils begin to plague,
If loneliness is all you see, and silence flirts with nothing,
Tell me, my dear, whose voice you'll hear,
And whose will lead you forward?

The slap of water against stone brought Sam to semi-consciousness, but the echo of voices along the canal roused her enough that she threw back the covers and moved to the window. Outside, sunlight dappled the water. A bright day. Another day in Venice. Another day to wrap her mind and heart around freedom and healing.

Hearing nothing from the sitting room, she climbed in the shower and let the spray flail against her skin. The luxury of cascading hot water made her want to weep.

She patted dry with an oversized towel and spread lotion again on her aging face and body. She wouldn't examine the lines or the dimples that kept cropping up where they shouldn't be. Her skin tingled.

Yes, ma'am, that's all she'd needed. A little sleep. A hot shower. A slathering of sweet-smelling lotion. Sunshine outside and what she hoped would be breakfast next. She wrapped herself in a silk robe and peeked into the salon.

Teo sat with a book in his lap beside a table spread with treats. "Good morning, sleepy head." He glanced at his watch. "Though it's almost good afternoon. Come see what a feast the hotel provided."

"Is it really that late? I'm sorry." She surveyed the chocolate-filled croissants, melon and berries, slices of prosciutto and cheese, and strong coffee. Her stomach rumbled as she slid into a chair.

"I waited until I heard your shower running to order this. I assumed you'd be hungry."

"Famished." Spreading the linen napkin in her lap, she accepted a cup of coffee and stirred in sugar and cream. "Thank you again for last night."

"You're welcome. Any time."

Sam sipped and felt decadent. It must be the place. Well, that and Teo's spoiling. "Are you going to live here always?" she asked. "I mean, in Italy?"

"I might." He scooped a bite of melon and seemed to concentrate on it and the food on his plate more than any of it deserved.

Sam nibbled, waiting.

"I can write here." He studied several fascinating bites. "The views are glorious."

"They are."

"Of course, if things changed or I had a reason, I'd leave."

Sam ducked her head quickly so she wouldn't have to respond, but that stupid, telltale heat crept all the way to her hairline.

It had to be a hot flash. Women in their forties could have hot flashes, couldn't they?

Fortunately, distraction came as Teo's cell phone rang from the bedroom. He excused himself.

His expression had sobered by the time he returned, carrying the phone. "That was Tootie. All of your plants are turning brown or wilting. All of them."

"The azaleas and the ones in the beds?"

He nodded. "I told her you'd call her back. Use my nickel. Lots of unused minutes."

Tootie picked up on the first ring. "Oh, Sam, I'm so sorry! I don't know what happened. I didn't do anything, really!"

"Calm down, honey. Of course, you didn't. Just tell me what's going on."

"I saw some of the damage last night, in the porch light. We'd been out on the water, and Holland was just leaving, so it was too late to call you." Her voice sounded breathless as she continued. "This morning, I walked all around, and, oh, Sam, every one of your beautiful plants looks like it's been doused with poison, all up the lane, the beds in front of the cottage. Everything dead or dying."

"I see. Well, I would have thought the vandal would have quit, now that I'm gone."

"You still think Jack was right?"

Sam squeezed shut her eyes and whistled out a deep breath. Of course she didn't. "Is Pete continuing to drive by? You need to report this."

"I already talked to Pete, last night. He said he'd be by today."

"I'm worried about you staying there if someone is still trying to hurt me."

"I thought I'd call Jack. Tell him about it. You know, in case he has any ideas. I mean, he might."

"Yes." What a mess. "For now, can you get Holland to drive you to and from home? Or ask him to stay there with you?"

"He already said he'd chauffeur me so we can make sure the coast is clear. I'll ask if he wants to stay at the house."

"I'd appreciate it. I really don't want to worry about you. If you're at all frightened, or if anything more happens, I want you to go back home. You're worth a whole lot more than any property, Tootie."

That brought sniffles through the phone. "I love you, Sam."

"I love you, too. And I'm absolutely serious about you not staying where there's danger. See what Jack says and call me back, okay?"

"I will."

Sam set the phone on the table as Teo pulled his chair close. He took both of her hands in his, rubbing warmth into them. "It'll be okay," he said. "Tootie is a smart young lady. I think we can trust her to use good judgment."

"I'm sick about this. I certainly hope India's still coming around merely because she doesn't know I'm gone. Maybe if Jack tells her, she'll leave things be."

"Whoever's responsible must have some serious issues that go way beyond wanting her man back. If it's Jack's girlfriend, she needs professional help."

Sam just nodded.

"Come on," Teo said, folding his napkin and pocketing his cell phone. "If you've finished eating, let's go do something, get some exercise. Sitting here brooding won't accomplish anything."

He was right. All they could do was wait to hear from Tootie and hope the girl took precautions—and that her deputy cousin kept a close watch.

Still, playing tourist felt wrong. Sam tried for enthusiasm when she saw the Tintorettos and other Renaissance masters at the Doge's Palace. She put on a game face when Teo led her through the dungeons where Casanova supposedly spent time before he escaped. Unfortunately, the torture chambers provided more visual information than she wanted. "That's enough of museums for now, please."

"You're worried."

"I can't help it. I need to know Tootie's okay."

He draped an arm around her shoulders and pulled her to his side. "If we don't hear from her by bedtime, we'll call her."

"Thank you."

As they walked out into the brilliant light toward their hotel, Sam stopped him. "Here's the deal. If we're going to remain in Venice any longer, we can't continue in gold-plated luxury. *I* can't. I mean, I've loved it, but it's way too extravagant."

He laughed, a simple, joyful sound. Did he have a clue how much his enjoyment of her, no matter what her mood, helped? There was something so freeing in being *liked*.

The memory of Jack's jokes, which had always surprised her into a hoot of laughter, made Sam tilt her head and smile in response to Teo's simple delight. That was it, wasn't it? Both men were quick-witted, but Teo filled his humor with compassion and real pleasure—a distinction she'd never considered before.

He touched the tip of her nose. "We can stay as long as you wish. Or return to Reggio tomorrow. It's up to you."

"Thank you."

"But we won't be moving from our hotel." He held up a palm as if to stop her objections. "I've no need to pinch pennies, my dear. I live very frugally on my own and am delighted to spend some of what I've hoarded. You can't imagine how much fun I'm having, seeing the city with your eyes instead of my own rather jaded ones."

She lowered her gaze as her heart sprinted. "Then, perhaps you'll think of something I can do for you. If this is a research trip, couldn't you find a job for me? Help me earn my keep?"

"Independent?"

"I want to be. I always have been."

"Did you always pay your own way, even when you were married?"

"Well, I always worked." She turned to stare out over the square, distancing herself as she spoke, as if the memories were a mere matter of course. "I supported Greg in the beginning, and once my business was making money, I contributed to the household. He earned a great deal more than I did, but I liked adding to the family coffers." She had been capable once, hadn't she? She wanted Teo to see her that way, not as the weak creature she'd been with Jack.

She wanted to—no, she needed to—see *herself* that way.

"If I can think of any job I need help with, I'll know just where to come," he said lightly.

"Don't patronize me."

"I wouldn't dare." He touched her jutting chin with a fingertip.

This would be a good moment to flounce something, a long skirt, unbound hair, but all she said was, "Good."

"Now that we have that out of the way, why don't we take a boat trip to the islands across the lagoon? The hotel can fix us a picnic."

"My sweet spot. The only thing better would be to sail there."

"Forget it."

The disgust in Teo's voice reminded Sam of the one person who had loved sailing with her, center-punching Sam's thoughts with images of the mess she'd left behind along with her boat. She turned away so that her suddenly blinded eyes aimed at the water and not at the man beside her.

What a waste of life and energy occurred when one behaved badly. She'd not only ruined any possible friendship with Jack, but she'd also sullied memories of both her boat and her once-friend, had tarred and feathered each until not even a good dunking in naphtha would clean them up.

~

THE DAY HAD BEEN GLORIOUS, but her niggling worries didn't succumb even to sun, water, and friendship. She punched in the numbers for *Samantha's* in Beaufort.

A breathless Tootie answered. Sam's first words were, "Did you talk to Jack?"

"I did. Sorry, hang on." It sounded as if Tootie set down a glass, and then she was back. "Just taking a bathroom break while the shop's empty. Yes, I spoke with him. Seems he's not been feeling very well. He thinks it's the flu, but he's waiting on tests. Oh, and Pete said they wrote up a report. The sheriff complained that you should have reported all the other times."

"I know it. What did Jack think about possible culprits?"

"He said he'd speak to India. It made me curious."

Sam wouldn't enlighten her. She hated not being able to fix this. Being able to control this one thing in her uncontrolled world? That would be a real boon.

"Holland said I should pull up the dead plants, then leave the area alone. He said we need to let the poison, whatever it is, leach out before we plant anything else in the spring."

"Oh, honey, you don't have to worry about that."

"I know I don't. I'm just sorry I can't put it back the way it was."

"Look, if you need help, you know, someone to do the

heavy lifting or digging, hire one of the boys from the nursery. I'll send you some money for it."

"No, no, it's not a problem. If we need anything, I'll e-mail or call. And don't worry about me. Holland's going to make sure everything's fine here. He may hang out more, but I don't know about him moving in."

"Remember what I said. If you get frightened at all, don't stay there. And make sure you turn on the alarm when you're home."

"Yes, ma'am."

Disconnecting, Sam followed Teo out to the balcony and leaned next to him against the balustrade. "We don't know much more, except that Jack will speak to India. At least he's thinking."

"How did Tootie sound this time?"

"Amused by my worries for her safety. Holland said he'd hang around more."

They sat on the bench to watch the moon climb over the water. Teo's quiet presence felt soothing. As always.

Soothing was seductive. And seductive was a bad idea. She knew that.

Too bad the wires got crossed when she tried to tune in to the knowing bit while she was in the middle of the feeling bit.

She straightened her spine, imagining Stefi offering something that lame as an excuse. "I think I'll go to bed now."

"Well, then, good night," Teo said, holding open the door for her. *"Sogni d'oro."*

Dreams of gold, he said. Sweet dreams...of gold.

She climbed under the silky covers, pulling the sheet up to her chin. What had that expression meant, the one she'd caught just before he'd turned out of the lamplight, when he and his eyes had retreated into shadow again?

If that had been the only thing on her mind, she might have

slept well. But visions of her ruined plants appeared and reappeared, along with India's face contorted in anger.

Pits certainly had a way of deepening if you turned your head for a moment.

25

JACK

Sticks and stones may twist my bones,
But broken vows will kill me.

India zipped her overnight bag and approached the bed. "You sure I can't fix you any breakfast? If you need me to stay, I could cancel, call in sick. If you want."

Jack waved her away. "I'll be okay. I'm just going to sleep a little longer. Then I'll be able to get to work."

Her expression seemed watchful, even wary. His eyes slid closed, and he wondered what that meant. Everything meant something.

"When do you see the doctor again?" she asked. "When will he have the test results?"

"Maybe today."

She stood over him for a few moments before bending toward his lips. Jack turned to offer a cheek. His breath was foul. He tasted like a body gone wrong, as if he were rusting on the inside.

Then the door clicked shut behind her, and he was alone.

Too many places hurt. Edgy, nervous, unable to sleep, he longed for the strength to get out of bed.

It was ten-thirty when the phone rang. Jack reached for the receiver. "Hello," he said, expecting to hear his secretary's voice. "Hello?" he repeated.

He was about to hang up when a faint voice whispered something.

"What? I can't hear you."

"It's the alcohol." The voice scratched out the words.

"What's the alcohol?"

"Examine it."

And then Jack heard a click.

He stared at the phone, wishing they'd invested in caller ID. Star sixty-nine's droning voice stated the number was unknown. Someone had called who didn't want to be identified. Why? What did he—or had it been a woman?—mean by "Examine it"?

Jack tossed off the covers, shoved his feet in slippers, and shuffled into the kitchen, bracing himself on furniture as he went. India had decanted the stuff she'd given him into an empty vodka bottle because she claimed it sat better on the shelf. Two vodka bottles stared at him. He took down the first, dabbed some on his tongue. Okay, vodka. The second had to be it.

He sniffed the open bottle. Nothing odd.

What had the caller meant? Was there something wrong with the stuff, some mistake the bootlegger had made in this batch? How did the caller even know Jack had it?

He wished he could get hold of India, but she was halfway to someplace. He hadn't paid any attention to her destination, just knew that she'd be gone until tomorrow. So it was up to him to figure out what to do, and, considering the state of his faculties these days, that would take some effort.

"Think, brain, think." He supposed moonshine could be lethal, assuming the bootlegger used faulty mechanics or bad grain. But India said she'd gotten this from a friend at the airlines. A co-pilot. Besides, it tasted great.

Jack shook his head. No, she'd been drinking it, too. Maybe not as much as he had, because she really liked her vodka, but she was fine. It couldn't be the liquor.

But what if it were bad and had somehow gotten to him first? Maybe he was already debilitated because of stress, the mess of Sam leaving, trying to get himself together. Okay. He needed to have the stuff examined and right away, because India could become ill any day now. He hated to think of her on the road as much as she was and suddenly tossing up her lunch or passing out.

Lumbering back to the bedroom, he yanked on a pair of jeans and a shirt, then went to the bathroom to splash water on his face and brush his teeth. He wasn't going to take the time to shave. The lab wouldn't care anyway.

Dr. Lennon's nurse said the doctor was with a patient. Jack didn't let her finish. "Tell him this is Jack Waters, and I may have found out what is poisoning me. I need to get it tested."

"Hold on a minute, Mr. Waters."

He held on. It didn't take long. "Jack, what's this about poison?" Jack told him about the phone call. "Are you the only one who has had any? Okay, I'll call the lab. No, better the Health Department. They can expedite things, get the tests done right away so we can find out if we've got some kind of epidemic brewing."

"It was just India."

"What about the person who gave it to her? We don't know how far back this goes, who's going to be affected. Take it in. I'll let them know you're coming."

~

JACK FORCED himself to sit up so he could answer the phone. It was five-fifteen.

"Your informant was correct, Jack. Remember back when I asked if you'd been chewing on lead paint? I couldn't guess you'd been drinking it instead."

"Lead paint?"

"Lead. You are being slowly poisoned with lead and mercury. The alcohol we tested is lethal."

"Sure doesn't taste like it."

"It doesn't have to."

"So, what's next? Will I just get better if I quit drinking it? What about India?"

This was unbelievable. Any minute India might tilt into this unreality with him.

Dr. Lennon was saying something. Jack forced himself to listen. "I need to run some more tests on you. But we've got to begin chelation therapy as soon as possible."

"Chelation?" The words made no sense. None of it made sense.

"It's not something we can manage here. There's a clinic in Durham. I'm going to see about getting you in right away."

"So what's this, this chelation?"

"We introduce a chelating agent into your system to bond with the metals and flush them out. I'm afraid it's quite a long process, and it doesn't correct any damage that's already occurred. But it will stop the progress." Dr. Lennon cleared his throat. "I want you to check into the hospital today, now, so we can begin the necessary tests. We'll move you to Durham as soon as we can get you a bed."

"Whatever you say."

"I've already called and made the arrangements. They're expecting you."

Jack pressed his fingers to his temples, picked up the phone, and left India a message.

∼

HE LAY HALF-NAKED on a bed on the third floor. They'd taken more vials of blood. He stared down at the bandages covering the holes they'd poked. Tainted blood. It had looked normal enough as it filled the syringe. But it wasn't, was it?

A bag dripped something into his hand, through his veins, into his system. He wished they'd knock him out. If they let him sleep, maybe he'd wake to find the nightmare ended.

Instead, he let his gaze travel up toward the ceiling. He was tucked in this hard bed with time to think. But who wanted to think?

Odd that India had no symptoms. None at all.

She was smaller, slighter. Anything poisonous should have affected her a lot sooner than it had him. Her liver had already been compromised by heavy drinking. No way it could filter better than his. Oh, sure, he drank, but nothing like India. So, if she had consumed even half the amount he had, she ought to be the one done in and dragged out.

She wasn't sick. Not even a headache. No nausea. No diarrhea. No coughing. Nothing.

26

SAMANTHA

The vision's waiting out there, the impetus to see,
To soar to other places, to grasp at something more,
To dare for something higher
Than you've ever known before.

The elevator to the top of the Campanile of St. Mark's Basilica overflowed with bodies, some of them malodorous. "I hope this thing doesn't collapse again." Breathing through her mouth made her sound adenoidal.

"Not likely," Teo said, smiling with those crinkly blue eyes of his. "Unless all of Venice sinks. Look, down there to the right. That's our hotel."

Sam tried to ignore the gentle pressure of his hand at her back, the limey scent of him when he pointed over her shoulder at something.

Stop. Her eyes slammed shut. She concentrated...on... Rhea.

Rhea had warned her. Rhea knew her truth, and she mustn't let Rhea down again.

She mustn't let *herself* down again.

She would *not* imagine herself attracted to every stray male who paid attention to her. Or who made her laugh. Or whose touch lit something in her.

She squinted at the view. What was it with this laughter thing? So Teo made her laugh. Big deal.

She could just go watch a funny movie. Read a funny book. That should do the trick.

She was strong. Strong, independent, and happy in her own skin.

Not needy.

She should *never* have picked up a romance novel. *Ever.* Look at the expectations she'd fostered of happy-ever-afters.

She should never have daydreamed.

Or grown intimate with another woman's man. Or with any man who hadn't put a ring on her finger.

She shuddered at that particular memory. She couldn't help it.

"Samantha?" Teo's voice startled her.

Oh, right. Teo. The person with his arm around her. "Sorry. I'm fine."

"Thinking about your vandal?"

After a momentary pause, she was able to say, "I don't suppose we'll ever know for sure."

"Just don't worry about Tootie."

"I'm trying not to."

As they ambled through the Basilica—and she did her best to keep to his slower pace and not run far and fast, just to get away—she tried to listen to the facts he presented. But she couldn't care about them. Because, really, what did it matter in the scheme of things that the remains of St. Mark the Evangelist were smuggled out of Egypt and reburied in 828 AD?

Teo took her arm to lead her out and across the square. "Come, this is Florian's. A landmark. Shall we have some tea?"

Sam preceded him into one of the most opulent restaurants she'd ever seen. Red velvet covered the seats. Ornate woodwork surrounded doors and painted wall panels. The staff wore white, with white or black bow ties and black vests. Their jackets had gold braid on the shoulders. Sam straightened her back and held her head just a little higher as they trooped after their gorgeous host.

And there, behind some ferns, was India.

Sam jerked to a halt, bringing Teo up short. "What?" He touched her arm as she peeked around him at the plants.

She looked more closely. No, not India. *Thank God.*

But it gave her pause. Did India ever fly internationally? And would India ever escalate beyond localized warfare?

The waiter held out her chair. As Sam slid into the seat, she hesitated only a moment. "I thought that was India back there. It wasn't, of course."

Teo studied her face. "But you're afraid it could be?"

She nodded, picking up the menu without seeing it. "I don't even know if she flies to places like Italy. But she could. I imagine she could find out where I am."

Teo nodded when the waiter offered tea and pastries. "Would she?"

"I don't know." Sam spread an overlarge linen cloth on her lap and pointed to a chocolate croissant from the tray. *"Grazie,"* she told the waiter, who aligned the cup and plate just so. The chocolate was warm enough to ooze from the side as she bit into it. She stirred in sugar, sighed, and said, "India once threatened me with Rick, some friend of hers."

Teo took his time as he sliced into a portion of cheesecake. "Do you think this Rick could be a danger to Tootie? Is India that far out of control?"

At that, the pastry stuck in Sam's throat. "Oh, Teo. I don't know."

"Finish your treat, and then let's call home."

"Perhaps just the tea? Maybe they'd let me save the croissant."

"Of course."

~

TOOTIE ANSWERED on the third ring. "I'm fine, really. Holland is driving me back and forth. You don't have to worry."

Sam needed to mention this Rick person, but her eyes snapped closed. Each time she spoke of India or Jack and those days, she exposed more of herself, and a little bit more of her shriveled inside.

Maybe humbling herself was a good thing, some extra bit of pride that needed to die. Maybe. But she didn't have to like it.

She heard Tootie's voice, but the words didn't register. Instead, a picture intruded of her, the mother, trying to get across some lesson to Stefi or Daniel. Had they ever once been grateful or enjoyed the process?

Never. So what made her think she'd get to?

Her sense of the ridiculous rose momentarily. *Very* momentarily.

And then she fell back into worry. Because she'd like to know when the check marks or stars or whatever she was trying to earn here would fill enough spaces so she could quit.

Too bad her own penance wasn't enough. Too bad she had to drag someone as innocent and sweet as Tootie into the slime.

Sam took a deep breath. "I remembered something." This was just information. Best get it out there. "India actually threatened me with a friend of hers, somebody named Rick. I don't remember her exact words—although you'd think they'd be seared in my brain." She paused, and Teo rubbed a hand up her arm, smiling sympathetically. "I'm worried she might escalate things."

"Whenever I've heard Ms. Monroe mention Rick," Tootie said, "I thought she was talking about her brother. That was his name. Only, isn't he dead?"

"Oh?" Sam turned to Teo, mouthed *her brother*. He did that facial-shrug thing. "Then why would she say she'd been talking to him and that he was angry? It doesn't make sense."

"I don't know," Tootie said. "Unless there are two Ricks in her world. I'll ask Jack next time I see him."

"I really am worried about you, Tootie. What if this man is someone dangerous?"

Through the phone, Sam heard the door chimes announce store customers. Tootie's voice called that she'd be right there. "I've got to go. Can you call me later?"

"Look, just be careful, will you? Call or send me an e-mail if you learn anything, and I'll contact you immediately. And talk to Jack again. See what you can find out."

"I will. Bye."

Sam turned to Teo. "India had a brother named Rick. And he's dead."

"You think she knows another man by that name? One she'd use to threaten you?"

Sam shrugged.

"Odd, isn't it?"

"Very."

Teo took her hand. "Would you like to head back to Reggio tomorrow?"

Her eyes brightened. "I would. I'm sorry. I hate to break up this perfect vacation."

"Not a problem. We can come back again."

Sam didn't think that would ever happen, but she appreciated the offer. And knowing they only had the rest of the afternoon in Venice, she suggested they find more places he could use as backdrops. "Bring your camera and your notebook, and let's go."

Anything to take her mind off home.

~

"Oh, look," Sam said, pointing to a house laden with gargoyles. "There's your mystery house."

Teo shot pictures of the house and those that surrounded it. "Good eye," he said and followed her across another stone bridge to a maze of alleys and more photo opportunities.

He snapped picture after picture. He'd taken dozens of shots during their time in Venice, but this was different. Sam actually felt a part of story-making as they tossed out various scenarios to go with the architecture. Eventually, though, all she wanted was a glass of wine and a place to sit and relax.

Teo must have read her mind. He helped her board a water taxi for the trip back to the hotel and led her to the elevator. "I think it's time for dinner."

Brushing her hair out of her face, she gave him her most brilliant smile. "Yes, please."

"I think we should give Florian's another go as this is our last night."

"Really? Then you'll have to give me a few minutes to get ready."

"Take your time," he called, but she was already heading to her room.

When she came out, she wore a scooped-neck black dress

that Stefi had insisted she buy in Firenze. "Beautiful," Teo said, again making her feel as if she were.

That night, everything seemed perfect. Sam relegated the morning's fears to the place of improbables. If she couldn't fix things, it seemed best not to dwell on them.

Sated, she set down her fork and turned her smile on Teo. "Thank you. I can't tell you how grateful I am for this trip."

"It's been my privilege."

Even knowing what Florian's could do with pastry, she declined dessert. "I may have to go on a fast just to recover from all you've fed me. I'll pass on the extra calories tonight."

"Samantha, you don't ever need to worry about your weight. You're perfect as you are, and a few extra pounds won't change that."

She looked at him in surprise. "Then bring back that chocolate mousse."

TEO OPENED the long windows to the balcony and let in sounds of music and laughter that carried over the water. Sam sank beside him on the bench, closing her eyes as the gentle evening breeze tickled her face. Replete and feeling the languor that came from being well fed, she laid her head back, finding Teo's arm instead of the expected wall. He had a nice arm, firmly muscled but not huge, and it made an excellent pillow.

When his fingers grazed her shoulder, she didn't move. She should have, but the lazy circular motions just added to the spell of the night air.

Her stillness must have emboldened him, because the next thing she felt was his other hand on her chin, turning her head toward him. He paused, perhaps waiting for her to draw away. She didn't. She didn't think she could have, not really.

Slowly, he touched her lips with his. The merest touch, and she went weak. When he deepened the kiss, she responded. Boy, did she. As her palm touched his cheek, the electricity stunned her.

It may have shocked him, too. At any rate, he backed away, causing her to fall toward him.

She straightened awkwardly, with a *whoa* zinging through her head. Or as Stefi would say, *wowsa*.

"I'm sorry," he said softly. "I shouldn't have."

He was apologizing. A man was apologizing for having given her the best kiss of her life.

"No, no." Really.

"I know. I promised I wouldn't."

She touched his cheek, then took his hand. "I enjoyed it."

"You did?"

"I did. I probably shouldn't have. But, yes, I did."

"Oh."

"And now, I should go finish packing, and then it's to bed." She stood and let him walk her to her room. At the door, she turned, fearful and yet filled with something that felt quite lovely, so different from the heady rush of purely sexual tension she'd felt with Jack. Though there was tension here —oh, yes.

Once again, she touched Teo's cheek and whispered, "I think this has gone a bit beyond friendship. I didn't want it to, but it has."

He touched her lips with one of his sweet kisses and said, "I hope so." Then his eyes twinkled. "So glad to know you aren't simply toying with me."

"Mr. Anderson."

"Yes, ma'am?"

"Good night."

~

SHE'D FOLDED and packed the last of her things when she heard the door to the hall opening. "That you?" she called.

"It is," Teo answered, laughter in his voice. "And if it weren't? What would you do then?"

She met him in the salon. "Scream?"

He held out a gaily wrapped package. "For you."

She slipped her fingers under the paper and loosened the tape. Gently prying the top off the box, she peeked inside. "Oh, Teo." She lifted out a gloriously decorated mask, all gold and white with glittering jewels outlining the features and feathers tufting off the top. "It's magnificent. Thank you, thank you."

"It's not the one you first saw, but I hope you like it as well."

She touched his sleeve with her hand, then moved closer and wrapped her arms around his chest. It felt right, incredibly so, to hold Teo and to feel his heart thump next to her own.

"One of many gifts I plan to give you, my darling Samantha."

"Oh?"

"I'm thinking over a long span of years."

"Re-eally? That sounds promising."

"A promise, yes." He kissed her fingertips.

"But not yet."

"No, not yet."

27

TEO

A cormorant's head slips through water,
Its body submerged like a half-coiled cobra,
Ducking for fish, then flying off boldly,
Does this spell trickery or merely dead weight?

The breezeless air wouldn't last, not when forecasters promised thunderstorms by morning. Teo kicked off his shoes and carried a glass of water to his terrace. Venice had been delightful, but he was glad to be home.

Lights flickered from the beach and from boats at the quay. Music filtered up from a waterfront café, discordant notes almost overwhelmed by a neighbor's loud stereo. He leaned back in one of the deck chairs and turned up the volume in his head.

It was strange, being alone after all those days in Venice. Yes, he and Samantha had spent time together before the trip, dinners mostly, but he hadn't enjoyed the closeness of shared breakfasts for two in... well, he couldn't exactly remember when. The time with Janet didn't count, because, obviously, their marriage hadn't included true closeness—not if she could end it with an outstretched pen.

Returning inside, he flicked on his computer and waited for it to boot up. He hadn't checked on his e-mail since he'd left, a treat, that vacation from social media chains he felt compelled to endure for his writing's sake.

One hundred twenty-nine unread messages showed up, and those didn't include the ones that automatically went into various folders. He scanned the list, surprised to find one from David.

Dad, David's note skipped the "dear" part and then tossed out this: *Tootie tells me you're spending a lot of time with her boss. What's that all about?*

Teo shot back with, *Dear David, lovely to find a note from you. As to your question about Samantha, I'm enjoying the friendship of a delightful lady.*

As he glanced down at the rest of his e-mails, trying to decide which to keep and which to toss, David responded. Ah, so the boy was online, hovering.

David: *You took her to Venice?*

Teo: *I did.*

David: *Dad, wake up. You don't know anything about her. Besides, she's older than you.*

Teo lifted his hands, dropped them into his lap, and tried to calm the sizzle that made him want to hit the Caps Lock button and yell back at his son. What did David know about Samantha? Older, *bah!*

When his breathing had slowed enough for him to answer, Teo typed: *So what? I'm older than you are. Is that a problem?*

He huffed and hoped that would be the end of it. It wasn't. David's next line read, *You don't want to mess with a cougar.*

Teo snorted. A *cougar?* Samantha? Where did a nineteen-year-old get off thinking he could talk like that? And to his father? Teo ground his teeth, wishing he could reach out and smack the boy.

How did David even know such a word?

Teo closed the messaging box until he'd cooled enough to respond and spent the next minutes deleting unwanted e-mails. Finally, he opened the box again and typed, *David, I love you. You're my son. But you're not my keeper. And I won't allow you to be rude about a friend of mine. Do I make myself clear?*

David's next: *Abundantly. As long as she stays just a friend, I'll shut up.*

Big breath. Big sigh. Fingers to keys. *And if she doesn't, I'd advise you to remember your manners.*

My manners? David wrote. *Manners don't have anything to do with this. You're setting yourself up to be taken. I mean, vulnerable like you are? You've got to be careful, Dad, real careful. Women like that? They're bound to be after your money.*

Teo was surprised that he could want to correct his son's grammar in the middle of an overwhelming desire to club the kid. *What, are you worried that there will be less for you if I find someone to love? Or are you implying that, because your mother couldn't stand my deformed leg, any woman with whom I spend time must only want my money? Let's drop this now before we say more that we'll regret. I do love you, but my relationships are not open for discussion.*

Period. Have a good night.

Closing down the computer, he rolled his chair away from the desk and just sat there, drumming his fingers on the chair's arms. The nerve of the boy.

He crossed and uncrossed his legs. He felt like hitting something. Instead, he grabbed his cane and wandered back out to the terrace.

The sky had opened itself to a full moon, a huge orb that rose over the eastern hills. It would be hours before David would see it. Of course, the San Francisco sky might be too overcast to reveal a moon—and David's mind might still be hanging out in the gutter, unable to see the orange-yellow of first rising, the lighter, paler, but no less brilliant white-yellow as it made its slow path through the night sky.

Years ago, a young David had sat with him, enthralled as they'd watched the moon and planets through a backyard telescope. That David would never have used words like *cougar* to describe a woman. Any woman. Much less Samantha.

~

THE MORNING BROUGHT an ability to sling off the sheets along with his anger. Boys of nineteen, on their own for the first time, did a lot of chest beating. That's all it was. If anything ever came of his relationship with Samantha and his son had a chance to know her, David would discover just how wrong he'd been.

Samantha.

Her face appeared. Of course, it did.

Teo laughed slightly, without much humor. She was constantly on his mind. He pictured her eyes closed as they'd kissed, the flush on her cheeks when she'd broken away. He saw her fussing outside Florian's, worried about Tootie. But the image that stopped him was of her teeth chattering, not from the cold, but from emotion as she'd told him of loving Jack.

No. Teo shook his head. The past tense of her affair didn't seem to be the stumbling block, but he'd seen the expression in her eyes the moment he'd spoken in future tense.

It was too soon. She didn't seem to be commitment phobic. Just that it was much, much too soon. He'd seen it, that momentary panic before she'd said, "But not yet."

The realization of how much he wanted a now and a forever with Samantha surprised him. All his fears had been supplanted by a craving for this woman, this friend.

Yes, she was attracted to him. She couldn't have kissed him like that if she weren't. But she'd been attracted to Jack and had hopped into bed with him, which certainly had erected a wall she seemed unable to scale.

He hoped she'd learn to forgive herself. If she couldn't, the two of them didn't stand much of a chance.

There was still the issue of his crippled leg and scarred flesh. He'd surprised himself by this new willingness to risk another woman's reaction. Another woman's revulsion.

After changing shoes, he picked up his cane and clopped toward the beach to clear his head. And there, ahead of him and entering an Internet café, was Samantha. Of course, she'd want to check her e-mail for word from Tootie. And from her children and that other employee. The one from Raleigh. And all those questions about India and that brother/ghost named Rick. Too many questions and no answers.

Sighing, he limped on down the hill, ignoring the tug of that café and an espresso, hoping for patience, his old, familiar friend.

Ha. Friend? Companion, certainly. On the lonely nights after Janet had left, on the long slog toward healing, he'd learned to wait. To bide his time.

But that didn't mean he liked it.

He'd rather be proactive and find a way to solve the problem for Samantha. But that was impossible. To do so, he'd need superhuman powers not only to investigate, but also to travel in space and intervene.

Ah. He knew One who could manage that. They weren't as intimate as he'd have liked yet, but the last months had been edging them into a unity of purpose, if nothing else.

28

SAMANTHA

Patterns in the universe, stars upon a course,
Oh, that I were yours today, and yesterday was not.

S am logged on to the computer as soon as the Internet café
opened. Tootie hadn't called, but perhaps she'd written.
And yes, there it was.

Jack got sent to some kind of clinic in Durham. Believe it or not,
they're treating him for lead poisoning. Seems he got very sick very
quickly. You know what the grapevine's like in a small town, so they
may be exaggerating. I'll keep you posted.

Jack with lead poisoning? Forget waiting for a written
answer. She punched in the house phone number on her way
out of the Internet café.

"Hello?" Tootie's voice sounded tinny.

"Did I wake you? I'm sorry. I forgot. You want me to
call back?"

Tootie cleared her throat. "Hold on." Another cough to
clear it and then, "Sorry. No. This is fine."

"I just got your e-mail about Jack. What's going on? Is he all right?"

"Yeah, well, it's like a twenty-eight-day treatment. Sounds horrible to me. They have to put this stuff in him to flush out the lead poisoning."

"So what's...I mean, do you think I should...?"

"According to India—"

"You saw her?"

"Yeah, last night on my way home. According to her, he should be almost back to normal, maybe a few side effects, but they don't know. Anyway, she's taking care of him. She said he lives with her now—or rather again—so she's got it covered. She didn't seem all that worried."

"Did she say how he got sick?"

"Breathing lead dust on a job site, something like that."

"That's horrible. But wouldn't his workers be in worse shape, I mean, exposed to it all the time?"

"You got me. We've all been wondering, but what do we know?"

"Can you find out where he is?" Sam fought the images that kept popping into her mind. "I would like to send flowers or something."

Tootie did a little *ahem* thing. "Do you think that's such a good idea? I mean, with India camping out there and everything? She, uh, she said he didn't want to see anyone."

"That doesn't sound like Jack." Not when he loved being the center of attention. "Okay. Could you at least let me know if you hear anything else?"

"Sure thing. Anything I learn, I'll send an e-mail."

"Or you have my new cell number. Use it if you're at the store."

"So, are you having a great time? When do you go back to Reggio?"

"We're already here. I'll tell you all about the trip some other time. I'm sorry I woke you." Sam clicked the *End* button.

Jack might be wasting away in a hospital bed, tubes running in and out of his flesh. She needed to know he was okay, but, of course, she had no right.

Intimacy lingered, didn't it? Even one that carried this much pain. And India's years with Jack had to count for something.

Sam tucked the phone back in her purse and sighed. She didn't want to go back to her room. Instead, she turned toward the boardwalk. And there, moving away from her, was Teo's limping form. She felt a stab of regret as she turned off along the water's edge.

She shed her shoes to feel the touch of sand. It was warmer than the air and squeaked when she planted her feet on it. She bent to pick up a handful, let it sift between her fingers into tiny piles at her feet before she grabbed another handful and then another, until the piles grew to form one larger hillock. If she left it there, it would keep its shape until the tide flattened it and shifted those grains into something new and different.

Here in Reggio, her life had done just that—shifted. But was the new thing she'd found real or illusory, too easily formed, something that would wash away on the next tide? Something based on need and propinquity?

She shivered as she stepped gingerly around the sand pile. Maybe if she talked to Teo, he'd help her make sense of things. But not today.

Today was for worrying.

～

HER FRETTING HADN'T DISSIPATED, but she eased it the next afternoon as she and Teo strolled along their favorite path next to the sea. She tucked her arm in his before delivering the latest news.

"Breathing lead dust?" He stopped to face her, and his frown formed crevices between his brows. "That doesn't sound right."

"I didn't think so either."

He resumed his limping gait. "I'm no expert on poisoning, but in my line of work you pick up a few things. I'd be surprised if you could inadvertently inhale enough lead dust to put you in the hospital."

"What then?"

"I haven't a clue, but I would think he'd have to ingest it in some form."

As the sand turned to rock, Teo led them away from town. He balanced with his cane, continuing to hold her arm, and Sam took care to stay on level ground.

"I hate not knowing," she said. "Tootie told me people are talking, but no one other than India has any answers."

"Do you think India's a reliable witness?"

"Oh, Teo." She pressed her cheek against his shoulder. "I don't know what to think."

Bringing them to a stop, he rubbed her back with his free hand, a soothing motion that evoked a sigh. He spoke softly. "Whatever's going on, he's being treated for it. He'll be okay."

"I hope so," she said, leaning in. "I certainly hope so." As she lifted her head, she noticed he wore a different, lighter scent, not the lime. She sniffed. "Something new?"

"You noticed, did you?" There was a laugh in his voice as he backed toward the sea wall and set his cane to one side. "Come here." His hands slid to her face, his lips eased upon hers lightly before he let her go.

They stood side by side, listening to the gulls shriek, to the sound of waves in the background, and farther away, the roar of traffic, the occasional horn, a shout, laughter.

Tomorrow, as soon as the Internet café reopened, she'd investigate lead poisoning. Tomorrow, she'd figure out what was going on.

∽

"You were right," she told Teo over the remnants of her seafood stew. "Lead poisoning is cumulative."

"I thought so."

"The article said that unless a grown man ingests it in substantial quantities, the poison would take a long time to affect him." She ripped apart a chunk of bread and dipped it in the last of her broth, staring at it before she popped it into her mouth.

"And you don't imagine Jack chomped on paint chips or drank solder."

She just glared at him.

"Of course not," he answered for her.

At that, she pushed her plate away. "You almost finished?"

Looking down at his half-eaten stew, he didn't answer.

He liked mussels and clams. She was a shrew.

"I'm sorry. Please, eat, enjoy," she said, waving toward his bowl.

He pulled meat out of another shell. "Feeling restless?"

"My muscles are all twitchy." She twirled her spoon between her fingers. "And I went for a walk this morning." The spoon went back in the bowl. "Maybe just not a long enough one."

She tried to calm the jitters, because she had absolutely no reason for feeling this way. None at all.

Teo set his fork and spoon at the proper angle on his plate and waved toward the waiter. *"Il conto, per piacere."*

Leaving bills and an apologetic smile because of his leftover food, Teo ushered her out of the restaurant.

"This is driving me crazy," she said, finger-combing hair out of her face and tucking it behind her ears.

"I can tell."

Instead of taking that as it was probably meant, she glared at him. "I need to walk."

"I'll join you." His voice remained pleasant.

She didn't want pleasant either. She didn't know what she wanted. Probably someone to take charge and make everything better, but then she'd manage to feel guilty about that as well. She sped up the pace, which was not easy for Teo and his cane. Now, wouldn't a friend have slowed and been sympathetic? Obviously, not this one. Fine, she wasn't a nice person.

A mile later, her muscles still twitched and the bones in her thighs hurt. What was that, arthritis?

Yep, she was old.

Once, Teo reached for her swinging hand, but she snatched it away. She didn't want to be touched. She caught his puzzled frown and couldn't even muster the energy to apologize.

He suggested the beach and led the way to a bench at the sand's edge. Sam leaned forward, bracing herself with her elbows on her knees.

"He'll be fine," Teo said.

She jerked up her head and glared. "How do you know? You can't. No one knows. And for him to be in the hospital, it has to be very, very serious."

Teo flicked up sand with his cane. "Does he still mean that much to you?"

"How can you ask? Yes, he means a lot. He always has."

"Not always. You didn't even see him for more than half your life."

"What's that got to do with it? I loved him when I was young, and I loved him when I was older. I don't want him to hurt. Or die."

"Certainly not. Only, don't we have something here, you and I, that can rise above your sympathy for him?"

She wiped her palms down her blue-jeaned thighs once and then again. "I thought so."

"What do you mean, you *thought* so. You don't know so?"

"Right now?"

He nodded.

"To be honest," she said, "no."

Teo stood up and sucked in a deep breath. "I see."

"I don't think you do. Sit down, Teo. Please."

He looked back. Sam held out a hand. He didn't take it, but he did sit.

"Look. I've been thinking about this." She waited, but he continued to stare at the sea. "The problem is, I can't tell if we've imagined things, if this is all some fairy-tale romance I've dreamed up because I am such a mess. You've treated me like a princess, wined and dined me, taken me to Venice, given me gifts. You've been wonderful."

"I love you." He didn't look at her as he spoke. His cane rested between his knees, and he leaned both hands on it. "I know this is premature, that you're not ready, but I need to tell you."

This was one of those moments when Rhea would have advised her to keep her mouth shut. Why couldn't she? Words tumbled out, words that scared her as much as they obviously hurt Teo. "Would any of this—this thing between us—have happened if we hadn't been here? If I'd just been running my shop, and you'd just been living in the States? It's been so quick, you know?"

"Not for me."

"For me, then." She gazed at a gull plunging after something it imagined might be dinner, then watched it come up empty-billed and begin circling the area.

"Are you going back?"

The words startled her. She hadn't actually formed the thought. "You knew I would someday."

"No. I thought *we* would go one day."

A sigh, a shrug, and she leaned forward on the bench, her hands clasping the edge of the seat. Sand had accumulated on the tops of her sneakers. She kicked up and shook first one foot and then the other.

What could she say that would fit the mood and her purpose? After all, she'd begun to hope for the same thing. Sort of. Accidentally.

How on earth had she become such a wimp that she let things happen to her, instead of making her own decisions? Where was the woman who'd opened two shops and made successes of them, even in a bad economy? The vibrant, go-to woman she'd imagined herself to be?

Well, wimp-dom seemed to be glorified in her. Jack, Teo, Italy. Leap in the deep end, that was Samantha Ransom.

Teo stood again and said quietly, "I think I'll head back to my flat now. I've a lot of writing to do."

"Will I talk to you tomorrow?"

"If I can find the time."

As she watched him limp away, the lump in her throat grew. If calling him back and unsaying her words would have helped, she'd be up and doing. But it wouldn't, because then she'd just have to say them all over again.

~

THE NIGHT TOOK A VERY long time to pass. Her eyes may have closed once or twice, but she remembered hours of watching green numbers flick forward very slowly. Around one, she decided she was a fool. She cared about Teo. Probably even loved him. Of course, she did.

The clock advanced. One-thirty. Two. And then, suddenly, a knock sounded on her door.

"Signora," a voice called.

"Sì?"

"A man, he is calling on the telephone. From the United States. Does the Signora wish to take the call?"

She flicked on the overhead light and pulled on her robe, then followed the tousled daughter of the house down the stairs. Her heart thudded as she imagined all sorts of horrid scenarios. Who could it be? Everyone had her cell number. Why hadn't whoever this was used it to call her?

When Daniel's frantic voice said, "Mom, is that you?" panic blossomed.

She swallowed it, tried to speak in a normal, non-croaky voice. "What's wrong? Why didn't you call my phone?"

"It went to voicemail. Twice. Anyway, it's Cindy, Mom. Cindy. They rushed her to the hospital. She's having contractions. Big ones."

Sam calculated quickly. "She still has three months to go."

"Her doctor said it's okay, she'll be fine. They put her on a monitor, and they've given her stuff to stop everything." Daniel's voice sounded as if he didn't believe a word of it.

"Where is she? If she's at Duke, you don't have to worry. They're the best."

"Can you come?"

She paused.

"Mom?"

"Of course. I'll see if I can get a flight out tomorrow. Everything will be okay."

"I appreciate it. Cindy will, too."

"Give her a big hug and tell her I'm on the way." Sam hung up the receiver and slowly climbed back to her room. Well, she had her answer. She was going home.

TEO'S ATTITUDE aped the stoic as he set about helping her book a flight. She'd called him early in the morning to give him the news, and he'd rallied, but she could feel the distance he'd carved out for himself.

She hugged the Garibaldis. "Nonna says we light candles every week," the daughter told her. "You will come back to visit, *sì*?"

"I'll try. You've been so good to me. *Grazie, grazie.*"

Teo picked her up and drove her to the Milan airport in quasi silence, their random words mere pleasantries.

"I forgot to call Martine," she said as they passed an off ramp for a travel center. "Will you do that for me?"

"I will."

"Tell her thank you, for everything?"

"I'll tell her to keep *Belle* ready."

"I don't know how long I'll be."

"I'll let her know."

He pulled into the parking area at the airport. "You don't need to come in with me," Sam said.

"I want to."

He lifted out her bag and rolled it to the ticket counter. Boarding pass in hand, she followed him to the security line. She turned to say good-bye.

"You'll think about things, about us? And come back?" Only his eyes revealed emotion. If Sam hadn't known better, she'd have thought he didn't care.

She nodded. "I'll come back."

"Because if you don't, I'll have to come fetch you." His tone hardened on the words.

A shiver shot through her. Sam studied the middle button on his leather coat, because that forceful note had jarred her back to the present. She didn't know how to explain it: one minute she was walking in a fog, the next she was there, with him, remembering how he made her feel.

He raised her chin and touched his lips to her cheek. She turned slightly so that their mouths met. His lips slipped into a feather kiss, increasing the pressure until she thought she'd swoon. How easily she swooned with him, so different, really, from the frantic heat of her response to Jack.

A loudspeaker droned in Italian, interrupting the moment. "You'd better go," Teo said.

"I know."

"Call me? Let me know where I can reach you?"

"I will."

"Samantha..."

She pressed a fingertip against his lips. "Don't say anything."

He took her hand and brushed a kiss against her palm. "What I don't say, I will think."

29

TEO

If I were a mockingbird, singing in a tree,
I'd know the story's endings, if we were meant to be.

He left the sunroof open on the drive back to Reggio. Who cared if it rained? Or if he froze. Not he, considering.

Considering what? He wasn't sure, not about it or about much of anything. Oh, he'd been full of force and determination when he'd told Samantha he'd come get her if she didn't return. But would he? Could he?

She was an enigma, this woman he loved. She'd begun as one, certainly. As more than one. In Venice, she'd seemed to smooth out, her image and reality merging into flesh that felt real and a mind he understood.

Ha.

Either he was a fool or he was—all right, a fool. He couldn't see any other options floating around.

His foot pressed on the accelerator as the highway ahead cleared of traffic.

Did his prayers avail anything?

He wouldn't go there. Fine, he'd keep up the conversations —no, the monologues—but a hint that they were being heard would be much appreciated.

Was he asking too much?

SAMANTHA

I've skewed the F-stop on my lens,
And darkness shutters all the light.

S am leaned over to kiss Cindy's cheek. Her daughter-in-
law looked so small and scared lying in that hospital bed,
attached to the IV and monitor. Her straight dark hair was
mussed and damp around her face.

"How are you?" Sam asked.

"Okay." But Cindy began to cry as her fingers turned in
Sam's and held on tightly. "They say I'm going to have to stay
in bed the whole three months!"

Daniel pressed his lips to his wife's forehead. "Shh, honey,
you know it'll be worth it. You're my girl. You can do it."

Though Cindy nodded through her tears, she didn't look
convinced. Sam traced the girl's knuckles with her thumb. "I
remember when I was pregnant with the twins," Sam said. "I was
blimp-like and thought it was unreal. I knew two babies were in
me, and I loved feeling them move, but when I had to rest so much
of the time and still cope with all the responsibilities in my life,

frankly, they often felt more like a huge, fat lump sticking out in front of me that was changing my life in not very pleasant ways."

"Mom."

"And then they were born." Sam smiled at the memory. "Oh, my, what a difference holding them made. It was all worth it. Every stretch mark, every backache, every hard day was worth it, because they had given me the two most wonderful gifts of my life."

"I guess maybe—oh, I hope I'll feel like that." Cindy pulled her hand free to swipe at a stray tear.

"You will."

"It's just, I can't finish the semester. I've only got a month and a half left, and I'll lose it all."

Sam sat down on a free spot at Cindy's hip and brushed the young woman's hair off her forehead. "You won't lose what you've learned. Sure, you'll have to take the classes again, and that's tough, but think how easy repeating them will be. Then, after the baby comes, you can finish your degree."

"That's what I've been saying. I'll be working. It'll be okay. A few extra semesters won't matter." He touched the round belly, smoothed his hands over it, and smiled down at Cindy. "They won't, because we'll be together, and we'll have this little one."

Cindy sniffed. She looked at them with watery eyes and reached again for both their hands. "You guys make it seem possible."

"It is. I told you, it is," Daniel said.

When Cindy dozed off, Daniel suggested he and his mother grab a bite in the hospital cafeteria, where he insisted on paying. Sam thanked him as if this were an everyday occurrence and watched her barely twenty-two year old dole out funds with his head held high.

"Thanks so much for coming, Mom." Daniel set the cups and straws on the table. "I'm sorry you had to leave ahead of schedule. I know you were having fun."

"I was, but it was time to get back to real life. Your call just spurred me to action."

"Cindy's mom said she'd come help later, but Cindy's sister's got the flu, and she's miserable." He wrinkled his brow. "I hope it's not the really bad kind."

Sam lined up the sugar packets in a neat row and stacked them. "Cindy's going to need a lot of help at home if she has to stay in bed. Have you thought about that?"

"We'll figure something out. We'll have to."

He reminded her so much of the young Daniel, trying to keep from crying when one of the guys chucked an unexpected ball his way, doubling him over in pain. He'd bit his lip and shrugged when she'd asked if he were okay, but she'd seen the shock of it. Now he was an adult, scared and unwilling to let his mother see how badly.

"You're not going to have much time, not with work and school."

"I know, but I'll figure it out. I have to."

Responding to his dejected look, she laid her hand on his. "Maybe I can help."

"How? Beaufort's not exactly around the corner."

"Tootie seems to be doing a great job managing that shop, so why don't I hang out here for a while?"

His face paled. "The apartment's only got one bedroom."

She couldn't help the snort that was supposed to be a laugh. "Oh, not with you! I'll rent a small place. Just until the baby's born."

Daniel swallowed hard. She could almost hear him reigning in his emotions. "That…that would be great."

"It'll be fun. I can come by for a few hours every day and still have time to visit Raleigh and Beaufort occasionally."

Her big, grown-up son choked on a sob and dashed renegade tears from his eyes. When he could talk, he said, "I love you, Mom. You're the best."

~

SAM NEEDED to find a motel where she could stay for a few days while she looked around for a cheap, furnished apartment. But first she had to call Teo. She hadn't reactivated her stateside cell service, so she borrowed Daniel's phone.

"I wish I were there," Teo said.

Sam heard the wistful tone. "I do, too."

"How long do you think you'll stay?"

"Cindy's going to need help at least until the baby comes."

"That's three months."

"I know."

The line went silent. Sam waited. Finally, Teo came back with a very quiet, "I'll miss you."

Still, she didn't speak. She couldn't.

"You might be interested to know that my cleaning lady's sister is now helping that little boy's family, the child we took to the hospital."

"Oh, really? How nice for all of them."

"She needed the work."

"And they can afford her?"

"Yes."

Or someone named Teo paid her wage. That would be just like him.

"Is he doing well?"

"Healing nicely."

"Tell him I asked about him."

"I will."

Good-byes came next, because what else could she say? They'd exhausted all the news.

As she stood under florescent lights in a sterile American hospital, disconnected even from Teo's voice, the Italian Riviera seemed a world away. This place, *this* was her new reality, for however long it took. With all the changes in the past year, she knew that things left behind soon became mirages, barely seen, hardly remembered except as glimpses in a mirror.

The closeness she'd felt with Teo had grown too quickly. Their relationship was like the fairy story she'd called it—very pleasant, sure, but you knew all along it was fiction.

JACK

Twisted visions hide the truth,
And spill their messes upside down.

Jack angled his bristly cheek away when India leaned in for a kiss. Her smile slipped sideways. Like the drooping bird-of-paradise petal on the windowsill.

Odd how it looked just like India's expression this morning. He considered the resemblance while she fussed. Had she picked the gift because she recognized something in herself? Like a skinny person might buy a greyhound and a jowly fellow, a bulldog?

She touched his shoulder, smoothed his hair back from his forehead, let her fingers caress his cheek. He stoically submitted to her caress but remained silent.

"Hurry and get well enough, darling, so you can come home, where I'll take good care of you." She promised to return in the morning and then left.

Man, he hurt. He almost considered praying, he hurt so much. This chelation stuff was supposed to clean him out, but it only seemed to be concentrating the aches. Or maybe the poison was so strong in him, it was taking gallons of anti-poison to get rid of it all. The doctor in charge here in Durham wanted him treated as an inpatient instead of giving him the stuff orally on an outpatient basis. That must mean he was sicker than most. Yep. He'd go with that diagnosis.

Some incompetent painter had swished streaks of yellowish bile over a puke-gray on the ceiling. Jack's insides felt like those colors, ready to heave or cramp or burn, sometimes all at the same time. He'd have fired that fool painter faster than the guy could spit if he'd been contracting the job.

Maybe he was going to die in this bed, staring at bad paint and a television that only pulled in six channels. Either he was going to die, or he would go crazy from the toxins, or he'd end up a cripple. Then what? He'd lose his business and be stuck on disability, living check to check and barely able to scrape enough together for meals at the end of the month.

He made two fists until he could feel what was left of his nails cutting into flesh. It refocused the pain momentarily.

Morbid wasn't going to do squat, but how was he supposed to be all bright and cheerful? India'd been bubbly enough for the lot of them when she'd first bounced into the room—not that she'd left that way, but too bad for her. And that night nurse, all smiles while she puffed pillows and stuck thermometers in a person's mouth. They weren't the ones having their blood sifted.

Again and again, he heard the voice on the phone whispering, "It's the alcohol. Examine it."

Who had called? Who had known?

Whoever it was had saved his life.

A curse skittered around in his head, flashing on his closed lids until he spat it at the room. He felt like the aging star of some stupid melodrama, the old guy they were dumping in favor of the young stud, killed off in this crazy way 'cause the script writers had used up their quota of bullet holes, car wrecks, and heart attacks. Might have even been some do-gooder producer who wanted to send out a warning to the viewers about poisoned alcohol.

Ha, ha. Real funny. The ceiling squiggle changed and tore his thoughts away from that absurdity. What, was he beginning to believe in his own plot?

Who got poisoned from bootleg liquor outside of West Virginia or the Tennessee hills? This was the Carolina coast. Only poor kids who chewed paint chips got lead poisoning, and nobody suffered from mercury poisoning that he'd ever heard of.

Only some crazy fool would dream up something like moonshine as a murder weapon. Had to be a soap opera. Or one of those made-for-television movies chock full of weeping, moaning, hand wringing, and teeth gnashing. Not real life. Not happening to him.

He'd wake up and find it was a dream. The craziest dream he'd ever had.

He turned on one side, with his needle-packed arm extended along the sheet, but he couldn't get comfortable.

Nope. People didn't dream all this pain. So he wasn't asleep.

Who had phoned him? Who had known he even had the stuff? Who, other than India and the person who'd given it to her?

He had to assume the call had come from the supplier. Had India known what she was pouring every night when she'd smiled and handed him his glass?

The million-dollar question. And not really a question, was it?

If she'd drunk it with him, she'd have needles poking into her—or be buried six feet under.

His head swirled with the realization. It had niggled at him. Now it slammed him full in the face. She'd only pretended to drink from that bottle. She—this woman who said she loved him—had known exactly what would happen to anyone seduced by the taste of that clear, sparkling liquor.

She'd tried to murder him. Not that he could prove it, his word against hers, but he knew.

The machine next to his bed beeped. He looked up at the bag. Empty.

A nurse would come soon. One of them always seemed to be creeping in to poke, prod, or sound him out with cold hands or sweaty hands. The skinny ones had cold hands. The fat ones tended to be nicer. He wondered why. His favorite was a big black lady whose laugh bellowed when she opened her mouth. Great sense of humor, and smart. She was the floor supervisor, day shift five days out of seven and sometimes nighttime. She said they were understaffed, so sometimes she just didn't go home. He warned her she'd be next in bed if she didn't quit that. Mattie was her name, from farm country just outside Newport. That probably explained it. Good people, those Carteret County locals.

Unless they were trying to poison you.

One thing he knew for sure, if he lived through this hell, you wouldn't catch him touching a drop of booze again. Not him.

3 2

TEO

He angled closer to the hole,
To peek, to peer,
And tipping, fell.

Teo did what he always did in times like this: he wrote.

His fingers flew across the keyboard as page after page developed. Sophrina, it seemed, was his only faithful companion, a woman in a million.

He sat hunched over, bending in ways he knew weren't good for his spine, but he needed to focus. He was almost there.

And then he was. The last period on the last line and a *The End* slapped on the bottom.

He leaned back in his desk chair and reached for the water glass he kept filled at his side. Lifting it, he found bare sips left. Even the gallon jug at his feet seemed to have emptied without him noticing.

He got up to refill both and wobbled. What the...? Where had that come from?

He glanced at his watch. Ah. It was almost five o'clock, and he hadn't eaten since last night. When had he last showered?

He lifted an arm and sniffed. Not nice. Not nice at all.

He'd better eat something so he wouldn't collapse in the shower and drown. And so he'd have the energy to get to Tonio's for dinner and that game of chess.

The refrigerator stared at him, its light bulb glowing against the almost-empty shelves. Pulling out a quart of milk, he noticed the curds had separated out. He held his breath as he emptied the contents down the drain. Dry cereal was obviously out of the question.

There wasn't much else. Some cheese.

He sliced away mold. So what if he got a little penicillin with his snack? He'd run out of bread sometime in the last day or so, but he found stale crackers in the cupboard.

That and a full glass of water ought to get him from here to the shower and on to Martine's.

"MY VERY DEAR FRIEND," Martine said as the housekeeper ushered Teo into the solarium. "You have been working too hard again, have you not?"

Teo kissed her cheek and leaned over to shake Tonio's hand. "I finished the book."

"Ah," Tonio said. *"Tanti auguri."*

"Indeed. Many congratulations. Now do you send this to your editor or must you do more?"

Teo took the seat she offered next to Tonio. "A reread at least. I dashed this one off so quickly that I've no idea what it looks like."

"And your editor?"

"Val doesn't know yet. She'll be pleased." He accepted the glass of sherry Martine offered and raised it to her health.

"Thank you. I drink to yours as well. And to my Tonio's, though he is doing so much better. You see, he sips his lemon water."

"I'd rather have a glass of red wine, but I obey."

Passing a tray of caviar and thinly sliced bread, Martine asked, "Will you travel to the States with the book when it is ready to go?"

"No. E-mail's faster. No need for me to leave town."

"I thought perhaps you might wish to visit your niece," Martine said with the air of one who meant only to make casual conversation. "And perhaps Samantha."

Teo's hand stilled, even though he'd known this was coming. "Have you spoken to her?"

Martine sipped delicately and inclined her head. "I am afraid not. You said she might telephone to me here, but I have heard nothing."

"Ah," he said. So, she'd cut them off, too. "I think she has taken a vow of silence toward all of us."

"What is that?" Tonio asked.

"She asked me not to call her again."

"No..."

The shock in Martine's voice should have felt comforting, but Teo's own *no* had resounded in his head since Samantha had tilted his universe in their last conversation. *We were just too soon, Teo. You and I. Too soon. Maybe all we experienced was the romance of a romantic place.*

Maybe that's all it had been for her. But not for him. No way.

"Teo?" Martine said. "Are you unwell, my friend?"

He shook off the melancholy. "Fine. I'm fine."

He didn't tell them that he'd spoken to Stefi, too. Stefi,

whose brother had called because he was worried about their mother. Oh, Daniel was grateful to have help. They couldn't have managed without her, Stefi said, but what neither of them got was why the mother who loved to surround herself with beauty had rented an appallingly ugly apartment.

Teo set his empty glass on the side table. Wouldn't he have liked an explanation himself? Why would Samantha do something like that? Weren't there any nice apartments she could afford?

"Teo, come," Martine said, when the housekeeper announced that their dinner had been served. "Let us eat and speak of pleasanter things."

Yes, pleasant things. There must be some of those left on his horizon. Because it looked as if his few Italian friends would be the only ones he could presume upon for companionship—beyond the world of make believe.

Thank God for worlds he could imagine. Thank God.

TEO PRINTED out his manuscript and began reading. He found it jarring, because the chapters he'd crafted just before Samantha had blown into his life—first in her shadow-form and then in the flesh—and the ones he'd written during her stay in Reggio differed so from the latter ones, post-Samantha. His voice had been so breezy, so carefree in the earlier chapters. He could hear the lightness as he read aloud, but he didn't recognize that writer. Had that been he?

His cell phone jangled Tootie's particular ringtone. Tootie must have noted his lack of attention to her or her mother. He hadn't checked in with them in weeks. Really, the façade of cheerfulness was just too hard to maintain.

He answered, pleasantly, he thought.

"Unc, I'm so glad to hear your voice!" she said in that chirpy tone she carried so well.

He closed his eyes, trying to picture her. "And I yours."

"So, what's been happening? You've been really quiet over there. Have you been traveling?"

"Just writing. I finished at last, and I'm rereading it now."

"I'm so excited. I can't wait to read it!"

"It'll be a while, love, you know that."

"Yeah. Well, have you talked to Sam recently?"

That question again. Why did he hold the key to Samantha for so many people? Didn't Tootie work for the woman?

"No," was all he could manage. *No*.

"I don't think she's doing well, Unc."

Well, neither was he. But there wasn't a single thing he could do to fix that for either of them, was there?

"I'm sorry to hear that," he said. Perhaps she'd leave it alone now.

"She hardly comes to the shop. And Rhea—that's her other manager, the one from Raleigh who's been helping me so much—said the same thing's going on for her. I mean, Sam's just up the road from the Raleigh shop, so you'd think she'd visit it, wouldn't you?"

"Yeah, well, you would." He guessed. What did he know about anyone, much less Samantha? "So," he asked, trying to make it casual, "what's going on with her friend Jack?"

"I don't know any more than I did before, because India said Jack doesn't want callers or visitors. I saw her last week, and she said he's getting better. But she didn't look so great herself, so she may be worried."

"Ah. Well. That's too bad."

"You're thinking Sam might have seen him? That maybe it got her all down again?"

He had, of course. Because how else could he explain her

refusal to speak to him? Hadn't she intimated that she cared for him? *Him*. Not Jack.

Well, maybe Jack, too.

Fine, he just bet that was Samantha's problem, no matter what Tootie imagined. Sam had gotten home and found herself all panicky about her lost love—*gag*—and so she moped. That would be it. Hadn't she started moping before she even left Reggio?

Double-minded female. Jack was probably really good looking. And he was a sailor. Why would she even be remotely interested in a cripple who hated boats?

Tootie's voice barged into his thoughts. "I don't think it's Jack. I mean, not completely. She couldn't have seen him. It's got to be something else."

"Ah."

Articulate, wasn't he?

"When are you coming to see us again?"

"I don't know. Lots to do before I send this next story off to my editor. And then there's the next one waiting in the wings."

"Okay. But call more often, will you? Mom likes to hear from you, too."

"Yes, ma'am."

"Oh, I forgot to tell you. I talked to David again. He keeps asking questions about Sam, like he's worried or something. Anyway, I told him she'd come home to take care of her soon-grandbaby and the mother. You should have heard the way his voice squeaked when he repeated the grandmother word. Like it shocked him." One of her laughs gurgled over the line. "I guess he was thinking about Grandma Lil. You think? I mean, I guess it's kind of a shock to imagine a friend about to be a grandmother."

"I guess it is."

"But he seemed kind of glad she was back in the States. Was he worried?"

Well, yeah, calling David worried was putting it mildly. And look, all for naught. "I think the idea of me seeing another woman probably got to him."

Tootie's laugh was a giggle this time. "And an *older* woman."

"That, my dear Tootie, was your fault."

"I know. I'm sorry."

"It's not an issue any longer, so no harm done."

"It isn't?" she asked. "Are you sure?"

"Tootie, good-bye."

Her voice drifted to him as he clicked off the phone. "Bye!"

Yeah, he was sure. How could he not be?

Shadows passing in the night. A vision he was allowed to explore, but only superficially. He obviously hadn't known Sam— *Samantha*—at all.

SAMANTHA

Disasters stuck to her like glue,
And clumped in piles, one by two.

M aybe she made Cindy uncomfortable. Sam glanced
over her shoulder at the small figure on the couch—
well, small except for the middle part—and tried to imagine
having her own mother-in-law hanging around, a woman she
barely knew.

She pasted on a smile and asked Cindy if she'd like a cup of
herbal tea.

"No, I'd like to get up and go to the movies."

Ah. Well. "Shall I put on something? Do you get cable?"

"Just the basic channels. For the Internet. Daniel said we
couldn't afford the rest."

"Well," Sam said, "I can fix that."

Cindy brightened. "Really?"

Sam picked up the phone book and started flipping
through it. By the time she'd finished chatting with the nice
lady at the cable company and had given her credit card

number, she'd been promised a service upgrade that very afternoon.

"After they've installed the receiver, you'll be able to watch any movie you'd like," Sam said. And she'd have Cindy's eyes off her while she worked around the too-small apartment.

Cleaning someone else's rooms while that someone watched her every move and chatted on about anything and everything—but nothing of interest—made Sam feel acutely self-conscious. Why did the girl chatter so much?

"I don't know how to thank you."

Sam waved away the thanks and got started on the refrigerator, no longer worried that her daughter-in-law might be offended when she tossed out zoological experiments. She'd already tackled the dust bunnies behind the curtains and under the bed.

Maybe Cindy worried that she judged her for getting pregnant in the first place. For trapping Daniel into marriage? As if her son had been an innocent party. Sure. But perhaps Cindy felt guilty.

Well, Sam knew all about guilt. And hadn't she said all the loving things, done the hugging things when they confronted her with their news? She'd tried to, but maybe she'd been so caught up in her own mess that she'd missed some of the cues.

She pasted on a happy face for Cindy when she next caught the girl's eye. "Dinner's in the oven and should be ready about the time Daniel gets home. Can I get you anything more before I leave?"

"Oh, no, thank you so much," Cindy said. A tad too heartily?

Sam had some work to do there.

She had work to do everywhere.

~

SHE CARRIED a plastic container of leftovers to her drab couch. Her stomach had rebelled as she'd cooked for Cindy, but she knew better than to starve herself. So eat she would. Soon.

She wouldn't look at the walls. She wouldn't remember her beautiful cottage. Why had she been in such a rush to rent something just because it was convenient? She'd forgotten how much difference a pleasing environment made. Fine, she was spoiled. She hadn't stayed in a place this awful since that first off-campus house she'd shared with two other girls. But that had been then, and they'd been young. This place? She could have kicked herself for pooh-poohing her need for light and airy or at least tasteful. Something would have to be done if she had to remain longer than a month or two, like painting the walls and covering this couch with a throw that didn't make her eyeballs hurt when she looked at it.

She'd done nothing but make poor choices since the day Greg announced he was leaving. Now she was back to wallowing.

Off with that self. On with someone new.

Right. Even that thought seemed ridiculously self-conscious.

When the phone rang, she didn't answer. She'd already spoken with Rhea and Tootie about the shops, and she couldn't imagine Daniel or Stefi needing anything that was worth the effort of getting up. Teo was the only other person who had the number here, and she'd told him she wouldn't be returning to Italy, that she didn't have the energy to talk to him now—or to see him. It had been a painful conversation, and she didn't want to repeat it. She remembered his silence after she said good-bye, a silence but no click to show he'd disconnected. She'd listened to that silence until, finally, she'd been the one who hit the *End* button on the handset.

She took a bite of the lasagna and then two more before

shutting the container and returning it to her refrigerator. She tried to read. That failed. A shower then.

She undressed and stood beneath the steady flow of water, remembering those shallow baths and quick showers of Reggio. And then the glorious ones from Venice.

Which tossed her memories back to the days with Teo and his dear self. And his stricken face when she'd left.

Stop. That had been a lovely interlude, but it was over. Her life was here.

Where she had excellent water pressure and all the hot water she needed at the twist of a knob. Nothing to complain about.

Until she turned off that water and stood drying her body and saw again the cracked tiles and missing caulking. When she'd donned her nightgown, she pulled on socks so her bare feet didn't walk on someone else's carpet.

She picked up her brush from the brown, faux-wood dresser. As she brushed the required strokes, her gaze shifted to the orange-and-lime colored spread that coordinated perfectly with the green upholstered chair at the far wall. She always pulled down the covers and tucked them beneath a roll of sheet.

Maybe tomorrow she'd find time to pick up another spread and perhaps a couple of new towels so she could give the kids back the one they'd lent her. She also should get new cell service. Tomorrow.

Or maybe the next day. It didn't really matter.

34

JACK

A tilted universe pulsed
Or expanded or wavered,
But it never, ever
Seemed to right itself.

India pushed open his door, all smiles, another plant in her hands. A Christmas cactus this time. Jack clenched his fists.

She set the plant on his table and stooped over him, her eyes widening when she saw his. "Jacky, what? Are you okay?" She turned as if to go after the nurse.

His voice stopped her. "You tried to kill me."

She snapped around. Her blonde hair whipped across her shoulder, and she grabbed the bedrail to balance herself. "Wh...at?" Her words came out in a high-pitched stammer. "What do you mean?"

"That bottle. That moonshine. Who gave it to you?"

She was shaking. He could see the vibration thrumming up her body. "Marty. I told you. One of the co-pilots. His brother gave it to him. I told you."

"Did you tell him I'd been sick?"

Now she merely seemed confused. "Why?"

He waited.

"Well," she said, rubbing her hand back and forth along the metal tube of the rail. "I probably did."

"He called me. Told me the bottle was poison."

"No." She breathed the word, her eyes round and frightened.

"That's why I had it tested, India. I was afraid for you." She stood, mute, a deer in the headlights. He wanted to hit her. Hit something. "I thought you'd get sick, too."

"I didn't."

"No. You wouldn't have. Not when you gave it only to me. So I'd die."

"No, never."

"It almost worked, India."

"I would never have killed you, Jacky. Never."

"You. Almost. Did."

Big drops formed in her eyes at that. "I never wanted to kill you. It got out of hand. You were just supposed to get sick."

He felt like puking again. India's normally pretty face contorted in front of him. She reached to touch his arm. He jerked it away.

"I'll take care of you, Jacky. I will."

He barked out a laugh. "I don't want you to come near me again. Ever."

"I will quit my job. I'll do whatever it takes. Whatever you want. You'll need someplace to go. Someone to help you."

"It won't be you, India."

"You had sex with her, Jack. I have pictures."

He winced and silently clutched the sheet with his fists.

"You left me, after all we'd been to each other. You left me for that slut. You ruined my life."

"I'm sorry," he said, finally. "Sorry you were hurt."

"But you're not sorry it happened. You lied, Jack. You said there was nothing between you. But I've got proof." She waited, staring at him.

He knew what she saw when she looked at him. He'd looked in the mirror: eyes shrunken and circled in black in a face bleached white.

"You lied," she repeated. "Ricky told me you would. But he didn't want me to hurt you."

"Your brother's dead, India. He's been dead for years."

"No, he's not. He loves me. He's the only one who ever has."

Jack whispered, "I treated both you and Sam badly, but did you have to kill me?"

"I didn't kill you, did I?"

"You tried."

"Well, we're even now." She tucked her hair behind her ears and turned on that smile of hers. "I'll forgive you for what you did with Sam, and you can forgive me for hurting you. We can go on with our lives."

"What life?" His eyes narrowed, and he pulled the sheet as high as it would go. "What life have you left me?"

"You'll get better. Everything will be okay, and I'll take care of you while you're healing. I won't leave you."

"I told you, India. I never want to see you again."

"Jacky..."

"I should have left you, never looked back, and never let you come near Sam. Then I wouldn't be almost dead, or as good as, and I might be married to the only woman I ever really loved."

"You are cruel, Jack Waters. Cruel and heartless, just like I told Rick, but he said I should forgive you. He stuck up for you! You are wicked and cruel and the worst person on this earth. You hear me? The worst!"

She dug a package out of her purse and tossed it on the bed before flouncing out of the room. At the door, she stopped and hissed out the words. "I'm going back to Rick. He'll take me back. I know he will."

Her heels clomped along the corridor. And he sighed.

India claimed he was the worst person she'd known? What, had she forgotten her daddy? And that brother of hers? What did she mean, Rick wasn't dead? That he'd take her back?

Had her past all been a lie?

35

SAMANTHA

Thoughts hurl like ready darts,
While words attack the flesh and sense.

Sam heard her cell phone ring from the depths of her purse as she tucked groceries out of the way. Where was the thing?

Ah, in the outside pocket. Stefi's number flashed.

"Mama, I'm so glad you finally got your cell phone fixed so I can call you anytime. Where are you?"

"I just walked in the door."

"Okay. Good. I wanted to tell you, I met with Signora Tascini. She liked my drawings! Isn't that exciting!"

Sam fit a carton of milk in the refrigerator, picturing her auburn-haired beauty as she'd last seen her. "Absolutely. But we knew she would."

"I didn't. I was dying there, I tell you."

"Then I'm glad you've revived." She wandered into the bedroom, propped up some pillows, kicked off her shoes, and fell back in semi-comfort, missing a few of Stefi's words as she rid her feet of too-tight socks.

"What was that?" she asked, hearing female laughter in the background, then Stefi's voice coming back on the line.

"I'm supposed to go see Signora Tascini when my program ends. Don't you think that sounds promising?"

"I think it sounds very promising."

"I called Teo to thank him."

"Excellent. Good." Then, "How is he?"

Stefi said something to one of her flat mates, practicing her Italian. Sam waited, relieved when Stefi didn't forget the question. "He's good, except I think he misses you. He was excited about the meeting. I dumped Guido."

Sam laughed. Good for Stefi.

"You mean," her daughter said, "you're not going to say 'I told you so'?"

"I wouldn't dream of it."

"Teo told me you aren't coming back to Italy."

Ah, well, there it was. The elephant. "Probably not. You know I have to help Cindy. And then I think I need to get back to my real life."

"But, Mom."

"I do. Italy was great fun, and I'm glad I had the experience. But that's all it can be."

"Why?"

"Because this is where I live and work."

Stefi sighed loudly. Sam could imagine eye rolling. "You sure?" Stefi said.

Sam closed her own eyes and spoke to herself as much as to her daughter. "I am."

"Daniel kind of described that awful place you live in. He sounded like he's falling all over himself being grateful, but I hope you won't have to keep on rescuing them for much longer. Isn't her own mother coming to help?"

"Soon. She was dealing with Cindy's sister, then her husband caught the flu and she's been feeling pretty putrid herself."

"Oh, great." More chatter in the background. "Sorry, Mom, gotta run."

"Bye," Sam told the phone. "Bye," she told that other world, the world of romance and sailing the Mediterranean, the world that hadn't been real.

~

SHE DROVE over to see Rhea early Saturday morning, her first trip to Raleigh since she'd returned. Stuck in first gear, that's what she'd been, but the day was crisp under a cloudless sky, and she didn't even mind the heavy traffic. Classical music blared from the stereo.

Okay, she could do this.

She clung to that attitude until Rhea held her at arm's length. "Girl, you look terrible. What you been doing with yourself since you got back? Come on now, sit down and let me fix you a nice cup of something. What d'you want?"

Sam turned to hide sudden tears and pointed to the coffee. "You don't know how good you look to me." She wiped the corners of her eyes with her fingertips, keeping her back to the few customers and to Rhea's assistant, a new girl she hadn't met. She certainly didn't want to meet anyone while showing off her less-than-confident self.

Rhea bounced over with a cup of coffee and the fixings Sam needed and pulled up a chair for herself. "So, talk."

Sam twirled a spoon in her cup. "I've missed this place."

"Honey, it's missed you. Now, you just tell me what's put

those circles back under your eyes. It can't be just 'cause you're taking care of your daughter-in-law."

Sam condensed the story of her time with Teo and then said, "But I told him I won't be going back."

"Too early to know if it was real, I suppose? You hear from God at all about it?"

Sam shook her head. "No." She didn't mention that she hadn't asked either. "There was all the glamour of Italy. And I was, once again, on the rebound." The last she tried to say with humor. It got stuck on depressed.

"Well, if it's supposed to happen, it will. But that's not enough to make you look like that." Rhea took off her glasses, wiped them on her shirt, and squinted at Sam before setting the frames back in place. "Nope. There's got to be more."

Sam looked everywhere but across the table. "It's just, Jack's in the hospital. They say it's lead poisoning."

"You got to be kidding me," Rhea said, her palms coming down hard on the table.

"Afraid not."

"How bad is it? I mean, I've seen it in kids, and, honey, it's not something you want to mess around with."

"I haven't been able to find out. I've thought of visiting..."

"Call. Get someone else to go. You need to steer clear of that man *and* his girlfriend."

"I know."

"Okay, then. Don't you let it get you down. Jack got himself in some sort of trouble, he's not your concern. Hear me?"

Sam started to speak, but Rhea raised her hand to stop the words. "I know he was your good friend once upon a time, but, honey, he led you right across a line that neither of you should have crossed, and he didn't act much like a friend ought to. He was carin' more about Jack than about either you or that girlfriend of his." Rhea's hair bounced on a loud huff. "You keep that in mind, you hear? You broke it off like you needed to, now you just leave it there." Then she gentled her voice and touched Sam's arm. "Honey, you can pray for him from a nice safe distance and trust the One who's in charge."

Sam didn't speak.

"I been praying," Rhea said. "Haven't stopped, but, honey, you're the one needin' to get yourself hooked back up with God in the right way so you can get past the mess and on into some good territory."

Rhea was right, but how, Sam wanted to know, did you go about making that happen?

She turned down Rhea's offer to show her the accounts and promised to come back another day when she didn't have so much on her mind. Rhea handed her a brownie for the road. "Eat, girl. You need the calories. You're turning into bones only, and, honey, that's not an attractive look."

Sam tried to laugh as she waved herself out the door. In and out, and it was barely eleven-thirty. She still had the entire day to kill.

She could hit the shops. Go out to lunch in some lovely little pub. Or she could drive the couple of hours to Beaufort, stop in *Samantha's*, and head out to see her beautiful home. Oh, and, by the way (and who did she think she was fooling?), she could ask Tootie for an update on Jack.

THE DRIVE SHOULD HAVE BEEN pleasant with the new interstate —fields of seed corn, stalks cut and withering; geese in V-formations that rarely broke, their honks audible when she slowed for a stoplight once the interstate ended. It should have felt exhilarating, being in the country again, but her eyes began to glaze as Highway 70 wandered and wandered, endlessly east.

She didn't recognize the very young woman behind the counter at the Beaufort *Samantha's*. She ordered a latte and asked for Tootie.

"Oh, she's at home. Taking the day off," the girl said, handing over a latte. "You want me to give her a message?"

"No, thanks." Sam left without introducing herself.

She drove east again on the narrower highway. Her eagerness grew as 70 turned into Merrimon Road and eventually to the smaller lane that would lead to hers, its macadam surface creating a rumble under her tires. She turned right onto the gravel and felt the crunch of it. So familiar.

Why had she been afraid to come?

Tootie and Holland had certainly spruced things up after removing the dead bushes. She liked their choice of planters with the bright and bushy chrysanthemums to distract the eye. Especially the yellow ones and the burgundy. One almost didn't notice the naked patches.

Tootie's car wasn't there. Sam parked, walked to the front door, and for courtesy's sake, rang the bell. When no one answered, she headed toward the bank to see if Tootie had already put *Alice* up for the winter.

Sun shimmered on the water. A heron rose, wings batting majestically, its raucous call too rude for such a sleek creature.

At the top of the steps, Sam's heart did a little flip at that first glimpse of blue hull. "Hey, *Alice*," she called and waved. "Hey, baby."

Her hand touched the railing, felt the wood beneath her palm as she began her descent. And then she really looked at her boat and the dock. Something rested on the wooden boards, and, in *Alice*, something dark lay partially hidden by the centerboard well. She hurried down, and then she was on the dock, approaching *Alice*, peering inside at black shoes, purple pants, and a draped hand.

Bile backed up in Sam's throat. Her hands flew to her face as the nausea threatened, and she stood, momentarily paralyzed, staring at the pool of dark, deep red that spread on the once-white floorboards under what was left of India's head.

Oh God, oh God.

The bile rose as she turned and raced back down the dock, up the steps, across the grass. She choked it back. "Tootie!" she screamed, pounding on the door. Tootie needed to be here. *Someone* needed to be here. She had to get in, had to call for help. She looked around, remembered the potted plant. Digging out the key, she unlocked the door, yelling again as she pushed her way in.

The 9-1-1 operator made her go over everything, took interminable minutes questioning her in a monotone that did not breed confidence, forcing her to repeat what she'd seen, where she was.

"No, this isn't a cell phone." Sam had forgotten she owned a cell, but did it matter? "No, I don't think anyone else is here. No, I won't leave."

The shakes made her legs wobbly. She managed to get to the front steps, where she huddled and tried to slow her breathing.

The sirens stopped as a fire truck and ambulance pulled into the drive. Sam didn't know why the firemen had come. They only needed an ambulance.

And the police. The police would probably be along soon.

On that thought, the sheriff's car skidded to a halt, churning up gravel. Sam remembered the bluff official from news photos. He'd probably relish this mess.

She pointed to the river.

She had moved to the back porch by the time several men huffed past. The cold had spread beyond her limbs. She couldn't equate the sunlight with that dark-clad body, the dappled water with a blood-soaked boat.

She couldn't let her body curl the way it wanted to. She couldn't let down her guard. There were policemen out there, in her yard, on her boat, on her dock. They had come to take away the woman who'd been India Monroe.

She pressed her palm against her stomach, bit hard on the side of her mouth. She would not cry. This was not the time for tears. They would want to speak to her in a few minutes. She had to be ready.

Perhaps she could make herself some hot water. Maybe hot water would stop her teeth from chattering like this, calm her nerves, keep the revolution in her belly from tossing up the brownie and the latte.

As she turned to enter the house again, she noticed the first men coming over the cliff edge, hauling something. She hurried through the back door.

Taking down a mug, she filled it with water and put it in the microwave, hitting the two-minute button. She heard a door slam and then another. An engine roared to life, and there was silence.

She looked out the kitchen window as she opened the microwave door and took out her scalding mug. The sheriff now headed up the path, past the house, holding a baggied gun in one hand, a purse and large envelope in the other. When he knocked on the door, he carried only a little notebook. She invited him in and introduced herself.

"You want to tell me how you found the body?"

Sam did. She worked at keeping her voice steady as she clasped the mug tightly between her palms, both to center herself and to eke out what warmth she could. The water stayed in the mug. Nothing could pass her lips except words, some she sucked in, some she let out.

"You know who it was, don't you?" the sheriff asked. "India Monroe? Why do you think she'd shoot herself in that boat?"

Sam had tried to shut out the image, but her mind flashed to India's dress shoes—black leather with a bow on the toe—their tips pointing skyward in the exact spot that Jack had pulled her onto his lap.

"Are you okay, ma'am?"

Sam tried to nod and must have, because he asked if he could look around. "Outside, I mean?"

She managed a feeble, "I don't suppose Tootie would mind."

"Tootie? Deb and Frank's girl?" And then he seemed to remember. "That's right. Pete said she's living here. You back for a while or what?"

She gave him the abbreviated version of their arrangement.

He tapped his pen against the notebook. "That your car? The Toyota?"

She nodded.

He touched his forehead with two fingers. "Thank you, ma'am." His shoes hit the flagstone and noisily crossed the gravel as he moved off toward the side of the property.

Sam just stared at her hands, at the mug in the hands. She took a sip of the lukewarm liquid. It didn't taste very good, but she was only after the heat, not the flavor.

Besides, how could anything taste good right now?

Her eyes slammed shut. *Oh, God.*

No, she couldn't close her eyes. She had to stare at something, anything, so she wouldn't see India.

The plants. Her driveway. Okay. The plants looked good. Not as lovely as her azaleas had. But azaleas could be replaced.

The woman who'd killed her plants couldn't be replaced or fixed or found again.

Poor, poor India.

Have mercy, please have mercy.

The sheriff walked back up to the house. She went out to meet him.

He tossed his head toward the back side of the property. "She's got Jack Water's truck parked back there. Found the keys on the front seat. Jack's in the hospital, isn't he?"

"So I hear. What're you going to do with the truck?"

"I dunno. I'll have to get hold of him. Got a letter for him, too. Probably a suicide note in there, but it feels like a book. I'll see. You know, that boat woulda sunk if she'd aimed over a couple inches. The bullet lodged itself right in the thick part, a brace or something. It your boat or Tootie's?"

"Mine."

"I need a phone number where I can reach you."

Sam got a pen out and scribbled the number to her cell phone. Ushering him to the door, she locked up, got in her little car, and thanked God Tootie hadn't been the one to find India.

No, she was the one who'd have to live with that image branded behind her eyes.

36

TEO

Deeper shoot the tendrils,
Deeper dig the weeds...

Teo shuffled up the hill from Il Mare Turchese toward his flat. The night air bit his face, and he pulled his scarf up over his chin. Passing a nightclub, he imagined the warmth of bodies snuggled in booths, listening to jazz or pop, liquor flowing. It didn't attract him, except for the idea of warm anything. He leaned on his cane more heavily this night. The damp cold and his bones were not friends.

Rain had fallen earlier, and puddles caught headlights before the tires splashed water at unwary pedestrians. He dodged to his left, but his foot caught on an uneven crack in the sidewalk. He barely corrected in time to balance with the cane and keep from colliding with two schoolgirls, still uniformed and giggling as they headed home.

"*Mi scusi, per favore.* " He begged their pardon, which set them giggling again.

Such sweet innocents, their plaid skirts rolled to show more thigh than he imagined they revealed to their teachers, many of whom still wore traditional habits. Though there, too, things were changing, just more slowly than in the States. The girls paused in front of a shop window. He imagined they watched his lopsided gait. Something new to talk about, the odd old man with the funny accent.

When his cell rang, he almost ignored it, but he recognized Tootie's tone. His primary fan. He answered.

"You won't believe what happened," she began, her voice more tense than he'd ever heard it. "Sam found India Monroe's body. Here! On *Alice*. Lying in the cockpit!" She gave him all the gory details, most of which she'd learned from that cousin of hers, Pete. It sounded to Teo as if she knew a little too much.

"Has Samantha moved back to her house?"

"Oh, no. She just came to visit, but I wasn't here."

"Maybe you ought to move back home for a while." He'd stopped walking when she first gave him the news. Now his feet shuffled up the hill.

"Oh, no. It was suicide, so there's no danger. Not now. Not from her. And Jack's in the hospital."

"What about that Rick fellow?"

"I don't know. I mean, I haven't heard anything about another Rick. You know, other than her brother. Who's dead."

What a mess. "Let me know if you learn more, will you?"

"As soon as I hear."

Teo sighed as the call ended. Not only did Samantha live in some hovel in a Durham suburb, but she'd found a dead body. *That* woman's dead body. She must be horrified. And reeling from guilt.

His cane handle fit one calloused palm. When he saw the sign for the café, he shouldered open the door and entered the cheerful room.

He felt aged. His bones might not have been particularly old in years, but they carried an old man's aches. As he sipped the hot *liquore di mandarino*, he remembered Samantha's graceful fingers holding the glass and her tongue licking the sticky remnants from her lips.

3 7

SAMANTHA

We choose the words that we will say.
We choose the action, sometimes the deed,
Always the posture and whether to pray.

Sam pulled on a pair of jeans and a turtleneck. They'd had a nasty ice storm yesterday, and the streets were full of brown slush. Slush about equaled her mood.

She slid her feet into boots and her arms into a warm jacket and headed for the diner where she'd promised to meet Tootie, though why the younger woman had picked a place in Durham, she couldn't imagine. There'd been something slightly frantic in Tootie's voice.

Tootie waited in a booth, a cup of coffee clutched between her palms. It looked like mud.

"Tea, please," Sam told the waitress as she slid in across the table.

"You want pancakes, too?"

"No, thanks. Tea will be fine."

The waitress set a mounded plate of doughy things in front

of Tootie. Tootie thanked her, drowned the pancakes in syrup. After the waitress brought Sam's tea and left, Tootie finally spoke. "I saw Jack."

Sam dunked her tea bag in barely warm water, focusing on the up and down motion. "How was he?" She tore open a packet of sugar. And then a second. Maybe it wouldn't all dissolve.

Tootie swallowed, forked another bite, and held it suspended over the plate. "He looks horrible. I mean, really, really sick. And he seemed kind of angry that no one except his foreman had come to visit. I told him India'd said he didn't want company, that he was supposed to be getting better. He laughed, but it wasn't a ha-ha laugh, you know?"

"What did he say about India?"

"That's the thing. It's so awful."

"What do you mean, awful? Besides the fact she killed herself."

"I guess we know why she did it now," Tootie said. "She'd been poisoning Jack and he found out."

That tea wasn't doing a thing to warm her as a deeper cold took hold of her belly and spread. "Poisoning? The woman must have been mad."

"Yeah. There's not much doubt about that. She'd been killing him with moonshine."

Sam couldn't have commented on that if she'd tried.

"Incredible, isn't it?" Tootie swirled another bite of pancake in the sugary goop. "Jack said the stuff India gave him tasted like a smooth tequila. He was touched that she'd thought of him, started drinking it occasionally even before you left. Then, when he moved back in with her—"

"Ah." What else could she say? "Ah" seemed to work as well as anything.

"Yeah. Said he hadn't been well, so she offered to cook for

him, make soup and stuff so he'd feel better. He figured it was easier, being there."

When she'd absorbed that, Sam asked, "And this moonshine was poisoned?"

"Yep. When India finally confessed to Jack, she claimed she'd only wanted to make him sick, but what no one can figure out is why this friend—someone from the airlines, Jack said—gave it to India in the first place. Maybe she stole it."

Sam had imagined India a crazy, rather pathetic figure, but she'd never suspected the woman would hurt Jack. And she'd thought her own small life miserable when she trudged through muck to do her laundry in the basement next door—because the dryer in her building just tumbled with no heat.

Tootie wiped her lips and continued. "It's fascinating in an awful sort of way. I mean, the poison aspect, not India's death or the attempted murder. Just how they made the stuff. Jack said the doctor at the clinic explained how all the poisons had probably gotten in the alcohol. It must be common enough."

Sam raised a brow. "You think? In what universe?"

"I know. Crazy, isn't it? Anyway, he said the bootlegger who made the liquor must have accidentally added some seed corn to the mix. Seed corn won't ferment because of the way it's treated, and this batch had been preserved with an agent containing mercury. Jack said treated seed corn scattered as bait has been known to kill shore birds. That was poison number one." Tootie held up a finger.

"There was more than one?"

"Three, actually. Poison number two was lead." Up went the second finger. "Our brave fellow used auto radiators in the condensing process. Lots of lead in the solder, and we know what lead poisoning does."

Tootie took a small bite, chewed, and swallowed again. Sam couldn't have eaten anything if she'd been force-fed.

"And," Tootie continued, "if that wasn't enough, the galvanized pipes leached zinc into the mixture." She wiggled the three fingers, then went back to forking more food. Obviously, the grotesque subject wasn't affecting her appetite. "So, poison number three. This harmless looking—and delicious, according to Jack—stuff was chock full of heavy metals. Sixty days or less, and you're dead if you consume up to six ounces a day. What's that? Two stiff drinks? Three?"

Yeah, Jack drank at least one glass of something every day—vodka, whiskey, the occasional gin and tonic. But more? Sam had never seen him even tipsy, so how would it have occurred to him to think danger from that source? Maybe he'd upped the ante when he started feeling lousy.

She tried to imagine the scene, but she couldn't wrap her mind around it. "How could India have done such a thing? She said she loved Jack."

"I know." Tootie's eyes sparkled as if her thoughts amused her. "Sort of the wolf dressed in granny's clothes, you know?"

Sam didn't smile.

Her normally perceptive assistant pressed on as if this were a snatch of gossip instead of a horror story. "You remember my cousin, Pete, the deputy? The one who watched the house after India poisoned the plants?"

She nodded.

"He said that package India left on the dock was her diary."

A *diary?* But the question wouldn't even croak past Sam's lips.

"That's what Pete said. He called me the day after. Okay, he shouldn't have, but it happened in my —your—backyard. He knew I'd want the details."

Sam's fingers began shredding the napkin. She noticed and folded her hands in her lap, waiting.

"Well, he overheard the sheriff say India wrote pretty much

every thought that came into her head and wanted it sent to Jack, if you can believe that. Even addressed the envelope to him. I've kept a diary before, but no way would I want somebody to read it. I guess that's how you know a person's crazy. Sheriff says her death was obviously suicide."

"Everyone read the diary?" Her stomach sent the tea water straight up her throat. She swallowed it back down. She just hoped she could keep it there.

"Oh, no," Tootie said hurriedly. "Only the sheriff. It's just, he made some comments while he was reading it. Pete heard about them from one of the other deputies."

Sam's eyelids shut over the image of those deputies, that sheriff, devouring words that would include her name. Coupled with Jack's. She wanted to die. Right here. Right now.

She must have groaned, because she felt Tootie's hand touch hers.

"It's okay," Tootie said, in what she must have imagined a soothing voice. "Pete promised he wouldn't tell anyone else." A pause and then, "But that's not all."

What more could there possibly be?

Sam opened her eyes and pulled free of Tootie's grasp, trying to warm her frigid hands beneath her armpits. She didn't want to hear more. She really didn't.

Tootie grimaced after another sip of coffee. "This stuff is terrible. Anyway, Jack got the diary from the sheriff, I guess because she wanted him to have it. That's really sick. But can you believe? On her last visit, India gave him photographs, ones she'd taken." Tootie shook her head, obviously puzzled. "I don't get why he was so chatty about all of this. Why tell me? I mean, would you?"

Not on your life. Tootie was a kid. What had Jack been thinking? "It...it doesn't sound like him."

"No, I didn't think so either. But I got the feeling he wanted an audience. He acted really put-upon that no one had been to see him until this all happened."

India was dead, and Jack felt *neglected*?

"Jack wouldn't tell me what the pictures showed, but I got the idea that they were somehow compromising and were the reason she was so mad at him. Well, he almost admitted that when he said she'd tried to poison him because of what was in the pictures."

Yep, she was going to be sick. The bile this time was more than just tea rising. She bit her lips together, tightly. The pain helped. Some.

"Like I said, absolutely crazy." Tootie stared at her plate for a few moments, then looked at Sam with sympathy. "Maybe I shouldn't tell you this. I mean, I don't want to hurt you more, Sam. But then I thought you'd want to know."

"Know what?" Why would she want to know anything more? No, she just wanted to go home and die.

Tootie still hesitated.

Sam tasted blood. "What?"

"Jack said her diary was pretty explicit. She wrote that she was going to shoot herself in *Alice* because she wanted to kill your boat. I'm so sorry."

Lightheaded and feeling slightly battered, she braced herself against the table. She would not collapse. She would not faint. "Did...did you tell Jack I was here?"

"Yeah, but he doesn't want to see you now. I think because he's in such bad shape."

She pushed away from the table. "I've got to leave."

"Sam..."

"I'm sorry," Sam called over her shoulder as she raced toward the door.

She had no idea how she made it into her car and back to the apartment without her stomach emptying itself. And she didn't remember that she'd forgotten to pay for the tea until she found herself on her own bathroom floor, spent and aching.

∼

SHE WAITED for the next axe to fall. How long before her name was splattered all over the local papers? Word would get out—it always did. The sheriff had read the diary. His deputies gossiped—and not just among themselves. Pretty soon all of Carteret County would know. They'd find out in Beaufort. They'd know *everywhere*.

The consequences of her affair had played out in Jack's body and India's death. Her portion was bound up in these, but there would be more. There always was.

Her cell phone, set on vibrate, bounced around on the living room table. She brushed out her hair, slipped her feet into wooly socks and padded out to check caller ID. Tootie.

Sam thought about their meeting and Tootie's revelations as she brewed a cup of tea, spooned a dollop of honey into it, and sliced a banana over a bowl of oat cereal. The yellow floating on yellow in a cream-colored mess did not look appetizing. Still, she carried both bowl and cup to the table, pulled out a chair, and sat down. Her hands rested on the table's surface.

This time of morning, Tootie would probably be skipping around the cottage, doing interesting things to her body: a new hair color, different makeup, perhaps replacing hoops with dangles in her earlobes, studs up the outside edge. Maybe she'd be flipping through her wardrobe to search for something apricot or turquoise or—horrible thought—magenta to brighten the day.

Brown surrounded Sam. Dirty, cracked brown. Okay, not

dirty. She'd scrubbed until her hands were raw—why did she keep forgetting to buy rubber gloves?—but the cracks and the flaked Formica *felt* dirty, like grit in her teeth from badly washed clams, the sort of meat to swallow whole (or spit out, if home alone).

That image brought on goose bumps.

She glanced at the phone again. Tootie might need to discuss the business, and, as much as Sam might prefer to crawl under a rock, she couldn't.

She picked up the phone and called Tootie back. Yes, she assured Tootie, all was well. She'd certainly evolved into a liar, hadn't she? Put on a cheerful face or a cheery voice and pretend.

"I'm glad." Tootie sounded unconvinced.

Sam probably hadn't sold the "all is well" bit with enough faked enthusiasm.

"Everything's fine here," Tootie said. "Busier than ever. Must be the weather, you know, everyone wanting something hot to drink."

Yeah, right. "Thanks for checking in." Sam disconnected.

She picked up her cereal bowl. As she chewed a spoonful of soggy oats, she blocked the image of a soon-to-be-repaired *Alice* and instead pictured old ladies who had never before stepped foot in *Samantha's* ordering a latte—would they even know what a latte was?—just to check things out, because even if India had been crazy, she'd belonged to the area. Sam was almost a foreigner, she'd been gone so long.

She rinsed her bowl and dressed to go to Daniel's. If only Cindy's mother would get over her bout of flu.

Cindy sat propped up in bed today instead of on the couch, which made Sam's cleaning-lady status more palatable. Daniel had loaded the dishwasher, almost house-trained. And he'd put a load in the washing machine.

Sam added these to the dryer and started on their dinner. She made a pot roast, full of good vitamins. Daniel could make their salad when he got home.

She stuck her head in the bedroom. "You need anything? Herbal tea?"

"I've got water," Cindy said, looking up from her laptop. "Dinner smells divine."

"I hope it is. Well, I'll just fold the laundry and then head out."

"I hope you know how much we appreciate you, Sam." Emotional as always, Cindy brushed away her tears. "I'm a mess."

"You're pregnant. It's allowed."

Sam was carrying folded linens to the bathroom closet when her son opened the door. "You're early," she said.

"It's supposed to get nasty out there again this evening. I wanted to get here in time for you to make it home before the mess hits the streets."

Sam set the towels on their shelves and met Daniel in the kitchen, where he sniffed at the roast. "This smells amazing, Mom."

"I'm glad."

When he turned, his eyes narrowed. "You look terrible."

It's true he hadn't seen her in recent days, but he didn't have to be mean about it. Sam smoothed her hair back and tried to shrug off the hurt.

Grabbing her shoulders, Daniel held her at arm's length. "I'm worried about you."

"I'm okay." She reached out to pat his cheek. "Really."

He helped her into her jacket, calling out to Cindy that he'd be right back. He stuck his hands in his jeans' pockets and hunched his shoulders as he walked her to her car, quiet until he saw her settled behind the wheel. Then he leaned in and said, "Is it the whole thing with Jack? You're not tripping on some guilt thing, are you?"

"No, of course not. Sorry I've worried you."

"I love you, Mom. I just want you to take care of yourself. Maybe get more exercise when the weather's better?"

Sam nodded. "I am. I will."

She drove home—no. Erase that. She drove to that *place*, wondering what Daniel's question about guilt meant. What did he know—or assume?

See. Even her son expected guilt to be an issue.

As far as exercise went, how could she run in yucky weather and with no energy? And who'd want to run in this neighborhood anyway? She didn't think it was dangerous, just ugly. Okay, maybe a little dangerous.

Only, not as dangerous as tromping on someone's heart.

～

DANIEL MUST HAVE CALLED STEFI, because now Stefi phoned daily. On Saturday, Stefi caught up with her mother while Sam was kicking around the apartment, vegging. "Mom, how come you still won't talk to Teo?" was Stefi's first question after they'd exchanged a couple of pleasantries.

Sam slammed shut her eyes and took a couple of deep breaths before saying, "Where did that come from?"

"Well, I called to chat with him about the possibilities for next year with Signora Tascini."

"Stefi, honey," she began, her grip on the phone tightening, "I love you, but I don't think my relationship with Teo is something you need to fret over."

"Don't be angry at Teo, Mama. I asked. The thing is, I know you like him and he likes you. Maybe you could use a friend like that. A real one."

Sam did not want to have this conversation. Why couldn't everyone just leave her alone? Besides, hadn't they already talked about this?

"Mama?"

Sam sighed. "Remember how you felt about Guido when you first met him, the excitement of something new in a romantic setting?"

"Sure."

"Well, I think that's what happened between Teo and me. Now that I'm back here, it doesn't seem real."

"But it might be, if you gave it a chance. I think he's perfect for you."

Daniel wanted to fix her eating and exercise habits. Now Stefi was interested in her love life. "And you know him so well?" She couldn't keep the sarcasm out of her voice.

"Enough to see that he's fun and nice and likes you. A lot. Besides," —and here Stefi's voice waxed enthusiastic— "he's been awfully good to me. And to you."

Good? Good like old Jack had been, helping the twins find a motorboat, helping Daniel with a good-paying job so he and Cindy could marry and stay in school? But Jack hadn't been good for their mother at all.

"I'm glad Teo's been able to help you." The conversation exhausted her, but she couldn't hang up. This was her daughter. "Okay, yes, Teo was very good to me, too. But things like the Venice trip aren't real life."

"They could be. I think you sell yourself short."

"Sweetie, it's not a question of selling myself one way or the other. I appreciate your concern, but right now I just need time to get over all that's happened. Okay? Maybe not so many phone calls."

"I just want you to be happy." Stefi's hurt tone made her feel terrible, but she didn't have the energy to fix things just then.

She did her best with, "I know. I love you."

And then she sat back and imagined Stefi closing her cell phone, calling to the other girls in her apartment, asking if one of them wanted to go out with her. Because that's how Stefi dealt with hurt and disappointment. Or at least, that's how she always had. Go out, have fun. Stefi would smile that bright smile and charm the world. She'd certainly charmed Teo. And obviously been charmed by him.

Sam let the thought of Teo linger. She allowed herself to imagine, just for a moment, what he was doing on that Saturday afternoon. Was he still in Reggio? Or had he gone traveling, hunting up new ideas for another of Sophrina's adventures?

She hung a clean towel in the bathroom and got out the liquid cleanser to scrub the ancient tub. As she rubbed at scum lines (were there any, or was that just where the finish had been denuded?), she wondered how long it would take Teo to shrug her off, decide she wasn't worth worrying about.

She wasn't. But the thought etched at her, like a burnishing tool on a metal plate. She poured on more cleanser and rubbed harder on the rust stains underneath the drippy faucet. They wouldn't come out, no matter how much bleaching agent she used.

She got off her knees and went after the week's accumulation in the sink. When she finished the bathroom, she'd give the kitchen floor a good mopping.

If only she could scrub her soul clean while she was at it.

38

SAMANTHA

I picked up shells and hid them well,
Collecting pails of woe.
It overflowed and bent my back,
Buckling my knees to the sand.

Sam was still in her sweat clothes when the knock came on Sunday afternoon. She hadn't taken a shower or washed the breakfast dishes—or maybe they should be considered lunch dishes. The last thing she wanted was company.

"Who is it?"

"It's me, Sam. Open up."

No mistaking that voice. Sam should have known the only one left to hound her was Rhea. She finger-brushed her hair and opened the door. Rhea breezed past, stopping in the middle of the living room and letting her eyes roam over the drab space. "So, this is where you've been hiding." Her friend's voice hummed disapproval. Rhea slipped out of her coat and flung it on the couch. "Girl, go get yourself ready. I've come to take you out. Becky's off with friends, and I decided I needed some Sam time."

Sam swiped at the wet that overflowed onto her cheeks. "I'm a mess."

"So, go get un-messy. We'll find ourselves something delicious to eat. Maybe go have sushi at that new place downtown. I know you like sushi, and I can have the scallop dish."

"I need a shower."

"Then have one. I can wait."

Sam hurried into the bathroom and turned on the water. While it was heating up, she snatched a pair of jeans, a silk turtleneck, and clean underwear from her room. She smiled as she soaped down, rinsed, and dried herself. She was still smiling while she dressed.

"Good job," Rhea said as she turned from the kitchen sink and looked her over.

"I didn't mean for you to do the dishes."

"Didn't take a minute. Get your coat, and let's go."

They drove into town and found a parking garage. The cold bit Sam's cheeks on the walk to the restaurant. She ordered a mixed plate of sushi rolls, Rhea, her scallops, and then Rhea got down to business.

"You been worrying me, Sam. Now I see that apartment of yours—honey, I'm scared."

"You don't need to be. I'm okay."

"No, ma'am, you're not. Look at you. You talk to me from Italy, you're happy and enthusiastic. You get back, and you fall off the edge again. What happened this time?"

Sam squeezed lemon into her hot tea, then added a packet of sugar. She concentrated on stirring, watching the miniature whirlpool her spoon created, waiting for it to settle. Little pieces of lemon pulp rose to the surface and floated. She sipped and felt them slip into her mouth. "Nothing. I'm fine."

Rhea waited. The waitress came, delivered their order. Rhea thanked her, said, "Bow your head and let's get this going." Rhea thanked God, and, oh, Sam missed her, missed *this*, with a mighty tug on her heart.

She reached across the table and squeezed Rhea's hand. "Thank you."

"Eat," Rhea said, taking a bite, waiting.

Sam picked up her chopsticks, but couldn't bring herself to do more than dunk a piece in her small bowl of soy sauce. Rhea would probably sit there all day if she didn't say something. "Has Tootie talked to you at all?"

"Hellos a time or two. But since you've been back, I haven't been bothering her. Figured she'd come to you if she needed anything."

"You remember I told you about Jack being in the hospital."

"That got you all crazy again?"

"No."

"Then what?"

"His girlfriend shot herself in my boat. I found her."

Rhea set her fork back on the plate. "Whoa."

Sam shredded her napkin as she spoke, making little distinct piles, and caught herself. When had she picked up that habit? She brushed the piles away and pulled another napkin from the holder. "Yeah, India tried to poison Jack, and then she killed herself."

Sam saw it again, India's body, dark red blood starkly outlined against white floorboards. She could still hear Tootie's voice, as if in another dimension, telling her about some photos and the poison. The photos because of her actions, the poison because of the photos, the suicide because of the poison. No matter what Tootie said, the photos were the catalyst, and she, Sam, had starred in those. She and Jack. The sour rose in her throat again, hard and fast.

"'Scuse me," she said, barely making it to the restroom.

When she returned to the table, she sat down and tried to focus on Rhea and not the plate of food she'd never be able to eat. "Maybe I ought to go home. I'm not feeling well."

"You blaming yourself for it all?" Rhea asked, taking another forkful of her rice. "It's no good holding all this blame, Sam. You need to let it go."

"Easy to say." Her voice still shook. So did she.

"It's a lot to carry if you don't. You know perfectly well where you're supposed to take guilt and shame. Better get on those knees of yours and work up some calluses, girl, or this is gonna kill you. Hear?"

Sam forced her lips to spread in the semblance of a smile. "Yeah, well, let's talk about something else. You came to cheer me up, so let's get cheerful." She lifted her chopsticks.

"Amen. Let's you and me do just that." Rhea patted her hand. "You tell me about this man you spent all that time with in Italy, the writer. Love his name. Teo." She let it glide over her lips. "You heard from him?"

"I did, but I can't. You know? I mean, he's a great guy, but I'm here, he's there." Sam shrugged, clamping the sticks around another piece of roll, but not lifting it off the plate. "I'm recovering. It wouldn't be fair to him. Probably not fair to me either. Another man, another issue."

Rhea shook her head. "Sam, honey, much as I love you, I gotta tell you, you're a mess."

Her "ha" took the place of laughter. "Thanks so much."

"It's time to wise up and get with the program, girl, or you're going to be moaning through life, looking for more sadness to heap on those shoulders. And, let me tell you, it'll be happy to find you."

Sam pushed her plate away and wiped her lips. "I appreciate you trying to help, but you're not. Maybe this wasn't such a good idea."

"Seems to me, you get yourself right with God, then you look things square in the face. It's not like Italy's at the end of the earth. He'd come, I just bet you. And if he likes you as much as I'm guessing, and you like him..."

"Let it alone, Rhea." Sam collected her jacket and waved for the bill. "I'm paying," she said, pushing Rhea's hand away when she tried to take the slip from the waiter. Dropping a couple of bills on the table, Sam slid her chair back. "I'll meet you outside." She left Rhea asking for to-go boxes.

They both seemed focused on the roads—or inside their thoughts—as the car headed back to the apartment. Sam didn't even mention that Rhea'd been the one to warn Sam away from a new entanglement. A bit hypocritical, wasn't it, this new line of Rhea's?

"Take your lunch," Rhea said, handing over one styrofoam box after she'd stopped the car.

She thanked Rhea and exited the car. Then, without a backward glance, she hurried up the sidewalk, jogged up the stairs, and tried to fit the key in the lock with hands that wouldn't stop shaking.

The world needed to leave her alone. All her friends, her children. Her head.

She'd be okay. She would. Grief didn't last forever, even when it felt like it would.

"I'll be fine. You hear? *Fine.*"

Never, the walls seemed to scream back at her, louder than her own words, heavier in her mind. They traced tendrils down her body, neck to back to legs, down her front until they grabbed her around the middle and poked like a bully's taunt. *You lie.*

~

SAM WOKE EARLY MONDAY, still in Sunday's jeans. She kicked them off and climbed right back in bed. Dawn hadn't yet happened. And besides, why should she bother to get up? Cindy's mother had finally come yesterday, so she was off the hook there.

Yeah, fine. She winced as she thought of how much she'd become the whiner she despised. She hated whiners. She hated wimps.

Samantha Ransom, depression personified. Didn't she once think people who caved in to blackness weak? What a hypocrite.

Ah, so not only Rhea, but she herself fit that mold. Double-minded.

Hypocrite, the walls hissed.

She hated this spiral she'd fallen into, this down-the-rabbit-hole-but-not-into-Wonderland place she inhabited. But the on-her-knees thing just wore her out and left her wearier than when she'd started. The door between her and heaven seemed closed and locked.

She groaned and shut her eyes, trying to block out the thoughts that rattled loudly. She wasn't hungry. If only she were. She needed something to propel her out of bed.

Parents teach children that all actions bring about consequences: touch fire, and you'll be burned; misbehave, and you'll be punished; run into the road, and a car could hit you. She remembered her own, "Stefi, no! Hot! The stove burns!" and, "Daniel, no! Stop! There's a car coming!"

Had she herself been deaf? Or merely a lost fool?

There was no blaming her own childhood, because what good did that do? She was a grown woman. Responsible for her own failings. And her own choices.

And yet. She'd been the sort of wife a man leaves. Why? What had been so terrible about her that Greg couldn't have kept their marriage?

If that weren't enough, she'd become the sort of woman who took from another, pushing that other into such pain that death had seemed a better alternative than life. How could she, Sam, atone for such a thing? India would never hear her "I'm sorry." No matter how loudly Sam shouted it. Or how often.

Sam pulled the sheet over her head, whimpering, her head full of *Oh God, oh God, oh God.*

She, of the strict moral code. *Whoosh.* A few hormonal urges, and she'd behaved as if the rules had never existed.

Tossing back the sheet, she drew in a deep breath of stale apartment air. She had to get out, go, do something. She'd suffocate otherwise.

She didn't bother with a shower, just pulled on sweats, a jacket, and her running shoes. A swig of orange juice for energy and a quick granola bar, and she hit the dry sidewalk, slowly at first to let the granola settle, picking up the pace when she felt able.

Who cared if the neighborhood were ugly? It wasn't any uglier than this ragged body she inhabited.

She was going to beat this thing.

Please. Oh, please.

Her thighs hurt first, a deep stinging that traveled down, then up to grab her torso. How had she gotten so out of shape? Her lungs told her to quit, and lazy slug that she was, she obeyed.

The walk back to her prison did nothing for her mood. She heard a beep from her cell phone when she pushed open the door, and her apartment phone blinked its message light.

Ignoring these, she shed her clothes and got in the shower. Water scalded her back, but it worked in lieu of a cat-o'-nine-tails to scourge her. Her skin was red and sore when she climbed out, but not sore enough to make her forget her other lives: the one as Greg's wife, and the one who'd let Jack in.

She bent over the bathroom sink. She didn't want to look in the mirror. She didn't want to see this self, this taker.

This thief.

Holding her hand up against the light, she stared at it. Fingers intact, a few veins visible where there'd been only smooth skin. She could feel it. She could see it. It could touch her cheek and recognize sensation both on the fingertips and on the facial skin.

Tangible things, tangible feelings. But what about the inner woman? Who was that person?

She picked up her clothes, put on her last clean anything, then wiped down the bathroom and decided to tackle the kitchen next. She had so little to do. No one needed her. Rhea and Tootie could handle the shops. Cindy had her mother, but Sam couldn't seem to move on, so she had an ugly apartment and places she didn't want to go.

The doorbell rang as she was scrubbing the kitchen floor. She closed the bedroom door before answering.

"Hey, Mom," her son said.

"Daniel. Is everything all right? Cindy?"

He smiled reassuringly as he looked over her shoulder at the room. "She's fine. May I come in?"

"Oh, of course." She backed to let him enter. "You want some tea?"

"Coke?"

"You know I don't keep sodas."

"Water then."

She tiptoed across the damp linoleum to fill a glass. Daniel saw her. "Don't bother. I didn't realize it was wet."

"It doesn't matter."

"I left you a message. Both phones. I went to see Jack." Daniel pulled out a taped packet. "He called and asked me to visit. And then he asked me to give you this."

Why had Jack used her son as a courier? He had no right. "Did he say why he was giving it to me? Why he wanted to see you?"

"He helped me when I needed it. You know that. So I think he wanted company, and he knew I'd come." Daniel waved toward the bundle. "He thought you should read what's in there. He said it explains a lot."

She bet it did. "How is he?"

"He doesn't even look like himself. I can't believe India would do something like that. I mean, almost kill Jack and then kill herself? She must have gone completely off the reservation. I just can't figure out why Jack missed seeing how badly she needed help."

Good question. Maybe India'd been crazy, but then maybe she'd had reason for her madness. Sam didn't know. "Did he want me to visit?"

"No. He asked me to tell you not to, at least not now. He said when you read what he sent, you'd understand better."

She smoothed her hand over the package. Understand? Was that even possible?

"Are you okay? I mean, you're just hanging out like this. Why don't you go home?"

"I can't, honey. Not yet."

"Because of what India did there?"

"Mostly."

"Stefi called me. She's worried."

"She shouldn't be. I'm fine. No one needs to worry." Sam tried to smile reassuringly. "Tell me how Cindy's doing."

"Her mother's been a big help." He glanced at his watch.

"I've got to get back. I told her I'd take her grocery shopping this afternoon."

She stood and gave him a hug. "Thanks for coming by."

"Call me if you need anything?"

"Of course. I'm fine, really."

After he left, Sam stared at the brown padded envelope. At least Jack had sealed it so Daniel wouldn't be tempted to peek. She set it on the counter, near the phone, and backed away. It screamed like the tell-tale heart under Poe's floor.

She had to escape. She couldn't listen another moment to those thurumping floorboards.

More people were out and about, a couple of old men lounging in front of the all-night grocery, a woman sitting just inside the Self-Wash with two babies in a twin stroller. Sam never passed the Self-Wash without wishing the name were true: eight quarters in a slot and she'd be cleaned.

The renewed exercise did her some good. It must have. At least it gave her the energy and enough hunger to pick up a small pizza on the way back to the apartment. She carried it inside and turned on the television.

Thurump, thurump.

She turned up the volume and watched nothing at all.

39

TEO

We choose the doing
And also the done,
Some for the future,
And some for today.

Silence pervaded Teo's world as he balanced precariously in the stillness of his flat. His fingers worked remotely from his brain as he rewrote and revised. Abroad, his lips sucked liquid, and his throat swallowed food, and he lived.

He even answered the phone and spoke into it. He heard updates from Tootie, his sister's fears about trauma after a suicide, Val's cheerful sales data and blandishments meant to encourage him to do more, write more, speak more, travel more.

But the words he remembered came from that last phone call to Samantha. "It wasn't real."

The hell it wasn't.

Sorry, Lord, but *really*?

And, um, God, what on earth had he done so wrong this time?

When the phone rang, he didn't answer immediately. But it was Stefi. He had to take it.

"Go help her," Stefi said. "Go."

"I can't."

"She's in terrible shape. If you care at all, please go."

"Look, I'll talk to you soon. This really isn't a good time."

It might never be a good time.

The words festered, a boil ready to pop. Stefi thought her mother needed rescuing and said there was no one else. But Samantha didn't want him.

Or perhaps she merely couldn't.

"What should I do?" His whisper echoed back at him. "What?"

He stared at his computer screen, answerless. When the phone rang again, it was Nicco calling to invite him out. *"Mi dispiace*, Nicco. I'm working on a project right now. Another time?"

"Sì, sì, certo. Another time."

To get out of his flat, he wandered down to Le Stelle and knocked back an espresso. But he didn't stay. His cane tapped on the sidewalk. Passing Il Mare Turchese, he thought of going in but changed his mind.

His rooms grew chilly in the evening air. He couldn't write. Or think.

His head fell forward. "God, please."

And he heard *her* voice, which voice he didn't know. She wept soundlessly and yet he heard the wail.

It was time. He picked up the telephone.

40

SAMANTHA

Lies steal breath. Shape changers,
They morph facts and those of us who listen.

She ignored the package for three days, girding up her loins and telling herself that no amount of crazy, dead heartbeats would break her down.

But she didn't throw it away. And that gave her pause, the why-not of it.

The package stared at her as she brewed her morning coffee, as she toasted a slice of bread. It moved to the table, because its place under the phone was too awkward. Too something.

Loud, maybe?

She pulled a chair up to the table and pushed the bundle just out of reach. A few sips into the coffee, a few bites of toast later, and she picked it up. Holding it, weighing its heft, didn't hurt. She had almost expected it to explode beneath her fingers.

The book slipped out easily once she tore the wrapping.

The diary wasn't locked, though a key was taped to the outside. She opened it gingerly.

It acted like any book begging to be read.

But this was a horror story.

It wasn't long before Sam's gut convulsed, and those sips of coffee and three bites of toast wanted out.

So, out they came.

She hated Jack for sending such a thing. She hated herself for reading it.

When the knock sounded, she ignored it. It came again. And then again. Whoever it was must have seen the Toyota and known she was home. She tried to keep her vowels clean when what she wanted was angry.

She got up to look though the peep hole and couldn't believe whose face stared back through the distorted glass. As if he could see her, she ducked, then flattened her back against the door, her palms at her sides, her eyes rounded. What was *he* doing here?

She had to open the door. He'd come all the way from Italy.

The chain rattled. She turned the lock and gazed at him. He wore a jacket she'd never seen before. It was leather. Of course it was leather. Tan and soft and—what was he doing here?

"May I come in?"

She backed out of the way. She'd just pretend this was an ordinary visit, that she was in ordinary shape. That she didn't look like a Holocaust victim.

"Would you like to sit down?" She motioned vaguely in the direction of the room.

He did a visual tour, then stared at Sam. "*This* is your place?"

"Temporarily."

He looked angry. It stirred something in her. "I sure hope

it's very temporary," he said. "Come on, get dressed, and let me take you out for breakfast."

"Breakfast?"

"You know, as in waffles, pancakes, juice. Maybe we can even find a chocolate croissant."

She smiled slightly at that but shook her head. She wished her hair felt clean against her neck. His probably smelled clean and fresh and... *Stop it.* "I can't. I'm busy."

He cocked a brow. "Now?"

She nodded and walked toward the kitchenette where she put on the kettle. "You want some coffee or tea? I have some bagels."

"Tea, please. A bagel would be fine."

Making tea took great concentration. So did toasting a bagel and putting out jam and cream cheese. She checked the cheese before offering it to make sure it wasn't mottled with green.

Teo leaned against the wall and watched. She knew what he was seeing, the same face and body she cringed from whenever a mirror caught her. Her cheekbones protruded and dark circles removed any hint of beauty she may have once claimed. Her hair had woven itself in tangles.

She handed him a mug and a plate and brushed past him into the living room. "Why did you come?" she asked once she'd settled on the sofa.

"I had to see you, to see for myself that you're okay."

"Now you've seen me."

"And you're not okay."

"I'm doing fine, Teo. I just need time." She finished her tea in deep gulps and got up. "Excuse me, will you? I've got to wash my face."

He was standing over the open diary when she emerged in jeans and turtleneck. The jeans were a little baggy now, but

Sam hoped that the turtleneck hid most of the bunchiness where she'd cinched her belt into the last slot.

"What's this?" he asked, pointing to the open pages.

"India's diary."

"Why do you have it?" His tone still had an edge to it, but the anger sounded laced with curiosity.

"Jack gave it to Daniel to give to me. Said he thought I ought to read it." Sam tried to sound nonchalant while she shivered, remembering the scrawled words, India's last testament.

"Have you?"

She nodded. "Some."

"And?" He looked fully at her.

She stood across from him. Her fingers touched the open page, lingered a moment, and then she backed up until the wall stopped her. Pressing her palms down the side of her thighs, she spoke with all the stoicism she could muster. "I got through the mess when her father essentially took over molesting her from her older brother. After the brother killed himself. Her brother *Rick*." Sam shook her head, felt shakes start again in her belly. "Can you imagine? She threatened me with him as if he were right there with her. In the moment."

Teo continued to stare at her silently. Sam wiped her face with both hands, tucking strands of hair behind her ears. She sucked in a deep breath and released it.

"So, in there," —Sam nodded to the diary— "India was writing to a man who died when he wasn't much more than a boy."

Pulling away from the wall, she sank into a chair. Teo eased down next to her.

"She wrote as if he were right there, talking to her, listening to her," Sam said. "I don't know if she thought she saw a ghost or a person. In most of the last part, she wrote as if he were occasionally hiding from her. She kept begging him to come back."

"And Jack didn't have a clue?"

Sam waved as if to brush off the question. How many times had she asked that same question? "He hinted at a closer than normal relationship between the siblings and some abuse by the father."

"I still don't understand why he wanted you to read and rehash it."

Sam sighed. "He told Daniel that it helped him understand India's actions. But I don't know if he meant the poisoning part or the suicide part."

"Because it shows her to be mentally unbalanced?"

Sam picked up the book, flipped through it, then pushed it aside. She couldn't stomach reading any more about good old Dad Monroe. Or about India's physical relationship with her brother. Maybe the clues Jack talked about were at the end.

"Do you really think you need to finish it?"

She lifted her shoulders again. "I'm this far. If I don't figure this out, I'm never going to get rid of the images already there. Her descriptions are horribly graphic—and you know how I feel about that."

"Would you like some help with it?" Teo asked, his tone neutral. "I could read to you if it's too much, or you could read to me. It might take some of the sting out of the process. I don't know."

"What? Are you just morbidly curious? The writer has to know?"

Sam hadn't meant it to be humorous, but Teo grinned. "A little of both? Plus a sincere desire to help you move past this place you're in."

"If reading the thing doesn't dig a deeper pit."

"Well, at least you'll have a friend to help you climb out."

That elicited the first smile she'd been able to arrange in a while. He was a nice man, in all the meanings of the word. "You read to me, then."

He picked up the book and flipped forward a few pages as Sam retreated to the sheet-covered monstrosity of a couch. She motioned him over. "Might as well make the best of bad furniture."

"She seems to be recording a visit to Jack in the hospital here," he said, flipping through pages, "so that's pretty late in the game. I won't go by days, because I think that will make it too choppy. Shall we see what this says and then go back if we need an explanation of anything?"

Sam nodded. She did have the slightest, and thoroughly morbid, curiosity. At least having Teo with her took away some of the horror.

~

I SHOULD HAVE JUST STAYED AWAY from that horrible place. Let Jack rot in his bed. His nasty words still sting, but I answered the only way I could—by reminding him he'd started things. He'd lied. He had. He was no better than any of them. And then I dropped the envelope of pictures in his lap. I wish I could have seen his face when he looked at himself on that nasty boat with That Woman.

~

SAM HELD a fist in front of her lips, but lowered it enough to whisper, "Oh, Teo. To have taken pictures. To have had to look at them again and again." The cold seeped back in, solid, like a lump of ice in her belly. "Tootie said something about Jack having photos." She remembered India's midnight knock on her door. How had Jack explained that one away?

Teo continued reading.

~

PART of me is glad Jack looked so bad. Sick. At least he's still suffering even if the treatment is working. He deserves it for lying.

When I told him we were even now, he said get out. Just like that. Even when I reminded him we had to forgive each other because that's how it works.

I hate him. I really hate him.

He said he couldn't stand to look at me. And when I reached for his hand, he snatched it away, turning his whole body from me. He told me not to come back. He called me a murderer. Okay, not a real one, because he didn't die, but it doesn't matter to him that I didn't mean to kill him.

I think he'd have called the police on me, that's how mad he was.

Here I am, alone again.

I am always alone.

I found a poem about him and Sam. Oh, not about them, not really. But it fits.

You want to hear it? I'll write it here. You used to write poems for me when I was little. This one fits Jack and her so well, I feel a cackle rise up in my throat when I read it now.

Get it? Cauldrons?

It's called "The Other Woman." Catchy title, don't you think? Sorry, but I didn't write down the poet's name.

> *Witches' cauldron,*
> *Potions brewing,*
> *Out of her belly chants a-spewing.*
> *The other woman wove her spell,*
> *Cast her net and reeled it in.*
> *And he, entrapped by various wiles,*

"Enthralled, in love,"
Her victim smiled.

See what I mean? That's Sam. A witch who wove a spell around my Jack. I wonder if she's happy over there in Italy. Probably. People like Sam always come out on top. They always get what they want.

Only Sam didn't get Jack. No sir. And, you know what? If Jack goes to Sam now, well, there won't be all that much left, will there?

Sometimes writing is the only thing that keeps me sane. It certainly is the only friend I have, now that you're so quiet. That and the lovely liquid in my glass.

Where are you, Rick?

≈

SAM CONTINUED to cradle her head in her hands as Teo stopped. How had India managed to survive? What she'd needed had been someone to listen to her. Someone who really cared. Not a betraying boyfriend or a witchy other woman.

Oh God.

"She pauses there," Teo said. "There are some squiggles as if she tried to write and then quit." He turned a couple of pages and began reading again. Sam had nothing to add, certainly nothing to say.

≈

JACK IS JUST like my father. I knew it. I told Rick so a long time ago, but he kept saying to have patience.

Yes, Rick came again, but this time it was only sort of. I mean, I sort of could see him, just not clearly. Or hear him clearly. It scared me, how far away he seemed. I told him what Jack said, and he reminded me who made Jack sick. Like I could forget.

I've disappointed Rick. He's not mad, he says. Just sad. And, you know, when he says it in that croaky whisper, it's worse than ever in his real voice.

Rick says he still loves me, that he'll always love me, but I can't feel him anymore. I can't touch him like I could before. He's only a shadow image when I look at him. I hope it's not because he's mad at me. I hope he isn't hiding to punish me.

He says no, he wouldn't do that. He says maybe it's something else. A spirit thing. Like a barrier because of the bad things I did to Jack. But if that's true, if I can't ever touch or see Rick again, I'll die.

∾

"ANOTHER PAUSE. Do you want to take a break here?"

"What I want is not to know anything, to be in a state of innocence again. But that's not likely, is it?"

Teo touched her cold fingers. "Honey, you've got to come to grips with what happened and forgive yourself."

"How? When I don't deserve forgiveness?"

"No one does. Remember, unmerited favor?"

She pointed to the book. "Just read."

∾

I FEEL COLD ALL OVER, or at least I did before I got warmed. Liquid fire works better than any furnace. The thing is, the black place is growing. The hole has always been deep and dark, but now the edges are jagged, like it's creeping into parts of me and leaving some things alone, outlining my stomach and kidneys in black. I wonder what's supposed to be in the blackness and isn't. Did I get born without a part, something everyone else has?

It was shallower before. I wonder if Jack made it bigger. I wonder if you can dig holes in yourself just by doing something mean. Rick says I was mean to Jack. I don't think I was meaner to him than he was to me, but maybe I'm wrong. And maybe it doesn't matter. Maybe Jack has a hole of his own that's getting bigger, but he's never said. Maybe my hole will go deeper and deeper if Jack doesn't get well. If it gets too deep, what will it do to the parts of me that are outside, especially the parts with that black ring around them? Are they doomed? Does a growing hole push things out of its way or does it absorb things, like black holes in space? Will I just disappear into it?

I tried to nap, but I couldn't. I walked around my garden, but I couldn't do more than pull a couple of weeds. I felt wobbly, so I came back in.

If only Rick would let me see him—no, that's wrong. He said he can't. It's not like he's not letting me. He isn't the one doing it, the one keeping us apart. I guess he thinks it's my fault. But if it's me, I don't know how to make it different. I don't know how to make things better, to make the bad go away so I can get him all the way back.

I said I was sorry. So Jack's supposed to forgive me. You don't have to forgive someone who doesn't apologize, like I don't have to forgive my father. I never could do that. Never. But you're supposed to forgive the person who says sorry. The Bible says so.

Mother kept forgiving Father, even after Rick went away, but I can't. Not ever. She said he apologized to her. Well, he didn't say a thing to me. Why didn't my mother get mad and stop him when he did that to me? Or when he made Rick leave?

That made him a murderer of his own son. MURDERER. Mother should never have forgiven him. So maybe I'm wrong and Jack shouldn't forgive me. But Jack was wrong first. He should forgive. Now his wrongness and mine are making everything horrible.

Too horrible.

And if the horrible stays and the black hole eats me, how will I ever find Rick again?

~

TEO LOOKED up and shook his head. "I can't believe no one caught how unbalanced she was. And you said Jack is intelligent? Where was his head when she was off talking to Rick and drinking herself silly?"

"I don't know. You'd think that sort of illness would manifest itself enough to be seen at work or among friends. Some place. The couple of times I saw her, I thought her behavior slightly over the top, but Jack couldn't see it."

"Or didn't want to." Teo sighed. "And her misperceptions about God?"

She couldn't comment. Or wouldn't.

Teo lifted the book again.

~

LIES STEAL BREATH. I finally know what I have to do. I know how to get to Rick.

~

HE READ that and then turned the page. "Blank again," he said, flipping to another page. Then he continued.

~

I FAILED. I got in my car and tried to go to the place Rick drove off the bridge, but the battery was dead again. Jack said I needed a new one, but I didn't believe him because it always worked after he charged it. Dumb. Super dumb. I planned everything so carefully. I was going to find Rick, and the best place seemed to be the bridge. That sounded painless enough, driving off the edge, a quick fall, probably like one of those roller coasters, and then splash. If I didn't wear a seat belt, it should all be over pretty quickly.

Then I thought of drowning, of sucking up water, panicking, screaming, and decided maybe my battery dying was a sign. Maybe Rick remembers how it was for him and doesn't want me to go that way. So I'm sitting here trying to figure out what he does want me to do.

I have a gun Jack bought for me. I don't like guns, but Jack said he wanted me to be protected when he wasn't home, so he taught me to shoot it. Guns are fast. And it would only take one bullet.

That feels right, which I think means Rick approves. Now I just have to collect the gun and the bullets and figure out where.

Okay. Got it. And you know what I realized while I was collecting everything?

Sam is getting off scot-free. It's not fair. Not when Jack has to pay and I sure am paying. So I have the perfect solution. It came to me as I fit the bullets in the spinning cylinder.

Her boat.

That was it, that stupid little boat. Sam made the witchy things on that boat and seduced Jack there. This time I won't fail.

Okay. I'm going to have one more drink to get me through the next part.

What shall I wear? I'm thinking my favorite pants suit, the dark purple crepe with the blue silk shirt. I'll use Jack's truck. And one more thing. I want Jack to understand, so I'm going to leave this diary for him. He needs to know I didn't want to kill him. Just like I won't kill Sam. But I will kill that Alice boat because without the boat Jack would never have gone to Sam. I should have let him keep his.

Now Sam won't have a boat, and Jack won't ever go to her again. At least I can take care of that.

Dear Diary, I'm back. Or maybe I should write, Dear Jack. It's time. I'm here. The sun is shining, so it will be a good day. Geese are calling up there in the sky. I told them to fly away or someone might shoot them.

I'm completely sober now. I'm not crazy or drunk. I'm just going to be with Rick. Soon, I'll be with the only person who has ever loved me and then I will feel his arms around me again. I'm coming, Rick. I'm coming.

~

TEO CLOSED the book and looked up. "Someone should have known."

Sam hated to imagine what it must have been like to be India. To think about things the way she had. "Oh, Teo."

He reached over and pulled her into his arms. The cold pierced all the way to her toes.

SAMANTHA

I've a flashlight in my pocket, I'll shine it in the dark,
Under stones and bedclothes, until I find you out.

"Come on," Teo said as he rubbed her back. "Let's go somewhere. You don't need to stay in this place another minute."

She sat up and looked at his dear, kind face. All the emotions she'd suppressed since her return slid into place. "Do I have time to take a shower? I feel filthy."

"Take your shower. It'll warm you, and I'm not going anywhere."

She hadn't done her laundry, but she did have a clean pair of slacks and a silk blouse to wear under one of her angora sweaters. She hadn't dressed in anything like this since she'd left Italy.

Water splashed off the tile walls and gurgled down the drain, the semi-clogged drain. Shampoo slid into her eyes, but she let the spray clean it from her face, from her body.

The knobs squeaked as she turned off the water. She reached for a towel. A hand slipped it behind the curtain. She stared at the hand and the towel hanging from it, and then she tugged it free.

She had wiped dry and covered herself before Teo pushed the curtain out of the way. She clutched the ends closed at her back.

He didn't speak, just looked at her with darkened eyes that revealed a heat she recognized. Her expression must have changed as her heart sped. Her lips parted, half in shock, half in anticipation. He waited. She took the hand he extended, stepped onto the bath mat with that towel covering all the embarrassing parts. Teo rested his cane against the basin cupboard without moving his gaze, lifted his free hand, and touched the side of her face, gently tracing her lips with the edge of his thumb. She moaned, ever so slightly, but enough, she supposed, to give him courage.

"Samantha," he breathed as he lowered his lips and moved one hand to the back of her head, the other to the base of her spine, keeping it on top of the towel and the towel from slipping. She couldn't believe how sweetly encouraging his lips felt, how strong and warm the hand on her back. When he deepened the kiss, she had no choice but to respond.

"Oh, Teo," she whispered when she could, as her arms circled his neck.

Teo's grasp tightened on the towel that still separated them, holding it shut as he finally unwound one arm and put a few inches between them.

Sam stared up, momentarily bereft, and quickly secured the covering as she backed away. She bowed her head to hide the rising blush. "Why did you do that?"

His words were softly spoken, but she could hear his breath catch. "Why did I kiss you or why did I stop?"

She shrugged, fixing her gaze on the tip of his polished shoe.

"I think you know why I kissed you. If you're wondering why I stopped... Honey, there are rules."

"Oh."

"You know I want you. It's got to be obvious."

She looked up quickly. His reddened cheeks elicited a slight smile. "I should get dressed."

"Yes, of course," he said, turning and closing the door behind him.

She moved to the mirror and stared at the smile that continued to widen. How had she let that kiss happen? Okay. She was glad it had. But it still felt odd that she could have gone from the pits of misery to hungry in less time than it took to say the words. She hoped she'd slid into his arms because she'd trusted him not to take advantage, but had she? Or had she hoped he would?

She blew her hair dry and wandered out with a brush in her hand. He turned. "Let's go find some real food. We need to talk."

You'd think that after the statement, "We need to talk," they'd have said something substantive once Sam slid in beside Teo in his rented SUV. Instead, the conversation took the form of reminiscing, which led Sam straight back into that place of comfort combined with fun that she'd known in Italy.

That buzz lasted until she gazed at her reflection in the restaurant's bathroom mirror as she washed her hands, and an unwelcome thought dropped like a water balloon to drench her mood.

She had gotten all dewy-eyed with Teo. Might have succumbed to lust if he hadn't backed away. So. Was she still the needy, grasping woman she'd been?

Being a victim was exhausting work, but she felt as if she

were back at it again. She tossed up a prayer right then, because the idea of being the needy yes-sayer again, the same hurting yes-sayer from her days with Jack—who'd swallowed every no she should have spoken—tightened the knot in her gut.

"Who are you?" she asked that woman in the mirror. "Have you changed at all, or is Teo merely the one in front of you now?"

And was she any better, any stronger than India had been?

She shuddered at that thought. She didn't want to be either weak or needy. She wanted to be the strong woman she'd once imagined. She wanted to be a woman capable of making relationship choices that were healthy. But how could she know if she'd arrived there, or if she remained stuck on replay?

The love she'd imagined for Jack might have been merely gratitude that a good-looking man had found her attractive. Had actually wanted her. But look what she'd done with that imagined-love, that gratitude. Let it and him seduce her.

Was this different? It felt different. *Teo* felt different. But, honey, she'd better figure out what *different* meant so she wouldn't fall back down the other side of the sliding board again.

She'd climbed to the top twice, teetered there for a while, and landed smack on her face in the sand pit. Now she was back on that ladder, aiming for the top—and for stability. Not for another fall.

She glanced toward the ceiling and whispered, "Please, show me."

~

CANDLELIGHT FLICKERED in Teo's eyes. The restaurant setting breathed romance, but Sam braced herself.

Be rational. Be careful. Wait.

They'd finished the salad course when he reached across the table and touched her hand. *Oh, no.* She suddenly felt so overwhelmed with emotion that tears gathered, but they weren't from sadness.

It might have been the place. It must have been. They'd shared so many meals together and had so much fun. Their afternoon spent walking hand in hand through Chapel Hill reminded her of the days in Italy.

Perhaps those internalized responses surfaced as she stared into Teo's face now. His generous nature, his kindness, and his humor compelled her to turn her hand into his as her heart flopped against her ribs like a hooked fish on the deck of a boat. Her lips opened, and she whispered, "I am so glad you're here. I missed you."

"I did hope that's what the kiss meant."

She grinned. "At least that."

And on those words, he grew serious again. "You know how I feel. I haven't changed my mind."

Ducking her head, she tried to slow that battering going on in her chest. But she couldn't say the words. The kiss had been pretty convincing—or rather her reaction to it. Or maybe it had been him pulling away that got her attention.

To feel valued enough, treasured like that, seemed so rare.

"I mean," she said, trying to get it all clear in her head, "I didn't feel anything but lousy this morning when I saw you at the door. I just wanted you gone."

Teo laughed out loud. "I don't know where I got the courage to hand you that towel or to stand there waiting for you to scream me out of the place. I don't even know why I did it, but something compelled me."

"I was so shocked, I guess I dropped my guard." She couldn't look him in the eye as she thought of the barrier he'd

thankfully held between them. "From there to here in eight," —
she paused to check her watch— "no eight and a half hours is
rather hard to believe."

He did his fingertip-kissing thing again, which sent shivers
down—or maybe that was up—her spine. Her grin expanded at
that irrelevant thought.

"Do you think you can bring yourself to imagine loving
me back?"

Oh, my. He was seducing her. Right here. At least, that's
what it felt like. But more an affectional seduction.
Romancing.

She wasn't ready for romancing or seduction, affectional or
not. She wasn't ready to admit she felt more than friendship.
But her mouth seemed to open all by itself and say, "Yes."

He whooped. And then he covered his mouth with his linen
napkin and cleared his throat, faking a cough. "Sorry," he said,
his eyes laughing at her over the linen. "I expected you to say no."

"Teo." Sam did her best to frown. She failed. "Why did you
ask me if you thought I'd say no?"

"It just slipped out."

"Well, so did my yes."

And with that, he really did laugh, but he kept it low so as
not to attract more attention. "You, my dear Samantha, are
a fraud."

"If I am, you are too."

"Perhaps. Which means we'd better join forces to keep each
other honest."

"What, some kind of honor pact?"

He ignored her words. "I see only one solution." And here
he paused for just a moment, perhaps two breaths' worth,
before he cleared his throat and said, "My very dear Samantha,
will you marry me?"

That dropped her jaw almost to the table. She hadn't imagined he'd propose. How could he propose so soon? "M...marry?"

His grin slipped. "Well, yes. That seems the logical next step. I love you, and it's obvious I'd like the right to take the towel down next time. And when that towel comes down, it needs to be official enough to keep you from tumbling into more guilt, don't you think?" He paused a beat. "I also want to be here to help you through everything." His fingers squeezed hers gently. "I'd like the right to do that."

As much as her stomach fluttered at the prospect of being able to wake up next to this dear man—okay, and not have those rules, like a clung-to towel, between them—and as much as she really did seem to love him, the thought of marriage petrified her.

The waiter set down plates of broiled flounder. Hovering momentarily, he asked, "Will there be anything else?" When Teo thanked him and said no, he bowed and left.

Teo again cleared his throat. "It's too soon. I'm sorry. I shouldn't have asked in such an unromantic way."

"Could we think about it later?" Sam tried to keep her voice steady as her whole body drummed with tension. "When there's not so much going on?"

"Of course. Now, let's see what they did to this poor fish."

HER FIRST THOUGHT on waking the next morning was that she couldn't marry Teo. She couldn't move forward in any relationship without first settling all the residual mess. She had to talk to Jack and had way too much left to fix. Besides, how could she consider marriage when she didn't know if she were yet strong enough to make it on her own? Hadn't that been her priority?

She'd failed rather miserably since she'd been home, but kissing Teo had been a tonic. He'd definitely woken the sleeping princess.

Now this princess just needed to figure out how to be strong enough emotionally so she wouldn't *need* a man. It was fine to *want* one. That was a different issue entirely.

She poured boiling water over the coffee grounds. As it dripped through, she considered visiting Jack. It wasn't a new idea. Initially, India had loomed like an armed sentinel. Then Jack had said not to come.

Now? Now, she'd read—they'd read—the diary. She needed closure.

Teo's knock came as she searched the larder for something to eat. One thing she hadn't done yesterday was buy groceries. She opened the door. He extended India's horrible epitaph.

She set it aside. "You read all of it?"

"I did. It explained a lot."

"Let's eat first. Options, I'm afraid, are limited to a plain bagel and a plain bagel."

"Then I guess it's a bagel. I'll fix it, if you'll fix me a cup of coffee."

She smiled. "Deal."

After they'd eaten their Spartan breakfast, Teo suggested they look for a new apartment. "You really can't stay here."

He wasn't the first visitor to be appalled by the place. Even she knew it hadn't been a good choice for someone who'd been wallowing enough for three. Nodding, she headed toward her closet.

"I don't think you'll need a jacket," he said, "unless it's light one. We've got an Indian summer day out there."

She hated to mar the day and Teo's enthusiasm in it. She cleared her throat. "There's...there's something I have to do. Before anything else."

He quirked a brow.

"Jack. I've got to see Jack. First."

His face closed, hard and fast.

She reached toward him. "Please understand. I have to finish things."

The hard expression slowly eased. Finally, he nodded and let a smile just touch his eyes. She caressed his cheek lightly. "I've got to face this full on before I can think of any future."

"You know how to get there?"

"No."

"I'll look it up. Put it in the GPS."

They didn't talk as they climbed in the car and headed toward the clinic, but when Teo hit the turn signal that would bring them to the front of the building, she cleared her throat. And mentioned her other qualms, the needing versus wanting thing. He focused ahead. She used too many words, spoke too quickly, until suddenly she heard herself. "I'm sorry. I don't even know what I'm saying."

"Let's take it a step at a time." His voice was quiet and restrained. "Jack first."

Her stomach pressed bile upward, burning her throat. She dug in her purse for an antacid, ripping loose the pink chewables. She hated the thought of hurting Teo, but more than that, she dreaded confronting Jack.

THE SLAP of her shoes echoed on the tile floors, a counterpoint to the beeps and bings from monitors. The halls reeked of cleaning agents. She hesitated at Jack's door. He didn't want to see her, but now it wasn't only their own behavior they had to face. She knocked and entered.

His gaze followed her as she approached the bed. His scowl increased her nervousness. "Sam," he finally said.

She'd expected him to look terrible, but her expectations and this reality were worlds apart. Maybe he'd started to improve, but his sallow face and the black circles accentuated bones she'd only imagined. His once salt-and-pepper hair had gone completely gray—gun-metal instead of an attractive white.

"How are you?" She slid her fingers along the footboard.

Jack's stare moved to her fingers, making her so nervous that she shoved her hands in her pockets. "Fine." His voice had a bit of a rasp to it. "And you?"

She shrugged. "Fine."

"You don't look fine."

"Neither do you."

"I know." He pressed the lever to raise the bed's head and tugged the covers toward his chin. The knuckles on his hands had extended, as if he had newly acquired arthritis or newly lost tendons. His once muscular arms had shriveled into thin, sinewy sticks. "How was Italy?"

"Great. I had a wonderful time."

"Tootie said you were the one who found India."

She didn't even flinch at his abrupt words, but crossed to the window and peered down at the dirty street. Hospitals always seemed to have terrible views, either of rooftops full of power transformers, the worst-part-of-town streets, or back alleys and dumpsters. The temperature outside was unseasonably warm and the sky bright and sunshiny, but in here the air smelled stale. With her back to him, she said, "Yes. I found her."

"I'm sorry about that."

"I read the diary you sent. How could you not have known how bad it was?"

She expected some contrition, some puzzled wonder. Instead, he barely paused. "I just didn't. She never showed me that side of her."

Sam turned to stare at this man who spoke so calmly.

He ran a hand over his eyes and pinched the bridge of his nose. "I failed her, but she'd obviously been sick for years."

"I just don't get it—I don't get how you could have missed the signs."

"Hey, look, I said I don't know. I didn't know."

"You must have had hints." Her frustration built as she watched him. "Even I had hints from the way she talked when she came to the shop."

Jack reached over and with those claw-like hands picked up his cup of water, took a sip, and set it back on the table. "You want anything to drink? I could ask the nurse to bring you a juice or something."

"No. I just want to understand." She returned to the foot of his bed. "Don't you see? We killed her. You and I."

Jack blew a breath between his lips. It sounded disgusted, disgusting. "Don't be ridiculous. She was crazy. Her diary was full of rantings about finally going where her brother was. I mean, she used to talk to his ghost, for crying out loud, as if she actually saw somebody. She thought he came to her." Jack used the edge of his sheet to wipe off sweat that beaded on his forehead. "You saw what she wrote. And she's the one who pulled that trigger."

"But if we hadn't betrayed her, none of this would have happened. We were the catalyst."

"I don't think so. Seems to me she was doomed from the

beginning. Something else would have set her off if my leaving didn't."

Sam stared at the set of his jaw, at the coldness in his dark eyes. His only emotion seemed locked in those beads of sweat. Then memories flashed.

Why was she only now remembering Jack's squared shoulders, his fists balled at his side and eyebrows lowered until the rest of the world either gave in or watched his back as he walked away? She pressed her eyes shut, as if closing them would block the images and slow the blood that pumped loudly in her neck.

Maybe she hadn't remembered because she'd always been the one standing next to him. Or maybe it was because she'd always acquiesced before his shoulders squared.

Opening her eyes, she picked her words and slowly spoke them. "The times India came by—" And here she paused, choking down her anger so she wouldn't raise her voice at him. "She was over the top. But I told myself I must have been mistaken. If something were truly wrong, if she were ill, you would have noticed. That's how I rationalized it. I thought her crazy, but crazy as in odd, not as in sick."

"I only saw her alcoholism."

"You didn't look deeper. *I* didn't look deeper. And now she's dead. In my boat."

"I'm sorry about that. You understand why she picked *Alice*, don't you?"

Sam stared at him. "That's all you're sorry about? The boat?"

"Look, I'm sorry she was sick. I'm sorry she felt she had to kill herself. I'm sorry it happened in your boat and that you found her. But I'm not going to be sorry you and I loved each other."

"Did we? I'm beginning to think not." She glared into Jack's face to see if she could find any traces of the boy she had idolized. "Lust, yes. Love, no."

What stared back were a stranger's eyes. The signs had been there ever since she'd met up with him again, but she'd never let herself believe them. She shuddered. "I've got to go." She heard him call her name as she hurried down the hall.

42

SAMANTHA

The hairshirt prickles, scratching worry lines
Between my tears, because I turned things inside out
And lost the altruist.

Teo didn't say anything as she climbed in and buckled her seat belt. Nor did she. It was a shame. Lovely weather, messy lives.

He gave her hand a quick squeeze. "You can tell me what you want when you want, okay?"

"Do you suppose we could just drive around? Out into the country?"

"We can do that. I don't know about you," he said, picking up a paper bag and opening it, "but that bagel didn't quite cut it. I'm ready for food. You prefer chicken salad or ham?"

"Chicken salad. Thanks."

He started the car and pointed it into traffic. "Which direction?"

"East? At least that will get us away from this urban sprawl."

She bit into the sandwich and stared out the window,

nibbling more to keep busy than because she was hungry. When she'd finished a quarter of it, she reclined the seat and closed her eyes. Teo remained mercifully silent.

Her stomach growled. Maybe food hadn't been such a good idea after all. She pressed a hand against her abdomen, trying to silence it.

She'd spent so many years thinking she loved Jack. If that were an illusion, if she'd been that stupid once—okay, twice— what about now? With Teo?

Was she capable of loving a man? Any man?

The more she thought about her romantic history, the more she convinced herself that she shouldn't be here, pretending everything was fine. Pretending she might actually have a future with Teo. It wasn't fair to him. She ought just to tell him the truth and be done with it.

She took a deep breath, turned her face to the window, and said, "I don't think I should be with anyone."

"I'm sorry to hear that," he said in his calm, matter-of-fact voice.

She mumbled, "So many mistakes."

"Sorry, I didn't hear you."

Facing forward, she repeated the words. Out of the corner of her eye, she noticed his fingers loosen on the steering wheel. So, matter-of-fact had been only in tone. As miserable as she felt, that thought encouraged her. Which made her think she must be sick, too.

"Ahh," Teo said, drawing out the sigh. "The guilt thing."

Sam chewed on her lip.

"I was afraid it might be the gimp thing."

That jerked her around. "You mean, because you walk with a cane? Why should that bother me?"

"Remember I mentioned that Janet—my ex-wife—couldn't even stand the *thought* of mangled limbs and scars. Frankly, my dear, the image—up close and personal—is much worse." He cleared his throat and said in his best deadpan, "I have rather eschewed relationships myself."

She reached over to touch him. "Oh, Teo, your scars wouldn't bother me."

He kept his focus on the road. "Then, if it's merely the guilt thing," he said, "I need to remind you that none of us deserves much of anything. We certainly don't deserve forgiveness, but we do need to seek it."

"I can't believe how Jack acted. He doesn't even regret what we did! How can he not, with all these repercussions?" As the traffic thinned, Sam told him what Jack had said and about her final fear.

"So, it *is* more than just guilt. You're not sure you love me."

"Oh, Teo, you make it sound so cold. I feel as if I love you, but what if that's just an illusion, too? I don't have a very good track record."

"I have a solution for that." He glanced at her and flashed that smile of his, the one that made her insides turn all gooey. "We can wait as long as you need to. I'm a very patient man, and I'm in love with you."

She fumbled in her purse for a tissue to blow her nose. "There's something else."

"Oh, no." He was doing that twinkling-eye thing again.

"Not about you or us. About the guilt thi-ing." A hiccup caught her mid-word. She blew her nose again and took a deep breath. "I think what gets me most of all is that India hurt and all I did was abandon my post."

"Explain."

"I only made things worse for her by my self-centeredness." She twisted the tissue around her index finger. "I mean, who's going to listen to someone who's trying to steal her man? And I was. Me!" She jabbed toward her chest. "I wanted Jack to want me, not her." The tears started up again, but now they only made her mad. "See." She swiped at the wet with both hands. "I'm no better than I was then, 'cause here I am, feeling sorrier for myself than I do for India. She's the one dead, and I'm the one who could have offered her hope. If I hadn't been so focused on *me*."

Teo smiled gently. "Stefi was right."

"What do you mean?"

"She said you're good at guilt. Honey, you're not just good, you're first rate. How many people would heap that one on their shoulders? Especially considering the emotional shape you were in while you were dealing with India and Jack?"

"But it's true."

"Sure, it's true. But give yourself a break. You were hurting, too. You needed healing, too."

"But India's dead."

Teo took his right hand off the steering wheel and lifted her fingers to his lips. "Darling Samantha, you are not India's healer, nor her counselor, nor the one who consigned her to death. Trust just a little? Let yourself off the hook?"

"I hate it."

"I know, and maybe if Jack had been more observant, he would have realized how badly she needed help. If he hadn't been so tuned into what Jack wanted and needed and so out of tune with what his selfishness caused. He was the one living with her. Not you. And without help, India's illness doomed her."

"Jack used that same word. Do you think she would have killed herself if I hadn't come along?"

"Maybe, maybe not. Jack's failure to be what she needed stemmed as much from his humanity as from his selfishness. He was trying to compete with a superhuman lover, a memory who would never let India down, who would never be imperfect, because he was dead."

"Her brother," Sam said.

Teo nodded and hit his turn signal to pass a slower car. "Her brother would always remain the exalted one who saved her from misery when she was a child. He died before he could fail her, although, of course, in dying he abandoned her to their father, which merely made things worse."

He paused as he finished passing and eased the car back into the right lane. Then he said, "From what the diary reveals, my guess is she would have held on to the image of Rick in the immediate, Rick with her, if she could have believed herself worthy enough to keep him. Once she tried to kill Jack and knew she'd been caught at it, she was convinced her meanness drove Rick away. She was no longer able to get to him. She had failed."

"So, you're saying that if she hadn't tried to kill Jack, she wouldn't have killed herself."

"No, I'm only saying that I think the attempted murder hastened things. Jack would always fail India. And whatever catalyst worked to change her from a woman who took it out on herself by drinking too much to one who wanted vengeance for sins committed against her, that thing would mark the beginning of the end. Her negative self-image would be validated."

"And so she would imagine Rick leaving her?"

"Yes, and she'd need to find a way to get to him. Ultimately, to punish herself as Rick punished himself, thus sending her wherever Rick was."

"Incredible. And you got all that from reading her diary?"

"And from listening to you tell your story. From knowing you."

"Too bad," she said, turning away. "Too bad I couldn't have

figured it out way back when. Or Jack couldn't have. She so desperately needed help. And hope."

"You didn't have access to her thoughts. You didn't have the diary. And Jack had no hope to give her because he didn't have any himself. Which made him someone who used her —and you."

~

SHE'D SLEPT SO LITTLE the night before that her eyes grew heavy. She yawned.

"Lean the seat back" Teo said, "and close your eyes. You need a nap."

She smiled over at him. "I'm so tired I hurt."

"So, sleep. I'm fine."

~

OBVIOUSLY, she slept and for a while. She sat up, adjusted the seat back, and sighed. "Thank you. I feel so much better."

"I'm glad."

They'd left the highway. It looked familiar, but pine woods and fields often resembled each other. And then she spotted a barn she knew. And a lane. "Why are we here?"

"I thought you might need to visit again. We're burying ghosts today, aren't we?"

The car crunched over the familiar gravel as it rolled up the drive and came to a stop next to Tootie's Volvo. Sam didn't understand what Teo thought they'd accomplish, but as she climbed out, she felt a compulsion to head to the dock. She wanted to see if the yard men had returned *Alice* to her slip.

Her sweet little boat bobbed on the water as if nothing had

ever wounded her. Teo's hand touched Sam's back. "A lovely boat," he said.

"Uncle Teddy!" The screen door slammed, and Tootie bounded toward them. "I didn't know you were here!"

Laughing, he caught her on his good side and gave her a one-armed hug. "I am indeed. What are you doing home at this hour?"

"I just came back to get some papers I promised to run to New Bern for Holland." She turned to Sam. "How're you doing? Did you see *Alice*? Doesn't she look wonderful!"

"Absolutely."

"Do you want to sail her? The sails are back on, she's ready to go."

Sam's breath caught.

"Oh, I'm sorry," Tootie said, reaching out to touch her arm. "I didn't think."

"No." Sam laid a hand on top of Tootie's. "Don't be sorry. I do want to go. I didn't realize it, but I do. I think I need to."

"You want company?" Teo asked.

Sam relaxed enough to grin at him. "You want to brave the water again, O mighty mariner?"

"I could. For you, I would."

"Maybe next time. Now, I've some ghosts of my own to settle."

"You can hang out with me, Unc." Tootie squeezed Teo's arm, her smile stretching across her face as she rocked on the balls of her feet. "Maybe you'd go with me, you know, so we can visit. We've got so much to catch up on, and Jenny's watching the shop, so it's okay," she said in Sam's direction before whipping her gaze back toward Teo. "Maybe after, we could have dinner with Holland. You liked him, didn't you?"

"I did."

"Then, will you come?"

He raised his brows in Sam's direction, and Tootie's expression changed quickly. "And, Sam, you could meet us for dinner if you want. Or I've got leftover meatloaf at the house. My special recipe."

Sam smiled. "The meatloaf sounds delicious. Thank you."

"Wonderful!" Tootie said. "Oh, this is so perfect."

"Samantha?" Teo stepped toward her and asked quietly, "What do you really want to do? Tell me."

"Sail. And then enjoy the porch and the view. I'll be fine."

"You don't want me to come get you so you can join us for dinner?"

She shook her head. "No, you guys go and enjoy yourselves. I need some time alone."

Tootie shielded her eyes with her hand and looked up at the sky. "Those clouds don't look bad, do they? I think they're far enough away, but if you need a jacket, I'll run and get one. And boat shoes? You have some in your closet?"

"The navy canvas ones."

"Be right back," Tootie called over her shoulder as she dashed back to the house. Teo seemed slightly bemused as he watched his niece.

Taking his hand, Sam led him down the steps to the dock. "It's fine," she repeated. "I'm looking forward to a peaceful sail." When they stood in front of her boat, she said, "Let me introduce you to *Alice*. Isn't she sweet?"

"She's safe? I mean, you'll be okay? Those clouds don't mean anything?"

"I'll be fine. I won't go far."

She climbed on board, holding the starboard shroud for balance. As she removed the sail cover and ties and handed them off to Teo, she said, "You need to spend time with Tootie. She's thrilled you're here."

Teo glanced toward the house. "Just don't stay out too late, will you? It'll get dark early. And it might cool off."

"Tootie's getting me a jacket. And I'll come in early."

The jib was in its bag but already hanked on, as if someone were expecting to go out soon. Pulling off the bag, she ran the sheets through their blocks and tied off the ends. Tootie handed her the jacket and a bottle of water and waited while Sam changed shoes and hoisted the jib. At Sam's command, Tootie tossed the dock lines on board and shoved against *Alice's* bow.

Sam pulled in the jib sheet and pushed the tiller hard over, smiling as *Alice* slipped quietly into South River. Once they were far enough out, she hoisted the main, then turned and waved at Tootie and Teo.

"Here we are, *Alice,* just the two of us." Her whisper lifted with the breeze that filled the sails.

Were there ghosts? Sam wasn't admitting any. She was too busy thinking sail trim.

She rounded the point into the Neuse and set the sails for a beam reach. With the wind across *Alice's* midsection, they could make the return trip without the work of constant tacking. She lost track of time as the wind caressed her cheeks and the water slapped against the hull. She waved to a man paddling out in a red kayak, but he was across the river, keeping close to shore, and probably hadn't seen her. Gulls squawked at one another, providing the only other company on the water.

She barely noticed the wind dying. The motion slowed, the main slacked, and soon *Alice* began to drift lazily.

Sliding one of the boat cushions behind her, Sam leaned against the gunwale and watched the kayaker. With no wind to fight, he had ventured farther into the river and paddled steadily. At that rate, he'd soon catch up with *Alice.* She smiled.

There were so many different ways people chose to move across water—the kayaker with his paddle, her children with their outboard motor, Sam with sails.

The sun's warmth relaxed her. She loved the gentle lap-lap of the water, the peace of just *being*. She hadn't felt the pure pleasure of that in a long time.

She closed her eyes and let the small movements, like the faint rise and fall of *Alice's* slow advance, adjust her rhythm, the in and out of her breathing. Her chest rose as the bow did, then fell with *Alice's* dip. Tuning out thoughts of the cloudy horizon, her guilt-ridden past, and her uncertain future, she focused only on the moment.

43

SAMANTHA

Better watch out. Better stay good.
Better not wait. Better just pray.

Moving past the inertia took effort. Sam glanced up at the still slack sails and sighed. She shouldn't have drifted so far downriver without a cell phone or hope of a tow. Now she tried not to remember how much effort paddling took.

Oh, well, the exercise would be good for her muscles, all that stretching and pulling on the oar. She yawned as she sat up. She'd just tie off the tiller and play boatman again, paddling on one side and then the other.

The oar lived up under the foredeck on the port side. She crossed behind the centerboard well and moved a cushion aside to look for it, surprised that she didn't see it extending into the cockpit.

It wasn't there.

She searched the starboard side. No oar. She couldn't

believe it. How had she left the dock without checking? She *always* carried something to make sure she could get home.

Okay, but *Alice* had been in the repair yard. Maybe the men had taken it out and not put it back. Or maybe Tootie had stored it in the shed.

"Look at me," Sam said to the gull staring from its height some ten feet off the deck. "I broke another cardinal rule: sails on, oar on. I assumed. I know. Never assume." The gull soared in a circular pattern and squawked. "Exactly. Stupid."

She glanced from the gull to the bank and saw no sign of the kayaker. He must have turned around and paddled his way home. Lucky fellow.

Flopping back on the cushion, she remembered that Teo would send help when her white sails didn't zip around the headland.

But that euphoric thought only lasted as long as it took to think it. The truth was, Teo was driving to New Bern with Tootie and then to meet Holland in Morehead. Who knew when they'd be back? She'd even told them not to worry.

Great. No oar. No Teo.

Still, she wasn't alone. She had *Alice*.

She knew her boat so well. And *Alice* knew her. Sam had never been afraid when she was in *Alice*, except momentarily when she'd faced an approaching storm. *Alice* had always carried her home.

Except...that was before. She shook off the thought. She wouldn't believe that *Alice* was tainted—or cursed—because of what had happened on board. She wouldn't.

Without wind, the sun felt quite warm. She reached over the side and scooped handfuls of water, then let the wet drip through her fingers. Touching the rail, she rubbed her palm over the recently varnished brightwork. How smooth and lustrous it felt. *Alice* was so clean, the cockpit so white. No vestiges of....

India had climbed in—right here. She'd stretched out on the cockpit floor. She'd picked up the gun.

What had it felt like, the gun in her hand? Sam shuddered and imagined touching the cold metal, lifting it... *Oh God.*

And the blood. There'd been blood all over. She could see it now, the picture she'd suppressed, the ugliest, most horrible, worst sight she'd ever witnessed. And the saddest. *Oh Lord.* The saddest.

The blood must have seeped into the caulked areas near the centerboard well, imbedded itself in the nonskid so it showed as a lumpy, granular red.

And just there to the left—what was that? An indentation in the floor. It hadn't been there before.

She crawled forward, stared.

A messy putty job. She had to see what was under it. If she could just get a little off the top, pull a little out, not all of it, just enough to see its shape. To know.

As she dug, a fingernail snapped, then tore. "Ow!"

She bit it off, smothering the words in her head. There had to be some tool she could use.

There it was, the small box that always stayed under the foredeck. Why had it found its way back on board when the oar hadn't? She rifled through the box, then backed up and aimed the clutched screwdriver. A quick stab. The putty gave, soft under the paint. Pressing the blade deeper, she twisted. A tiny chunk caught. Not enough.

"Come *on.*" She raised her fist, stabbed down, then pushed the blade under and twisted again. It popped out in one gross blob of gunk. She stared into the hole.

And saw why the putty hadn't stuck.

The color wasn't red now, more a dark brownish. The

bullet had gone through India's head into that hole. Forcing blood and who knew what else in with it.

Sam exhaled the breath she'd been holding. As counterpoint, a wind rose and grabbed the sails. She was far from the tiller, without control, when the wind slapped the boom over in an accidental gybe. *Alice* rocked crazily. Shaking from the near miss of the boom mere inches above her head—inches that had saved her from being knocked flat, or knocked overboard, or killed—she scurried aft and clutched the tiller as *Alice* heeled out of control, close to being swamped.

Dear God, please, Sam prayed silently, then whispered, "Please don't let us capsize," as she grabbed the main sheet and yanked it free of the jam cleat—which she never used except in very light winds. Never in anything like this. The boom flew to port, spilling the wind and setting *Alice* on her feet again. Slowly, Sam felt the blood easing in her neck and head.

The gust had come so suddenly. She looked around, unbelieving. She'd been so concerned about a stupid lump in her boat that she'd missed the cloud, missed the catspaws ruffling the surface, which had abruptly turned to waves as the wind shifted and built.

She knew that *Alice* wouldn't sink in a capsize. They'd gone over once, she and the kids when Daniel had the helm and hadn't been paying attention to a gust. Over they'd flipped, landing with all their goodies in the drink. He'd been embarrassed, especially when they'd discovered that bailing a righted *Alice* was an exercise in futility. The boat filled so far up the gunwales that more water flooded in than they could empty. They'd clung to *Alice's* sides and floated to shore on an incoming tide, while Stefi berated her brother and grew slightly hysterical, even though Sam assured her that there were no sharks in the Neuse River, that they'd get home, and that Stefi needed to think of this as an adventure.

"I hate adventures," her daughter had said, not really meaning it.

But that day the air had been ninety-five degrees, with the water just chilly enough to be fun. Today? After a month of frigid nights, some very cold days, and even one slight snowfall, the river would not be a benign friend. Besides, the tide was headed out to sea, not in.

"Just keep your head, Sam."

She felt the wind grow with each gust and looked up to see clouds rushing to cover the sun. How had they filled the sky so quickly? And with the wind came waves that grew and splashed at *Alice's* topsides, drenching them both and threatening her as much, if not more than the wind.

A drop of rain hit, then another. She thought of Tootie's jacket, tucked forward under the deck, but she was afraid to cleat the main sheet. One gust of wind could heel *Alice* past her righting moment, and over they'd go. Sam's heart bounced along with her stomach, and, in spite of the chill, sweat seeped from her pores as she held on for the ride, trying to think ahead, to decide where to tack and change direction to get *Alice* pointed home.

And then, just as she began to think she'd gained some control, she heard a sharp twang, then a thud that reverberated through the deck, and finally a splash. Her fingers tightened as she searched frantically for the source of the sound.

"Oh, no, please no."

The starboard shroud had snapped and trailed uselessly in the water.

If her heart had been pumping double time before, now it raced. She shoved the tiller hard over, trying to use forward momentum to get the bow into the unrelenting wind and waves. If she didn't haul those sails down immediately, the mast might snap and break, putting a hole in the boat. *Alice* might sink.

A sob followed and another "Please."

She yanked the jib sheet free and tied off the tiller to keep the boom centerline. Batting the flogging main out of her way, she struggled to keep her balance as *Alice* bucked in waves that seemed to slam from fore and aft. Each surge became the moment before disaster, each creak a drum roll. She scurried forward, released the main halyard and then grabbed fistfuls of sail, tucking the heavy new Dacron into the cockpit as it fell. The wind fought to catch the sail and toss it overboard.

Why had she gotten rid of that old, floppy main? She bemoaned her wilted, easily handled, though badly stretched mainsail. The last ring settled on the boom. "And why on earth did I think I wanted to be out here alone? Fool. *Fool.*"

She uncleated the jib's halyard and yelled at the sail as it whipped across the foredeck, "I need help!" Then she reached for the downhaul. Her hands fumbled, found the two halyards, both jib sheets, the tail of some line. They did not find the one narrow nylon line attached to the head of the sail that would keep her from having to go out on that messy deck to haul it down. With the downhaul, she could handle the jib from where she stood, safely in the cockpit. It had to be here.

But it wasn't.

"Okay, fine. Okay, *fine!*"

It was all too much. Way too much. Hanging on to the mast, she watched *Alice* dance and slam as waves sprayed up and drenched her. Sam's attention focused on the slippery deck, the flailing jib. She had to crawl over that deck, then balance on it, hanging out over the bowsprit while she yanked the sail down. The rain vied with the waves to see which could make her more miserable.

"This...is...not...fun...any...more." Her voice rasped out the words as she bent to hunt up sail ties. "You listening, wind?" She pushed the anchor line out of the way, trying to find the bucket where she normally kept the ties.

"No sail ties either?" What had she done with the ones on the main? Oh, right. Handed them to Teo along with the cover and the jib bag.

She squeezed shut her eyes. "Okay, get a grip." She had to keep her head and her balance, no matter how disgusted she was. She climbed up on the foredeck, one hand firmly on the mast until she had no choice but to let go, and then she crawled—very carefully—toward the bowsprit.

The rough non-skid pricked her knees and bare ankles, but she pushed on until she was far enough out to reach the forestay. Leaning forward over the very slippery, very shiny, very *narrow* mahogany sprit, she grabbed hold with numbing fingers that didn't want to fold over the skinny metal wire. She tried to focus on the stay and the sail so she wouldn't see the dark waves below.

One move at a time. Slowly...

A wave curled under the bow, raising, then dropping the bowsprit, the deck, and Sam, before *Alice* plowed through the back of the next wave. Blinded by the water, Sam let go to wipe her eyes, but immediately felt herself slipping and lunged for the stay again.

The water was so close. So cold. "Hold on, girl," she told herself, hearing Rhea's voice in the echo of her words. If only Rhea were with her now. Rhea would shake her fist at that wind.

And know how to pray.

Tears stung Sam's eyes, but she told herself to concentrate and tugged hard on the sail with her free hand. "Now'd be a good time for one of those calm-the-seas miracles, God. You know, like back when your boys were out in the storm?"

He must not have heard—or cared—because the wind continued to howl, and the rain pelted with renewed vigor. Trying not to feel slighted, Sam spat at dripping hair that flipped in her face. She brushed it ineffectually with her shoulder because she couldn't spare a hand. "Soon as I get back, the hair goes."

She didn't have enough hands to keep the sail from trailing overboard as she lowered it, or ties to keep it on the deck once she had it down. Improvising, she looped a section of the jib sheet over the bunched sail and knotted it to the Samson posts. Too cold and exhausted to worry about how well the knots would hold, she edged back to the cockpit. Her feet landed on heaped mainsail, squishing into the puddled water.

She thought about bailing and rolled her eyes. There probably wasn't even a bailer on board. "With my luck?" She shook her head and imagined the old bleach bottle sitting in the barn next to the oar and the sail ties.

When the wind tried to grab a loose foot on the sail, she stomped it down. Pulling the jacket over her wet shirt, she wiped a sleeve across her face, took hold of the tiller, and squared her shoulders.

Fine, she didn't have sails. Fine, there was way too much wind and too much rain. But she wasn't out of the game yet. "Right, *Alice*? You're still with me in this, aren't you?"

Another wave slapped the starboard quarter, sending spray into the cockpit. Sam tucked her hair behind her ears and held on.

"Okay, *Alice* old girl." She patted the stern area near her perch. "Can you help me out here?"

She did *not* want to imagine potential disaster. She didn't want to think what could happen if the current shot them straight toward the widest part of Pamlico Sound, toward Hatteras, toward the ocean. Jack had told her stories of boats tackling the sound in a storm and losing, and those were big boats. Little *Alice* rocketed along with no motor, no oar, no sails, and only one scared woman clutching the tiller for dear life. And clutch was exactly what she had to do if she wanted to control the rudder and try to point the bow into the back of the wave and not let *Alice* take any of them beam on. If a big enough wave grabbed the boat's side, it could tip them right over. And keep them there.

She never, ever took *Alice* out when a storm threatened, but it hadn't looked like anything other than a beautiful afternoon with a few clouds hovering on the horizon. And then, all full of herself, she'd told Teo and Tootie to have a grand time and not worry about her. "See you later," she'd said.

"*Ciao*."

It might not even be raining wherever Teo and Tootie were. She glanced over her shoulder to check on the size of the storm, but couldn't see beyond the near bank.

Considering the drive from New Bern to Morehead and then here—plus Tootie's errand time, plus traffic and maybe even coping with rush hour around Cherry Point—they could be gone for hours. Sam pictured them laughing, certain that she was having a gay old time on the water. Because, even if they also had to cope with rain, they might not have wind. And, even if they had wind, they might think the storm local. And, even if they knew it rained down here, they'd tell themselves that Sam would have sailed *Alice* right on back to the dock and tucked her safely in her slip. They'd toast Sam's health, imagining her up at the house, sipping something hot and warming up dinner. They might phone, but when she didn't answer, they'd just shake their head and laugh at Sam for not carrying her cell.

Had she ever talked to Tootie about boating disasters? No. She'd made it all seem glorious and fun. And she'd portrayed herself as a woman with experience. Someone who could handle herself and her boat. She'd puffed herself up, and she'd felt good doing it. Now look at her.

What a fool! An arrogant, in-too-much-of-a-hurry *fool*.

Her only hope lay in Teo's horrible sailing experience. Maybe he'd see the wind and be frightened for her. Maybe the dark sky would get him moving.

44

SAMANTHA

One breath can tatter demon hoards,
And we've but a few to scatter.

Sam glanced away from the waves long enough to scan the horizon. Rain and heavy clouds obscured any sun, but it looked as if full darkness would soon descend because of these wretchedly short days. She had no idea how far they'd drifted, but the river had widened quite a bit, which meant she was definitely in the sound.

She had to get off the water. If *Alice* had sails up, she'd tack until she reached the populated side of the river. The drift of the current carried her forward, and the wind-waves pushed *Alice* at a good clip toward an unlit shore. It was time to take advantage of whatever force worked and let the waves move the boat wherever they would take her, because any shoreline beat the alternative. From what she could see, there were only trees, a field or two, then marsh grass, which would be a soft landing but hard to walk through. The best Sam could do was hope for a decent landing spot before it got any darker.

"Come on, girl, you can do it." She hoped *Alice* believed her. Up went another prayer. This was her foxhole, all right.

It took all her strength to battle the push of the waves on the rudder and point at an angle toward the bank. She hoped to land near a field and follow it to a road of some kind, though she had very little control of the landing spot. Keeping her eyes on the bank, she scanned the landscape. An uprooted tree loomed, its arms menacing. Sam pushed the tiller hard to port, but *Alice's* bow continued to aim for that tree as if the tree were a magnet slurping up slivers of iron.

"Not that way!" Sam's yell competed with a grunt as she leaned over and fought the force of the waves. "Over there. Just a little more to the right. Come on, *Alice*, you can do it. Work with me here."

Her trajectory lined up with one of the biggest limbs on the tree, big enough to poke a good-sized hole in *Alice's* side. It didn't seem to matter how hard Sam pushed on the stupid tiller. The boat wanted to commit suicide.

Bad analogy, Sam.

"Whoa!" She cried out at the last minute, squeezing her eyes shut and ducking her head. But she didn't let go of that tiller. Her breathing might have stopped, and her shoulders might have hunched up into her neck, but she pressed on the tiller as hard as her poor muscles would let her. And she groaned, unable to form words.

It was over in a moment. Instead of the impact she'd expected, she heard only a few scraping sounds against the hull and felt only the scratch of small branches against her arms and hands. She had barely opened her eyes to look around when the centerboard crunched into sand, stopping them dead and knocking Sam forward into the cockpit. As she fell, she flung her right arm forward to brace herself. This time, she spat out a curse with no apologies.

Carefully, she tested her arm. It wasn't broken, though it sure had whacked the centerboard well. At least her head hadn't hit anything.

And at least they'd landed.

The wind turned the boat beam to, and the waves smacked against *Alice's* side. Each time the hull slammed down, the centerboard hit, jolting everything within reach, including Sam's bones. She grabbed the nearest cleat for a handhold, stood, and yanked up on the line that raised the board, praising the boat as she drifted toward shore. Bending down to drag out the anchor, she found its line bunched and tangled.

Of course, she did.

She untangled the line. With no space to secure the anchor rode to the already cluttered Samson posts, she tied it to the base of the mast and slipped over the side. Mistake. The freezing river splashed past her thighs and felt like stabbing ice picks.

Stupid, stupid. Why hadn't she just tossed the anchor? Sure, *Alice* might have pounded against the bank, but she wouldn't have risked freezing to death. Her mind must be dulled. Or she was getting old. In all her years of sailing, she'd never compounded so many life-threatening mistakes.

Her boat shoes slurped up water with each step as she towed *Alice* toward shore. She set the anchor as high up the bank as the line would reach, then looked in vain for a path through the woods—which she was *not* investigating in the dark—or for a way to walk in either direction to search for cleared land. Fallen trees blocked the left side, and, on the right, the woods met the river where the water had eroded an undercut in the bank.

With her face to the sky and rain hitting it square on, she called, "I'm here. What's next?"

Shivering, she couldn't think. She was drenched, freezing, lost, hungry, and without any land-based shelter from the rain except in those gloomy, wet woods behind her. Not that they'd exactly keep the rain out unless she dug a hole. She could cover herself with leaves. Didn't Boy Scouts do that or something like it?

But she wasn't a Boy—or Girl—Scout. She'd never had the slightest interest in camping, and she didn't want to start practicing wilderness techniques now. What she wanted was someone to hold her, to make the cold go away, to make the hunger go away. To make the *day* go away.

Okay, she didn't actually mean that. She'd take daylight over this encroaching darkness anytime. She jumped up and down, trying to force some warmth back into her limbs, but the rain and wind were not helping. Woods or boat? Which was it going to be? The boat was wet and cold, but she could hide under the sail. The woods were wet and cold, but she could shelter, a little bit, under the trees.

As if from the bowels of those same dark woods, something screeched in a long, high note. In seconds, she was back in the water, high-tailing it out of there just as a second scream pierced the air. She was *not* going to wait for some cougar to sniff her out and make *himself* warm by eating *her*.

She was trying not to get depressed here. Really. She was.

She hooked a leg over the side of the boat, but waves caught the hull broadside and bounced it so much that all she could do was hop around like a one-legged jackass and yelp as she collapsed backward into the water.

She came up spluttering and began to blow the freezing water out of her nose. She grabbed a stern line with shaking hands and dragged it to one of the large branches they'd just missed on the way in. The taut line kept *Alice's* bow pointed inland so the waves slid more easily under her transom. The boat still bounced, but not as forcefully.

Now so cold she couldn't stop shivering, Sam clambered back in the cockpit and hunted for the bailer, just in case one was on board. Her hands shook violently as she pushed away a soaked life jacket and found it.

Thank goodness. One right thing.

Scoop, toss, scoop, toss. Her teeth chattered. Tears filled her eyes, and her nose clogged.

Hadn't she said just that afternoon that she wanted to be independent, to learn how to stand on her own emotionally?

"I think I've...I've changed my mind. Y...you hear?"

Finally, when she'd bailed as much as she could, she took the two boat cushions and crawled under the cold, heavy, dripping mainsail. She had to stay low to keep the wind from whipping the sail out of the boat, but she managed to place the cushions under her and to cover herself.

And the rain continued to fall, splat, patter, splat, patter against the wood, against the Dacron sail.

Please, please let someone come.

She pushed dripping hair out of her face and rubbed her arms, avoiding the bruise. *Alice* rocked and rolled, jamming Sam's knees against the side of the hull. She repositioned to brace herself, shifting the cushions to protect her bones.

That wasn't any good, because now her shoulder and hip felt the beat of wood on water. Her head rested on bunched sail, which crackled with every movement as only new Dacron could.

Had Teo left Morehead? Had he missed her yet? Was he worried? How many hours could she survive like this?

She huddled under cover, but the wet still dripped on her from the sail, and her dunking had soaked what the rain hadn't. Her toes wouldn't even wiggle. And the shivering wouldn't stop.

She'd already decided Teo wouldn't worry if she didn't answer the phone. He'd just think her out of range or busy. And when he did get back and did worry and did think to send someone, it could be hours from now. She might never warm up.

The Indian summer day was a thing of the past. What would night bring? If the storm lowered the air temperature to freezing when her body temperature was already precariously low, and all she had for protection were sopping clothes and a soaked mainsail... How long did it take for hypothermia to set in? How long before the numbness climbed up past her toes and fingers and slipped into her blood? Before her interior thermostat just quit, and she went to sleep forever? She could actually die right here, and all they'd find would be her stiff body.

Because, even if they looked, how would anyone find *Alice* in the dark, this many miles from home? On the wrong side of the sound. Her dark blue hull invisible against the black woods.

In between shivers and chattering teeth, Sam tried to calm herself. She tried to picture a rescue boat zipping over the water, straight toward her, Teo at the bow, directing them.

Teo? Teo, who'd never been on this river, who barely knew the front from the back end of a boat? The image almost brought a smile, but it turned to a cackle, which nearly choked her as tears dripped across her already wet face.

Stop it. Get a grip.

She was a big girl. She could manage. She hated the self-pity she made friends with for too long. Wasn't this whole trip about coping? Dealing with issues?

She rubbed harder on her upper arms and tried to think of a song that would cheer her, but her mind blanked. Night had fallen completely now, making her cocoon pitch black. They might postpone any search until morning. Considering the storm. The waves, the rain, the wind. No one would want to go out in this. She didn't want to be out in it either.

She wouldn't think about that. She didn't want to imagine dying out here like this. Not yet. Not with so much left unresolved.

She'd just turn her mind to other things. Happier things.

She pictured Venice, the canal below the window. The smell of the water tinged with salt, the buildings with age. Old stone. Old lives. Old memories.

And Teo so gentle, so loving and patient. If only she could feel those sensuous lips playing over hers, warming her blood. She moaned at the thought.

He'd take her in his arms, his hands would rub her back, his breath would heat her flesh.

Did she love him as she'd begun to think?

Not a good question right now.

She wished...she wished for so many things. Mostly, she wished for warmth. And Teo's arms.

That was almost worse, imagining things so far from what she had or was likely to have anytime soon. So far from what she might ever have.

No, no. No more negative thoughts. Curling into herself, she lay with her arm pressed to the cockpit floor, trying to stop her muscles from convulsing. Shivering was supposed to be the body's way of warming itself, but it *hurt*. And she was growing so tired.

A rough edge, rougher than the surrounding non-skid, pricked the skin of her hand, and she rubbed fingers across it.

There it was again. That bullet hole.

She couldn't get away from it. Not from the blood, nor from the image of that dark spot shadowed on the white. She tried to breathe deeply, but she felt as if she were suffocating. She lifted the edge of the sail and took a long, slow breath, in and then out again. In and then out.

Please, oh, please.

Here she was. Lying right on top of where India had died. She touched the hole.

Poor, poor India. *If only.* But India couldn't offer forgiveness. She was dead.

I wish...I wish.

What? What did she wish for? She could never undo the harm. Or the death.

Her fault.

So sorry. So, so sorry.

She didn't know how much time passed as she wept. At some point, her thoughts evolved into a different kind of plea. And though hiccups finally stopped the flood, she lay curled in the dark, seeing years of choices that had brought her to this moment. Years of acting the victim. Years of blaming her past, her present, her father, her husband. Years when she'd filtered perfect love—like a sunscreen held up to dampen the light— and basked in the little slivers she'd let through. Thinking, that's all there was. Thinking, that's all she deserved.

Realizing, finally, that the fist in which she'd clutched her tiny portion had been the fist that had opened her to the mess with Jack.

Her stomach hurt from hiccupping. And her heart hurt from peering behind the screen.

Okay. She was a mess. Fine.

Could she ever get past here?

As she asked that, she felt a gentle whispering that enveloped her. Not words. More like the soughing of wind through a pine woods.

The whispering inside grew louder. And a thought tickled her brain, slithered in there and grabbed her: she could let go of it all.

She squinched her eyes shut. She couldn't quite bring herself to ask about India. Or to wonder about the plan for Jack. But was it really so simple? She begged for it to be so. And as she begged, she again wept.

These tears were different, cleansing. For the first time in years, she felt her heart begin to ease. The hiccups stopped. And she lay waiting, hearing the whisper.

Until the shivers grabbed her teeth and clacked them against each other almost in time to the beat of rain against the sail. It hurt so badly as her jaw tensed more with each clack and her body shook, clutching at her muscles, tightening them, loosing momentarily, tightening again in shudders that took so much energy. She wanted to sleep. She wanted it to quit.

But it didn't.

If only she had a flashlight. No, a spotlight. Something big to signal any boat coming to the rescue. Because, surely, one would come. Sometime. Before it was too late.

Surely.

She felt so exhausted. So weak. Maybe she could just rest her eyes, rest her mind for a little while.

But, no, if she slept, she wouldn't know when rescue came. Or when the weather got too cold to bear. That's how folk froze to death. They just got so cold, they went to sleep. Instead, she went back to praying, asking again for calm. She knew she was helpless to change anything.

Nothing new there.

Why did she keep doing that? Focusing on the negative?

She'd just been touched, hadn't she? That had to count for something.

A picture flashed into her mind of a cat's cradle woven around her old self. As she watched, it morphed and finally unraveled.

So, how did she keep it that way? How did she keep herself from being cobwebbed by her past?

She heard again Teo's voice. "Trust," he'd said. "Trust," he whispered now.

FINALLY, a motor roared more loudly than the storm.

She wasn't dead. Oh, goodness, she wasn't dead.

She pushed aside the sail and tried to stand, but her legs wobbled. She could only scramble weakly to her knees, hanging on to the sides.

A beam of light scanned the water. She tried to yell, but the words sounded more like a whimper. The light moved slowly across the waves, just out of reach. She used her arms to hoist herself onto the side deck.

"Here...I'm here!" This time her voice cracked. "He-re!"

They had to hear. They had to. The beam hit the tree's roots, and she yelled again, her crying-and-cold-weakened voice warbling the sound. Then the beam slid away in the other direction. How could she get their attention? She searched frantically around her feet as if that might magically produce a flare or a horn. Something. Anything.

"No! This way!" But her cry wafted on the wind. A sob bubbled in her throat, forcing its way out on a barely heard scream. "No!"

The light flitted on down the bank.

It couldn't be leaving. *Please, no.*

If Teo were there, he'd hear her. He'd know. "Teo! I'm here."

The light and the engine noise both dimmed.

"No, please! Here!"

They couldn't go. They had to see. But the light continued to recede.

She dropped to her knees on the puddled mess of sail. Maybe this was what she deserved. Maybe this was where it would end.

She knew it had seemed too simple. A quick prayer, an ooey-gooey feeling, and then absolution? That's not how life worked, was it?

Foxhole prayers. She'd been tossing up a dying woman's prayer.

A gust of wind slammed *Alice* and rocked Sam off her knees. The wind wasn't lessening. The rescuers hadn't found her. Now they'd give up and go home. And she'd be here. Alone.

She didn't want to be alone and freezing. Hungry, hurting, angry that she'd gotten herself into this predicament.

Then, flowing into her anger, she felt it again, and the whispering murmured in the air. Her bones felt it: even if no one found her, she wasn't alone.

Was this the end, then? Was it her time?

She examined the thought as it flitted around her. She was so tired. So cold. And she'd hurt for so long. Carried the guilt and the fear for way too long.

Maybe that's how India'd felt. Tired of all her pain. Of a lifetime of pain she couldn't change.

Alice bounced wildly again, but Sam felt steadied. And suddenly she knew. She heard Teo's words: accept forgiveness and forgive. That was the thing she had left to do. Forgive Jack.

Forgive India, and Greg, and her father. Her past. Her present. And forgive the one person she couldn't seem to, herself.

Easier said than done.

Ah. The whisper covered her. It spoke, and she felt the love. She actually *felt* it. Could it truly be that easy?

Could it? She let that thought and the wonder of it slide around inside her as she waited. "God, is that you?"

Jesus?

Then, above the soft sighing voice in her mind, above the wind and waves, she heard, again, an engine.

She raised her head, pushed herself up and held on to the boom to keep from falling. As she strangled out a "Here I am! Here," the light approached, inching along the bank toward her. It glanced off the beach, caught the branches, then *Alice's* stern, until finally it blinded Sam. She blinked and turned away. *Oh, thank you! Thank you!*

She heard voices, the boat's engine revving. Then a splash, and Teo yelled, "I'm coming!"

For a man who limped along with a cane, he certainly moved through that water. The river was too shallow for the big boat to come all the way in, so poor Teo got soaked as he slogged toward shore. Then he lifted her over the side of *Alice* and hugged her to him.

"You came," she whispered.

"I heard you call," he said, tightening his grip. "I drove like a madman to get back." Another shiver passed through her, and he bent lower. "Oh, baby, you're freezing. Come on, let's get you dry."

Sam's head dropped against his shoulder as he carried her across to the other boat. A man yelled that he had the anchor and would set up a tow line. And then Teo handed her up to waiting arms.

Soon, someone draped a blanket over her and someone else

tried to hand her a cup of steaming broth, which she couldn't hold. Teo took it below, before he helped her maneuver down the steps and over to a bunk. Gently, he stripped her of her sodden clothes. He dried her off, pulled a huge sweatshirt over her head, and stepped her into a pair of pants way too big, but they and the wool socks he slipped on her feet were dry. After wrapping her hair in another towel, he held her hands between his and blew warm breath over them.

Then he turned his back and unzipped his own dripping slacks, letting them fall to the floor. His wet shirt and jacket suffered the same fate. Sam watched as he picked up the towel he'd used on her and wiped himself dry, lifting one leg and then another. When he stuck his feet in oilskins, she wondered what it would be like when he first turned so she could see him full on. The thought made her grin. What it would be like when she had the right to touch those rippling back muscles, skin to skin. She felt warmth zipping through her veins for the first time in hours, and a heat that had nothing to do with dry clothes built in her belly.

He donned a dry sweatshirt and turned to catch her staring. She blushed.

Grinning, he sat down next to her and touched her cheek with his fingertips. She felt a smile curve her lips, though she knew it was still small and a tad crooked. "Oh, Teo. I was so scared."

His arm circled and drew her toward him until she nestled close. "I'm sorry it took me so long to find you. But you're safe now." The oilskins crinkled when he moved to kiss her, and more warmth suffused her insides as those lips worked their magic.

She forgot to ask him how he'd heard her from the car. How he'd found her. How they'd known which side of the bank to search. Instead, she slept.

~

S<small>AM DIDN'T KNOW</small> who steered *Alice* as the powerboat towed her poor, bedraggled boat, or who helped tie the sails once they got back to the dock. She remembered thanking her rescuers profusely as Teo helped her up to the house, where Tootie waited with a hot shower and clothes that fit.

"I'm cooking up some dinner for everyone," Tootie said, propelling her toward the bathroom, "so come on down when you're ready." And to Teo, "I'll toss your things in the dryer while you use the other bath."

Sam stayed under the spray until the water cooled. Finally warm again, she descended the steps to the living room. Tootie rattled about in the kitchen, doing something with pots that sounded very loud and smelled very good. Teo stood with his back to her, watching what was left of the storm, *her* storm, wear itself out over the river. He turned and smiled, then held out his hand. Sam pressed herself into his hug as he set his cane aside.

How glorious he felt as her arms circled his neck. The big sweatshirt he still wore smelled slightly of diesel, but there was no mistaking the underlying scent of the man.

Her man. Her very own. Incredible.

"I love you, Mr. Anderson."

His grin flashed as he looked down at her. "You finally sure about that?"

"Absolutely."

Laughter bubbled out of Sam as he pulled her into his arms and whispered, "About time." Over his shoulder, she saw Tootie and Holland grinning from behind the center island. "Are you guys hungry yet?" Tootie asked.

That's when Sam noticed the table set for four, the platter of spaghetti waiting on the counter, the bowl of salad next to it. She heard a log shift on the hearth and breathed a deep and satisfying sigh. She'd finally found home again. As she took Teo's hand, she knew it didn't matter where that was—here or nearer Raleigh and her children or even part time in an apartment in Reggio. As long as she had a place for *Alice*. And Teo beside her.

EPILOGUE

TEO

Notes tinkled on piano keys, a lens's vision on the screen
Of floating ice, rocks rimmed with snow,
Deserted sky, and screeching gulls,
An octave up, then scaling down,
And we are in the scene and of it,
Moving across space.

A stone plopped into water forms ripples, creating concentric circles that move out from the center and subside gradually if nothing impedes their progress. Whether or not they ever come to a full stop, Teo wasn't scientist enough to know. It looked to him as if the molecules touched by movement become propelled in an infinitely wider arc, slower perhaps as they achieve distance, but still there, still moving, still affecting other molecules and pushing them to confront whatever lies in their path.

Last night, they'd spoken of the stones that had started their circles and brought them to this place. He'd told

Samantha of his visions. The evening had ended... Well, he didn't need to go into details of those hours at the end.

The memory of her touch, of her skin against his, of the way his physical imperfections lost significance every time she loved him, made him bite his lip to keep from insisting they return home right then. Forget about meeting their friends.

The barman approached for his order.

"*Due cappuccini, per favore,*" Teo told him.

"*Subito, signore.*"

Teo paid and tap-tapped back to the table. Samantha looked up with that full-lipped smile of hers as he pulled out his chair and leaned the cane against another.

"What time did Martine say they'd be here?" he asked.

"Soon. Yesterday's sail did Tonio so much good."

"I'm glad."

She accepted a cup the barman set before her and began adding sugar, stirring slowly. "You don't find it so bad now, do you?"

"What, sailing?"

A nod. "You seem to have more fun each time we go out."

"Well, it's growing on me. I'm not sure I'd ever have been comfortable on *Alice*, not with this leg."

"I know. She's a better boat for young people."

He sipped his own coffee. "You couldn't have given Tootie and Holland a better wedding gift, you know."

For a moment, he thought a shadow passed over Samantha's features, but then it vanished, replaced by a softened expression. "They'll have fun. And *Alice* belongs with the house. It will be a great place to raise children."

"And no unpleasant memories."

"No."

"Are you happy here? I promised you we'd live wherever you wish."

She reached toward him, her slim fingers touching his. He turned his hand and clasped the smooth skin. "I love Reggio," she said.

He pulled a folded paper from his pocket using his free hand. "Then perhaps you'll appreciate this little something I bought for you."

Her brows tented as she accepted the paper, then settled as she opened it. "A present?"

"Would you like me to translate?"

She looked up. Her widened eyes said she'd absorbed the gist of it. "Is it what I think?"

"*Belle Journée* is yours, my dear."

"Why...but...I don't understand. Tonio and Martine. They love her."

"Yes. And they will continue to sail with you or with us."

"Oh, my." She stared down at the official title change and then clasped it against her chest. Her eyes glistened dangerously.

He spoke as calmly as possible to stave off an emotional deluge. "They offered to give the boat to us, but I said I'd rather buy it for you. It seemed more fitting. And though they are not poor, they will need more and more care for Tonio in the years to come. This is better."

"Oh, Teo. Oh, Teo, thank you." She leaned closer, touched his cheek with her palm. "You beloved man."

"Well," he said, straightening his back. "I'm glad you like it. I hope it makes up for relinquishing your little *Alice*."

"More than." The glitter in her eyes made them sparkle. "We can cruise, Teo. We can go to all sorts of places. Maybe even Greece."

His eyes narrowed. "Greece? The Aegean?"

She laughed. "I forgot. But if we sail there, we'll be careful.

We'll watch the weather. Really. No more storms for either of us."

"And you can predict that accurately, Madam Weather-guru?"

"There are electronic toys on *Belle*. And there's always the Internet."

"Fine," he said, sighing. "Let's start with local cruises. Okay? There's plenty to see right around here."

"Yes, sir."

"Now, before our friends arrive, I thought I'd mention an upcoming research trip." He tucked the deed away and drew out the suspense. How he loved to see those eyes, bright and interested instead of deeply shadowed. "Sophrina and I need to visit Tokyo. Would you like to go?"

"Tokyo? You mean, as in sushi and kimonos?"

"I thought we'd fly in the other direction on the way home. Pause in Hawaii and then to California to see David and his new girlfriend."

Thinking of David reminded him of the wedding and David's apology. He'd known his son would love Samantha once he had a chance to know her. It hadn't hurt that Stefi and Daniel had taken David under their wings. Siblings, even late in the game, made life just a little fuller for a boy who'd been so torn by divorce. Teo remembered the squeak in David's voice when he first learned that the gorgeous Stefi was now his sister. And that he'd become an uncle to boot.

"I'd love to see him again," Samantha said. "He's a great kid."

Smiling, Teo agreed. "And after California, we could drop in on our grandson."

"Oh, Teo. See Christopher? Daniel said he's sitting up already."

"We wouldn't want to miss that. Precocious little fellow,

isn't he? And I've been in touch with Robert. He said he and Lizzie want to meet us in New York."

"Of course. A meeting with Val." Her eyes had lost none of their luster. She was undoubtedly counting all the museums she could visit—and drag him through. "Ah, Mr. Anderson. I do like your life."

"Well, Mrs. Anderson, it seems to be your life, too."

ACKNOWLEDGMENTS

So many people helped bring this story from its ragtag beginnings to its present form. *Sailing out of Darkness* would have foundered without the hours of reading time my beloved husband and best friend, Michael, provided. He prodded me with prayer and encouragement and was the first to say, "Off with its head," to bits that bogged the story down or took it in the wrong direction. I am so blessed that he has my back.

Many thanks to the encouragement of my long-time critique partner, Jane Lebak; to my writing and editing friends, Robin Patchen, Jane Shealy, and Linda Glaz; I'm also immensely grateful to writing friends Lynne Hinkey, Ane Mulligan, and Denise Falvo for their help in yanking a sagging beginning out of the mire. Leonardo Carelli of Montecassiano (MC), Italy, read the manuscript to correct my failures of memory. It hasbeen a long time since I actually lived and studied in Italy, and Leonardo is so very gracious. *Grazie, signore!*

Many, many thanks to my former agent, Terry Burns, for his friendship and faith and for the encouraging circle he provided his clients. Thank you to Roseanna White and everyone at WhiteFire Publishing, including Dina Sleiman, for believing in the story and pushing me to make the first edition of this book the best it could be.

My darling children, Ariana Milton Scoville and Joshua Milton, have always been my cheerleaders. No mother could be more proud of the adults they've become. And I adore my grandchildren, the next generation.

This second edition of *Sailing out of Darkness* sports a new cover and new eagle eyes in the reading and proofing, including those of DJ Sakata.

AFTERWORD

I'm like most authors: we take bits we've overheard, bits we've experienced, bits we've read about or heard about or pondered, and we fashion them into a what-if that becomes the genesis for a story. Each character in *Sailing out of Darkness* is a figment of my imagination. None of the events in this story actually happened to anyone I know or have known. But the lovely thing about crafting stories is that I can allow my imagination to people places in ways that seem interesting or fitting to me.

I hope you carry away something from the story, even if it's only an awareness that there are hurting people all around who just may need someone—you—to listen and care. And I'm not only speaking of the Indias in our world, but also of the Samanthas, who can become so mired in guilt that they have trouble climbing out of the muck. I've met an India or two, women who couldn't climb out, and their pain haunts me.

In crafting the second edition, I moved my characters from the Eastern Shore of Maryland down here to North Carolina so I could tuck them among the friends of the Carolina Coast novels. I've branched out a little, though, moving Sam to South River, about thirty minutes from Beaufort. It seemed a good place for her to get into trouble.

I hope you enjoyed the story, and that you'll pick up another one of my books to see what else is happening.

ALSO BY NORMANDIE FISCHER

Becalmed Carolina Coast Novel, Book 1

"It's a rare book that draws you in from the first page, wraps its cover around you, and warmly envelops you in its unfolding tale. This book did that for me…" ~Lita Smith-Mines, *Boating Times of Long Island*

Heavy Weather Carolina Coast Book 2

"…the book's strengths lie in its suspense and vivid characters, whose personalities and small-town relationships are truly believable. A heavy, suspenseful North Carolina novel about parenthood, human connection, and how to make peace with the cards you're dealt." ~*Kirkus Reviews*

Twilight Christmas Carolina Coast Book 3

"A charming Christmas story full of mystery and love." ~Amazon reviewer.

From Fire into Fire An Isaac's House Novella

"…a riveting story pulled right out of current events"

"…an excellent novella written by an accomplished novelist." ~Amazon reviewers.

Two from Isaac's House, An Isaac's House Novel

"…Fischer's novel is nothing less than thoroughly gripping!" ~Top Pick, *Romantic Times* Book Reviews

Sailing out of Darkness, 1st edition

"…beautiful, gorgeous imagery… It is take your breath away awesomeness. The storyline could absolutely suck and I wouldn't care half as much because I just wanted to read more descriptions of people, places, feelings and thoughts. This is true writing talent here. And she's a wonderful storyteller too." ~*Samantha Coville, Sammy the Bookworm*

www.ingramcontent.com/pod-product-compliance
Lightning Source LLC
Chambersburg PA
CBHW030650120726
47905CB00001B/146